IT'S ALL
ABOUT HIM

COLETTE CADDLE

**POCKET
BOOKS**

LONDON • NEW YORK • TORONTO • SYDNEY

First published in Great Britain by Pocket Books, 2007
An imprint of Simon & Schuster UK Ltd
A CBS COMPANY

1 3 5 7 9 10 8 6 4 2

Simon & Schuster UK Ltd
Africa House
64–78 Kingsway
London WC2B 6AH

www.simonsays.co.uk

Simon & Schuster Australia
Sydney

A CIP catalogue record for this book is
available from the British Library

ISBN-13: 978-1-4165-2194-5

Typeset by Rowland Phototypesetting Ltd, Bury St Edmunds, Suffolk
Printed and bound in Great Britain by Cox & Wyman Ltd, Reading, Berks

Also by Colette Caddle

For Seán

Thanks to my son Peter for his help and advice about young boys; what would I do without him? To Seán, for making me laugh and reminding me what it's all about. Thank you to my mother for her constant and solid support. And last, but by no means least, thank you to Tony for still putting up with me after all these years. I love you all.

Chapter 1

A wave of nausea swept over Dee as she read the letter. She'd been expecting it, of course. The bathroom had flooded the Sunday before last. The ancient tank had finally given up the ghost and burst, sending hot water spewing out at a frightening rate. The old floorboards couldn't take it and had buckled under the weight of water, devastating the room underneath. The fact that the room was now leased to the Happy Days crèche owned by her friend Lisa meant that, for nearly two weeks, Lisa and her assistant Martha had to crowd the eight children into one room and it was far from ideal. It had been an awful experience all round but now it had just got worse.

Dee stared in horror at the piece of paper documenting the cost of a call-out on a Sunday night, of replacing the tank and the pipes – 'they've had it, love' – and there was another bill sitting on her desk for the installation of the new bathroom floor and dining-room ceiling.

'The insurance will cover it,' her boyfriend Conor

had assured her as they mopped up after the plumber had left, and she'd nodded with a pained smile. She didn't have the courage to tell him that there was no insurance; he would think she was stupid.

It was madness, of course, but Dee had allowed the policy to lapse as there simply wasn't enough money to go round. She had to have public and employer's liability insurance for the crèche and medical insurance for Sam was imperative. The house, well, the house had been standing for the last eighty years and it would probably survive another few.

'Mum? I feel sick again.'

Dee shoved the letter into her dressing-gown pocket and led her little boy back into the bathroom. He looked pale and his lips had a blue tinge but his eyes were reasonably bright. Still, she'd take him to the surgery just in case. He'd been up half the night throwing up for no apparent reason and though Dee had gone over and over in her head what he'd eaten the previous day she still couldn't figure out what might have upset him.

When Lisa arrived for work, she took one look at mother and son, sent Dee for a shower, and took the little boy down to the kitchen. After Dee had dressed in her uniform of jeans and T-shirt and twisted her long hair into a knot, she ran downstairs. Sam, clad in clean pyjamas, was curled up on the battered sofa in the corner of the kitchen, nibbling toast and watching *Pokémon.*

'Thanks,' Dee said as Lisa passed her a mug of strong tea.

'Bad night?'

Dee nodded, rolling her eyes. 'Awful.'

'Why don't you go and have a lie down? Once the other kids arrive and he's distracted he'll be fine.'

'I have to do the shopping,' Dee looked at the clock, 'and if I just go to the local supermarket I'll be back in time to take Sam to morning surgery.' Dee usually did her shopping in the wholesaler's twenty miles south on the outskirts of Dublin as it worked out a lot cheaper, but that was out of the question now.

'I'm sure it's nothing,' Lisa tried to reassure her.

'Still, I'd like Bill to check him. Do you need anything at the shops?' Dee pulled a pen and pad towards her and added another couple of items to the already long list.

'Plasters and some fish fingers, please.'

'There are two containers of my homemade fish nuggets in the freezer,' Dee reminded her.

Lisa grinned. 'Sorry, they're just not orange enough for the kids.'

Dee grunted and added the items to her list. She and Lisa chatted about the day ahead and then Lisa went through to prepare for the imminent arrival of three babies and four toddlers. 'I'll be back for Sam in a minute,' she called over her shoulder and Dee nodded her thanks and crossed the room to crouch down in front of her son.

'How are you doing?'

''kay,' Sam said, not taking his eyes off the television.

'Do you think you might be sick again?'

He shook his head.

'Great! Then let's get you dressed.'

'Ah, Mummy, do I have to?'

Dee smiled. 'No, I don't suppose so. I've got to go and do the shopping and when I get back I'll help you dress and we'll go and see Doctor Bill.'

'But Mummy, I'm fine now,' he protested.

She stood up and fluffed his thick mop of hair. 'We'll let Doctor Bill decide that. See you later, sweetheart.'

As Dee drove the short distance to the large supermarket on the outskirts of Banford, she thanked God for Lisa. To have someone on-site on days like today was a godsend and it suited Lisa, too.

Her best friend since childhood, Lisa Dunphy adored children and had trained both in childcare and Montessori. Her dream had always been to run her own crèche and it had finally occurred to Dee that she could both help her friend realize her dream *and* solve some of her own money worries at the same time.

Lisa had been thrilled with the idea and Dee had begged and pleaded with the bank for a loan so that they could carry out the necessary work that would transform the bottom of the house into Banford's most popular childcare centre. It had been the best move Dee had ever made. The dark, old house was now alive with the sound of children's voices, Sam loved having the company of the other children, and the extra income helped towards the maintenance of her family home. At least, it used to, she thought, as she remembered the bill that had arrived that morning.

She had no idea how she was going to pay it. Between her income from her catering business and Lisa's crèche she could just about manage but there was nothing in the kitty to cover events like this. She would have to go to the bank or credit union and beg for help. Either that or arrange a payment plan with the plumber and builder.

She turned into the supermarket car park and groaned as an ominous rattle came from under the car. 'No, not now, you bloody rust-bucket,' she growled, resolving to ask Conor to take a look at it later. Thank God she had a boyfriend who not only was attractive but also knew something about cars, too. In fact, although he was a farmer, Conor could turn his hand to most things and seemed to spend much of his free time either fixing something in her house or tinkering with the car. Sam followed him around like a lapdog and Conor always made a big deal of giving the child something to do and calling him his little helper.

'You should make an honest man of him while you have the chance,' Lisa often told her. 'Men like that don't grow on trees.'

'No, they don't,' Dee would agree.

*

She parked the car, grabbed a trolley and pushed it through the automatic doors, rummaging in her pocket for her extensive shopping list. 'Oh, no,' she groaned as she searched fruitlessly through all her pockets and bag, realizing that it didn't matter how much she looked, the list was at home on the kitchen table. 'Great,' she muttered, heading for the fruit and vegetable aisle, 'just great.'

She tried to remember what was on her list, then gave up and threw a bit of everything into the trolley. If she had too much it would simply mean more cooking and freezing; they couldn't afford to throw anything out. She would make a hearty soup, she decided, and freeze it in small portions for Lisa to reheat on days when Dee wasn't around. Cheered at the thought, Dee moved on to the freezer section and peered dubiously into the cabinets at the range of fish fingers. She hated buying this sort of stuff but Lisa would murder her if she came back without them. 'If you can feed them healthily four days out of five you've done an amazing job,' she'd argue and Dee knew she was right. So she relented and bought the processed food that Lisa demanded but not before agonizing over all the labels.

She was studying the tiny print on the back of a pack of waffles when a young girl appeared at her elbow.

'Hi, I'm Carrie Lambe from Forever FM, can I talk to you for a moment?'

'I'm in a bit of a hurry . . .' Dee started.

'Oh, *please.*' The girl looked at her with large, pleading eyes. 'This is my first stint as a reporter and no one will talk to me. I promise it won't take long.'

Dee glanced at her watch. She was making better time than she'd realized and, after all, everyone deserved a break. 'Okay, then.'

'You're a star, thanks a million!' Carrie switched on her tape and shoved a microphone under Dee's nose. 'We're just asking people today if they have any opinions about food labelling.'

Dee's eyes lit up. 'I have an opinion, all right; it's a bloody disgrace.'

Carrie nodded excitedly. 'Really? And why's that?'

'Do you know exactly how misleading some labels are?' Dee demanded.

'Well, yes, that's why—'

'Look.' Dee pulled a pack of chicken nuggets from the freezer. 'Read that,' she instructed.

The girl frowned. 'One hundred per cent chicken breast.'

'And what does *that* tell you?'

Carrie blinked. 'That it's made from one hundred per cent breast of chicken?'

'No!' Dee flicked over the packet and pointed at the ingredients label with its tiny writing. 'It means that the chicken in the pack is one hundred per cent chicken breast.'

'Okay,' Carrie said slowly, giving her an odd look.

'Read it,' Dee was saying.

Obediently, Carrie screwed up her eyes and studied the label. 'Chicken forty-seven per cent – huh?'

'Exactly.'

'But I don't understand. On the front it says one hundred per cent; that's a lie.'

'Not at all. It's just clever marketing,' Dee explained. 'It's telling you that the chicken in the pack is chicken breast, but what it's *not* telling you is that less than half of the product is actually chicken.'

Carrie wrinkled her nose. 'So what else is in there?'

Dee shrugged. 'God knows.'

'I had no idea.'

'Because you do what most people do and read the label and believe it. You look at one hundred per cent chicken breast and think you're buying a reasonably healthy meal.'

Carrie double-checked that her tape recorder was working and she was getting all of this invaluable information. 'Are there any other products that you feel are misrepresented?'

'Oh, yes, but I'm afraid I don't have time to go through them all now.'

'Oh, please, I won't keep you long,' Carrie promised.

Dee glanced at her watch again. 'Tell you what, let's talk about breakfast.' She pushed her trolley quickly towards the aisle with the breakfast cereals, Carrie scurrying after her. 'The best way for a kid to start the day is with a healthy cereal, right?'

'Right.'

'And cereals are sweet even before you add any sugar.'

'Well, certainly the chocolate- and sugar-coated ones are,' Carrie agreed.

'No, *all* of them,' Dee assured her. 'Almost all cereals have sugar added and something else, too.'

'What?'

'Salt.'

'Salt? In cereal?'

Dee nodded solemnly. 'Oh yes. So you'd give your little one a bowl of cereal with milk and sugar and then maybe a slice of toast?'

Carrie nodded.

'More salt. Not just in the butter or spread but in the bread, too.'

'But that's terrible.'

'So before your kids have even left for school they've probably consumed their recommended daily intake of salt. Most people don't stand a chance with this kind of labelling,' Dee continued. 'For a start, some labels talk about sodium and some about salt and they're not the same thing.'

'That's scandalous,' Carrie protested. 'How can you possibly make healthy choices unless you're a trained nutritionist or dietician or something?'

'It's hard,' Dee agreed, 'but there is a way.'

'There is?'

'Home cooking. The only way you truly know what goes into anything is if you make it yourself.'

'Yeah, well, that only works if you have the time and you can cook.' Carrie made a face. 'I'd poison myself!'

Dee laughed. 'You're not alone and some people are always going to depend on processed food, which is why there should be more restrictions on labelling.'

'How come you know so much about food?'

Dee rummaged in her bag and pulled out a business card.

'Dee's Deli Delights,' Carrie read. 'Oh, you're a chef!'

'A cook,' Dee said modestly. 'I'm self-trained. I cook all the food for the Happy Days crèche and the café in Better Books.'

'Yes, I know it! They have that amazing chocolate cheesecake, do you make that?'

Dee nodded. 'All natural ingredients and only three hundred calories a slice,' she said proudly. She glanced at her watch and groaned. 'I'm sorry, but I really have to go now.'

'Oh, of course. Listen, thanks a million, that was great.'

'No problem.'

Dee finished her shopping at break-neck speed. In little over an hour she'd returned home, put away the groceries and was walking with Sam towards the doctor's surgery. It was nearly twelve and surgery would be over soon so she quickened her step, tugging Sam after her.

He seemed fine but Dee wasn't taking any chances. She would never forget the time when Sam was just twenty-six months old, and she had put him to bed coughing. She had assumed it was just another cold – he got so many – but in the early hours of the morning he had been fighting for breath. Terrified, she'd called an ambulance and prayed as they sped down the motorway towards Dublin. The staff in the emergency ward had quickly eased Sam's breathing and within two days he was home again, the doctors assuring her that though it had been an asthma attack it had been a mild one and it was something he would undoubtedly grow out of. They had been interested to see the rough, red skin in the creases of his arms and knees and had told her that eczema and asthma often went hand in hand.

Dee had gone straight to see Bill Green, her GP, and though he had agreed with the diagnosis and told her that Sam might get mild attacks from time to time until he grew out of it, she'd pestered him as to what she could do to prevent it. He had told her that a healthy diet with plenty of fresh fruit and vegetables might help and that she should restrict Sam's exposure to additives. She could also keep a diary, noting when Sam's skin flared up or when he started wheezing, and see if there was any pattern to it.

Then Dee had begun a crusade, promising herself that she wouldn't rest until she found the causes of Sam's health problems. It turned out that dog and cat hair – some breeds more than others – were a trigger of some of his skin problems and also that processed food was definitely an issue. Dee spent hours in the local library researching food and the damage that additives could cause and began to cook everything from scratch herself, even their bread.

Bill Green assured her that Sam would probably be fine given time and that she shouldn't get too stressed about his condition, but Dee was determined to do everything in her power to cure her son. She never wanted him to go through such a horrible experience again. Her hard work paid off and with a change of diet and a bit more care around animals, Sam's attacks became fewer and milder.

'How are you feeling now, sweetheart?' she asked, putting a hand down to caress his dark head.

'Okay. I don't want to go to see Doctor Bill,' he grumbled.

'But Doctor Bill's your friend, Sam. I'm sure you're fine, but let's get you checked out just to be sure.'

When they walked into the surgery, the receptionist looked up and smiled. 'Hey, Dee, hi, Sam, how are you?'

Dee smiled at the girl who'd become a friend over the years. 'Not very well, Sheila.'

'Oh, dear.' Sheila shot Sam a sympathetic look. 'Well, you timed it well, honey. Doctor Bill is just finishing up with our last patient and then you can go in.'

Dee perched on a stool as Sam wandered over to the small play area.

'What's up?' Sheila asked when he was out of earshot.

'No idea; he's been vomiting half the night but I can't figure out why.' Dee stifled a yawn.

'You look terrible,' Sheila told her.

'Thanks a lot.'

'You need a break. Why don't you get away for a few days?'

'You are joking,' Dee laughed. Even if she could afford a holiday, who would take over her workload? Anyway, it would be too stressful, worrying about what was in the food Sam was eating, never mind the worry of him sleeping between strange sheets.

'Then at least let's have a night out,' Sheila was saying. 'I'll organize it; you, me, Lisa and Lauren.'

'I haven't seen Lauren in weeks, how is she?'

'Tired,' Sheila chuckled, 'but that's par for the course with six-month-old twins.' She turned her head as the surgery door opened and Bill Green shepherded out an elderly lady.

'Okay, Mrs Doyle, you take care now, bye-bye.'

'I will, Doctor, thank you.'

Bill Green turned to smile at Dee. 'Hello, Dee. Hey, Sam, are you coming in to see me?' Sam nodded and offered a weak smile. 'Ooh, you do look a bit peaky, let's have a look at you.'

Dee followed them into Bill's office and waited as Bill did a thorough examination.

'What do you think?' she asked anxiously after sending Sam back out to the waiting room.

Bill sat down in his chair and pulled his stethoscope off and shrugged. 'I'd say it's just a virus of some sort.'

'He definitely didn't eat anything out of the ordinary.'

'He's four,' the doctor told her, smiling kindly. 'Four-year-olds get bugs all the time.'

'I suppose,' Dee said with a tired sigh.

'You need a break,' Bill said.

'So Sheila was just telling me,' Dee said, smiling. 'I'll hop on the private jet and go down to the Bahamas for a few days.'

'A couple of early nights and a babysitter would probably do the trick,' he said, ignoring her flippancy. 'Just keep him on very simple plain foods for a couple of days.'

Dee nodded as she stood up. 'Will do.'

'And call me if you're worried.'

'Thanks, Bill,' she said and went back out to reception to pay Sheila.

'I'll be in touch about that night out,' the receptionist told her.

'I'll look forward to it,' Dee lied. She loved going out with the girls and it had been a long time since they'd done it, but the thought of the unnecessary expense when money was so tight put her off.

*

'Can we go to the playground?' Sam asked Dee as they walked out of the surgery and turned for home.

'Oh, I don't know, sweetheart, that might not be such a good idea—'

'Oh, please, Mummy!'

Happy to see him a bit more enthusiastic, Dee relented. 'Well, okay, then, but not for long. I have a lot of work to do this afternoon.'

As he played on the swings and the slide in the small playground next to the beach, Dee stared out to sea and went over in her head what she had to make that day. A vegetarian quiche, a steak and kidney pie for the café and a beef stew for the children's lunch tomorrow. To simplify life and her budget, Dee usually used similar recipes for both the crèche and the café. Although for the most part she kept the children's menu simple she had become adept at tailoring many sophisticated dishes to suit their tastes, too.

The owner of Better Books, Ronan Fitzgerald – Conor's dad – was delighted with Dee's food and his café had turned from a place for morning coffee to a thriving lunchtime venue largely because of her dishes.

It was Lisa who had first suggested to him that he should buy his cakes from Dee – homemade and local, she'd told him – and a few days later, he'd called and they'd struck a deal. He had steadily increased his order as the months had passed and now Dee was his largest supplier. While Dee was thrilled with this development – she needed every penny she could get – it was also a lot of hard work. Conscious of how little time she was spending with Sam lately, she'd taken to getting up at six and doing some of the cooking before Sam woke.

Planning was the key, she'd found in this business, and the freezer was her greatest tool. She always cooked greater quantities than she needed and then froze some of the food in small portions so that there was always something healthy for Lisa and the children and for her and Sam, too, on the rare occasion that she took a day off from the kitchen. Though Saturdays and Sundays were largely her own, she usually did some baking while Sam 'helped'.

Dee's thoughts returned to the bill she'd received that morning and she sighed wearily. Every time she seemed to get her head above water, something seemed to happen and it usually involved money or, rather, the lack of it. The house absorbed most of her income, but Sam's medication and creams and his frequent visits to the doctor added up, too. As she watched him climb up the slide she also realized that he would need a new pair of shoes before long; that would be another forty euros or so which she couldn't afford. Glancing at her watch, she called to her son. It was time to get back to the kitchen and earn it.

*

Lisa was in the dining room on her hands and knees cleaning up after lunch when they got back. 'So, is everything all right?' she asked Dee.

'Yes, it's just a bug.'

'Poor little man.' Lisa smiled affectionately at her godson. 'Why don't you go and play with Tom and I'll bring you some milk and crackers?'

'Thanks,' he said with a grin and skipped off to join his best friend.

Lisa got to her feet and she and Dee went back out to the kitchen.

'You look like you could do with a cuppa,' she said.

Dee yawned. 'I think I'm going to need a gallon of tea if I'm to keep going today.'

'Why don't you lie down for an hour? You'll be a lot more productive if you've had a rest.'

Dee rubbed her eyes. 'But I haven't made anything for lunch yet—'

'There's a plate of ham in the fridge and that lovely soda bread from yesterday, that's more than enough.'

'But—'

'Dee, just go.'

Dee saw the determined look in her friend's eye and gratefully capitulated.

She gave Lisa a quick hug and made for the stairs. 'Call me if you need me.'

'We'll cope.'

Dee collapsed on to her large bed and pulled the duvet up around her. Closing her eyes she tried not to think of all the jobs she should be doing. Lisa was right; she'd get a lot more done if she had a catnap, just a little one, an hour at the most . . .

Chapter 2

Ronan and Julia Fitzgerald worked in companionable silence as they got ready for opening at ten. It was a beautiful spring morning and the sunshine lit up the pretty café with its yellow curtains, faded floral cushions and pine floors. The eight tables were draped in blue and white check oilskin cloths and four tall stools stood at the bar for those who came in for a quick cuppa and a gossip. Ronan glanced at his watch. 'You're going to be late, love.'

'I am,' she agreed, and hurried to get her bag, cardigan and keys from the counter. 'Right, is there anything else you need me to do?'

'No, you go. Zoe will be here in a minute.'

Julia looked at him from under raised eyebrows. 'The day that girl's on time I'll eat my hat. Now, I'll be going to the shops later, do you need anything?'

'No, love.'

'And if you want to go home for lunch there's some salad—'

'I'll have something here,' he said hurriedly.

'And don't be late home this evening,' she warned.

'Of course I won't,' he said affronted.

'Okay, then, see you tonight.'

'Glasses.' Ronan held up her spectacles and she hurried back to him, planting a kiss on his cheek.

'Thank you, darling.'

Ronan chuckled as she hurried off. Julia ran herself ragged between helping out at the church, working at the nursing home and looking after him, but if it made her happy then that was fine by him. He was grateful that she was such a busy woman. If they worked together too much they drove each other mad. Ronan was too relaxed and easygoing as far as Julia was concerned and she too critical and demanding in his view. Anyway, a bit of space was always a good thing for a marriage, Ronan thought. It was also quite pleasant working alongside a pretty young thing like Zoe. He liked to be surrounded by young people. They didn't moan or whinge the way his age group did, or if they did, it was in a light-hearted sort of way. Ronan had no doubt that Zoe's pretty smile and sunny disposition was very popular with his customers and not just the male ones.

'Hiya, boss.'

He looked up to see the young lady in question slipping in the back door and tossing her backpack behind the bar. 'Morning, Zoe, how are you today?'

'Don't ask.' She pulled a face. 'I was out last night.'

'Ah, feeling a little delicate?'

'Let's say I'd prefer if you didn't put on your big-band CD today.'

Ronan chuckled as he went behind the bar and opened the fridge. 'I have the perfect cure for you,' he said, extracting tomato juice, a lemon and an egg.

Zoe looked on suspiciously. 'Are you trying to kill or cure me?'

'You've a full day's work ahead of you; of course I don't want to kill you. So what was the occasion?'

Zoe pulled herself on to a high stool and dropped her head on to the counter. 'It was Tracey's birthday so we decided to have a few drinks and then we went on to a club in town and bumped into a few mates and, well, it's all a bit of a blur after that.'

'How did you get home?' Ronan asked, trying not to sound too much like her father.

'Someone poured us into a cab,' she assured him, a smile playing around her lips. 'Don't worry, boss, I didn't take any lifts from strangers.'

'Glad to here it. Now, try this.' He banged the foaming mixture down in front of her making her wince.

'I'm not sure I can.'

'Hold your nose and down it in one. Trust me, you'll feel better.'

Zoe sighed. 'That wouldn't be hard.' She raised the glass and lowered half of it before coming up for air, her face twisted in disgust. 'That is bloody awful!'

'It will be worth it,' he promised, glancing at the

clock. 'Now, are you ready to open up or do you need more time?'

'No, no.' Zoe stood up and waved him away. 'I'll be fine, I just hope it's a quiet morning.'

'Thanks a lot,' he said dryly, heading into the shop.

Zoe grinned. 'Ah, sure it's not like you need the money, boss!'

'That's right,' he called over his shoulder, 'I'm just here for the fun.' He smiled to himself as he went to unlock the shop door of Better Books. It was true he didn't need the money. When he took early retirement from the civil service he had enough put aside to live a very comfortable life indeed but he wasn't the sort of man to sit back and watch the world go by.

Returning to live in his home town and taking over the local bookshop was exactly the challenge he'd needed. He loved working here and enjoyed the eclectic mix of people who came through his door. It attracted all sorts from the young girl looking for a juicy romance, to the academic in search of a book of poetry, to the art collector attracted by the prints and landscapes that graced the window and walls.

The tea shop had been Julia's idea as there was such a large, open space at the back of the shop and now the café brought in more money than the bookshop with a steady flow of customers throughout the day and a positive frenzy some lunchtimes. All in all, it was a thriving business and a valuable asset but Ronan wouldn't dream of selling it. He was only sixty-one and in good health so hopefully it would be a long time before he would have to consider that.

Ideally he'd love to pass it on to his son but Conor had no interest in taking on the business. He was a farmer and Ronan had never seen a man who enjoyed his job more. Though there had been no farmers in the family and Conor had largely grown up on a housing estate near Dublin, the outdoor life seemed to be in his blood. Conor reminded Ronan a lot of his own father – a solid, bear of a man with a quiet voice and a rather dry sense of humour.

Today was Conor's thirty-second birthday and Ronan was half hoping it would be marked with an engagement. For as well as being a wonderful cook, Dee Hewson was also his son's girlfriend. Ronan had to applaud his taste. Quite apart from being a very pretty girl with serious brown eyes and a fine figure, Dee was both kind and clever. Ronan had no idea how she managed to run that house, a business and raise a child and he admired her hugely.

Julia, however, didn't share his views. While she acknowledged that Dee was a great cook and a loving mother it was clear that she was suspicious of Dee's single-parent status. It was quite common these days, Ronan pointed out, and they had no idea of the history concerning Sam's father, but Julia dismissed his arguments. 'She's hiding something,' she said. 'I bet he's a married man. She wouldn't be the first to get pregnant in an attempt to get a man to leave his wife.' The fact that all of this conjecture had no basis in reality made no difference to Julia and so Ronan gave up arguing the point. He did, however, make it very clear to his wife that she'd better not meddle in their son's love-life. Ronan had never seen Conor as comfortable with a woman before and he was wonderful with the little lad.

The bell on the door jangled noisily and Ronan turned to greet his first customer of the day. His smile broadened when Vi Valentine staggered in, weighed down with canvases. 'Vi, I wasn't expecting you! I thought you were in Youghal doing seascapes.'

'It rained and you know how I hate the bloody rain. Still, I got some nice harbour scenes before the weather broke.'

Ronan relieved her of her load. 'Let's take them through to the back and I'll get you a cuppa.'

Vi followed him into the café and waved at Zoe. 'Hello, darling, how are you?'

'Don't talk too loudly,' Ronan warned, 'Zoe's a little sensitive this morning.'

Vi laughed. 'Good for you, girl. Oh, to be young again.'

'I'd say you were a wild woman.' Zoe grinned.

Vi's green eyes twinkled. 'I've had my moments.'

'Vi, these are wonderful,' Ronan marvelled as he stood the four canvases against the wall and studied them.

'I am quite pleased with them,' Vi said modestly.

'There's something wonderful about the light down there at this time of year; quite, quite beautiful.'

'Is that where you come from, Vi?' Zoe asked curiously.

'Lord, no, I was born and raised in Banford.'

'But I thought you only moved here a couple of years ago.'

'Moved back here,' Vi corrected.

'There must be something about this place,' Zoe marvelled.

With her café-au-lait skin, blonde afro hair and hazel eyes, Zoe was a perfect mix of her Irish mother and Ethiopian father and it was a shock to most people when they heard her strong Dublin accent. When her family moved to Banford – Zoe's dad had accepted a position as registrar in the local private clinic – she had been horrified at the thought of moving out of the city and had said she'd find herself a flat in Dublin instead.

As it turned out, though, Banford had worked its magic on her and she hardly went near Dublin these days. Her original plans to go to Dublin City University to study marketing had been scrapped and instead she came to work for Ronan and put her studies on hold.

She looked wistfully at the paintings. 'I wish I could paint.'

Ronan nodded at the walls of the café.

'You can have a go in here if you like; it could do with a fresh coat.'

'Ha ha.' Zoe made a face at her boss. 'Coffee,Vi?'

'Yes, please, and a scone would be nice, too,' she added.

'Sorry, Dee hasn't been in yet.' Zoe looked worriedly at the clock.

'I'll give her a call,' Ronan said and left them to chat.

'Sorry, Ronan,' Dee answered her phone, breathless, 'just loading up. I'll be with you in five.'

'Okay, love, I was afraid that Sam might be sick again.'

'No, he's as right as rain this week.'

'That's good. I'll see you soon.' He hung up and went back to join the two women in the café. 'She's on her way. So Vi,' he said, pulling out a chair and sitting opposite the artist, 'what price are you putting on these?'

'One hundred?' Vi suggested, taking a sip of her coffee.

'Too low,' Ronan retorted. 'Way too low.'

'Absolutely,' Zoe agreed as she placed a coffee in front of her boss. 'You could easily get twice that.'

'You think?' Vi said doubtfully.

'If the paintings are displayed properly, I'm sure they'll sell in no time.' Ronan tugged on his white beard as he pondered how he could rearrange his stock to showcase Vi's work to full advantage.

'So why did you leave Banford?' Zoe asked Vi

when Ronan had to go through to the shop to tend to a customer.

'Itchy feet,' Vi said, smiling.

'And where did you go?'

'Here and there.'

'You're very mysterious,' Zoe said with a grin.

'I don't mean to be, there just isn't much to say. I've had quite a boring life.'

'Were you always an artist?'

'Lord, no,' Vi laughed. 'I only started painting a few years ago.'

'And yet you're so good!' Zoe shook her head.

'Well, thank you!'

'Can you give me a hand?' Dee said, staggering in the door of the bookshop, her face hidden behind a pile of plastic food containers.

Ronan rushed to her aid and brought the food through to the café.

'Hi, Zoe.' Dee followed him through.

'Hey, Dee.'

Ronan poured Dee a cup of tea and she took it over to Vi's table.

'I didn't think you were due back for another week,' Dee said.

'Hello, darling! Rain, I'm afraid,' Vi replied.

'Oh, hard luck.'

'She didn't do too badly.' Ronan gestured at the paintings leaning against the wall.

'Oh, Vi,' Dee breathed, 'they're fantastic.'

'Well, thank you,' Vi said with a regal nod.

'I think I might buy one,' Ronan announced. 'That stormy scene would look very nice over our fireplace.'

Vi and Dee exchanged a look. 'It'll never happen if *she* has anything to do with it,' Vi muttered when Ronan had wandered off again.

'I'm sure it will,' Dee said not altogether convincingly.

Vi and Julia were complete opposites who had never got on. Julia sneered at Vi's hippy clothes and made comments about mutton and lamb and Vi called Julia a do-gooder who stuck her nose in where it wasn't wanted.

'I can't believe she's Conor's mother,' she would say to Dee. 'He obviously inherited all of Ronan's genes.'

Privately Dee agreed, but she wouldn't dream of saying so; it would be very disloyal to Conor. She drained her cup and stood up.

'Going already?' Vi looked disappointed.

'Sorry, I must get back to work.'

'Will we see you tonight?' Ronan asked, walking with her to the door.

'Sure,' Dee said, stretching up to kiss his cheek. 'See you then.'

'Birthday tea?' Lisa giggled. 'I haven't been to one of them since I was twelve.'

'Shut up and pass me the garlic.' Dee continued to chop onions.

Lisa rummaged in the vegetable rack behind her. 'I'd have thought you'd be baking a cake, not making chilli.'

'I'll leave that to Julia.'

'And what does Conor think of this? I mean he's thirty-two, for God's sake.'

Dee shrugged. 'He's like his dad. They go along with whatever Julia wants because it's easier that way.'

Lisa rolled her eyes. 'Men; they do anything to avoid hassle, don't they?'

'You can't really blame them; I mean, it is Julia we're talking about.'

'She is a total control freak.' Lisa helped herself to a muffin from the cake tin on the table. 'I don't know how they put up with her.'

'Ronan just switches off. In fact, they both do,' Dee said as she peeled and crushed four cloves of garlic. 'They tell her what she wants to hear and then do their own thing anyway.'

Lisa looked unconvinced. 'You're still all going to a birthday tea at seven,' she pointed out.

Dee chuckled. 'True, but what harm is it? I'll probably be just as bad when Sam's grown up. By the time he's sixteen he'll be dying to move out!'

'He won't move far, though. He'll be back to eat and to drop off his washing.'

'No way,' Dee retorted, 'he can look after himself.'

'Yeah, sure, I believe you.'

Dee sighed as she poured some olive oil into a large frying pan and turned on the gas. 'Yeah, who am I kidding? I'll probably be even worse than Julia. You know, she still irons Conor's shirts.'

'She doesn't!'

Dee nodded. 'He says it keeps her happy, so why should he object.'

'I don't know how she gets time to do it all. I mean, there's the nursing home, the parish council, the Women's Institute.'

'The church flowers,' Dee reminded her.

'And she cooks, cleans and irons too!' Lisa shook her head. 'What a life. You know, when you and Conor marry he'll probably expect you to do all of that.'

'Who said anything about marriage?' Dee scraped the onions and garlic into the pan and stirred.

'Maybe that's what this tea is all about,' Lisa said, her eyes lighting up. 'Maybe he's going to propose!'

Dee looked at her, horrified. 'In front of his mum and dad?'

'Ah, so you don't mind the idea of a proposal, it's just how and when he does it you're worried about,' Lisa surmised.

'Lisa, haven't you got a nappy to change or puke to clean up?'

Lisa glanced at the clock and jumped to her feet. 'Damn, I didn't realize what time it was. I'd better go or Martha will murder me. She was supposed to go home ten minutes ago and she's got a hot date this evening – just like you!'

'Get out.' Dee shook her spoon at Lisa's fleeing back but she was smiling as she stirred the mince into the pan.

Lisa always made her smile. She teased and joked continuously but there was no malice in her and Dee had never seen anyone as good with children; such a shame that she had none of her own. And despite her constant smile and effortless good humour, Dee knew Lisa would give anything to have children.

It was never going to happen with Ger; at least, Dee shuddered, she hoped not. Ger Clancy was a waste of space and it was clear to everyone except Lisa that he was just using her. Lisa, however, couldn't do enough for him. She talked about Julia waiting on Ronan and Conor but she was worse. She would love nothing better than to move in with Ger and to clean up after him. Dee couldn't understand how an otherwise clever girl could be so gullible. Ger never took her out, saying he preferred to keep Lisa all to himself – but it was because he was mean. He said he preferred her cooking to any restaurant rubbish – but he was mean. And the couple of times Conor and Dee had met them for a drink, Ger had rigged it so that he only ever bought a round when the girls weren't having anything – he was mean.

Dee couldn't stand it. Ger had a reasonable job

working in the council, he had his own house, and yet he lived off Lisa at every opportunity. Conor went mental one night when they went on to the local Chinese restaurant and Ger had chosen the cheapest food on the menu and then produced a calculator when they were splitting the bill. 'He argued with me because I'd had the spring roll and he'd only had the soup and it was twenty-five cents cheaper – twenty-five cents!' he'd told Dee.

Dee chuckled as she added chilli powder, chopped tomatoes and tomato purée to the pan. Maybe Sheila was right and they should have a night out. Lisa might meet someone nice and finally dump Ger. Though that was unlikely in a small town like Banford where everyone knew everyone else and there were few eligible men available. Still, they could always go into Dublin city and really do something special. Maybe Sam could even spend the night with Aunt Pauline; surely one night with the old dragon wouldn't kill him?

Anyway, she had noticed that Pauline was slightly less austere when Sam was around. She certainly wasn't the strict disciplinarian that Dee remembered from her childhood. Pauline had taken over when Dee's mother died of breast cancer when she was only nine and she was a very different person from her softer, younger sister.

She shivered slightly as she remembered times when

all she'd wanted was a cuddle and what she'd got was a sharp direction to 'pull herself together'.

Her dad hadn't been much better. He'd been devastated when he lost his beloved wife and had been too caught up in his own grief to notice or care about his young daughter's feelings. As the years had passed, Arthur Hewson had become more remote, if that was indeed possible, and by the time he died just after Dee left school, she didn't feel as if she'd lost a father; rather, she felt as though she'd buried a loved but distant relative.

The phone rang, interrupting her reverie and, wiping her hands on a dishcloth, she hurried to answer it. 'Hello, Happy Days Crèche, can I help you?'

'Oh, hi, may I speak to Dee Hewson, please?'

'Speaking.'

'Dee, hi, my name is Don Reilly, I work for the *Daily Journal*. I wonder if I could talk to you about your comments on Forever FM?'

Chapter 3

It was almost five past seven when Dee rang the doorbell of the Fitzgeralds' handsome detached house in its own grounds on the hill overlooking Banford. As she waited, she turned to look at the twinkling lights of the village below with the harbour silhouetted in the background and breathed deeply. She loved living here. It was a small town where everyone knew everyone, but the anonymity of Dublin was less than thirty minutes' drive away; definitely the best of both worlds. The door was thrown open and Dee whirled around to see Julia smiling at her.

'Dee, darling, there you are. We thought you'd got lost.'

'Sorry, Sam was—'

'Conor and Ronan are in the living room, go on through.' Julia strode back down the hall towards the kitchen.

Dee sighed and went in search of the two men. They were standing by the fireplace drinking beer and chatting and in the moment before they spotted her, she had a glimpse of the unspoken closeness between father and son.

'Dee!' Ronan turned and smiled and came over to hug her. 'Don't you look lovely?'

She laughed. She had just swapped her customary jeans for a denim skirt so this was a slight exaggeration.

'What will you have to drink?'

'One of them, please.' Dee nodded at their cans. 'Hey, birthday boy, how are you?' she said, smiling at Conor when Ronan had left them.

'I'll be better once I've had my birthday kiss,' he murmured, pulling her into his arms.

Dee turned up her face to oblige and marvelled, as she always did, at how tiny he made her feel and, at five foot seven and nine and a half stone, that was an achievement. He was only three inches taller than her but he was broad and thickset and substantial, the kind of man that made you feel safe. She kissed him gently on the lips and when she drew back he protested.

'Is that it?'

'For now,' she murmured, and handed him a gift as his dad returned with her drink.

'Here you go, love.'

'Thanks, Ronan.'

'This is great, Dee, thanks.' Conor kissed her again and held up the shirt for his father's inspection. 'What do you think, Dad?'

'Very nice.'

'And the DVD, is it the one you wanted?'

'It certainly is. You should come over tomorrow night, Dad, and watch it with me.'

'I'm sure you'd prefer to watch it with Dee.'

She shuddered. 'Oh, no, I couldn't watch one of those blood and guts films; it would give me nightmares for weeks.'

'So are you doing anything tonight?' Ronan asked the couple.

Dee looked at Conor. 'What do you think? Would you be up for a wild night out in Banford's hotspots?'

Conor shook his head worriedly. 'It is a week night.'

'Live dangerously,' she urged.

He grinned. 'Okay then, a pint in Casey's it is.'

'You're as mad as each other,' Ronan said.

'Want to come along?' Dee asked.

'Come where?' Julia bustled in. 'Tea's ready.' She looked pointedly at the beer can in Dee's hand.

'The pub,' Conor said, leading the way into the dining room and smirking at the array of tiny sandwiches and cream cake on the table.

Dee smothered a giggle and avoided his eyes. 'This looks lovely, Julia, thank you.'

'I'd have preferred steak and chips,' Ronan murmured.

'What was that?' Julia's eyes glittered.

'Nothing, dear.'

Julia proceeded to pour stewed tea into tiny china

cups as her son picked up two ham sandwiches and bit into them together. 'Conor, really!'

'It's my birthday,' he pointed out, helping himself to two more.

Julia's eyes misted up. 'Thirty-two years ago today; I can't believe it. Your father cried when he saw you.'

'Yeah, you were such an ugly little bugger.' Ronan loaded up his plate.

'He was not,' Julia said stoutly, 'he was a chubby little chap with a mass of black hair and the most wonderful dimples.'

Dee grinned at Conor. 'Have you any pictures, Julia?'

'Yes, of course!' Julia was on her feet.

'She's joking, Mum,' Conor said.

Julia sat down again. 'Very funny.'

'I'm sorry, Julia,' Dee apologized. 'I'm sure he was gorgeous. Not like Sam; he was all wrinkly and as bald as a coot.'

Ronan laughed. 'I've never understood all of this business of "Oh, he looks just like my father" or "He's got my mother's eyes". The only person babies ever resemble is Churchill.'

Conor stuffed another sandwich into his mouth and reached over to cut the cake.

'Wait!' Julia stopped him, 'We have to sing "Happy Birthday".'

'Oh, Mum, for crying out loud.'

But Julia was already sticking candles in the cake. 'Lighter, Ronan.' Her husband obediently handed over his lighter and Julia lit the candles. 'Now.' She smiled tenderly at her son. 'Happy birthday . . .'

'Peanuts?' Conor asked as they climbed on to two barstools in Casey's.

'Oh, yes please.' Dee was ravenous as she usually was after eating at Julia's. She had only nibbled on one of the 'plastic' ham sandwiches and had pushed the birthday cake around the plate hoping the woman wouldn't notice. If only Julia had bought a cake instead of insisting on making her own. Dee had watched in astonishment as Ronan and Conor had polished off two portions each. The Fitzgerald men had obviously been born with cast-iron stomachs and no taste buds. Conor bought them two packs of nuts each and grinned at her as he raised his pint. 'If your son could see you now!'

Dee laughed. She always tried to eat healthily in front of Sam and was careful not to eat things around him that he couldn't. Peanuts were definitely on that list. 'I think he'd forgive me on the grounds that I'm starving. Oh! I forgot to tell you my news. Remember that reporter who stopped me in the supermarket last week?'

He nodded.

'Another journalist from the *Daily Journal* is doing a follow-up article and he wants to interview me.'

Conor grinned. 'You're going to need a manager or an agent at this rate.'

'I doubt that. Still, at least the papers are interested in

the issue. Maybe it will make a few people think twice before they throw something into their trolley. It really annoys me that, because of clever packaging, people bring home something they think is relatively healthy.'

'You have mentioned that one or two hundred times before.'

Dee opened her mouth to protest but Conor held up his hand. 'I'm kidding! I think you're right and I think it's great that you care so much about stuff like this.'

'I never bothered until I became a mother. I used to live on takeaways and microwave meals before Sam came along.'

'So when are you going to meet this journalist?' he asked.

'He's dropping by tomorrow morning.' She made a face. 'He wants to see me at work in the kitchen.'

'You know, this could be good exposure for the café.'

'Gosh, yes, I never thought of that. I must make sure to drop the name into the conversation a few times.' Dee finished her peanuts and stifled a yawn.

'You look tired,' he said, stretching out a hand to push her hair out of her eyes.

She turned her face and kissed his hand, smiling at him. 'Not too tired.'

He smiled back, his hazel eyes dark in the dimly lit pub. 'Who's babysitting?'

'Paula.' The seventeen-year-old next-door neighbour was always broke and only too happy to look after Sam.

'Great, so I don't even have to walk her home.'

'Just watch her climb over the wall. So would you like another drink here or shall we have one at home?'

Conor shook his head as she yawned again. 'I think we'd better go.'

'I'm sorry,' she said as they strolled back to her house, his arm wrapped around her waist. 'This isn't much of a birthday celebration, is it?'

He stopped and cupped her face in his hands. 'It's perfect.' He kissed her, gently at first and then more urgently. He tugged at her shirt and moved his hand across the smooth skin of her back and she moaned softly as he pushed his fingers under the waistband of her trousers. She pushed him away, smiling. 'Stop, or we'll be arrested.'

'It would be worth it,' he murmured, pulling her close again.

'Could you imagine your mother,' she said, into his ear before kissing his neck.

'My mother can go and—'

'Dee? Dee Hewson? I thought it was you!'

Dee pulled away from Conor and smiled at the little man standing behind him. 'Uh, hello, Mr Dunne, how are you?'

'Fine, thanks. Nice evening for a stroll.'

'Yes, yes, it is.'

'I was just wondering if there's any fish pie on the menu tomorrow,' he asked hopefully and winked at Conor. 'She makes a wonderful fish pie.'

'Yes; yes, she does,' Conor said. 'She's very good with her hands.'

Dee stepped on his foot. 'Not tomorrow, Mr Dunne, but I'm making some for Friday.'

'Oh, okay then.'

'Tomorrow is steak and kidney pie; you should try it.'

'Maybe I will. Well, goodnight then, safe home.'

'Goodnight, Mr Dunne.' She turned her face into Conor's shirt collar and groaned. 'It could only happen in this town.'

'It's just as well he came along when he did; another five minutes and he might have found you in a very compromising position.'

Dee laughed up at him, her eyes twinkling. 'You're all talk, Conor Fitzgerald.'

He turned for home, tugging her after him. 'We'll see about that!'

When they let themselves in the back door, the kitchen was empty and the small TV in the corner was on but silent. Dee frowned. 'I'll just go and check if everything's okay.' As she got to the landing, Paula was just coming out of Sam's room. 'Is he okay?' she asked, suddenly worried.

Paula nodded and smiled. 'He had a bad dream, but he's asleep again now.'

Dee let out the breath that she hadn't even realized she was holding. 'Did he say anything?'

'Nothing that made sense.'

'Did he have anything to eat before bed?'

'Just one of your cookies and a glass of milk. Honestly, Dee, he's fine.'

They went back downstairs and Dee went to her bag for her purse. 'Thanks, Paula,' she said, handing over the money.

'Any time; he's a little pet. 'night.'

Conor watched from the door as the girl hopped home across the wall and then he came back inside and locked up. 'Is he okay?'

'Just a bad dream,' Dee said. 'It's probably something he ate.'

'I'm sure he's fine.' He drew her into his arms. 'Now, where were we?'

Dee stepped back. 'I just want to look in on him. You get us some drinks and I'll be back in a minute.'

'Fine,' Conor said, and after fetching a beer from the fridge, he settled back on the sofa with the remote control.

Dee crept into her son's room and sat down on the edge of the bed. He didn't stir, one hand flung out over his head, the other tucked under his chin. His cheeks were flushed and looked damp, and Dee laid a hand across his brow. He was warm but not hot, she decided. Still, to be safe, she pulled back the covers and felt his tummy. Sam turned over in protest at the feel of her cool skin against his and she took the opportunity to lift his pyjama top and examine his back. Despite the muted glow from the night light she could see that his skin was clear and, feeling slightly silly, she pulled his top back down, tucked the sheet loosely around him, and left the room.

Guiltily, she hurried back down to Conor. This was really turning out to be a very poor excuse for a birthday. As she walked into the kitchen she began to undo the buttons on her shirt. 'Okay, birthday boy, I hope you're ready for your pres—' Dee pulled up short at the sight of Conor sprawled on the sofa, snoring quietly. 'No way!' she murmured, kicking off her shoes and climbing carefully on to his lap. She started to open the buttons of his shirt, dipping her head to follow her fingers with her lips. 'Hey, birthday boy, you ready for your present?'

Conor smiled but didn't open his eyes as his hands slid around her. 'Oh, yes.'

Chapter 4

Lisa settled the toddlers on the floor with blocks and shapes before going into the baby room. Martha was burping one baby, there was another gurgling under a play-gym, and the third was asleep in the crib. 'Keep an eye on my lot, will you? I'm just nipping out to the kitchen. Do you want anything?'

'Yes, food,' Martha begged, 'I never got breakfast.'

'No problem. Dee's cooking up a storm this morning.' Lisa hurried through to the kitchen and sniffed appreciatively as she pushed open the door and was hit by a blast of heat and a host of wonderful aromas. 'God, I was hungry before but now I'm positively drooling!'

Dee laughed as she lifted a tray of scones out of the oven and set them carefully on the hob. 'This journalist is due at eleven and I want to get as much done as I can before he gets here.'

'What are we allowed eat? Martha hasn't had brekkie and lunch is a long time away.'

Dee nodded over at the other counter. 'There are apple sponges and blueberry muffins and, if you fancy a healthier option, there's some soda bread on the table. Or the fruit is ready for the children's snack; you could always have some of that.'

'Don't be ridiculous,' Lisa said, fetching the butter from the fridge and hurring towards the breadboard. 'Who's going to do the delivery to the café?'

'Conor said he'd drop by and pick it up.'

'Oh, I forgot to ask, how did the birthday tea go?' Lisa popped a piece of bread in her mouth and buttered some more to take inside.

'Brief, thankfully, and then Conor and I just went for a drink.'

'What did you give him for his birthday?'

Dee suppressed a grin. 'A DVD and a shirt.'

'Is that it?'

'Yes, why?'

'It's not exactly romantic, Dee.'

'And I'm not exactly rich,' Dee reminded her.

'You don't have to spend a lot of money, just get something a bit more personal.'

'Why? He wanted the DVD, and he likes to receive clothes because he hates going shopping.'

'Very practical,' Lisa murmured. 'Right, I'd better get back to work. Thanks for this.' Clutching her plate of food, Lisa left and Dee finished packing up the café's order and started to clean down the worktops. Once the interview was over she would be free for the afternoon and if the weather held, she could take Sam down to the beach to play in the rock pools.

Of course there were a lot of other jobs she could be tackling today but she liked to spend time with Sam whenever possible. He didn't have a dad to take him fishing or to football matches and, though Conor was great with him, she felt it was up to her to make sure he didn't miss out. His health placed enough restrictions on him as it was. There were foods he couldn't eat and places he couldn't go – some of his friends had dogs or cats. Still, it was a small price to pay if it meant he stayed healthy.

Dee vividly remembered times when her son had struggled to breathe, was racked with coughing, or was crying pitifully because his skin was red and raw. She hated having to say no when he wanted to go somewhere or do something that she knew would only result in pain for him.

She would always talk to him about it, explain that he couldn't do the same things as other children and, an intelligent child, he usually accepted the logic. Dee shivered, however, at the memory of the sometimes resentful looks he shot her whenever she had to say no.

There was a rap on the kitchen door and Conor stuck his head in and smiled at her.

'Morning.'

'You're late.' She shoved a large carton of food into his arms. 'Be careful with this, it's the curry.'

'Good morning, Conor, how are you, Conor, thanks for helping me out, Conor,' he retorted.

She grinned and reached up to kiss him. 'Sorry, I'm just a bit jittery at the thought of being interviewed.'

'You'll be fine,' he assured her before turning to carry the food to the jeep. 'What time is he coming?' he asked when he came back for the rest.

'Eleven. I hope he doesn't think I'm some kind of expert. I won't have a clue if he starts asking me about additives or colouring.'

'You know a hell of a lot more than most people,' Conor pointed out.

She helped him carry the last of the food outside and then stood watching as he climbed back behind the wheel. 'Drive carefully.'

'Don't worry, I won't spill the curry.'

'That's not what I meant.'

'I know.' He smiled. 'Good luck with the interview. I'll see you later.'

Dee waved him off and went back inside. Looking around the large kitchen she was satisfied that it was clean and realized that she should probably go and tidy herself up.

Upstairs, she quickly changed into a pair of black combat trousers and a purple long-sleeved T-shirt. She released her hair from its tight knot, brushed it thoroughly and decided to leave it loose. A touch of lip gloss and she was ready.

On her way back to the kitchen, Dee made a detour to check on Sam. When she went into the Happy Days dining room which doubled up as the arts and crafts room, she saw her son at the table with Tom, up to his elbows in paint and glitter. Lisa was on her knees beside them, glueing cotton wool on to multi-coloured card.

'What are you making?' Dee asked, crouching down beside Sam and peering over his shoulder.

'Sheep.'

Dee looked from the yellow and green soaked wool to Lisa. 'Sheep?'

'They're magic sheep,' Lisa affirmed, 'they can be any colour they want.'

'That's convenient,' Dee smirked.

'What's convenient mean, Mum?' Sam asked.

'It means it's handy,' she explained, studying his hands and arms for any tell-tale signs of irritation. 'You okay, sweetheart? Having fun?'

He nodded without looking up, intent on the job at hand. After complimenting Tom on his creation and going to admire the artwork of the three little girls who were busy painting, Dee said goodbye and went to the door.

'Good luck,' Lisa called after her.

'Thanks,' Dee said, jumping slightly as the doorbell rang.

'Well, go on, answer it,' Lisa urged.

'Right, okay, see you later.'

Dee hurried to the door, opened it, and smiled nervously at the incredibly tall, thin man on her doorstep.

'Dee Hewson?' She nodded. 'Don Reilly from the *Daily Journal.*' He stuck out a hand and smiled. 'Any relation to Bono?'

Dee took it and smiled. If she had a euro for every time someone asked that.

'Unfortunately not. Come on in. Did you find us okay?'

'Hard to miss,' he said, nodding at the large, colourful sign in the garden.

'Oh, right.' Dee grinned. 'My friend Lisa runs the crèche, she has the bottom of the house, with the exception of the kitchen, hence the décor.' She waved a hand around at the brightly coloured murals and the children's photos and artwork which covered the walls.

'It's a huge house, must cost a fortune to heat,' he remarked.

Dee sighed. 'It does.' She led him through to the kitchen and pointed towards the heavy oak table. 'Why don't you take a seat and I'll make some tea. Or would you prefer coffee?'

'Coffee, please,' he eyed up the cartons of food lining the worktops and winked at her, 'and whatever else is going!'

Dee smiled to herself. Men were all the same, put food in front of them and they were happy. She set out soda bread, muffins and scones in front of him and then went to the fridge for milk and butter.

'I'm surprised to see you eat all this stuff,' he gestured

at the spread in front of him. 'I thought you'd be into rice cakes and seaweed quiche.'

She laughed. 'No, I believe in eating healthily, not starving yourself.'

'And this is healthy? Oh, you don't mind if I use this, do you?' He held up a small tape recorder.

'Oh, no, go ahead.'

'Sorry, you were saying?'

'Right. Well, yes, this is all fine – in moderation of course. Once you eat a varied diet then it's fine to have some treats. I'm sure you've heard about the food pyramid.'

'Yeah, sure.'

'Also, all of this food is homemade, so there are no additives and I know exactly how much sugar or salt is in everything.' She smiled at him. 'Not a lot. Please, try something.'

'I'd love to.' He took a scone, cut it in half and spread it generously with butter. 'I'm surprised you don't use a spread. Isn't butter fattening?'

'Butter actually gets a lot of bad press. I use non-salted, and while the fat content may not be good for adults with cholesterol or blood-pressure concerns, it's very necessary for growing children.' She carried his coffee and her tea to the table and sat down.

'These are delicious,' he said, polishing off his scone and reaching for a muffin. 'You really seem to know your stuff. Are you a dietician or nurse or something?'

'Lord, no. My son was diagnosed with asthma and eczema when he was little and I've found that the best way of keeping him healthy is through diet. He hardly eats any processed food now, but when he does' – she rolled her eyes – 'he pays for it.'

'What kind of processed food upsets him?' he asked through a mouthful of muffin.

She shrugged. 'Chicken nuggets, oven chips, cheese—'

'Cheese?' He stared at her.

'The processed stuff,' she amended. 'You know, those orange, shiny slices or plastic triangles, that sort of thing.'

'I live on toasted cheese sandwiches; I suppose that's a bad thing.'

'Not if you use real cheese and wholemeal toast.' She smiled at his wiry frame. 'You don't exactly have to worry about fat, do you?'

'I can eat anything and never put on weight.'

'You must have a high metabolism.'

'Well, I'm always on the go, that's for sure,' he laughed. 'So, what about this little lad of yours; does he ever get sweets?'

'There are some sweets on the market now that have no artificial additives or colourings, so he can have those; he can eat some chocolate, popcorn is fine, and I make my own ice-cream which he loves.'

'What about drinks?' he asked.

'Sorry?'

'Lemonade? Cola? Is he allowed to drink that sort of stuff?'

'He drinks homemade lemonade, juice, milk and water and I wouldn't give him fizzy drinks even if he didn't have allergies. Those drinks make children hyper, destroy their teeth, and set them up with a bad habit for life.'

'You feel strongly about this sort of thing.'

She laughed. 'Sorry, I'll get down off the soapbox now. It's just that when children develop problems like asthma, they have to go on all these terribly strong medications. If their diet was tweaked a little, they might not have to use them as often.'

'It's an interesting point. Now, I wanted to ask you to expand on a few of the points you made about food labelling.'

The journalist helped himself to another muffin and started asking her about various foods. Dee answered his questions as well as she could, giving him examples of the worst offending foodstuffs and healthy alternatives.

'Right, that should do it,' he said finally, as he turned off the recorder and stood up. 'Thanks a million, Dee, I've got plenty here for a really interesting article.'

'Glad to help.' Dee smiled, relieved that it was all over. She had been perched on the edge of her chair throughout and now felt quite drained. Who'd have thought being interviewed could be so stressful? 'Would you like to look around before you go?'

'Yes, please.'

Dee led him back into the hall and then pushed open the first door on the right.

'This is a bathroom that I had installed especially for the children. You see there's a changing table for the babies, a potty area for the toddlers being toilet trained, and then the two cubicles to give the older children their privacy.'

'They're not adult-size toilets, are they?' Don poked his head in to look at the diminutive facilities.

'No. This facility is for children only, so it's fitted with their needs in mind. There's a separate staff toilet,' Dee pointed to another door, 'and over here is the yellow room where the children eat and do their arts and crafts.' The journalist nodded, looking at the low wooden table surrounded by tiny chairs and the built-in shelving that housed Play-Doh, paint pots and other art materials. 'It's all very colourful,' he remarked, grinning at the blue and green chairs, red table and yellow walls.

'To stimulate the children,' Dee said, leading him back into the hall and then into the next room. Here the walls were warm buttermilk and the children's artwork was dotted around the room, a large giraffe height chart stood by the door, marked with the children's names at various levels. 'This is Lisa Dunphy, the boss,' Dee introduced her friend. 'Lisa, this is Don Reilly from the *Daily Journal*.'

'Pleased to meet you.' Lisa smiled and shook his

hand. 'And that's Martha.' She pointed at the young girl who was cuddling a crying baby in an area to the right that was sectioned off by a red wooden fence. 'She looks after our three babies.'

'We have a reading corner over here.' Dee gestured at the area just inside the door with miniature armchairs and sofas and a long, low bookcase. 'And that's the nap room.' She pointed to the section next to the baby area and Don went over to peer in at the three cots, and the stack of small mattresses in the corner.

'Then we have a TV corner.' Dee brought him round the corner where the five older children sat curled up on the two sofas watching *Sesame Street*. 'Say hello, children.'

'Hello,' they chorused obediently.

'He's mine.' Dee pointed at the little boy with dark, curly hair at the end.

Sam looked up and smiled and Don waved. 'Hello, Sam.'

'They only watch about ten or fifteen minutes of children's programmes a day, and we try to make sure they get at least an hour in the garden. If the weather is bad, we have yoga or exercises in the hall.'

'So you work in the crèche, too?' he asked as they said goodbye to Lisa and went back into the hall.

She shook her head. 'I make their meals and help out from time to time but that's all. Most of my time is taken up cooking the food for the café in Better Books in the town. Do you know it?'

His eyes widened. 'I do indeed. And do you supply all of that wonderful food?'

'Most of it.'

'I'm very impressed!'

'Good,' she laughed. 'Feel free to give us some free advertising in your article!'

'I'll do that,' he promised. 'You've got a marvellous place here. I must get our features editor to visit you the next time she's doing a piece on crèches. It would be good advertising for you.'

'We'd be delighted.' Dee beamed at him. She gestured at Lisa and Martha's framed diplomas on the wall in the porch. 'We're very proud of Happy Days and we like to think it's home-from-home for the children.'

'It's a lovely place,' he agreed. 'Okay, well, I'd better get back to the office. Oh,' he paused, 'we'll need a photograph.'

Dee frowned as she mentally went through her photo album. 'I'm not sure if I have anything suitable, at least, nothing recent.'

'No problem, I'll send my photographer around later. What time would suit you?'

She made a face. 'Is a photo really necessary?'

He grinned. 'Absolutely! Readers always want to know the face behind the story. One of you with your little boy would be really nice.'

Dee could just imagine Sam's delight if he got his photo in the paper. 'Okay,' she relented, 'any time after four.'

'I'll have him here at half past,' Don said, sticking out his hand. 'Thanks again, Dee, you've been a great help.'

'Ooh, you're going to be famous!' Lisa teased when Dee went back inside and told her about the photo.

'Hardly, it's only the *Daily Journal*,' Dee scoffed.

'Today, the *Daily Journal*; tomorrow the world,' Lisa breathed theatrically.

Sam bounced up and down on Dee's knee. 'Why are we going to be in the paper, Mummy?'

'I'm not really sure, sweetheart.'

'When is the man coming to take our photograph?'

'After tea.'

'Can I wear my *Pokémon* T-shirt?'

'Sure you can.'

He looked up at her, his eyes round with excitement. 'Will everyone in the whole wide world see my picture?'

Dee laughed. 'Everyone.'

Chapter 5

Martha bent to pick the post off the mat and carried it into the kitchen. Dropping it on the table, she collected the tray of fruit from the fridge and took it back into the crèche. 'Dee gets an awful lot of bills, doesn't she?' Martha remarked as she set the little dishes of fruit in front of the children.

'Shush.' Lisa glared at her and nodded towards Sam.

'Sorry,' Martha mouthed and turned her attention to tying bibs on the younger children.

'Sam, Tom, Natalie,' Lisa called to the three older children who were playing with cards on the floor, 'will you go and wash your hands before snack time, please?'

Sam ran to the door and the other children followed. 'Please don't talk about Dee in front of the children,' Lisa murmured to Martha, aware that even though the two remaining toddlers were only three, they still had big ears.

'I'm sorry,' Martha said again, 'I wasn't gossiping or anything, I just noticed there seem to be a lot of bills lately and Dee does seem to be very preoccupied these days.'

'Well, with the flood and everything it can't be easy,' Lisa reasoned. She didn't want Martha talking about Dee nor did she want her needlessly worrying. 'It's not easy running a business, maintaining this place and looking after a child.'

Martha went to tend to the babies while Lisa settled the two little girls at the table and helped them with their fruit. Martha was right, she realized as she mentally rewound the last few weeks. Dee had seemed a bit glum, but then she'd had a parade of tradesmen through her house at all hours of the day, which was enough to drive anyone mad.

Dee had told her that Sheila was trying to organize a girls' night out and Lisa resolved to follow it up. It had been ages since they'd been out together – largely her fault, she realized guiltily. When she wasn't out with Ger, she was dolling herself up for Ger, cooking for Ger – well, microwaving – or just hanging around waiting for him to call. She smiled wryly. Love had a way of taking over your life but she shouldn't neglect her friends. She'd call Sheila this evening and set something up. Although, Ger was coming over tonight and she needed to wash her hair before he came and she wanted to stop off at the deli on the way home and pick up some of that pâté he loved. She'd call Sheila during her lunch break.

*

Martha returned and was settling the babies into high chairs when the phone rang.

'You go,' she said, 'I'll take over here.'

Wiping her hands on a cloth, Lisa ran to the hall to get the phone, her face lighting up when she heard her boyfriend's voice. 'Ger, how's it going?'

'Yeah, grand. Listen, I won't be able to get over tonight,' he said without preamble.

'Oh?' Lisa tried to keep the disappointment out of her voice. 'What's up?'

'The lads are meeting up for a pint to watch the match. I said I'd go. I just forgot it was tonight.'

'A match?'

'Liverpool versus Chelsea; it should be great.'

'Right. So, do you want to come over tomorrow night instead?' Lisa knew she wasn't supposed to sound so eager.

'I'll give you a shout, Lisa, okay? Listen, got to go, I have a meeting. Seeya.'

'Seeya.'

'He's cancelled again, hasn't he?' Martha said bluntly when she saw Lisa's face.

Lisa bent to clean mouths and scoop up stray fruit. 'What?'

'It was Ger, wasn't it?'

'Yes, it was,' Lisa retorted, 'and no, he can't come over tonight but it's not his fault, he has to work.'

'Right.'

Lisa glared at her and started to clear the table. 'Why don't you get the kids ready to go outside and I'll clean up.'

'Sorry, Lisa, I know I should mind my own business but—'

'Yes, Martha, you should,' Lisa retorted and, picking up the tray, she marched out to the kitchen. She shouldn't have snapped at the girl, of course, but they were together so much, sometimes they just got on each other's nerves.

For the most part, they made a good team, although they had to work quite hard. With eight children under five to look after, both of them needed to be on hand all of the time and only got a break at nap times or when Dee was able to help out. It meant a long and hard day but a better salary. Still, Lisa mused, if they hired another assistant they could take another couple of children on and make some more money. She resolved to discuss it with Dee as soon as possible and before she throttled Martha. Pasting a smile on her face, she went back into the crèche.

'Now then, who wants to do some exercises?'

Dee smiled as she got out of her car, punched in the security code and opened the garden gate. Lisa had the five older children marching around the play area, swinging their arms and warbling in various different tones 'The Grand Old Duke of York'. Sam's face was bright and happy and the cool, fresh air had brought a

healthy glow to his cheeks. And that was more important than anything. That was more important than
bills and bank managers and a supercilious, unhelpful
clerk in the credit union who'd looked at her as if she
were a complete imbecile.

'You had no insurance?' she'd said, her eyebrows
ascending into her hairline, and Dee had felt like punch-
ing her. How dare the smug old bat judge her when she
didn't know her circumstances? The bank manager had
been almost as bad. He'd sighed heavily, looked grave
and given her a lecture on managing her finances and
finally, Dee had exploded.

'I really don't have time for this, can you help me
or not?'

The man eventually agreed to loan her the money but
had set up a very stringent payment plan and made her
sign a page of conditions. 'And of course, I strongly
suggest that you take out an insurance policy. We can
help you with that if you want—'

'No, I have it in hand, thanks,' Dee had lied, just
desperate to escape his office.

Waving to her son, she went into the kitchen and
filled the kettle. If it wasn't so early in the day she'd
have poured herself a glass of restorative wine, not that
she could really afford wine any more. Dee realized
she'd have to make some changes to her lifestyle and try
and cut her costs although her budget was pretty tight

as it was. Perhaps she could persuade Ronan to take more food although that would mean more work and there were only so many hours in the day. She made a strong cup of tea and carried it upstairs to the smallest bedroom that served as her office. There were two other bedrooms that she could easily rent out but she baulked at the idea. She had no real privacy during the day and valued it hugely once the clock struck six.

Sitting down at her desk, she turned on her laptop and pulled up the three spreadsheets that detailed her private and business expenses. She scanned the private one first and as she suspected there was little she could do to improve her situation. The main drains on her finances were the basics like heating, phone, electricity, all necessities. She had a minute amount put aside for clothing and she used most of that for Sam; he went through shoes at an alarming rate. She switched to the Dee's Deli Delights accounts and studied the different categories. Ingredients were by far her biggest expense but there wasn't a lot she could do about that without letting the quality suffer.

Flicking to the next screen, she looked at the Happy Days spreadsheet and sighed. It was Lisa's business, but Dee kept records of the rent, the cost of food, the insurance and an estimation of the various services and utilities used by the crèche. She knew she was definitely undercharging Lisa but apart from paying the rent, Lisa had to pay Martha's salary, supply the various materials and toys used on a daily basis, and support herself. Dee dreaded raising the subject with Lisa but she realized she couldn't afford not to. Lisa would understand when Dee showed her the figures; she'd have to.

A shriek from downstairs had Dee on her feet in an instant. 'What is it, what's wrong?' she called as she hurried down to see what the problem was.

Martha held up the *Daily Journal* while Sam danced around her. 'Guess who's in the paper!' she said.

'We're famous, Mum, we're famous!'

Dee laughed. 'I don't know about that, sweetheart.'

'It's a lovely write-up,' Lisa said from the crèche doorway, 'he even gives Happy Days a mention.'

Dee took the paper and read. It was complimentary to both the crèche and her food but Don still made her sound a bit anal in her attitude towards processed food.

'God, listen to this: "she doesn't let her son eat chicken nuggets or sweets, convinced that they are causing his health problems." He makes me sound like a right monster.'

'I don't think so,' Lisa soothed, 'he's just a single guy who doesn't understand the responsibility involved in childrearing. Other mothers will understand.'

Dee tossed the paper down on the hall table and headed for the kitchen. 'Oh well, today's news, tomorrow's fish and chip wrapper! I need to go and make lunch.'

Chapter 6

Sheila had finally had her way, tonight was the girls' night out and Dee wondered if there was any way she could get out of it. Sheila had booked them into a fancy restaurant and between drinks and taxi fares and the cost of a babysitter it was going to be an expensive night. Dee had offered to drive but Lisa had vetoed that idea straight away. 'You wouldn't be able to drink which kind of defeats the purpose.'

'I can have fun without alcohol,' Dee had argued.

'You are not driving. Anyway, that rust-bucket of yours wouldn't get us down the road.'

And Dee had reluctantly agreed. At least Conor had offered to drop them into Dublin so they would only need to pay for a taxi home and she would be careful what she ate and drank. She still hadn't had a chance to talk to Lisa. No, that wasn't strictly true. She'd been finding reasons *not* to talk to Lisa. Maybe she didn't need to. If she tightened her belt just a little bit more . . . no, that was ridiculous. All she needed was one more problem – like, for example, her car giving up the ghost, and she would be in a right pickle. She had all the facts and figures to show Lisa and her friend would understand. Dee resolved to talk to her on Monday. Tonight, however, she might as well enjoy herself.

Lauren had insisted that they were going dancing after dinner. Her mother had offered to take the twins overnight and she was determined to make the most of her freedom.

'I haven't been dancing since I was pregnant and that was a very weird experience,' she'd told Dee. 'I can't wait to strut my stuff on the dance floor.'

Dee could just imagine it. Lauren was a wild woman when she got going and the prospect of not having the babies to look after when she got home meant she'd really let her hair down.

'Take care of her for me, Dee,' her husband, Phil, had joked. 'No stripping, no snogging and nothing illegal.'

Lauren had made a face. 'I may as well stay at home then!'

Dee had sometimes envied Lauren and Phil's relationship, especially when the twins had come along. Phil was a hands-on father who helped out every chance he could, despite putting in long hours as a taxi driver. Dee didn't think Lauren appreciated how lucky she was. Phil was handsome, fun and devoted to his wife and when she got annoyed or irritated or just plain moody, he'd ignore it and keep out of her way until she calmed down.

Conor wasn't quite as good at reading Dee's moods, in fact, he was lousy at it. Usually, when she was annoyed she just sulked but he never seemed to notice. Occasionally she'd lose her temper and tell him to get lost and he did – it was very annoying. He never shouted back, he just disappeared from her life until she finally gave in and called him. And she always called. Sam's constant whine of 'Where's Conor?' would finally wear her down and she'd pick up the phone. Sometimes, Conor would play it cool for a couple of days but then things would be back to normal until the next time.

'Mummy?' Sam's high-pitched, excited squeal came from downstairs. 'Conor's here.'

'Coming.' Dee put on her gold chain, hoop earrings and bangle, eyed herself up in the mirror and added a last touch of lip gloss. 'You'll have to do,' she told her reflection.

'Very nice.' Conor whistled appreciatively as she walked into the room. 'You should wear dresses more often.'

Dee twirled, and the silky burgundy material swirled out showing off her long, slim legs clad in opaque tights. 'I hope I don't break my neck in these shoes.'

'Are they new?' Conor eyed up the black stilettos.

'God, no, Lisa lent them to me.'

'Where are you off to?' Paula asked from the floor where she was doing a jigsaw puzzle with Sam.

'Dinner in Chapter One and then we're going to either Zanzibar or Traffic – Lauren and Sheila are still arguing about that one – and then we'll probably finish up in Barcode.'

'Cool!' Paula's eyes widened and Dee could see her trying to figure out what three 'oul wans' pushing thirty were doing going to such trendy nightspots.

'Never heard of any of them,' Conor said cheerfully. 'Give me a nice pub and a bit of live music any day.'

Dee rolled her eyes. 'I think I should have bought you a cardy and slippers for your birthday.'

Conor raised his eyebrows. 'Are you still looking for a lift?'

'Yes! Yes, please, sorry.' She kissed his cheek and then went over and gathered Sam into her arms.

'Mum, you're stepping on the jigsaw puzzle.'

'Sor-ry! Excuse me for trying to say goodnight.'

He grinned and hugged her. 'G'night, Mum, have fun.'

'I will, sweetheart, thank you. Now be good for Paula.'

'He always is,' Paula said, tousling the little boy's hair.

'Right, let's go.' Conor picked up his keys and handed Dee her jacket. 'You really do look gorgeous,' he murmured as they went out to his jeep and he opened the passenger door for her.

'You could come too,' Dee said, reaching up to kiss him. 'It's ages since we had a smooch on the dance floor.'

'I can just imagine what Lauren would say if I tagged along.' He laughed. 'Anyway, there's a match on telly.'

'Oh, well, that's that then.' Dee slid into the seat.

'Let's have a night out soon,' he said when he climbed in beside her, 'a proper one.'

She smiled and put a hand on his thigh. 'I'd like that.'

'Right. Where to first?'

'Lauren's, Sheila's meeting us there – mind you, that girl is never on time.'

'Is Phil babysitting?' Conor asked.

'No, Lauren's mum has taken the babies for the night.'

'Maybe he'd like to come to the pub and watch the match.'

'From what I hear he's working very long hours.'

'I suppose two babies must be a lot more expensive than one,' Conor acknowledged. 'Oh, well, no doubt I'll find someone to go with.'

'What about your dad?'

'Mum's dragged him off to an amateur musical production in the parish hall.'

'Oh, he'll love that,' Dee giggled. 'If there's no one in the pub you could always go with them.'

Conor shot her a withering look. 'If you keep this up I'm going to drop you lot there instead.'

'No, please, anything but that,' she groaned. 'I won't say another word.'

They drove in comfortable silence for a while and then Conor shot her a sidelong glance. 'I didn't think you wanted to go at all tonight.'

'I didn't,' she admitted, 'but now that it's here I'm quite looking forward to it. It should be a laugh.'

'You could do with that; you seem to have been a bit down lately.'

'Have I?' Dee considered telling him about her money troubles but what was the point? 'I suppose I'm just a bit tired. It's been a busy time.'

'It may get even busier now that you've been in the paper.'

'You think?'

'Dad's already noticed some new faces in the café. You might have to hire some help if he increases his order again.'

'No way, I can manage. Anyway, I couldn't work with anyone else.'

'You could operate shifts,' Conor pointed out.

'I never thought of that.' Dee pretended to give his idea some consideration but how could she possibly afford to pay someone? If the orders increased and she got an extra couple of catering jobs she would be able to cover her current debts and hopefully take out a new house insurance policy. So she'd have to work harder, it wouldn't kill her. She yawned widely and wondered what time she'd get to bed. Regardless of what time they got home or the fact that tomorrow was Sunday, she still had a busy day ahead.

'Why don't I take Sam out for a few hours tomorrow?' Conor said as if reading her mind.

'Where?' Dee asked, ever cautious.

He shrugged. 'We could go and watch the football up at the grounds and I have a new calf that I'm sure he'd love to meet. And yes, of course I'll lock up the dog,' he said as she opened her mouth to protest.

'Sorry. I think he'd love that, but are you sure you don't mind?'

'I wouldn't have offered if I did.'

And Dee knew that was true. With Conor what you saw was what you got. He was an uncomplicated man who said what he thought, not always showing the greatest tact. But Dee preferred it that way; at least she knew where she stood.

'Nice place,' Lisa murmured as they were led to their tables in the restaurant.

'It's a bit quiet,' Lauren complained.

Sheila rolled her eyes. 'Don't worry, you'll have plenty of time to go mad after we've eaten. We need to line our stomach's first.'

'Could have done that with a burger,' Dee murmured, running her eye down the prices on the menu.

Lauren rolled her eyes. 'Oh, shut up, it's not often we go out. Anyway, the good news is, Phil is going to pick us up so we don't have a taxi fare to worry about.'

'Excellent.' Sheila put down the menu and opened the wine list. 'Let's have a little bubbly to get us in the mood.'

Dee groaned inwardly; so much for trying to keep a tight rein on her purse strings. Still, like Lauren said, they didn't go out often and she could always be careful in her selections. Soup and the pasta vegetarian dish, she decided, shutting the menu before turning her attention to trying to persuade Sheila that the Spanish sparkling wine was much nicer than champagne.

They ordered and then settled down for a chat. Lauren produced photos of the twins and they all cooed over the baby girls.

'They're so cute,' Sheila said. 'I can hardly remember my three at that age.'

'That's 'cos you were in a haze of exhaustion,' Lauren reminded her.

'True,' Sheila agreed with a grin. 'Still, at least you have Phil to help you; my Matthew was worse than useless. Any time they woke, he'd pretend not to hear them.'

'Phil knows he has to pull his weight,' Lauren assured her. 'If I have them for the day, he has to do his share at night.'

'But if he's out driving he needs to get some sleep too,' Dee pointed out, wondering if she really did want Phil to take them home tonight.

'He gets lots of time to snooze between fares, believe me.'

'They're beautiful children,' Lisa said, wistfully. 'Who do you think they look like?'

The champagne had arrived and Lauren took a gulp before replying. 'I'm not sure, it's probably too soon to tell.'

Sheila laughed. 'Well, they have your beautiful eyes. They're such a strange shade of blue, almost like a stormy sea.'

'Very poetic,' Dee said with a grin.

'That comes from my dad's side. His mother was Scottish, they all had eyes like that.'

'I didn't know that.' Dee took a sip of her champagne and licked her lips. It might be horrendously expensive but it was gorgeous.

'My family are all from Dublin,' Lisa said, 'generations of them. Isn't that boring?'

'I don't think so,' Sheila said. 'They were all obviously happy here or they would have left.'

'I always wanted to leave.' Lauren drained her glass and held it out to Sheila for a refill. 'I wanted to move to London when I left school but my dad went ballistic and said no bloody way.'

'I didn't know that. What were you going to do?' Dee asked.

Lauren shrugged. 'Be a model or become an actress, something glamorous.'

'But if you'd done that, you wouldn't have your wonderful career in marketing, you wouldn't have married Phil and you wouldn't have the girls,' Dee pointed out.

'True,' Lauren acknowledged. 'Speaking of marriage, Dee, when are you and Conor going to take the plunge?'

'Yeah, I wish you'd hurry up,' Sheila added. 'It's ages since I've been to a wedding.'

'And I'm sure Sam would love a little brother or sister,' Lauren said with a wink.

'We're fine as we are,' Dee murmured, wishing they'd change the subject. Still, she'd known it was only a matter of time before it came up; it always did. Everyone always asked her. She wondered if Conor got the same hassle from his friends. Probably not. Guys didn't talk about stuff like that, did they?

'He won't hang around for ever, Dee,' Lauren was saying. 'He's not getting any younger and you can see that he's the kind who'd like to settle down.'

'Can you?' Dee asked curiously. She wasn't sure she could see that.

'Salt of the earth, as my dad would say,' Lisa laughed. 'They don't come much straighter than Conor.'

'So why don't you?' Lauren urged. 'You're not still hankering after Neil, are you?'

There was an awkward silence around the table at the mention of Sam's father and Sheila and Lisa shot Lauren reproachful looks.

'Course she's not!' Lisa said staunchly as Dee drained her glass and reached for the bottle.

'Then what are you waiting for, Dee?' Lauren said undeterred. 'Is there someone else?'

Dee bit her lip. 'No.'

'Then why not, love?' Sheila said gently. 'He'd make you so happy, you know he would.'

'Because,' Dee said softly, 'he never fucking asked me, okay?'

The women sat in stunned silence as Dee got up from the table and made her way through the restaurant.

'Shit,' Lauren muttered.

'Why did you have to push her like that?' Sheila said.

'I was only having a bit of fun. Anyway,' she nudged Sheila, 'you joined in.'

'I'll just go and make sure that she's okay.' Lisa stood up and hurried out to the loo after her friend.

'Well, well, well.' Lauren sipped her drink thoughtfully. 'I wonder what's going on there.'

Sheila shook her head. 'I don't understand it. I got the impression he was mad about her and she was the one holding back.'

'Maybe Conor doesn't want to be saddled with someone else's kid.'

Sheila's eyes widened. 'Oh, no, he's not like that and Sam's a great little lad.'

'Yeah, but not *his* little lad. Some men can't get past that.'

'I don't believe Conor's like that.'

Lauren shrugged. 'He hasn't asked her to marry him, have you any better ideas?'

'Should we go after them?'

Lauren shook her head and topped up the glasses. 'No. The best thing we can do is pretend it never happened and get her totally pissed.'

'Dee, are you okay?' Lisa rapped on the loo door again. 'Please come out.'

After a moment the door opened and Dee emerged, red-eyed and sniffing. 'Sorry.'

'Don't be silly, what have you to be sorry for?'

'Making a scene and spoiling the evening.'

Lisa grabbed some hand towels and shoved them into Dee's hand. 'You haven't spoiled anything. We shouldn't have been winding you up.'

'How come Lauren was going on at me about Conor and not you about Ger?' Dee protested.

'I would have been next,' Lisa assured her. 'Would you like to marry him?' she asked gently.

Dee sniffed. 'Of course I would.'

'I'm sure it's only a matter of time before he asks you because he is definitely mad about you. Has he ever used the L word?'

Dee shook her head and dabbed half-heartedly at her eyes. 'No. Maybe he's just staying with me until someone better comes along. Or maybe he already met her. All of those years he spent in Clare, Lisa – what if he met the love of his life down there?'

'Did he have a girlfriend down there?'

'I don't know; all he ever talks about is his mate Aidan, the farm and Aidan's mother's wonderful cooking.'

'I doubt if he lived like a monk when he was in Clare, Dee, but even if there was anyone special, he's not seeing her now, he's seeing you.'

'But he could be settling for me,' Dee insisted.

'Rubbish, the man is mad about you, it's obvious to everyone but you. Is he the right guy for you, though?'

Dee considered the question. 'I didn't think I'd ever be happy with another man after Neil left but with Conor everything's so . . . easy. Oh, lord, that doesn't sound very romantic, does it?' she chuckled.

Lisa shrugged. 'Ger isn't exactly 007 but he's mine and I love him.'

Dee nodded. 'Conor's like my other half. He understands me, we like the same things, have the same values, and, of course, he's great with Sam. We fit, if you know what I mean.'

'Have you told him you love him?' Lisa asked.

Dee shook her head vehemently. 'No way!'

Lisa grinned. 'You're so old-fashioned.'

'No, I just don't want to feel a total prat when he doesn't say it back.'

'Maybe you need to let him know you love him, without actually saying it,' Lisa suggested.

Dee wrinkled her nose. 'That sounds very complicated.'

'Well, we're not going to think about it any more tonight. It's a girls' night out, let's go and have some fun.'

'I can't go back out there,' Dee protested.

'You can and you will,' Lisa said, steering her towards the door.

'Sorry about that,' Dee murmured, taking her seat. She was relieved to see that their food had arrived and Lauren and Sheila were tucking in.

'Nothing to apologize for.' Sheila smiled. 'Eat up, the food is gorgeous.'

'Want to try some of my fish?' Lauren smiled at Dee. 'It's really good.'

'Thanks.' Stretching across she took a forkful of fish from Lauren's plate. 'Oh, yes, that's lovely,' she agreed and then bent her head over her pasta.

'How's your lamb?' Sheila asked Lisa.

'Very good, although not as good as Dee's,' Lisa said loyally.

'I had the shepherd's pie in Better Books last week and it was gorgeous,' Sheila agreed. 'You should open your own restaurant, Dee.'

'Too much work,' Dee replied.

Lisa laughed. 'And you have such an easy life at the moment!'

Dee shrugged. 'It's not so bad, really, and I can work my hours around Sam. I wouldn't be able to do that in a restaurant.'

'He seems to be much healthier these days,' Sheila remarked. 'I haven't seen him with a rash in months.'

'Would it not be better to expose him to more things?' Lauren asked.

'Sorry?' Dee looked up.

'I mean, you'd probably find that he'd get used to animals and foods if he was around them more.'

Dee thought for a while before answering. Her instinct was to tell Lauren that she didn't know what the hell she was talking about, but she'd already had one outburst tonight and she didn't want to ruin the evening completely. Anyway, Lauren didn't really mean any harm. She always shot straight from the hip when she drank and she'd made it clear in the past that she thought Dee was way too over-protective.

'It's an interesting theory, Lauren,' Dee said eventually, 'but I think I'll stick with the preventative strategy for now.'

'I think you've done an amazing job with Sam,' Lisa said, supportive as ever. 'You're a great mother.'

'Brilliant,' Sheila agreed. 'Do the twins eat well, Lauren?'

'So much goes all over them and the floor, it's hard to tell. I need a cigarette.' Lauren pushed back her chair and headed for the door.

'She's a bit prickly tonight,' Lisa observed.

'No more than usual after a few drinks,' Dee said with a grin.

'Now, now, ladies, no bitching on our night out,' Sheila warned.

'I think it's healthy to speak your mind,' Lisa said, slurring her words slightly. 'Much better than keeping it all inside.'

Dee and Sheila exchanged an amused look.

'I'm going to the loo,' Sheila announced. 'Order me a coffee, will you?'

'Not dessert?' Lisa asked.

'Oh, no, I'm stuffed,' Sheila said, patting her flat stomach.

'You'll have something, Dee, won't you?' Lisa said, signalling to the waiter.

'No, I'm fine.'

'Oh.' Lisa's face crumpled in disappointment.

'But you have something,' Dee urged. 'I believe the desserts here are really good.'

'Oh, okay then,' Lisa said, her eyes devouring the menu.

Lauren returned as the waiter came back to take their order.

'Oh, there you are, Lauren, want some dessert?'

Lauren shook her head. 'Just coffee for me.'

Lisa rolled her eyes at the waiter. 'Just the one cheesecake then, please, and I'll have a cappuccino.'

She looked around the table. 'Now, where are we going next?'

Chapter 7

Dee was very grateful that Conor had taken Sam out for the day. Her head ached and any time she bent down, the room went into a spin. After all her protestations she had ended up drinking as much as the other girls and had been more than a little unsteady when Phil dropped her off in the early hours. Despite the upset in the restaurant which she really didn't want to dwell on, Dee had rather enjoyed her night out. Once she and Lauren had hit the dance floor they'd forgotten their differences and let their hair down. Neither of them got the opportunity to do it very often and when they did they usually came home hoarse after singing their hearts out. Last night was no exception and despite her hangover, Dee was glad she'd gone.

Lauren drove her round the twist at times and they had totally different views on raising children but she was great fun. Long after Lisa had got maudlin about Ger and Sheila had started to yawn, Dee and Lauren were going strong.

'You're unbelievable,' Sheila had complained when she'd finally got the two of them to get into Phil's car. 'You never want to come out and once you're out, you never want to go home!'

'That's why I don't go out often,' Dee had told her, closing her eyes and snuggling up against Lisa.

Now, with a very delicate stomach and at least four hours of cooking ahead of her, Dee wished she'd stuck to water and come home early but then it was good to break the rules occasionally. All that dancing and singing was surely good for her stress levels, if not her feet and throat.

She took a couple of aspirin and swallowed them with a strong cup of tea before making a start on preparing the vegetables. Hopefully the pills would have kicked in by the time she started cooking and the smells wouldn't be too hard to handle. She had just finished peeling the potatoes when the doorbell went. Who on earth was that at this hour on a Sunday, she wondered, wiping her hands in her apron as she went to answer the door. Immediately her thoughts went to Sam, although, if there was a problem, Conor would phone. Still, she hurried through the house to the hall door and threw it open.

'Hello, Dee.'

Dee stood staring, her mouth opening and closing again like a startled fish.

'Aren't you going to invite me in?' Neil said gently.

'I'm not sure,' she said eventually, her voice barely a whisper.

'That's understandable.'

'Why are you here, Neil?'

Neil didn't reply but instead held up the newspaper with the photo of Dee and Sam.

She sighed. 'You'd better come in.'

Neil wandered around the kitchen as Dee went through the motions of making tea. She wondered why she was being so polite to this man; this man who had stolen from her and left her in a foreign country without a thought or a care for her well-being. She went into autopilot and tried to come up with a plan. What could she say about Sam? Could she convince Neil that he wasn't his father? No, she realized, he'd never buy that. Sam had his dad's lopsided smile, thick mop of dark, curly hair and grey-green eyes; there was no doubt that they were father and son. Perhaps he just wanted money and thought that because Dee had her own business she was rich. He was in for a shock. Still, it would be great if she could just pay him to leave them alone. She didn't want Sam to meet Neil; it would be too unsettling.

'I've interrupted you,' he said, indicating the chopping board and vegetables.

'Yes.' Dee carried two mugs of tea to the table. She watched him as he stirred in sugar and added milk. He looked well. His hair was shorter and he was wearing dark jeans and a heavy cotton shirt in a moss green shade that brought out the green in his eyes. His shoulders were broader than she remembered and he seemed in good shape. There were a few wrinkles around his eyes – laughter lines? – but on the whole, for nearly thirty, he looked good.

'You look great,' he said.

She realized that while she had been studying him, he'd also been studying her.

'That's a lie,' she said bluntly, knowing she looked her worst. Her face was pale, there were bags under her eyes from lack of sleep, her hair was in an untidy knot on the top of her head, and she was wearing yesterday's crumpled T-shirt and jeans. It annoyed her that he should catch her looking so unkempt. When she'd imagined this confrontation – and she had, often – she was wearing a suit and heels so she could look him in the eye and show him that she was confident and successful. But the reality was very different. She felt lousy, looked lousy and her confidence was shaky at best. In contrast, Neil looked great and relaxed, which was very annoying. He had no reason to feel comfortable.

'You've grown up,' Neil said, ignoring her irritation.

'Being robbed and deserted in a foreign country has that effect,' she spat.

His eyes held hers. 'I can't tell you how much I regret doing that to you. It's tortured me every day we've been apart.'

'Not so much to make you come back or return the money. You're only here now because of Sam.'

He produced a small envelope from the back pocket of his jeans and set it down on the table next to her hand. 'That's what I owe you, with interest.'

Dee stared at it. 'It still doesn't make it all right, Neil. It's been nearly five years!'

'I know that and you're right; I probably wouldn't have come if I hadn't seen the photo. But the only reason I stayed away, Dee, is because I knew you were better off without me.'

'Oh, right, you were doing me a favour, is that it?' she said angrily.

'Yes, Dee, I was,' he said, holding her gaze.

'Well, you did the right thing then. I didn't need you then and I certainly don't need you now and neither does Sam.'

'I can understand that you're angry—'

'Can you? Can you really? You know what, Neil, I don't think you know or understand anything about me and I certainly don't think you care.'

'You're wrong. I treated you very badly and that's haunted me since we parted.'

'That's bullshit and you know it!'

He sighed. 'Okay, it's true that when we split, all I could think about was the next bet. But once I stopped gambling, I fully realized how terribly I'd treated you and how much I must have hurt you.'

'Don't flatter yourself, I was better off without you,'

she said again. 'So are you back in Ireland for good now?' she asked, wondering exactly what he was after.

He kept his eyes on the newspaper in his hand. 'I'm not sure yet but when I saw the picture' – he smiled slightly – 'I had to come.'

'You can't see him,' Dee said hurriedly. 'He's not even here today—'

'It's okay, I didn't expect to meet him. I just wanted to talk about him and about you. I just wanted to catch up.'

'So what do you want to know?' she asked, thinking that the sooner she told him what he wanted to hear, the sooner she could get rid of him.

Dee was startled when his face split into a huge smile.

'Everything, every little detail,' he urged. 'When did you find out you were pregnant? You must have been so frightened. I wish I'd been here for you but I would have been more of a hindrance than a help.' He smiled at her again. 'I bet you were beautiful when you were pregnant.'

'I was big, awkward and I suffered badly with wind,' Dee said sharply but in fact he was right. She had blossomed when she was pregnant and she'd revelled in her round, ripe body and loved the sensation of her child moving within her. 'I was only home a couple of weeks when I found out I was pregnant. I did consider abortion because the last thing I wanted was your child,' she added, hoping to hurt him.

He winced but nodded in understanding and waited for her to continue.

'But they did a scan and I saw this tiny heart beating and I knew I couldn't do it.'

Neil smiled.

'I had a relatively easy pregnancy,' she continued, 'although Pauline was a thorn in my side at the time. Do you remember Pauline?'

'The aunt from hell, how could I forget? She hated me. Wasn't she at least happy that you came home without me?'

'She'd have been happier if I wasn't carrying your baby. Finally she'd thought I was getting my life back on track and going to college, and bam, I'm pregnant. She totally lost it with me. My Uncle Jack had to almost drag her out of the house. She screamed at me that I had destroyed my life but I'd made my bed and now would have to lie on it.'

'Good old Aunt Pauline,' Neil shook his head, 'she was always so supportive.'

'She improved once Sam was born,' Dee admitted, 'and he still sees her and Jack regularly. She's not the maternal sort but she does seem to have a soft spot for Sam.'

'Good, I'm glad he's had some family. My mother will be furious that she's missed out on a grandchild all these years. I don't think she'll ever forgive me.'

Dee stood up and went to put on the kettle again. She

didn't really want more tea but it gave her something to do. 'Have you seen your mother?'

'Yes, I'm staying with her.'

'Oh!' Dee kept her back to him so he couldn't see the shock on her face. 'So how long have you been back?'

'A couple of months.'

Dee digested this piece of information. 'She must be pleased to have you back.'

'She seems to be but, like you, she's not sure if she can trust me. I suppose it's up to me to prove to her, to both of you, that I have changed.'

Dee said nothing, simply made more tea and sat down again.

'Go on with your story,' he urged, 'please?'

She sighed. 'Sam was born on the 18th of December.'

He frowned. 'So that was 2002?'

She nodded. 'He was seven and a half pounds, was completely bald and cried non-stop for the first seven weeks of his life.'

Neil chuckled.

'You wouldn't have been laughing if you'd been there,' Dee snapped. 'I was incredibly tired, very depressed, and I blamed you for everything.'

'I can understand that.'

Dee wished he'd stop being so reasonable. She couldn't believe that he was here in her kitchen and that they were calmly discussing his behaviour over a cup of tea. She should be screaming and shouting at him and throwing him out of the house, telling him he'd never get his hands on his son. She should be telling him about all the times that it was so hard to be alone. But now as he sat here opposite her, all she felt was sad.

'So he was healthy?' he prompted.

'Yes, he was at the beginning.'

'What do you mean?'

'He has asthma and eczema. Not badly,' she added hurriedly when she saw his eyes darken in concern. 'If he avoids cats and dogs and sticks to a healthy diet, he's fine.'

'So they can't fix it?'

She shook her head. 'No, but he should grow out of it. In the meantime, he has steroid cream for when he gets a rash and an inhaler for his breathing. I've cut all processed food out of his diet and give him as much fresh and natural food as possible. That's how I got into all this.' She waved a hand around at the food. 'It started with the crèche, I cooked all the food for the children, then I started catering for parties and business dinners and it went on from there.'

'Yes, I read the article.' He gestured to the paper on the table in front of him. 'And Lisa Dunphy runs the crèche?'

'Yes.'

'Is she as mad as ever?'

Dee couldn't help smiling. 'Not quite. We've all grown up, I suppose.'

'Is she married?'

Dee shook her head.

'And what about you? Are you in a relationship?'

Her eyes met his. 'Yes, yes I am. How about you?'

'Who'd have me?' he joked.

'True.'

He smiled sadly. 'I suppose I deserve that.'

'You do and more.' She was surprised to realize that she was close to tears. It was nearly five years ago now, why did it still hurt?

Neil watched her steadily. 'I know you probably don't care one way or the other but I've stopped gambling.'

'Yeah, right.'

'It's true. After I left you, I went to North Africa and things just went from bad to worse. I stayed there for a few months and then moved to Spain. I bummed around the resorts, doing bar work when I needed the money and then spending it. I didn't lose all the time, once I even won a few grand.'

'And blew it all in a week.'

'A weekend actually,' he corrected with a sad smile. 'Anyway, I got friendly with a Scottish guy who was working as a bouncer in Benidorm and who was even more into gambling than I was. Honest to God, he was unbelievable. If you had diarrhoea he'd bet you how long it would be before you had to go to the loo again. He had a girlfriend and sometimes she'd show up at a poker game with their kid and beg him not to spend their money. He'd tell her to shut up nagging and send her home. One night, when he was completely cleaned out, he bet their flat. It was the only possession they had left and he gave it away, just like that.'

Dee gasped. She had been taking everything he said with a grain of salt but the look on his face told her that this was true. 'What did she do?'

'She took the kid and went home to her mother.'

'And what happened to him?'

He shook his head. 'I don't know. I never saw him after that. It was the wake-up call I needed and I joined Gamblers Anonymous.' He looked down at Sam's picture and smiled. 'I was probably at my first meeting the week this guy was born.'

'It's a pity you didn't feel I was worth changing for,' she said bitterly, 'and then you could have been with him instead of alone in Spain.'

He nodded. 'I know, I'm sorry. I suppose I had to hit rock bottom before I could start to climb back up again. Anyway, I started to work long hours so that I wouldn't have time to even think about gambling.'

'Were you still working as a barman?'

He shook his head. 'No, there was way too much temptation in the bars. I got a job as a bus driver. I took tourists back and forth between the hotels and the airport and when I wasn't working I'd go back to the flat. It was almost fifty miles inland and by the time I'd get there I'd only have time for a few hours' sleep before going back to work; there was little opportunity for me to get up to anything.'

'That was a clever move,' Dee admitted.

He nodded. 'It worked for me. Don't get me wrong, I had a few slips along the way, but I came out the other side. I've turned my life around, Dee. I saved every penny and when my boss decided he'd had enough of the sun, I bought him out.'

Dee frowned. 'When was that?'

'Just a few months ago.'

'So you're making Spain your permanent home.'

He shrugged. 'I'm not sure yet. I'm thinking of starting up a branch here.'

Dee's eyes widened. 'I see.'

'I'll be around for a few months anyway.' He looked at her and then reached into his pocket for a business card. 'I'd love to meet Sam, I'd like to get to know him, but I can understand that you might need time to think about it.'

'Neil, I really don't think—'

He stood up. 'Please, Dee, don't say anything now, just think about it. You can phone me anytime, anytime at all.'

Dee followed him out into the hall and opened the front door. For the first time she noticed the gleaming BMW convertible outside the door.

Neil followed her gaze and shrugged. 'Business is good.'

She turned the business card over and over between

her fingers. 'Don't expect anything, Neil. I'm going to have to give this a lot of thought.'

'I understand that, Dee. You say when, the ball's in your court.' He touched her arm lightly, and smiled. 'Thank you for listening. I can't tell you how much it means.'

Dee watched him walk down the path and climb behind the wheel of the expensive car and then went back inside. In the kitchen she opened the envelope and stared at the cheque. Five thousand euros! That was almost three times what he had taken from her and even with interest it was way too much. She'd have to return it. The last person she wanted to be beholden to was Neil Callen.

Chapter 8

'You bloody won't return it!' Lisa had retorted later when they were sitting at the kitchen table with two mugs of tea.

Dee had abandoned her cooking plans and just dumped the prepared vegetables in a large pot for soup. She had wandered around the house after Neil had left, running through their conversation and staring at the cheque in her hands. Finally, confused and distracted, she'd called Lisa. Ger was off playing golf for the day and Lisa was at a loose end so she'd agreed to come straight over.

'I can't believe it,' Lisa said, 'after all this time. How does he look?'

'Fantastic. He's filled out in all the right places and looks much more of a man.'

Lisa's eyes narrowed. 'I hope you're not going to fall for him all over again.'

'Don't be mad, after what he put me through?'

'Yes, well, don't you forget it. I don't know about you, but I can never forgive him.'

Lisa had been the one to pick up the pieces when Dee had arrived home from Greece, distraught and inconsolable. She had been the one to support Dee through her pregnancy and act as a buffer when Aunt Pauline had called her niece a slut and a tart.

'She's Sam's only relative,' Dee had reasoned when Lisa had asked why she had anything to do with the old witch. 'And she can't help the way she is; she's a product of her upbringing.'

'Your mum wasn't like that,' Lisa had pointed out. Her memories of Catherine Hewson were of a quiet, gentle woman who lived for her daughter.

'No,' Dee had agreed, 'but Pauline was the eldest and always much more controlling than Mum.'

'She's a bully,' Lisa had retorted, 'who walks all over everyone, especially poor Jack. How did he ever marry her?'

It amused Dee that Lisa could be so tough on Pauline and Neil and yet see nothing wrong with Ger and how he treated her. That was the problem with being in love with someone; you exaggerated the good points and tried to ignore the bad ones. Not that Dee for one moment thought that Lisa was in love, more likely she was in love with the idea of being in love. Lisa loved being in a relationship, she loved being part of a couple and she got very depressed when she was single. Whether that was because she missed a man's company or just craved to have children with someone – anyone – Dee wasn't sure.

'So are you going to let him meet Sam?'

Lisa's voice pulled her back to the present and reminded her of the conundrum she faced. 'I don't know.' It was nearly three weeks ago now since she had received that awful bill and wondered how she was going to manage. Now there was a cheque for five thousand euros burning a hole in her pocket.

'I really don't think it's a good idea,' Lisa continued. 'I mean, anyone can say that they own a huge company in another country, who's to say it's actually true?'

'I can. He gave me his business card and I went on to the Internet and found Continental Coaches, based in Benidorm.'

'He could have forged the business card,' Lisa pointed out. 'And even if it's true, it's still no guarantee that he's kicked the gambling for good.'

'No,' Dee agreed, 'but he's definitely different. He couldn't have been more understanding, not in the least bit pushy. He says the ball's in my court now and he'll wait for my call.'

Lisa laughed. 'How very big of him! Dee, have you forgotten this guy stole from you? You could pick the phone up right now and call the cops.'

'Aren't you forgetting about this?' Dee waved the cheque under her nose.

'If a bank robber brings back the loot they don't say, "Thanks very much, off you go".'

'It's not the same, Lisa, and I would never go to the police.'

'More fool you.'

'He's still Sam's dad.'

'Is he? Is he really? Conor's been more of a dad to Sam these last couple of years.'

'I know.' Dee sighed. 'I always thought that if he showed up I would slam the door in his face, honestly I did, but if Neil has really changed how can I stop Sam getting to know him? If he found out about it later in life he'd never forgive me.' She groaned. 'This is so bloody hard, Lisa, so bloody hard.'

Lisa took her hand and squeezed it. 'Don't rush into anything, Dee.'

'I'm not going to,' Dee assured her.

'Good girl. You need to think long and hard about this and then,' she shrugged, 'if you still want Sam to meet the asshole, I'll support you one hundred per cent.'

Dee laughed. 'Thanks.'

'Are you going to tell Conor?'

Dee frowned. 'I suppose so. God, I can't think straight. It's so hard to process all of this with a hangover.'

Lisa rooted in her bag and produced some paracetamol. 'Take two of these and we'll open a bottle of wine.'

'Don't have any.' Dee gulped down the tablets and took a drink of water straight from the tap.

Lisa looked at her watch. 'When are you expecting Conor and Sam back?'

'Not for a couple of hours.'

'Then let's go down to Better Books and have one of your marvellous lunches. What's on the menu?'

Dee grinned. 'Curry.'

'Oh, yes, that's exactly what we need!'

'Hello, you two!'

'Hi, Zoe, how's it going?'

'It's been crazy all morning and I think it's about to get worse; Sunday lunch is always busy.'

'At least you finish at four,' Dee consoled her.

'And I'm off tomorrow.' Zoe grinned. 'I can't wait. So are you two having lunch? I'll get the menus—'

'No need, we'll have two curries,' Dee told her.

Zoe looked from one white face to the other and grinned. 'Oh, of course, you were out last night. How did it go?'

Lisa rolled her eyes. 'When we remember, we'll tell you.'

'That sounds like my kind of night!'

'Hello, ladies.' Ronan had come through from the shop and stopped when he saw them. 'Come to eat your own food, Dee?'

She nodded and instantly regretted it as her head throbbed. 'Don't really feel up to cooking today. *She*' – Dee nodded at Lisa – 'dragged me out on the town last night.'

'*She* also dragged you home again,' Lisa pointed out.

Ronan laughed. 'I take it that means you enjoyed yourselves.'

'Yeah, it was a good night.' Though, Dee realized, after the morning she'd had, her night out was now a dim and distant memory.

'Well, you'll be glad to know your son won't be back for a while yet, Julia's taken him off out for the afternoon.'

Dee's eyes widened. 'I thought he was out with Conor?'

Ronan shook his head. 'Conor has a sick cow, so rather than have Sam knocking around the farm on his own, he dropped him off at our place.'

'He should have brought him home,' Dee said tightly. 'I'm sorry about that, Ronan, I'll go and fetch him right now.'

'What?' Ronan stared at her. 'Why would you do that? He and Julia are having a grand time.'

'Still, it's an imposition.'

'Ah for God's sake, girl, sure you're practically family. Now relax and enjoy your meal and don't worry so much.'

Dee gazed after him, wondering what she should do. Julia had no comprehension of Sam's allergies and was likely to feed him all sorts of rubbish.

'He'll be fine,' Lisa said, recognizing the look on Dee's face. 'He won't eat anything that will sicken him. He's a smart kid, Dee, and he's growing up.'

Dee nodded and was surprised to feel tears pricking

at her eyes. Sam wouldn't need her for much longer, he'd be starting school in September – six months! – and then he really would be independent.

'Practically family, eh?' Lisa's eyes twinkled.

'What?' Dee looked up absently.

'Ronan; he said you were practically family. That doesn't really tie in with what you were saying last night.'

Dee was lost for a moment and then she had a flashback to the scene in the restaurant and how she'd poured her heart out in the loo afterwards. 'Oh, God.'

Lisa made a face. 'Ah, sorry, I thought you'd remember.'

'I do now. Lord, I made such an eejit of myself,' she groaned. 'Lauren and Sheila must think I'm a right gobshite.'

Zoe arrived with two plates of steaming chicken curry and two glasses of milk.

'I've given you extra-large portions,' she told them.

'We didn't order milk,' Lisa said.

'No, I know, but it's perfect with the curry and will settle your stomach. Trust me, I'm an expert, I know what I'm talking about.'

'She's right,' Dee said when Lisa looked sceptical, 'you'll feel almost human after this.'

'No, I'll need a nap after this,' Zoe corrected. 'Then I just might feel human.'

'No time for naps,' Dee muttered, 'I need to get Sam before Julia poisons him.' As she tucked into her curry her mobile phone beeped, indicating she'd received a text message. Pulling it out of her pocket she read the message and smiled.

'What?' Lisa asked.

'"Sam with Mum but don't worry, told her I'd feed him, see you later, x, Conor."' Dee laughed. 'He knows me so well.'

'He does,' Lisa agreed, 'and that's why you should tell him you love him.'

'Oh, please, don't start that again.' Dee put down her fork and sank back in her chair.

'I'm sorry, but I just think it's so silly. He loves you, how can you doubt it? It's written all over his face every time he looks at you. And look at how great he is with Sam.'

'Then why doesn't he say something?'

'Maybe he's afraid it will scare you off. You are so independent, Dee, so capable, so self-sufficient.'

'Me!' Dee spluttered on her milk.

Lisa nodded and paused to eat some food. 'God, this is gorgeous.'

'Thanks.'

'But yes, you and Sam are such a tight, complete little family and you don't seem to need anyone else.'

'That's not true. I mean, who's minding Sam right now, sorry, is supposed to be minding Sam right now?'

'I bet he had to persuade you to let him,' Lisa said with a knowing grin.

Dee scowled at her. 'You'll understand when you have kids of your own and it's even harder to let go if you're a single parent.'

'Hey, I'm not having a go at you.'

'Good, because I'm really not up to it.' Dee bent her head over her food, annoyed with her friend. She knew Lisa meant well but did she have to go on so much? What gave her the right to pass judgement on her love life when she was making such a mess of her own? And yes, maybe she and Sam were close, but that was hardly surprising.

Dee felt her most important job in life was to be there for her son and he was, in essence, her world. Conor was wonderful and Sam adored him but she was terrified that one day he was going to turn around and tell her it was over. Though they had been almost inseparable for more than two years, Conor made no noises about making their relationship more permanent. Sometimes Dee thought she should break up with him just so that she would have control over the hurt that it would cause both her and her son but she could never quite work up the nerve.

Lisa scraped up the last bit of curry off her plate. 'That was good. I'm beginning to feel very slightly better. I wonder how Lauren and Sheila are doing.'

'I hope Lauren is suffering; it was her idea to order those tequila shots at the end of the night.'

Lisa shuddered. 'I wish I'd been as sensible as Sheila

and refused them. Do you know, for every drink she had, she had a glass of water?'

'She's very sensible,' Dee agreed. 'She was probably out for her constitutional at seven this morning.'

Zoe came to clear the dishes away and they ordered tea for Dee and coffee for Lisa. 'Industrial strength,' Lisa told the girl. 'So, what are you going to do about Neil?' she asked when they were alone again.

Dee said nothing for a moment as she thought back on her reaction when she'd found Neil on her doorstep that morning. She had been shocked, angry and, at the same time, thrilled to be finally able to discuss her son with his father. And maybe it was because he looked so much like Sam but she found it hard to maintain her anger especially in light of his supposed redemption. 'Talk to him again, I suppose,' she said finally.

'Why don't you play the detective in the meantime?' Lisa suggested.

'But if he's spent the last four or five years in Spain who can I talk to?'

Lisa chewed on her thumb as she thought about this. 'You could contact a couple of the big hotels in Benidorm and see if they know of him.'

Dee made a face. 'In my best schoolgirl Spanish?'

'I'm sure they all speak English or,' Lisa brightened, 'you could go and see his mother.'

'Yes, I suppose I could,' Dee murmured, thinking that could be a very interesting experience indeed.

Chapter 9

Sam and Conor didn't arrive home until seven, by which time Dee was feeling a little more human and well enough to prepare a thank-you dinner for her and Conor. She knew that Sam would have already had fish and chips – one of the few fast-food dishes that he could eat – and would be content with just a sandwich and a cookie.

'So where were you two?' she asked, hugging her son.

'I went to Sunday school with Auntie Julia and then me and Conor went to a football match and then Conor brought me for fish and chips,' Sam paused for breath and grinned at her, 'and then we went to the movies.'

'Wow, you have had a busy day. What film did you go and see?'

'*Cars*, it was ace.'

'Did you say thank you to Conor?'

'Thanks, Conor,' Sam said obediently.

'You're welcome, champ.'

'Can I watch some telly, Mum?'

'Just for a few minutes and then it's bath time,' Dee said as she cut up some peppers, courgettes and a red onion to accompany their steaks.

'I thought you'd be sending out for a curry tonight,' Conor said when Sam was sitting in front of *Thomas the Tank Engine* munching his snack.

'I already had some for lunch,' Dee admitted with a grin. 'Lisa and I went down to Better Books.'

'You must be one of a very small minority that can go out to eat their own food,' he observed. 'How come Lisa came over? Did she and Ger have a row?'

'No, he was playing golf so she was at a loose end and I felt too miserable to work.' Dee quartered three potatoes, put them on a baking tray with the other vegetables, drizzled olive oil over them, and carried the tray to the oven.

Conor was standing at the counter scanning the Sunday papers, only half his attention on her. 'That was nice.'

'I had a bit of a shock this morning and I needed to talk to someone,' she told him quietly after she'd checked that Sam was too engrossed in his programme to hear her. 'Neil was here.'

'Neil?' Conor looked up, frowning.

Dee nodded towards Sam. 'Yes, *Neil*.'

Conor's eyes widened. 'His dad?' he mouthed.

Dee nodded.

'What did he want?'

'I'll have to fill you in later,' Dee said, washing her hands. 'Okay, Sam, time for your bath.'

It was nearly an hour later before she came back downstairs and Conor immediately switched off the TV and came to stand beside her as she turned on the gas and heated a drop of olive oil in a frying pan. He had opened the wine he had brought and left her glass by the cooker. Dee hadn't planned on drinking tonight but after the day she'd had, she felt in need of fortification. She took a sip and smiled at him. 'Thanks, this is lovely.'

'So, tell me what happened,' he urged her.

She didn't need to ask what he was talking about. 'He saw that photo of me and Sam in the paper,' Dee explained, taking two fillet steaks out of the fridge and adding them to the pan. 'Sam is the image of his dad and between that and Sam's age, it wasn't exactly hard for him to figure it out.'

'So what does he want?'

Dee sighed. 'To get to know him.'

Conor watched her closely. 'And how do you feel about that?'

'Angry, scared, worried,' she admitted.

'He can't take him away from you; you're Sam's mother and you raised him.'

'It's not just that,' she said, turning the steaks.

'Then what is it?'

'It's a long story. Let me finish this first and I'll explain.'

Conor wandered back over to the TV and switched on *Sky News* while Dee quickly cooked the meat and then made gravy with the juices in the pan and some wine.

'It's ready,' she called five minutes later as she carried the plates to the table.

'Thanks.'

Dee topped up his wine glass and left the bottle beside him.

Conor eyed her full glass. 'Aren't you drinking?'

'I'm still recovering from last night,' she admitted, taking a small sip. 'I'm out of practice; my body can't handle that much alcohol any more. Once we'd eaten our curry, Lisa was all set to start again.' Dee shook her head. 'I don't know how she does it.'

Conor said nothing, concentrating on his steak.

'Is it cooked okay for you?'

Conor looked from his plate to her and then laid down his knife and fork. 'It's fine, Dee, but would you please just tell me what's going on?'

'There's nothing going on, Conor,' she assured him, 'but there is a lot about Neil I haven't told you.'

'Go on.'

'I told you we split up when we were travelling in Greece but I didn't tell you why.'

'He knew about Sam and didn't want him, did he?' Conor's fingers tightened around his wine glass.

'No, no, he didn't know about Sam, neither did I.'

'Then what?'

'Look, it's a long story and I need to start at the beginning so you understand. I first met Neil at a dance when I was just seventeen. I hadn't had a real boyfriend before; I was quite shy. But with Neil it was different; I felt I'd known him all my life. He was three years older than me and seemed so mature, so sure of himself. I couldn't believe he was interested in me.'

Conor said nothing but his mouth settled into a grim line.

Dee didn't really notice. She had drifted back into her past. 'After Mum died, Dad was devastated and shut himself off from everyone, including me.'

'That was when you were nine?'

She nodded. 'I know he loved me but he just couldn't seem to function properly any more. It was as though once she had died, his life stopped too. He spent all of his time working and left Aunt Pauline to raise me.'

'Poor you.'

Dee smiled. 'She wasn't so bad. She organized my school uniform, bought me my first bra, God help me, and went to parent-teacher meetings. She was fine when it came to practicalities but no good at the emotional stuff. If I was upset about anything she'd tell me to pull myself together, and if I did anything she didn't agree with she'd tell me that my mother would be turning in her grave.'

'I can't imagine you ever being in trouble,' Conor said.

'I wasn't really,' Dee agreed. 'I was a total mouse at

school but Pauline was very strict and if I as much as raised my voice she'd let me have it.'

'I've only met her twice but she struck me as a very cold woman.'

'Yes, but I think that's just the way she is,' Dee said reasonably. 'She could have left Dad to cope with me and God knows how I would have turned out.'

'If she had, he would have had to get his act together and realize that he had a daughter to rear,' Conor retorted.

Dee shrugged but she was touched at the anger he felt on her behalf. 'Well, we'll never know. Anyway, the point is that Neil was the first one to show me any kind of love since Mum died and I adored him.'

'Your knight in shining armour?'

'Something like that.' She smiled at the memory and the jealousy in Conor's tone. Maybe he did really love her after all. Maybe having Neil back on the scene would make him realize how much.

'So?'

She looked up, realizing he was waiting for her to continue. 'Sorry. Neil had also lost his father when he was young so he knew what it was like for me. The year after we met, I did my leaving certificate and was due to start university the following October. I wasn't bothered either way but Pauline pushed it and Dad agreed, so I decided to go along with it and applied for English literature in all the main universities. It suited me, really, as I hadn't a clue what I wanted to do with my life and it bought me more time.'

'So you went off to college.'

Dee shook her head. 'No. The week before the exam results came out, Dad dropped dead of a heart attack.'

Conor instinctively reached over and squeezed her hand. 'I knew he'd died before Sam came along, but I didn't know it was that long ago. My God, you lost them both so young.'

Dee smiled sadly. 'I suppose I was unlucky. Anyway, Aunt Pauline organized the funeral, packed his clothes off to the charity shop and then started talking about college again.' She shrugged. 'Well, to be honest, I hardly knew my own name at the time, let alone what I wanted to do. The morning the results came out I even forgot to go and collect them!'

'So how did you do?'

'Pretty good and I got offers of a place in three universities.' She laughed. 'For once, Aunt Pauline couldn't accuse me of letting my mum down.'

'But you didn't accept any of them.'

Dee shook her head. 'I intended to; I needed to do something and I just had to get out of this house and that's when Neil had the idea. He said we should take a year out and travel, that it would give me time to get over Dad's death and a chance to really think about what I wanted to do with my future.'

'What did he do?' Conor asked.

'He worked in his uncle's shop and absolutely hated it; he'd been talking about leaving for ages.'

'So this was the perfect opportunity. You don't mind me asking, Dee, but did your dad leave you much in his will?'

Dee shook her head. 'He left me this place and just under twenty thousand. Neil wanted me to sell the house but I couldn't bring myself to. Aunt Pauline had always said how much my mother loved the place. We had only moved here the year before she died and she had great plans to renovate it and extend it, but once she died, Dad didn't bother. It was a miserable old house back then and I hated it, but I knew I couldn't part with it, not when it meant so much to her.' She shrugged. 'Anyway, there was enough cash to ensure we could go and see the world and that's what we decided to do.'

'Did Neil have any money of his own?' Conor said shrewdly.

'Not a lot, no, and I know what you're thinking but you're wrong. Neil cared for me back then and if I hadn't had him I'm not sure I'd have got through it all.'

'Okay, sorry, go on.'

'So we finally set off on our travels the December after Dad died; that would have been 1998. We went to the States first, travelled the length and breadth of it. It was truly wonderful. It was like I'd been living in black and white and suddenly I'd been transformed into full, glorious, Technicolor.' Dee pushed away her half-eaten dinner and took a sip of her wine. 'I think that was the first time I was truly happy since Mum died.

Everything was perfect until we got to Las Vegas. I wasn't that keen on the place but Neil loved it and long after I went to bed, he'd be down in the casino. At first it didn't bother me but then he started to lose some serious money and I got worried. Finally, when he lost really heavily one night, I convinced him to move on and we crossed the border to a motel in Arizona. After a couple of days I realized that he kept making excuses to go off on his own and he finally admitted that he had been going back across the Colorado river to a small town just inside the Nevada border to play the slot machines.' She sighed. 'I went ballistic. I told him that either we left the States immediately or we were finished. He finally agreed but persuaded me I wasn't ready to go home yet and that we should spend some time in Europe first.'

'How long had you been away?'

Dee frowned. 'About sixteen months.'

'And weren't you homesick?'

Dee laughed. 'I didn't have a home, not really. There was just this place and I certainly didn't miss it or Aunt Pauline nagging me all the time. Apart from Lisa, Neil was the only one who mattered and I didn't want to lose him.'

'So you went to Europe.'

'Yeah, we started off in France, then moved down to Spain, then Morocco, Tunisia and then back up to Greece.'

'Over what time frame?'

Dee counted it up on her fingers. 'About two years. I turned twenty-two the November before I returned to Ireland.'

His eyes widened. 'I had no idea you were away for so long.'

'It certainly wasn't the plan, but I suppose we were afraid to come back to reality.'

'Did things improve when you went to Europe?'

'Initially, yes, but it didn't last long.' She shook her head. 'Neil had been bitten by the gambling bug and every so often I would catch him sneaking off to a betting office or playing poker with the locals. I didn't tell him I knew, though; I suppose I realized even then that he couldn't help himself so I'd just suggest it was time to move on.' She paused to take another drink, the glass trembling slightly in her hand.

'We were in Crete and it was coming up to Easter when things finally came to a head. We were arguing about what to do next; I wanted to go home but Neil wanted to go to Egypt. He said we should give ourselves one more month and finally I agreed. Then I got this awful stomach bug and I was really sick for almost a week. Neil was great. He took me to the doctor, went to the chemist for my prescriptions, and looked after me so well. He was really kind and it was the closest we'd been in months. He stayed in the room with me all of the time and, believe me, it was a tiny room. At this stage we could only afford to rent the tiniest, dingiest places.

'One evening I told him to go out and get something to eat and just take a break. I was a lot better but I had no real interest in food and I knew he must be starving. He didn't want to go but in the end he agreed, promising he'd be back within the hour. I fell asleep and I woke up at about eleven, nearly four hours after he'd gone out and he wasn't there. I had my suspicions but at the same time I was worried because he'd been so good to me and so caring and I just didn't believe he'd have left me to go gambling. I decided to go downstairs and have a look around. I was pretty unsteady and light-headed but I knew I wouldn't be able to sleep until I was sure that he was safe.

'There was no sign of him anywhere in the hotel or outside and I was about to go back to the room when I met one of the staff. He was laughing and telling me that I'd be moving to a four-star hotel in the morning because Neil was on a winning streak. I asked him where he was and he gave me directions.'

Dee had to stop and swallow hard as she remembered that awful night. 'I thought I must have got the directions wrong because I was heading out of the town and it was dark and deserted and obviously a poor area. I felt a bit nervous and I decided to go back when I heard a huge cheer. I followed the sound and suddenly

I was in a square and there were thirty or forty people crowded around, screaming, shouting and whistling. I pushed my way through and then I saw them.' She shuddered and closed her eyes. 'It was a cock fight. It was nearly over by the time I arrived, one of the cocks was covered in blood and its eye was hanging out, the other wasn't much better.'

'Jesus!' Conor muttered.

'Neil was there, right in the thick of it. He had a bunch of notes in his hand and was jumping up and down like a madman but it was the wild look in his eyes that really scared me. I knew then that he had a problem and there was nothing I could do or say to fix it. I went back to the hotel and packed.'

'Did you not see him before you left, to confront him?' Conor asked.

'Oh, yes,' she said with a twisted smile. 'I was determined to explain to him why I was leaving and why we were finished. I suppose I thought it might bring him to his senses and he would get help.'

'But he didn't?'

'He said he would, he said he was sorry, he cried, we both cried, and he begged me not to leave until the next day. He said I was too weak to travel and that I should get some sleep before I faced the journey. I was tired and miserable and very weak and I realized he was right; there was no reason to leave in the middle of the night. The next morning when I woke he was gone and he'd taken all of our cash, a ring he'd bought me in San Francisco and my dad's watch with him.'

'The bastard! What did you do? Did you go to the police?'

She shook her head. 'I was too embarrassed and humiliated. Luckily I still had my credit card and so I could pay for my flight home.'

He sat back in his chair, shaking his head. 'I can't believe it.'

'Yeah, well, it took me a while to believe it myself. I knew he had a problem but I never thought for a second that he would actually steal from me.'

'I can't believe he had the nerve to show up here today.' Conor stood up suddenly and started to pace. 'What is it, is he looking for more money? He saw your face in the paper and thought you were good for another few bob?'

She shook her head. 'No, at least I don't think so. He says he's stopped gambling and he's now running his own business, he was driving this very flashy car and he did seem changed, more mature and in control. And he gave me my money back, with interest.'

'So you believe him?' Conor shot her an incredulous look.

'I really don't know what to believe,' Dee said, slumping back in her chair. Suddenly she felt exhausted as if she'd run a marathon. Conor was studying her silently. 'What?'

'You need to be very careful, Dee.' His voice was quiet but she could hear the fury in his words. 'All you know about this man is what he's told you and he hasn't got a great history when it comes to honesty, has he?'

'No,' she agreed, 'but then he hasn't asked me for anything and he gave me my money back.'

'But he's asked to meet Sam,' Conor pointed out.

'Yes.' She chewed on her thumbnail anxiously. 'And though I don't want to stop Sam from getting to know his father I'm afraid of Neil letting him down the way he let me down.'

'And you're instincts are spot on,' he said, leaning forward and staring into her face. 'Sam's done just fine with you up until now; he doesn't need a father.'

'But if I send Neil away and Sam finds out about it when he's ten or fifteen or twenty-five he may never forgive me.'

'And if you let him into Sam's life he might hurt him. Why take the chance?'

Dee sighed. 'It's not that easy. I lost my mum when I was only nine and I know how much I missed her, still miss her. How can I deprive Sam of one of his parents?'

Conor gripped her hands in his. 'It's not the same at all. You knew your mother, you had her for nine years! There was someone for you to miss, but Sam's never known any different. Look at him, Dee, he's a very happy little boy.'

Dee smiled. 'He is, isn't he?'

'Yes, and that's all down to you.' Conor touched

her cheek tenderly. 'You're a fantastic mum and what makes you even more special is that you had no one to learn from.' He leaned across the table and kissed her lightly.

Dee's eyes glistened with tears. 'Thank you, that means a lot.'

'So what are you going to do?'

'I don't know, but I don't want to talk about it any more, is that okay?'

He nodded. 'Maybe you should sleep on it.'

She smiled, standing up and taking his hand. 'Maybe we both should.'

Chapter 10

Sam shrugged off his pyjama bottoms and bent to scratch his ankles. Immediately Dee was on alert. 'What's wrong, sweetheart?'

'Dunno.'

Sam continued to attack his ankles and feet and Dee watched in alarm as the area grew red and the skin started to flake. 'Please try not to scratch, Sam,' she begged, hurrying out to the bathroom for the steroid cream. 'You said that you and Julia went for a walk after church yesterday, where did you go?' she asked as she applied the cream.

Sam didn't look at her. 'Just around.'

Dee shot him a look. 'Where around?'

'On the beach.'

Dee frowned. There was nothing on the beach that should cause him any problems, unless ... 'Did you pet any dogs?'

'Of course not, Mum.' He looked at her reproachfully.

Dee smiled apologetically. Sam knew to his cost not

to touch dogs and anyway, if he had, the rash would have been almost instant and it certainly wouldn't have been on his ankles. 'Did you do anything different?' she asked.

Sam reddened and kept his head down.

'It's okay, darling, you're not in trouble, just tell me.'

'I was messing down at the rock pools with a twig, pretending I was fishing.'

'Go on.'

He looked up at her guiltily. 'I fell in and my shoes and socks got all wet and dirty. But Julia said not to worry about it and that she'd clean me up and she did.' He beamed at her before reaching down to scratch between his toes.

Dee realized the rash stopped at his ankles. 'I see, and did Julia wash your socks in the washing machine?'

Sam nodded, smiling. 'Yes, she said it was no trouble, she was just putting on a wash anyway. She's very nice, Mum.'

'Yes, she is.' Dee sighed. 'Let's leave off your socks and shoes for a while until the cream starts to work. Do you want to go down to the crèche or stay with me?'

'Crèche,' Sam said without hesitation, 'we're making hedgehogs today.'

She bent to hug him. 'Okay then, off you go but come back to me if the rash gets worse.'

It had been nice of Julia to take Sam out and, indeed, she had probably meant well in trying to clean him up. It was just a pity that she hadn't hand-washed the socks in plain water for Dee had no doubt that her son's rash was down to the washing powder Julia had used. But then why would that even occur to the woman? She wouldn't have any idea of the simple things that could trigger Sam's allergies. Thankfully it wasn't too severe but she should really ask Conor to have a tactful word with his mother so that she didn't make the same mistake again.

It was so hard to protect Sam from everything, Dee thought as she searched under the bed for the offending socks. The only way to do it successfully was to forbid Sam to go out with anyone other than herself and that would be as cruel as it would be unfeasible.

And what if Neil came back into her life? Would he want regular access? Would he expect Sam to spend weekends with him, maybe even take him to Spain? She shivered, horrified at the thought of having to share her son. It had always been just the two of them and she wasn't sure she wanted that to change. She shook off her thoughts, gathered up the rest of the washing and went downstairs. The aroma of Irish stew hit her when she walked into the kitchen and, glancing at the clock, she realized it would be ready in thirty minutes. She would take it straight over to Better Books for lunch, collect her other Tupperware containers and also get Ronan's order for next week.

Dee made deliveries on almost a daily basis but, by

Ronan putting in the order just once a week, she was able to organize her time to suit both her duties to the crèche and the café. She put on the washing, tasted the stew – it was excellent – and then turned her attention to the post which Martha had thrown on the kitchen table. As usual there were a number of brown envelopes and Dee steeled herself to open them. She'd much prefer to stick them in a drawer but that would be stupid, childish and irresponsible. Thankfully, there was nothing too scary today and once she'd sorted through them, she tidied the kitchen and went through to the crèche to check on Sam. He was busy painting his potato that would become Harry the Hedgehog before the day was out, stopping every so often to compare his efforts with Tom's.

Lisa looked up and smiled when she saw her. 'Hi, how are you?'

'Fine, just off to Better Books, but I wanted to check on Sam first.'

'I'm keeping his hands busy so he can't really scratch,' Lisa said with a grin, 'but he hasn't been complaining too much.'

Dee went over to her son and crouched down beside him.

'Do you like it, Mum?' He stuck the potato covered in orange paint into her face.

'Lovely,' she laughed. 'Just swivel around for a minute, sweetheart, and let me check your feet.'

Sam obediently swung around and stuck his feet

out. They were still red but the angry blotchiness was already fading.

'Okay, Sam, we'll put on more cream at lunchtime and then you can put your socks and shoes back on.'

'But Mum, we're going out to the garden before lunch,' Sam protested, his lip trembling.

'Not today,' Lisa said quickly before the tears could start. 'We're going to have skipping in the hall and we'll go out to the garden this afternoon.'

Dee smiled gratefully before turning back to her son. 'So, I'll see you later.'

'Bye, Mum.'

Dee grinned as he rubbed away her kiss leaving a smudge of orange paint in its wake. 'Charming! Just as well he's not allergic to that stuff, isn't it?'

'They can even drink it – and they do – and it won't harm them,' Lisa assured her.

'See you later.' Dee waved at the children, who chorused 'Bye-bye, Dee', and then she went into the kitchen to fetch the stew.

'You shouldn't be carrying that.' Vi Valentine was sitting over a coffee and sketchbook when Dee struggled through the door with the vat of food, beads of sweat standing out on her forehead. 'Ronan!'

'Yes?' Ronan walked in and quickly went to relieve Dee of her burden. 'Smells gorgeous,' he said, taking it in behind the counter and putting it carefully on the hob.

'Just keep it on a low heat,' Dee instructed Zoe, 'and it should be perfect through lunch.'

'Great, thanks.' Zoe put on the gas and gave the stew a quick stir. 'It's a bit nippy today so I'd say it will be gone in no time.'

'Have you any soup left?' Dee asked, climbing on to a stool as Ronan poured her a mug of tea. 'Thanks.'

'Yes, there are about ten portions of tomato soup left and about a dozen of the mushroom.'

Ronan pulled out a notebook and pen, poured himself a coffee and sat down beside Dee. 'Keep an eye on the shop, will you, Zoe?'

'Sure.'

Zoe left them and Dee looked around at the few occupants of the café. There was one middle-aged man nursing a coffee and doing a crossword; a couple of young women with babies in buggies having a chat over a cake and a cuppa; and Vi, sketching away in her corner, oblivious to everyone. 'It's a bit quiet in here today, isn't it?'

'Monday.' Ronan shrugged, 'Lunchtime will be busier.' He grinned at her. 'Don't worry, business is very good, I'm not going to reduce the order.'

Dee smiled. 'Good.'

'In fact, I may have to increase it.'

Dee flushed with pleasure but at the same time she wondered how she would cope. They discussed menus for the following week, increasing quantities of hot food for the Friday and the Sunday – Ronan had told her that since that article in the paper they were much busier on Sundays – and discussing new possibilities.

'I'd like us to serve more vegetables, you know, a choice of potatoes and some other options, but not the usual boring carrots and broccoli.'

Dee frowned. 'Mash, baked or boiled potatoes are the only real options in an operation like this.' She already supplied the mash and baked potatoes on alternate days and adding boiled potatoes wouldn't be too much extra work. 'Then you could have ratatouille with the fish pie or chicken stroganoff and a purée of carrot and parsnip with the heavier dishes.'

Ronan beamed at her. 'That's exactly the kind of thing I'm talking about.'

'Okay, good. Let me have a think about it and I'll come back to you with some other options.'

'You're sure it won't be too much for you?' Ronan said. 'You look a bit tired today.'

'I'm fine,' Dee said, draining her mug and standing up. Ronan was studying her, his eyes dark with concern, and Dee wondered for a moment if Conor had told him about Neil. 'I'm just still reeling from my night out with the girls.'

He chuckled. 'That was two days ago. Where's your stamina woman!'

'I know, I'm past it,' she admitted, laughing. 'Right, Ronan, I'll get back to you in a couple of days about this.'

'That's grand, love, thank you.'

'Hey, stranger,' Vi called as she saw Dee heading for the door, 'aren't you going to say hello?'

Dee crossed the room and bent to kiss the powdered cheek. 'You looked so immersed in your work I didn't like to disturb you.'

Vi tossed her pad aside. 'This rubbish?'

Dee rescued the pad and flicked through it. 'Rubbish? I don't think so!' She marvelled at the line drawings of some of Better Books' customers, a wonderful depiction of the food display and a profile head and shoulders of the proprietor. 'You've really captured him,' she enthused, 'you should do portraits more often.'

'Not really my bag, although' – she studied Dee – 'I wouldn't mind painting you.'

Dee rolled her eyes. 'That would be a waste of paint. If you're looking for a model, you've got one right over there.' Dee inclined her head as the lovely Zoe walked past.

'She's a stunner,' Vi agreed, 'but I'm interested in inner beauty too.'

Dee grinned. 'Is that your way of telling me I'm ugly?'

'Stop fishing for compliments,' Vi patted Dee's hand, 'you know you're gorgeous outside and in.'

'Stop, you're making me blush.'

'So will you?'

'What?'

'Will you pose for me?'

'Oh, Vi, it's really not my thing—'

'You would be doing me a huge favour,' Vi pleaded. 'I could come and study you while you worked.'

'I don't think so—'

'You wouldn't even know I was there.'

'Ah, Vi—'

'And in exchange, I'd do a portrait of young Sam,' Vi said with a triumphant grin.

Dee paused. A portrait of Sam would be something she would treasure, especially if it was painted by someone as talented as Vi. 'Go on, then.'

'Wonderful. I've a lot to do this week but I'll come over next Monday about ten.'

'Monday?'

'Is that a problem?' Vi challenged.

Dee sighed and shook her head, smiling. 'No, Vi, no problem.'

Dee felt stressed. Neil had come back into her life and was waiting for her to call him; Ronan was putting her under pressure to produce more dishes and although it would increase her bank balance she wasn't at all sure she could cope; she still hadn't had that chat with Lisa about increasing the rent and she wasn't sure she'd ever work up the courage to do it and now, to cap it all, Vi Valentine was going to become a semi-permanent fixture in her kitchen drawing her 'inner beauty' or more accurately her inner panic.

Dee had seen the keen observation in Vi's work and was afraid of it. There was so much going on in her head right now and the last thing she needed or wanted was to have that exposed; it would be worse than posing nude.

'I didn't know you were back.' Lisa breezed into the kitchen making Dee jump. 'Is everything okay?' she added when she saw Dee's sombre expression.

'Yeah, fine. How's Sam?'

'Not a bother on him, but I put some more cream on his feet just in case.'

'Oh!'

'Sorry, shouldn't I have? I thought you said that's what you were going to do and it's just when you didn't get back by lunchtime—'

'No, that's fine, thanks. Sorry, I'm just a bit distracted. I completely forgot about the cream.'

'Neil?'

'Among other things.'

'Did you tell Conor?'

Dee nodded.

'How did he take it?'

'He's worried for me and for Sam.'

Lisa filled plastic beakers with filtered water and put the lids on. 'So have you decided what you're going to do?'

Dee shook her head, went to the pantry and took out flour, baking soda and butter. She would make bread; that usually calmed her when she was feeling flustered or anxious.

'What about going to see his mother?'

'Sorry?'

'Neil's mother. Why don't you go and see her?' Lisa repeated patiently.

'Shouldn't you be getting back to Martha? The babies are probably awake by now.'

'If you don't want to talk about it just say so,' Lisa said with a scowl.

Dee grinned. 'I don't want to talk about it.'

'Fine, fine, I'm leaving.'

'Lisa?'

The other girl paused in the doorway.

'Thanks.'

Lisa smiled. 'No problem.'

Dee worked solidly through the afternoon in relative peace and then when Lisa and Martha went home, she buttoned Sam into a warm jacket and took him for a walk down on the beach. As they clambered around the rock pools, Sam's feet safely encased in cotton socks and knee-high wellies, Dee felt the tension begin to seep from her bones.

'Can we go on holidays, Mum?' Sam said, out of the blue.

'Not in winter time, sweetheart.'

'Then in the summer?'

'We'll see,' she prevaricated. 'Maybe we could go down to Tramore for a few days.'

'Natalie is going to Switzerland, skiing, and Tom is

going to Scotland in the summer,' Sam told her. 'It would be fun if we could go on a plane together, wouldn't it, Mum?'

He looked up at her, his large, beautiful eyes making her catch her breath.

'Lovely,' she agreed and, watching him run off to play, happy with her response, Dee wondered if his first flight would be with his father.

Chapter 11

Ger flicked the toast crumbs from his trousers and stood up and stretched. Lisa looked up from the newspaper. 'If you're making a cuppa I'd love one.'

Ger walked to the door. 'Sorry, no, I'm off for a pint.'

'But you've only just got here.' She looked at her watch. Ger had arrived only an hour ago, two hours late and an hour after Lisa had scraped his burnt dinner into the bin. He'd said he'd had to work late and of course she understood that and she'd made him a toasted cheese sandwich and brought it in on a tray so he could watch the news.

'Sorry but I promised Terry I'd meet him, he's having a few problems in work. Anyway, you'll be going to bed soon.'

Yeah but she hadn't been planning to go alone. 'I don't know why you bothered coming around at all,' she said sulkily.

Ger came back to the sofa and jumped on her. 'For a cuddle of course,' he said tickling her.

Lisa made a pretence of pushing him off.

'You don't really mind me going, do you?' he murmured into her hair. 'I kind of feel sorry for Terry, he's been having a tough time.'

'You're a big softy.'

'That's me.' He kissed her noisily. 'You go and get your beauty sleep.'

'Will I see you tomorrow night?' Lisa asked, remembering it was Friday.

'I'll call you.' He blew her a kiss and was gone.

With a frustrated sigh, Lisa turned to the telly page but there was nothing decent on. She may as well go and have a bath, shave her legs and do her nails. With luck she would talk Ger into taking her to the new Italian restaurant on the main street tomorrow night. Apparently they did a very good early bird menu and it was quite reasonable. That would appeal to Ger; he believed in value for money. And he was right of course, Lisa hadn't realized what a rip-off most of the restaurants were until he'd pointed it out to her.

'Five euros for two prawns!' Ger had said when he'd seen her starter in the Indian restaurant he'd taken her to for her birthday.

'It's really delicious,' Lisa had ventured.

'It would want to be,' he'd scoffed, 'at two-fifty a prawn.'

'But there's the salad and the lovely sauce too,' Lisa had pointed out.

He had rewarded her with a pitying look. 'God, Lisa you're so gullible.'

And of course he was right, the prices were a bit high but then they had to make a living too, didn't they? But she knew better than to say that to Ger. He felt very strongly about the huge mark-up on food, wine and even water in Irish restaurants. On the rare occasions they did go out Lisa had to listen as he went through the entire menu, putting a figure on what each dish had probably cost to make. It was wearing her down to the point that Lisa was now happier going to the pub and bringing home a takeaway or doing the cooking herself.

And Ger did love her cooking, a fact that greatly amused Dee. Lisa had never really got to grips with the whole healthy living bit, despite seeing and eating the marvellous things Dee produced every day. She didn't have the energy or the interest to prepare things from scratch and why would she when there were perfectly good sauces in jars? As for the ready meals you could get today, they were a far cry from what she had lived on when she first left home. Now she could present Ger with shredded duck with pancakes and plum sauce on a Saturday night and follow it up with a roast beef dinner for lunch the following day complete with roast potatoes and gravy. Dee had no idea how good the quality of this food was now and if she tried to tell her the other girl would just point to the ingredients and walk away. But so what if there were a few additives and sugar and salt – how could you have dinner with no salt? It hadn't done her any harm.

The bath was now full of foaming bubbles and Lisa stripped off, pausing to stand on the weighing scales before she climbed in. She groaned when she saw she'd put on another two pounds and decided that tomorrow she would just have cup-a-soups and coffee. If she could survive on liquids during the day she'd be able to enjoy her dinner all the more.

'How can you eat that muck?' Dee wrinkled her nose as Lisa stirred boiling water into her mug. 'A bowl of my soup would be much healthier and lower in calories.'

Lisa eyed the pot of chicken and vegetable broth on the stove with suspicion. 'It's got bits in it.'

'They're called vegetables,' Dee said slowly.

Lisa shrugged. 'I've made this now; it would be a shame to waste it.'

'Please yourself, but just don't let the kids near it.' Dee took the empty packet, crushed it into a ball and threw it into a bin. 'Do you know how big an insult it is that you prefer that crap to my homemade soup?'

'Don't nag, Dee, it'll give you wrinkles.'

Dee threw a cloth at her. 'So where are you going tonight anyway?'

'I'm not sure yet if Ger is free; he's got a lot on at the moment, but if he is I thought we could go to the Italian restaurant down in Swords.'

Dee raised an eyebrow. 'Council workers do over-time on a Friday night?'

Lisa laughed. 'Maybe not all of them but Ger sometimes does.'

Dee spread a thin layer of butter on a piece of soda bread still warm from the oven and pushed it towards Lisa. 'It might kill the taste of the soup.'

'If I can't get into my new jeans tonight it will be your fault.' Lisa took a bite and grinned at her. 'I don't know about your funny soup but your bread is yummy.'

'I'll be puréeing the soup for the kids – you could have some of that later.'

'You just don't give up, do you?' Lisa headed for the door with her mug. 'Are you coming?'

'Sorry?' Dee looked blank.

'Martha's got a doctor's appointment in half an hour, remember?'

'Oh, damn, I completely forgot.' Dee pushed her hair out of her eyes.

'If it's a problem, I could call the agency—'

Dee shook her head. 'No, just let me finish up here and I'm all yours.'

'Are you sure? You seem a bit flustered.'

Dee's smile was as bright as it was false. 'No, I'm fine.'

Dee ran through her list of jobs for the afternoon. There was still a lot of food to prepare for Better Books for the weekend. The only way she could get it all done was if she got some work done this evening after Sam had gone to bed. Conor wouldn't be too impressed. Friday night was their night and they usually got a takeaway, a bottle of wine and watched a video. Then they had an early night. Sometimes they never even made it as far as the bedroom; the sofa was amazingly comfortable.

She'd have to call him and cancel. Maybe it was just as well. Things had been slightly strained all week with Neil silently coming between them. Dee knew that Conor would love her to tell Neil to go to hell but she couldn't do that. She wasn't sure what to do; she just wanted to do what was best for Sam, if only she could figure out what that was.

Lisa kept nagging her to go and see Neil's mother, Peggy, until Dee felt that she might scream, but she couldn't tell Lisa why that was impossible. She knew at some stage she'd have to find people who were able to corroborate Neil's story but first she needed to talk to him and be sure that his intentions were truly honourable. It would be a lot easier to send him away and it would certainly make Lisa and Conor happy but she owed it to Sam to give Neil a chance. If she decided that father and son shouldn't meet, she wanted to be able to look Sam in the eye in later life and explain why.

Despite the huge amount of work that lay ahead of Dee and the worries crowding her brain, she totally enjoyed her afternoon with the children. When they went out to the garden, she spent all of her time running, chasing, lifting and swinging and it did her as much good as the children.

'And you wonder why I don't go to the gym,' Lisa

said, when they'd come inside and settled the children
down for a nap before tea time.

'I'm convinced, more than ever, that you eat too much
crap,' Dee retorted. 'If you stuck to my food every day
you'd be a size ten in no time.'

Lisa's eyes twinkled. 'Who wants to be a size ten?
Ger likes curves.'

Now, as the last child was collected and Sam had gone
up to his room to play, the two girls wiped, swept and
tidied the toys away. 'You go on and get ready for your
night out,' Dee said, 'I'll mop over the floors.'

'Great, thanks, Dee.' Lisa gathered all of her belong-
ings together and shrugged on her jacket. 'Are you
going out tonight?'

Dee thought of the mountain of work ahead of her
but she wasn't going to tell Lisa about it, the girl would
only be consumed with guilt. 'No, I think I'll just have
a quiet night in.'

'Is Conor coming over?' Lisa persisted.

'Yeah, he'll probably drop by later,' Dee said, though
she'd already called Conor to tell him she was working.

'Okay then, have a good weekend, see you Monday.'
Lisa gave Dee a quick hug.

'Have a good time,' Dee called, locking the front door
after her and going to fetch the mop.

When she'd finished in the crèche, Dee quickly made
some beans on toast and called her son.

'Beans!' His little face lit up when he saw his tea.

'Hands first, please,' Dee said and lifted him up so he could reach into the cavernous Belfast sink and wash his hands.

He sat up at the table and she poured milk into his cup before fetching her tea and taking the seat opposite him. 'Did you have fun today, Sam?'

He nodded, his mouth already full of toast. 'I like it when you come to play with us, Mum.'

Immediately Dee was filled with guilt. 'But you have fun with Lisa and Martha and the other children, don't you?'

'Yeah, but it's even better when you're there too. Can we play a game after tea?'

'Sorry, darling, I have to work.'

His face fell. 'Ah, Mum, but it's Friday.'

Sam got to stay up a bit later at the weekend and Dee usually played junior Scrabble or Snakes and Ladders with him before bedtime.

'Sorry darling,' she said again, 'but I'm trying to get all my work finished tonight so that we can have the whole weekend together.'

'What are we going to do?' he said excitedly. 'Are we going somewhere nice?'

Dee hadn't thought that far ahead. 'You'll just have to wait and see.'

'Ah, Mum!'

'Eat your tea and you can have some Buttons and watch a video while I clean up.'

'Is Conor coming over?'

'No, not tonight.'

'Why not?'

'I told you, I have to work.'

'But he could come and play with me,' Sam persisted.

'Sam, I told you, he's not coming,' Dee snapped.

Sam's bottom lip started to tremble.

'Look, Sam,' Dee said impatiently, 'grown-ups can't always drop what they're doing just to play with children; we're very busy.'

Sam climbed down from the table and went to the door.

'Where are you going?'

'Upstairs.'

'Don't you want to stay here with me?'

He looked at her, unblinking. 'Sorry, I'm busy.'

Dee listened to him stomp upstairs and sighed. 'Well, that's telling me.'

It was almost ten o'clock when Lisa followed Ger into the crowded pub and she grimaced when she saw there was a gang of his cronies from work in the corner and it was patently obvious they'd been there for some time. Now not only was she not getting a nice meal out – he'd convinced her to go for a burger and fries instead – but they weren't even going to have some time alone together. 'Let's sit at the bar,' she whispered in his ear, trying to drag him back.

'We can't do that, it would be rude,' he said, pulling her after him. 'Hey, everyone, you know Lisa.'

Lisa nodded hello and got some garbled responses and waves in return.

'Well, did she feed ya?' one of the lads jeered.

'Shut up, PJ, and buy a round,' Ger retorted.

'I will not, it's your round,' the man protested and belched loudly.

'So what did you make him, love?' A girl with strawberry blonde hair and thick horn-rimmed glasses moved up on the seat and patted the space beside her. 'Was it the shepherd's pie or the lasagne tonight?'

'Don't mind her, Lisa,' Ger said reddening. 'She's had one or twenty too many.'

'My mother always said', the girl continued, 'the way to a man's heart is through his stomach. I think it's quite nice that he goes home for his dinner every night.'

Lisa stiffened and raised an eyebrow at Ger. 'We don't live together.'

'And you still cook for him?' The loudmouthed PJ roared with laughter. 'Nice one, Ger.'

Lisa was seriously thinking of walking out and leaving Ger with his revolting workmates when she saw Conor Fitzgerald sitting at the bar alone. 'Excuse me for a minute,' she said and left, brushing past Ger. 'Hey, Conor, how's it going?'

'Lisa!' His face split into a wide grin. 'Fancy seeing you here.' He took his jacket off the stool beside him and pushed it towards her.

'Where's Dee, in the loo?' she asked as she climbed up beside him.

'No, I'm on my own, she's working tonight.'

Lisa frowned. 'She is?'

It was Conor's turn to look confused. 'Isn't she?'

Lisa sighed. 'Probably. She stood in for Martha this afternoon to help me out. She said it was no problem but it obviously was. Sorry, Conor.'

'Hey, don't worry about it. I don't think she was feeling very sociable anyway. I tell you what, have a drink with me and I'll forgive you.'

'Gladly.' Lisa looked back at where Ger and his pals were huddled in the corner, laughing uproariously. 'A bottle of lager, please.'

'So why do you think she didn't want to go out tonight?' Lisa asked after he'd bought her drink and settled back on the stool beside her.

'Well, I suppose it hasn't exactly been an easy week for her.'

'You mean with Neil showing up.'

Conor inclined his head and lifted his pint. 'Cheers.'

'Cheers.' She took a sip. 'It must have been a bit of a shock all right.'

Conor, a man of few words, nodded again.

'I told her she should check him out a bit more before she makes her decision. I mean, how are we to know he's really changed his ways?'

'You knew him before, didn't you?'

Lisa nodded. 'Yeah, we met him at a dance in town.

Dee's dad didn't really like strangers in the house and Neil lived on the other side of the city so they used to meet in town or they'd end up hanging out at my house.'

'What was he like?' Conor asked.

Lisa smiled. 'Fun. Dee was a different person when he came along.' Suddenly realizing who she was talking to, Lisa clapped a hand to her mouth. 'Sorry.'

Conor smiled reassuringly. 'Don't be silly.'

'It's just that she was always such a serious kid. I mean, first she loses her mum and then she's left to rattle around that bloody house on her own all day.'

'I thought she spent a lot of time with Pauline?'

'Not at all,' Lisa scoffed. 'Pauline would phone to make sure she'd done her homework or to check that she'd ironed her uniform or to warn her to go to bed early but she only saw her once a week and that was to take her to Mass on Sunday.'

'I didn't know that,' Conor said quietly.

Lisa shrugged. 'Dee doesn't talk much about those days, why would she? Anyway, we met Neil during our last school year and they hit it off straight away. Pauline would have gone mental if she'd known they were dating when she was supposed to be studying for her exams. Once we finished school, though, and the heat was off, we had a great summer until . . .'

'Mr Hewson died.'

Lisa sighed. 'It was awful and, of course, Pauline was as tactless and overbearing as usual.'

'So Neil talked her into going to the US.'

Lisa nodded. 'I thought he was right at the time but I had no idea that they would stay away for so long. Still, if she hadn't gone, Pauline would probably have driven her nuts.'

'And she wouldn't have had Sam.'

'True.'

'Lisa? Lisa, come over here, will you?'

Lisa looked up as Ger beckoned her over and climbed down from her stool with an apologetic smile. 'Sorry, Conor, got to get back. Thanks for the drink.' She reached up to kiss his cheek and then went back to sit with Ger.

Chapter 12

Dee was just tidying the kitchen when a rat-tat-tat-tat on the back door made her jump. It was almost eleven o'clock, who the hell would be coming visiting at this hour?

'Dee? It's me, Conor.'

Relieved, she opened the door and stood back to let him in. 'You scared the life out of me.'

'Sorry.' He leaned against the wall and glanced at all the steaming containers on the counter top. 'You've been busy.'

'Yeah, just finished. Want a cuppa or something stronger?'

'Just a coffee, please. I had a couple of pints down the pub.'

'Oh, yeah, anyone interesting there?' Dee put on a kettle for his coffee.

'Lisa and Ger and a very loud crowd from his work.'

'Poor Lisa, she thought they were going out for a meal tonight.'

'Ha! That miserable bastard, she'll be lucky if he bought her a packet of peanuts.'

'Were you talking to them?'

'Just with Lisa for a few minutes. Ger asked me to join them but I dragged myself away. I wanted to check you were okay.'

'Why wouldn't I be?'

He shrugged. 'It's just that we haven't had much of a chance to talk this week.'

'I've been busy,' she said, conscious of the defensive note in her voice.

'Me too,' he said, accepting the mug of coffee from her and sitting down. 'Thanks.'

Dee shot him an apologetic smile. 'Sorry, I haven't been much company lately, have I?'

Conor stretched out his long legs in front of him. 'You've a lot on your mind.'

'Doesn't everyone?'

'We don't all have ex-partners turning up on our doorstep. Have you heard any more from him?'

The question was casual but Dee could hear the concern in his tone. Maybe Lisa was right, maybe he was jealous. The thought comforted Dee. 'He hasn't been in touch but then he said he wouldn't be. He gave me his mobile number so I could call him if or when I was ready.'

'He's playing this perfectly, isn't he?'

Dee frowned. 'Playing?'

'He's sorry, he's reformed, he's rich and he's not

pushing you for an answer.' He shrugged. 'Isn't it all a bit too good to be true?'

Definitely jealous, Dee decided. 'Are you saying I shouldn't let him meet Sam?'

He shook his head. 'No, not at all, I'm just saying you should tread carefully.'

'I thought that was exactly what I was doing,' Dee said tightly.

Conor nodded curtly. 'I'm sorry, you're right of course. And I should just mind my own business.' He put his coffee down and stood up.

'That's not what I said; it's not what I meant!' Dee shook her head in frustration. 'I just feel you're judging me. You seem to have decided, firstly, that he's trying to con me and, secondly, that I'm going to be fooled. Well, Conor, he fooled me once and I can promise you he won't do it again. Having said that if there's a chance that he could be a good father to Sam I will do everything I can to make that happen.'

Conor sighed. 'Sorry, I was out of line. Now, it's late and we're both tired. I'll go.'

'Please don't,' Dee said, immediately sorry for lashing out.

'I have an early start in the morning.' He bent his head to kiss her lightly on the lips and headed for the door. 'Don't forget to lock up. Goodnight, Dee.'

'Goodnight.' She closed the door after him, turned the key in the lock and went upstairs to check on Sam. He was out cold, his skin pale in the glow from the nightlight, his hair an untidy cloud around his face. Dee stood looking at him for a few moments before bending to kiss him. Then, gently, she pulled the duvet up over his shoulders and crept out of the room.

She often wondered if it was the same with every parent but she was physically incapable of being near her sleeping child without kissing him and she couldn't walk by him without resting a hand on his hair or shoulder. She had this impulsion to touch him at every opportunity and thankfully he hadn't reached an age yet where he objected.

She dreaded the day when he would shrink from holding her hand or cringe when she kissed him in public; it would be like a knife through the heart. Maybe she was unnaturally close to Sam because it was just the two of them but she would never know for sure. What she did know was that she would do anything for him regardless of the cost to herself.

Conor walked into the café the next morning, ordered coffee and two scones, and spread out his newspaper. He was halfway through his first scone when his father came through from the shop.

'I thought you'd be having your morning break with the chef,' he said, his eyes twinkling.

'Thanks to you I'm not seeing much of the chef at all,' Conor retorted.

'What does it have to do with me?' Ronan scratched his head, puzzled.

'She seems to be cooking around the clock and she said something about working on new dishes for you.'

Ronan frowned. 'I didn't mean to add to her workload, I thought she'd be glad of the extra money.'

'She is, and she's not complaining,' Conor quickly assured him, 'I am. I'm a bit worried about her to be honest, Dad. She's under a lot of pressure at the moment.'

'She has seemed preoccupied lately,' Ronan agreed, 'and a bit stressed.'

'I think she's exhausted,' Conor said. 'She should really take on extra help. I mean, if she came down with flu or something what would you do?'

'I hadn't thought of that,' Ronan admitted.

'If you had a word with her—'

'Me?'

Conor nodded. 'She'd accept that from you because it's business; if I said it she'd think I was interfering.'

'Really?' Ronan looked at his son curiously.

Conor grinned. 'Have a word, Dad, for all of our sakes.'

It was several days and Dee still hadn't mentioned the new dishes that she was supposedly working on so Ronan decided it was as good an excuse as any to drop in and see her. As usual, her kitchen was warm and full of wonderful aromas although now there was also an easel set up in the corner.

'Are you extending your repertoire, or is young Sam starting early?'

Dee followed his gaze and laughed. 'No, worse; I'm posing for Vi.'

Ronan's eyes widened. 'How did she talk you into that?'

'I'm not too sure,' Dee admitted, 'but I'm giving it three days tops and then she's out.'

'We'll see. Vi is a bit like dandruff; relatively harmless but impossible to get rid of.'

Dee laughed. 'You wouldn't dare say that to her face.'

He held up his hands. 'Do I look stupid?'

Dee set a pot of tea and a plate of scones on the table and sat down opposite him.

'Well, what can I do for you, Ronan?'

He shifted uneasily in his chair and crumbled scone on his plate. 'It's about the revised menus we were talking about—'

'I haven't forgotten about them,' she said quickly, 'I just wanted to work out some figures before I got back to you.'

'There's no rush, none at all, in fact.' He shot her a nervous look from under bushy eyebrows. 'I don't think it's such a good idea after all.'

Dee stopped, her cup halfway to her mouth. 'Oh?'

'Yes, well, you see, Better Books is already heavily dependent on you, Dee, and I'm not sure that I should increase that dependence.'

'I see.' Dee stared at him, stunned.

'I mean, if you got sick then the café wouldn't have a lot of food to sell, would it?'

'But I never get sick,' Dee argued.

He smiled kindly. 'There are no guarantees, Dee.'

'But—'

'What you need is an assistant.'

'I don't know about that—'

'Now, hear me out, if you had an assistant – part-time would probably be sufficient – then we would be protected.'

'Protected?'

'I'd never be left high and dry.' He smiled broadly. 'Think of it as an insurance policy.'

Dee winced. 'Right.'

'I can't think why I didn't realize it before.' He shook his head, mystified at his own stupidity. 'We've been very lucky.'

Dee smiled faintly. 'Yes – yes, we have.'

'So that's settled then.' Ronan swallowed the rest of his scone and dusted the crumbs from his fingers. 'Will you put an advertisement in the paper or use an agency?'

'I'm not sure,' Dee mumbled.

'No, of course, you haven't had time to think about it. An agency is probably best though; you don't have time for answering applications.'

'No.' Dee could agree with at least that statement wholeheartedly.

Ronan stood up and walked to the door. 'Or you could try the Internet; Conor seems to do everything on the Internet. Get him to check it out for you. Farmers aren't half as busy as they make out, you know.'

Dee smiled. 'I'll talk to him.'

'Great, that's great. I'd better let you get back to work.' He paused in the doorway and turned concerned eyes on her. 'I haven't spoken out of turn, I hope.'

'No, Ronan, of course not, this is business after all.'

He smiled. 'I knew you'd understand, Dee. Keep me posted.'

'Will do,' Dee saluted and didn't allow her smile to falter until he was in his car and driving away. 'Oh, God,' she said to herself.

When Vi walked in it was to find Dee slumped over a pad, a pen gripped between her teeth, one hand tugging anxiously on her ponytail. 'What's up?' she asked without preamble, sitting down at her easel.

'Nothing.'

'It looks that way.'

'Please, Vi, leave it.'

'Fine.' Vi picked up her brush and started to mix colours on her palette.

Dee groaned. 'Do you have to do that now, Vi? I'm not really in the mood.'

'I'd never have guessed.' Vi dropped the brush into her water jar.

'I'm sorry.' Dee threw down her pen and flopped back in her chair.

'Tea?' Vi moved to the counter.

'Please.'

Vi said nothing until she'd made the two drinks, set them down on the table and then produced a small hip flask from her voluminous bag.

'Not for me—' Dee started.

'It works better than sugar,' Vi said, ignoring her and pouring a small shot into both their mugs.

'Sugar?' Dee frowned.

'For shock,' Vi reminded her. 'You look like you've had one.'

Dee nodded dumbly.

'Money worries?' Vi guessed.

'In a manner of speaking.'

Vi sipped her tea and waited patiently.

'It's been one thing after another, you know?' Dee said finally. 'I just about get over one hurdle and – bam – there's another one.'

Vi smiled. 'That's life.'

'No, that's Dee Hewson's life,' Dee grumbled.

'So what's today's hurdle?'

'Ronan says I need to hire an assistant as' – she drew quote marks in the air – 'an insurance policy.'

'Or?' Vi raised one pencilled eyebrow.

'Or I suppose he'll have to review his position.' Dee shrugged. 'He's right, of course. If I were to fall and break an arm, I'd be scuppered and so would he.'

'But you can't afford to take anyone on,' Vi surmised.

'Not really,' Dee admitted. 'I just about cover my costs at the moment but if there are any hiccups it's a struggle.'

Vi's eyes narrowed. 'Like that flood you had when that old boiler burst?'

'I wasn't insured,' Dee admitted.

'Oh, darling.' Vi patted her hand. 'Did you tell Ronan?'

'God, no! How unprofessional would that look?'

'But surely Conor knows?'

Dee shook her head. 'You're the first person I've told, apart from the bank manager.'

'And I'd say he was sympathetic,' Vi said dryly.

'He told me in a very polite way that I was stupid and irresponsible, which I'm not. Honestly, Vi, sometimes it's just so hard.'

Vi nodded. 'I know, darling, I know. But you are making it even harder by trying to do it all on your own. Sometimes the bravest thing you can do is to ask for help.'

'Who can I ask? My Aunt Pauline? She and Jack don't have that much and if she did give me a loan it would be accompanied by the obligatory sermon.'

'How about Conor?'

Dee shook her head. 'Everyone thinks farmers are loaded but Conor has to re-invest any profits in the farm. He's almost as strapped for cash as I am.'

'I wish I could help you, darling, but until some millionaire collector discovers me I'm afraid I'm just an impoverished artist.'

Dee looked horrified. 'Oh, Vi, I wasn't asking!'

Vi chuckled. 'I know that, darling. So what are you going to do?'

Dee thought of Neil and the generous cheque he'd given her; she could use that to pay some of her bills but she'd wanted to keep it for Sam. She thought of how she could increase Lisa's rent but that could mean solving her financial crisis at the expense of her friend. She could increase her price list but then Ronan might decide to source another caterer – she might be like family but business was business. Dee leaned on the table, her head in her hands. 'I wish I knew.'

Chapter 13

Ronan drove straight to Conor's farm after he left Dee. He wasn't feeling very good about himself. He'd seen the look of shock in Dee's eyes and he knew that he had completely knocked the wind out of her sails. Still, if it meant she stopped working around the clock it would be worth it. Sometimes the pace of Dee's life made Ronan's head spin. Even when she stopped for a cup of tea in the café it was only for a few minutes.

Yes, everyone had to work hard these days and there was a lot more responsibility if you were self-employed, but you had to take some time for yourself. Dee's social time seemed to revolve around her son, however, and her adult social life meant a couple of drinks in the pub with Conor or the occasional meal out.

It was no life, he decided as he turned into the farmyard, and so he had definitely done her a favour although she probably wouldn't agree right this minute.

*

Climbing out of the car, Ronan took care where he placed his polished brogue shoes. Gingerly, he picked his way through the cowpats and walked around the house to the back door. It was open and he could hear Conor talking on the phone.

Cleaning his shoes on the mat, he went inside, put on the kettle, and sat down at the table to read his son's newspaper while he waited.

'Dad! Sorry, I didn't hear you come in.'

Ronan laid down the paper. 'I've just arrived, how are things?'

'Great. That was Aidan on the phone. He's getting married.'

'Really?' Ronan smiled. Aidan Bow had gone to college with his son and Conor had subsequently worked on the Bow family farm in County Clare. 'Do you know the girl?'

Conor scratched his head. 'Aidan says I met her but I honestly don't remember. She lives nearby, apparently, and he's known her all his life but they only just got together a few months ago.'

'So will he stay on the farm or get his own place do you think?' Ronan asked. Aidan had spent all of his working life on the farm and he'd always said that he would never leave it. His aim in going to agricultural college was to bring the family up to date with the latest technological advancements and show himself as a worthy heir to his father. Now that he was getting married, Ronan wondered if his ambitions had changed.

'His dad has given him a plot of land so he can build a house,' Conor told him, 'so it looks like he plans to stay put.'

'His fiancée may not be that keen. It's not easy living so close to your in-laws.'

Conor laughed. 'Dad, the farm is over a thousand acres, I don't think that's going to be a problem.'

'It's not the land that counts,' Ronan retorted, 'it's who your neighbours are. Still, if you say she's a local she'll have her own family nearby. When's the wedding?'

'October.' Conor sighed. 'That gives me about seven months to work on my speech.'

Ronan chuckled. 'You're going to be the best man?'

Conor nodded. 'For my sins. He says he can't trust any of his friends in Clare because they know too much about him. He figures any story I'll come up with will be from his time in Dublin and no one will be able to check it out.' Conor grinned. 'He's forgetting, however, that I worked alongside him in Clare for nearly four years and we went on three foreign holidays together.'

Ronan shook his head as he thought about the quiet, skinny lad whom Conor was talking about. 'I can't imagine Aidan having ever got up to any mischief.'

Conor laughed. 'He didn't. That's why I'm going to need seven months to come up with something interesting.' As he talked, Conor quickly put teabags into two mugs and carried them to the table. Then he went to the fridge for the milk which he sniffed before pronouncing it safe.

'How can a cattle farmer have sour milk?' Ronan complained.

'It's not sour and they're not dairy cows.' He sat down opposite his father and carefully took the bag out of his mug. 'So, what are you doing up here, Dad?'

'Just reporting back,' Ronan said, peering cautiously into his mug and also sniffing the milk before adding a drop to his tea.

'You talked to Dee?'

Ronan nodded. 'I've just left her.' He took a sip of his tea and winced. 'Thankfully I had my elevenses there.'

'So, how did it go?' Conor asked.

'Fine, I suppose.'

'So she's going to hire someone?'

'I didn't give her a lot of choice.'

'You don't look too happy about it.'

Ronan sighed. 'I'm not. I don't like to force the girl's hand, but you're quite right; she needs the help and I need to know that she has some back-up. To be honest, I'm a bit embarrassed that I didn't think of it myself; not very professional.'

'The café was never your core business, Dad, you're a shopkeeper.'

Ronan nodded. 'True, but I have been very slipshod with the way I'm running the place. It should be an absolute goldmine at this stage and it would be if I put a bit more thought and effort into it. Maybe Dee isn't the only one who needs an assistant.'

'If Mum gave up her charity work she could help.'

'If your mother gave up the charity work we'd be divorced within a year,' Ronan retorted only half joking. 'So, anyway, I did what you asked. Now we'll just have to wait and see what she does next.' Ronan abandoned his tea and stood up.

Conor smiled. 'Thanks, Dad.'

Dee was still making lists, notes and prodding her little calculator later that afternoon when the phone rang. Vi had gone, promising not to come back for a couple of days.

'And hopefully by then you'll have your sparkle back,' she'd said, cupping Dee's face in her hands. 'There's always a solution, Dee, you just have to find it.'

But Dee couldn't. Well, there were lots of solutions but none she felt happy with. The easiest thing to do would be to use Neil's money but she wouldn't do that without his blessing and the thought of going to him, cap in hand, and telling him what a mess she was in didn't appeal.

She put down the calculator and went to the phone. 'Hello, Happy Days Crèche?'

'Oh, I'm sorry, I must have the wrong number. I was looking for Dee Hewson.'

'That's me.'

'Oh! I thought you were a chef!'

'I am, but I rent part of my home to Happy Days Crèche,' Dee explained. 'So do you need an event catered for?'

'No, no, nothing like that. Sorry, this is Carolyn Maher; I'm the producer on the *Right Now* programme on Seven TV.'

'Oh?' Dee frowned. She had seen *Right Now* a couple of times. It was a talk show that was on every afternoon where five people sat around drinking coffee and discussing the main topics in the news.

'We're doing a piece on tomorrow's show about the problems facing women when they are trying to buy healthy foods for their family and I wondered if you would be part of the panel.'

'Me?'

'We'd need you in the studio by about three tomorrow.'

'Tomorrow? Oh, I'm not sure—'

'And, of course, we'd arrange for a car to collect you and take you home afterwards.'

'I really don't know—'

'There would be a small remuneration to compensate you for your time,' the woman continued smoothly.

'What time will the car be here?'

'Oh God, was I completely mad? I think I'll phone and say I'm sick and I can't come.'

'You can't do that!' Lisa exclaimed as she went through Dee's wardrobe. 'It's twelve o'clock, they'd never be able to get someone to stand in for you. You've got to go,' she said as Dee opened her mouth again to protest. 'What are you going to do with your hair?'

Dee put a hand up to her ponytail. 'I wasn't going to do anything with it; I washed it this morning.'

'You can't go like that; you look like a—'

'Cook? Childminder? An overworked mother?'

Lisa sighed. 'You're going on TV, for God's sake, you have to make some kind of effort.'

Dee put a hand to her mouth. 'You know I may not have to pretend I'm sick.'

Lisa smiled. 'You'll be great. Just concentrate on what you want to say and you'll be fine.'

Dee stared at her, her eyes wide. 'But what if I can't say a thing? What if my mind goes blank?'

Lisa thought for a minute. 'Think of a couple of anecdotes that you can churn out if you can't think of anything else to say.'

'Oh, yeah, that's good.' Dee started to pace the room, chewing on her thumb. 'But what?'

'Tell them about some of the things you changed in Sam's diet and the mistakes you made. And why not put together a list of top grocery shopping tips?'

Dee looked at her in admiration. 'You're good at this.' She pulled her pencil out of her apron pocket, sat down at the dressing table and started to scribble on a scrap of paper.

'Good, now all we have to figure out is what you wear.' Lisa turned back to the wardrobe and gazed at the rows of jeans and T-shirts. 'I wish I had time to go home and get you something of mine. It would be two sizes too big but it would still be better than this lot.'

'I'll wear my denim skirt,' Dee said absently.

Lisa pulled out the narrow, knee-length skirt – one of the three skirts Dee owned.

'Okay, but you need something dressy with it.' Inspiration struck. 'Where do you keep your undies?'

'Over there.' Dee pointed at the chest of drawers under the window. 'But—'

Lisa rummaged in the drawers for a minute, muttering something about grannies and then pulled out some camisoles and vest tops. 'Ah, now, this is more like it.'

'I can't wear one of them, it's March,' Dee protested.

'You're in a studio under very hot lights,' Lisa retorted, 'you'll be roasting. This is the one.' She held up a silky chocolate brown camisole that would look great against Dee's creamy complexion and dark brown eyes. 'And you can borrow my boots.'

Dee looked up. 'You've only just bought them.' Lisa had shown her the fabulous, knee-high, brown leather boots and even she knew they were gorgeous.

'Yes,' Lisa agreed, 'and if you get a mark on them I will murder you.'

'You won't have to,' Dee said solemnly, 'I'll kill myself.'

'Now, what jewellery have you got?'

Dee looked blank.

'You need something colourful for around your neck,' Lisa prompted, 'or maybe some dangly earrings or a flashy bangle.'

'I don't have anything like that—' She stopped.

'What?'

'I have some stuff that belonged to my mother.' Dee went to the wardrobe and pulled an ancient jewellery box from a top shelf. 'I haven't looked in here for years but I'm pretty sure it's all just costume jewellery.'

Lisa pounced on it. 'Sounds perfect.' Her face lit up like a child at the ropes of crystal and pearls, a necklace of pink stones – 'What are they?'

Dee shrugged. 'Probably just glass.'

And then Lisa found a long gold chain with blue stones and a matching bracelet.

'This is perfect.'

'It is?' Dee looked at the pieces. They were pretty enough but nothing special.

'The stones will match your skirt and the gold will liven up the brown top.' She arranged the outfit on the bed and Dee had to admit it did look kind of funky.

'We just need to sort out your hair and make-up and you're ready.'

'The producer said they'll do my make-up.'

'You lucky thing! I'd kill to be made up by a professional make-up artist.'

'You could always take my place,' Dee volunteered.

Lisa grinned. 'Not a chance! Now, your hair.' She tugged at the band that was holding Dee's ponytail in place and fluffed her hair around her face. 'Yes, that's better, but it's a pity you don't have time for a trim; it's not in great condition.'

'Thanks.'

But Lisa wasn't listening. She went to the phone by the bed and dialled.

'Who are you calling?'

Lisa grinned. 'A friend.' She turned away from Dee and spoke into the phone.

'Lou? It's Lisa. Listen, I need a really big favour. My friend is going on the telly in a couple of hours and she badly needs your help.' She listened. 'Great!' She gave the girl directions and then put down the phone. 'She'll be here in thirty minutes.'

Dee's eyes widened. 'Was that Lou as in Louise Mulvaney from Short Cut?'

Lisa nodded. 'The very one, she's dating my cousin and the most obliging girl you've ever met.'

'But isn't she busy?'

'Don't worry, it's her day off,' Lisa explained.

Dee laughed and hugged her friend. 'You are amazing!'

Lisa looked at her watch. 'I doubt Martha would agree, I'd better get back downstairs.'

'Oh, has she been on her own all of this time?'

Lisa looked at her crossly. 'As if I'd leave her alone with eight children, what do you take me for? I asked Paula next door to come in and paint with the older children while I sorted you out.'

'Sorry.'

Lisa swatted her friend on the bum and headed for the door. 'Don't let it happen again.'

'Lisa? Thanks.'

Lisa blew her a kiss. 'Just remember me when you're rich and famous.'

When she was alone, Dee turned again to look at the outfit on the bed. It was the most feminine outfit she'd worn in years and she just hoped she could carry it off.

Louise, true to her word, turned up thirty minutes later and walked around and around Dee.

'I know, it's in an awful state,' Dee apologized. 'I've been meaning to make an appointment but I'm just so busy.'

Lou grinned. 'Don't worry, we'll have you looking like a star in no time.'

'I'd settle for presentable,' Dee laughed nervously. The last thing she wanted was some ornate, complicated hairdo that would make her even more uncomfortable and nervous. She cringed as Louise picked up bits of her hair, gathered them together, stood back and looked at her, frowning in concentration. Maybe this hadn't been such a good idea after all.

'Right.' Louise smiled. 'I think I've got it.'

Dee tried to smile. 'Do you?' she croaked.

'Yes. I think you should wear your hair loose but we'll take about an inch off so it just rests on your shoulders. Also, it's too severe the way you pull it back off your face.'

'I did have a fringe but it's grown out.'

'Yes, well, we'll bring it back again, but not a heavy fringe or you'll look like Cher. I'll feather it to frame your face, how does that sound?'

'Great!' Dee smiled, relieved that she wasn't going to end up with a beehive.

Two hours later, she was on her way to the studio in a chauffeur-driven Mercedes with a soft leather interior. She clutched her notes on her lap but reading them had made her feel queasy and she was terrified she'd throw up all over her lovely outfit or, worse, Lisa's boots. The phone hadn't stopped ringing before she left with Ronan, Conor, Zoe and Vi all calling to wish her luck. She was on her way out the door when she realized she hadn't told Aunt Pauline and the woman would be infuriated if she heard about it after the event.

'I'll call her,' Lisa said, propelling her out towards the car. 'What about Neil?'

Dee looked at her blankly and Lisa smiled. 'Well, there's hope for you yet. You hadn't even thought of him, had you?'

'No,' Dee admitted, 'I hadn't.'

'Good.' Lisa hugged her tightly and only let go when Sam came hurtling down the path and threw himself at Dee.

'Good luck, Mummy, good luck.'

Dee sank to her knees, gathered him into her arms, and buried her face in his neck.

'Thank you, sweetheart.'

'We're going to record it so you can watch yourself later,' he told her importantly.

Dee rolled her eyes. 'Great, I can't wait.'

Now, as the car swung through the gates of the television studio, the butterflies in her stomach took flight. Stuffing her notes into her bag she waited until the car came to a halt in front of a doorway and mumbled an embarrassed thank-you when the driver rushed around to open the door for her.

'Good luck, love,' he said with a kind smile.

'Cheers,' Dee said gratefully and went inside to be met by an attractive middle-aged woman who smiled and held out her hand. 'Dee? I'm Carolyn Maher.'

Dee shook it. 'Hi.'

'You're not related to Bono, are you?'

'Sorry, no.'

Carolyn laughed. 'Never mind. I'm so glad you could make it, I think this is going to be a very interesting piece and we're sure to get lots of phone calls.'

Dee nodded dumbly.

'I'll take you down to make-up although' – she scanned Dee's clear complexion, large dark eyes and wide mouth – 'you don't really need it.'

'Thanks.' Dee followed her down the narrow corridors and wished she could come up with something witty or intelligent to say but she couldn't. It didn't bode well for the show.

They came to a tiny room with a large mirror and three chairs in front of it. A plump, blonde girl was setting out palettes of colours on a side table and she looked up and smiled when Carolyn and Dee walked in. 'Hi.'

'Pat, this is Dee Hewson.'

'You can sit here.' The girl indicated the chair in the centre and Dee sat down.

'You can watch the show on that,' Carolyn pointed to the monitor, 'and we'll come and get you in about ten minutes. Can I get you some water?'

Dee shook her head dumbly. She could do with a drink but then she was afraid she might need to use the loo when they were going on air. No, she'd do without a drink. She licked her lips nervously and watched in amazement as Pat transformed her into a sophisticated and, if she did say so herself, rather pretty woman.

Pat chattered on about make-up, the show, the weather and holidays and Dee knew she replied but she couldn't remember afterwards what she actually said. Pat was just applying lip gloss when Carolyn returned.

'Don't you look gorgeous? That eye-shadow is fabulous, Pat.'

'It's nice, isn't it? I've been meaning to try it out for a while but it only really works well on wide-set eyes.' She appraised her handiwork critically. 'I think it will look good on camera.'

Dee thought she looked a bit like a panda but she thanked the girl anyway and followed Carolyn down more corridors and into another small, dark room.

'They're just going to an ad break and then you can go in. I'll introduce you to Marge Preston, our presenter, and the three other guests and then you'll be on in three.'

Dee nodded but said nothing.

'Are you going to be okay?' Carolyn asked, giving her an anxious look.

Dee nodded again and then mumbled an affirmative.

'Just remember what you've come to talk about,' Carolyn advised kindly. 'From what I've read about you, it's something you feel strongly about.'

'Yes – yes, it is.'

'And this is your opportunity to talk to thousands of parents out there and persuade them that they can feed their children healthier options. It's only a twenty-minute slot, Dee, and there are four other people in that studio. If you want to get your message across you're going to have to speak up loudly and clearly and not be intimidated by the other guests.'

For the first time, Dee looked through the window at the people already seated on each side of the presenter and gulped. There was a well-known male journalist who was always on the TV slamming one thing or another; a TV chef – surely she would be on Dee's side? – and another woman whom Dee didn't recognize. She was about to ask Carolyn who she was when the 'on air' light went off and Carolyn was ushering her into the studio.

'Marge, this is Dee Hewson.'

'Oh, any relation to Bono?'

'No, I—'

'Dee, if you sit over there next to John.'

Dee took her place beside the journalist and smiled nervously at him. 'Hi.'

He gave her a brief nod and went back to looking at his notes.

'And this is Polly Underwood.'

The chef waved and smiled at Dee. 'Hi.'

Dee smiled back.

'And this is Ann Baker, junior minister for agriculture and food.'

Dee's ears pricked up. 'Hello.' She nodded politely at the older woman. Ann inclined her head regally.

'Okay, folks, back on air in thirty seconds,' someone called and Dee swallowed hard.

'Right, people,' Marge said, 'I'll introduce this piece by reading a quote from the article in the *Daily Journal* where Dee slams the standard of food labelling in Ireland. Then, Dee, I will come to you and after that I will invite comments from the rest of the panel. If we have time, we'll take some viewers' questions.' She stared into the monitor. 'And that, as they say, will be that. Are we all ready?'

'Five seconds,' yelled the disembodied voice.

Marge smiled into the camera. 'Welcome back.

Joining me now is a lady who doesn't believe in chicken nuggets or cola, who won't give her child sweets and who has some very strong views on the labelling of food; particularly food which is aimed at children.' Marge read an excerpt from the newspaper article and then turned to smile at Dee. 'Welcome, Dee Hewson.'

'Thank you.' Dee managed a small smile.

'Dee, tell me, what made you decide to ban processed food from your home?'

'I wouldn't say that I banned it, exactly, but when my son started to get sick I realized that food had a large part to play in both the cause and the prevention.'

Marge nodded. 'Explain that to me.'

'Well, my son was diagnosed with both eczema and asthma just before he turned three. I did a lot of research into both conditions and I discovered that a healthy diet and an elimination of processed foods would help him.'

'Are we just talking about sweets and fizzy drinks, Dee?'

'No, not at all. I'm talking about any processed food and yes, that includes fish fingers.'

Madge's eyes widened. 'But fish fingers are the staple food of most of the kids in the country.'

Dee nodded. 'And for most kids that's okay, in moderation, but I would still suggest that parents read the labels carefully before they buy if they want to be confident their kids are getting a reasonably healthy meal.'

'Why, what kind of things should they be looking for? Give me an example.'

'In the case of fish fingers, buy ones that state there are no added colourants or preservatives, that are low in fat and low in salt,' Dee ticked the items off on her fingers, 'and if they don't mention any of these things on the front of the packet, don't buy them.'

'That seems a bit over the top, if you don't mind me saying so.' Marge smirked at her other guests.

Dee bristled. 'Not really. It's a very competitive market and if the producer has something to brag about you can bet it will be on the front of the packet. By the same token, I would always suggest that you read the full list of ingredients. If the writing is tiny, it's usually not a good sign.'

'What other things get your back up, Dee?' Marge asked.

Dee put her head on one side. 'Salt is a real problem in our diet and I think it's ridiculous that some labels talk about sodium and some talk about salt when it's not the same thing and their recommended daily allowances are different.'

Marge looked confused. 'I don't understand.'

'Not many people do, that's the problem. To get the salt content of food you need to multiply the sodium figure by 2.5. Our RDA—'

'Sorry?'

'Recommended daily allowance, that's basically what we should be having per day and the RDA of salt is 6 grams. It's a lot less than that for small children. Now some labels show salt content and some show sodium content and it's very confusing.'

'I have to interrupt here,' the politician said, with a patronizing smile. 'We've run a major advertising campaign telling people about the dangers of salt and it's been hugely successful.'

'But Marge still didn't know what the RDA was,' Dee shot back.

Marge grinned. 'She's got you there.'

'Also, did you know that if you added no salt at all to your food you would probably still exceed your recommended daily allowance?'

Marge looked shocked. 'That's if you eat processed food, right?'

Dee smiled sadly. 'You see, Marge, this is part of the problem. People think that processed food is chicken nuggets and fish fingers but it also includes sliced bread, cereal, sliced meats, packet soups, sausages. Ordinary foods that are in all our kitchens.'

'And it would be totally unfeasible to cut it all out,' John, the journalist pointed out.

'Yes, but we can make informed choices,' the politician said piously, 'and that's what our campaign is all about; giving people information.'

'But that's just the problem,' Dee said. 'The information is confusing and conflicting and as a result most people will end up buying the product with the largest advertising budget and the cleverest branding and packaging.'

'I have to agree,' Polly chipped in. 'I think there is huge ignorance in general about what is and isn't good for us and the Government is doing nothing about it.'

'Well, I'm not one to stand up for the Government,' the journalist said dryly, 'but I think you're under-estimating and patronizing the general public. Everyone knows these days what foods affect their cholesterol and their blood pressure. We are a nation that never stops talking about health and diet. Ms Hewson is completely overreacting. Our kids are still kids and they deserve some treats. For heaven's sake, we all grew up eating gobstoppers and crisps and it didn't do us any harm.'

'It's a different world,' Dee replied calmly, 'and when you were growing up there was a lot less processed food; there was no such thing as TV dinners and the microwave hadn't been invented.'

'That's true,' Polly chimed in. 'Our lives have got busier and busier and the choice of easy options in our supermarkets has increased dramatically.'

Marge grinned delightedly, 'Well, let's see what our viewers have to say on the subject. Joe in Santry, what do you think? Is Dee patronizing you?'

'Not at all; I'm gobsmacked at what she's been saying. I didn't know any of this stuff about the salt and I feel like a terrible parent because I've just been looking at the food in our freezer and it's all full of the stuff.'

'Thank you, Joe. Now I want to go to Ann-Marie in Newry. Ann-Marie, what did you want to say to our panel?'

'Hi. I just want to say that Dee is right. I try really hard to feed my children healthily but I'm a working mother and I don't always have time to cook everything from scratch. Also, I find fresh food is often more expensive than buying processed.'

'Minister, what do you say to that?'

'I would completely refute that,' Ann said haughtily. 'If you shop carefully, it's just as cheap to buy fresh ingredients.'

'But they're not as easy to prepare,' Dee said, 'and many children are no longer being taught the basic nutritional facts, let alone how to cook.'

'We have only time for one more call,' Marge cut across them. 'Nicola from Limerick. Nicola, what do you want to say?'

'I want to say that I'm fed up being told how I'm screwing up my children's lives. There's always some know-it-all on telly telling us what we're doing wrong but they should try raising six kids on one income. Half the things that girl said are processed and bad for us are what my kids live on. I can't afford to buy them steak and fish. They get sausages or fish fingers if they're lucky and stew once a week if I get a chance to make it. I don't have time to make fancy food, never mind read labels.'

'You're right, Nicola,' Dee said immediately, 'and that's why I'm saying labelling is so important. There need to be simple standards, clear labelling and stringent penalties for companies who don't keep to those standards. Then if you are buying processed food, you can pick the best of the bunch.'

'I have to agree,' the journalist said gruffly, 'and if such guidelines were properly enforced then the food manufacturers would be forced to produce better quality foods.'

'And finally, Dee, can I ask you, how is your son now?'

Dee smiled. 'He's doing very well. He hasn't had an asthmatic attack in two years and his skin is much better.'

Marge turned back to the camera. 'And I think you'll agree, that says it all. That's it for today. Thank you to my guests . . .'

Chapter 14

When Dee stepped out of the car it was to be met by Lisa, Martha, Sam and all the children cheering and clapping.

'You were fantastic,' Lisa said, hugging her, her eyes shining and her face flushed, 'we were so proud of you. We had to pin Sam down to stop him hugging the telly.'

Sam flung himself at Dee's legs and she swung him up into her arms. 'You were great, Mum,' he said shyly.

'Thanks, sweetheart.'

'I didn't like that nasty lady who was fighting with you.'

'She was just doing her job,' Dee explained.

'Why?'

'That's what the show is all about, people who feel differently about things discuss them and then the audience can decide who makes the most sense.'

Sam wrinkled his nose in confusion. 'But you were just trying to tell them about eating good food.'

Dee smiled. 'Yes, I was.'

'You made mincemeat of that minister, if you'll pardon the pun,' Martha grinned, 'and that stuffy journalist came over on to your side at the end.'

Dee nodded. 'Yes, I was chatting to him briefly afterwards and he seemed quite nice.'

'I liked that chef, Polly Underwood, she seems lovely.'

'Yes,' Dee agreed, 'and she really knows her stuff. She took my email address and she's going to send me some recipes.'

'Come on, let's go inside,' Lisa said. 'The phone hasn't stopped ringing since the programme finished. You listen to your messages and I'll get you a cup of tea.'

'Come on children,' Martha said, 'snack time.'

Dee carefully took off Lisa's boots, flopped on to the sofa in the kitchen and, tucking her feet under her, listened to the messages on her answering machine.

'Dee, Ronan here. You were fantastic! We had the TV on in the café and everyone was cheering you on. Well done, darling, but please don't run off to become a TV star; we'd never manage without you.'

The next message was from Sheila. 'Dee, tried to get you on your mobile but maybe stars don't answer their own phones. Seriously, you were wonderful and you really lit a fire under that old witch Ann Baker. Well done you, and don't forget your friends when you're rich and famous!'

Next there was a stilted message from her aunt.

'Hello, hello, Dee? It's Aunt Pauline here. I saw you on television this afternoon; I can't remember the name of the programme—'

Dee giggled.

'—anyway, I thought you were very articulate and composed, and you put your argument across quite well. You might have looked more authoritative with your hair up and I don't know where you got those boots from, but apart from that I think you made quite a good job of it. I hope Sam is well. Good bye.'

Next, Dee was surprised when Julia's voice rang out.

'Hi, Dee. I'm up at the nursing home and we've all been watching you on television. Weren't you marvellous? I had no idea you were such an authority on food. Anyway, the girls here want me to tell you that you looked great and well done. That's from me, too, of course. Not sure about those boots, though. Bye-bye, Dee, see you soon. Love to Sam.'

And lastly, Dee froze when she heard Neil's voice.

'Dee, Mum just called to tell me about your television appearance. Well done, she says you were great. Sam's a lucky boy to have you. See you soon . . . I hope. Bye.'

'Wow, was that Neil?' Lisa turned to look at her.

Dee nodded. 'He shouldn't really have left a message; Sam could have heard it.'

'Does Sam know his dad's name?' Lisa asked.

'Yes, of course.'

'Maybe you should phone Neil and tell him to be more careful.'

Dee sighed. 'I'll send him a text later.'

'It was nice of him to call, I suppose,' Lisa offered.

Dee grinned. 'Careful, you just said something positive about him!'

'Don't hold it against me.' Lisa handed her a cup of tea.

'Thanks.' Reaching into her bag, Dee pulled out her mobile phone and switched it on. Immediately it started beeping as message after message came through.

'You're popular,' Lisa laughed.

'I know, it's amazing, everyone seems to have been watching the programme.'

Lisa took a sip of her own drink. 'You'll be in demand now.'

Dee laughed. 'Well, if they're all willing to give me five hundred euros for twenty minutes work I won't object.'

'You'll be able to give up the day job and become a lady who lunches, albeit healthily,' Lisa joked.

Dee sighed. 'It will be a very long time before I can afford to give up the day job.'

Lisa immediately picked up on her tone. 'What's up?'

Dee's eyes met hers. 'Things are a bit of a struggle at the moment; funds are low, as they say, and Ronan wants to expand his menu.'

'Well, that's good . . . isn't it?'

Dee shrugged. 'It would be, except he wants me to take on an assistant. He's afraid that the café is too dependent on me and if I get sick or am knocked down by a bus, he's up a certain creek without a paddle.'

'I see.' Lisa nodded. 'And you can't afford an assistant?'

'No, if I pay someone else I'll just about break even. I'd be better off giving up the catering altogether and getting a job as a cook. At least then I wouldn't have the worry or responsibility of running things.' Dee dragged a weary hand across her eyes, smudging her beautiful eye make-up.

'What if Happy Days moved to another premises, would that help?' Lisa said quietly, her eyes riveted to Dee's.

'No! Oh, God, no, Lisa, I don't want that at all.'

Lisa visibly relaxed. 'Thank God for that.'

'But I might have to increase your rent,' Dee said quickly before she lost her nerve. Lisa nodded. 'That's fair enough.'

Dee stared. 'It is?'

'Sure. I mean, you haven't increased it since we opened and that's over three years ago now. How much were you thinking of?'

Dee pretended to consider the question. 'Annual inflation is usually about five per cent, isn't it? So if we say fifteen per cent, would that be okay?'

Lisa grabbed Dee's pad and scribbled down some figures. 'I'm not sure about that.'

Dee's heart sank. If she couldn't agree a reasonable figure with Lisa she didn't know what she would do, and the fact that she'd brought up the whole issue would probably come between them and ruin their friendship.

'It doesn't seem enough.'

'Excuse me?'

Lisa smiled. 'I said, it's not enough. You supply and cook all the food and you help out in the crèche. It's a routine we've sort of slipped into over the years and never formalized and maybe we should. I'm sure your accountant would be a lot happier if we did.'

Dee rolled her eyes. Her accountant, a conservative old buzzard, had been a friend of her father's and he came in once a year to prepare her tax returns and give her a lecture on the proper way to run a business which was basically not the way she was doing it. 'I don't want to impoverish your business in order to prop up mine,' she said now.

'We have to put our heads together and work something out. Happy Days is a successful business and so is Deli Delights, yet we're both working harder than ever. I'd love to take on another person and then we could increase the number of children, thereby increasing income, and at the same time giving Martha and me some more free time. I'm terrified of losing Martha to another crèche and I think I will if I don't reduce her workload soon. Also, I'd like to be able to offer the older children more variety and take them out on trips and that's just not feasible at the moment.'

Dee stared at her. 'You've given this a lot of thought, haven't you? Why didn't you say something before?'

Lisa reddened. 'I thought you'd want me out. Your business is doing so well I was afraid you'd want to expand and there wouldn't be space any more for Happy Days.'

Dee shook her head emphatically. 'No, whatever the future holds I want it to include Happy Days. It's important for Sam that you're here,' she smiled at her friend, 'and for me.'

'I'm glad to hear it.' Lisa stood up. 'Look, I need to get back to the troops but do you want to talk again later?'

'Why don't I make you dinner and we can talk then?' Dee offered.

'Great.'

'Right, just let me get changed and I'll give you a hand with the kids.'

'You don't have to do that—'

Dee grinned. 'I know, but there's no way I'm going to get any real work done today so I may as well be in there with you guys.'

Lisa laughed. 'I won't say no. The children will be delighted to have a TV star to play with.'

Lisa left and Dee read the text messages on her phone as she finished her tea:

WHAT A WOMAN!! PROUD OF U!! XX LAUREN

U WER GRT, DEE, WELL DONE. DINNER 2NITE
2 CELEBRTE? PAULA SAYS SHE'LL BABYSIT.
X. CONOR

Dee replied immediately:

SORRY, GOT A MEETNG WITH LISA.
CAN WE DO IT FRIDAY? X. DEE

She decided to text Neil before she forgot. It would
be a disaster if he called again and Sam answered or
overheard the name.

NEIL. TNX FOR GD WISHES BT PLEASE DON'T
PHONE AGAIN – SAM MIGHT BE HERE. DEE

She pressed send and within a few seconds got a reply.

SO SORRY, DEE, NEVER THOUGHT.
WON'T HAPPEN AGAIN. NEIL

She sighed, relieved, although he now had her mobile
number, she realized. Still, it looked as if he was keeping to his word. He hadn't been in touch in the three
weeks since his surprise visit and she did appreciate
that. She would arrange to see him again soon, she
decided. She'd had time to get used to the fact that he
was back in Ireland and she wanted to talk to him,
question him, study him, and see if he really deserved

to be part of her son's life. She would have to meet him in the city, though, Banford was too small and she didn't want to risk Sam seeing them or hearing about Neil's visit from a nosy neighbour.

If they eventually met, it would be in controlled circumstances and Dee would be the one in control.

Her phone beeped and Dee read the message that Conor had sent back.

FRI IS FINE. PAULA BOOKD FOR 8. X.

'GREAT, XX,' Dee typed and pressed send. Then, after she had put her mug in the sink, she went upstairs to change into more practical clothes for playing with children. As she walked through the hall, the phone rang and she went across to answer it. 'Happy Days Crèche?'

'Dee?'

'Yes?'

'Dee, it's Carolyn Maher from Seven TV.'

'Oh, hi, Carolyn.' Dee crouched on the bottom stair and smoothed her skirt down over her knees.

'I just wanted to say thank you for coming on the show, you were really great.'

'Oh, thanks, you're very kind.'

'No, seriously, the phone hasn't stopped ringing and we've got a ton of emails and texts and most of them are about you.'

Dee cringed. 'Did I upset some people?'

'On the contrary, a lot of the messages are from

people saying that they learned more about food in twenty minutes than they ever had before. As for the whole salt argument, you really touched a nerve there. One woman said that when the programme ended she went through her whole larder and sat down and cried when she realized how much salt she was feeding her children.'

'And we never even got to tell them about sugar,' Dee said regretfully.

Carolyn laughed. 'I think you have a lot to say, Dee, and one show isn't enough to do it. We're thinking of having a regular spot every week on the show about nutrition and diet.'

'That's a great idea,' Dee said, delighted.

'So will you do it?'

'Sorry?'

'Be on the show every week?'

'Oh, Carolyn, I don't know—'

'Obviously it would involve some research and more of your time, so we would pay you more.'

'Really?'

Carolyn laughed. 'Why don't you come in some time tomorrow and we can talk about it?'

Dee swallowed hard. 'I suppose there would be no harm in talking.'

'About eleven-thirty?'

Dee could hear a smile in the other woman's voice. 'I'll see you then.'

*

'Oh. My. God.' Lisa took a gulp of her wine. 'Oh. My. God.'

'I know.' Dee poured a glass for herself and sat down next to Lisa on the sofa.

She had spent the afternoon with the children and they'd gone out to the garden for an energetic game of leapfrog. Sam had adored having his mother around and it had made Dee more determined than ever to make some changes to her life. She would not get rich at the expense of time with her son. Putting all of her worries firmly to the back of her mind she had thrown herself into the childish games and, though she was tired and sore at the end of it, she felt happy.

Now Sam was tucked up in bed fast asleep, there was a homemade pizza in the oven, and she'd just told Lisa her news.

Her friend was gobsmacked. 'I wonder how much they'll pay you.'

'No idea,' Dee said, 'but it will have to be good if I'm to spend time on research and then there's the travelling. They're unlikely to send a car for me every week.'

Lisa sighed. 'Oh, it would be nice if they did. I could get really used to being driven around.'

Dee laughed. 'Me too, but I won't hold my breath.'

'So she wants to do a regular spot about diet?'

'Yes, and general nutrition. I don't know why she's asking me. I'm sure Polly would have been a much better choice.'

'Maybe Polly will be doing it too,' Lisa reasoned.

Dee nodded excitedly. 'You could be right; after all, there is always a panel of guests.'

'On the other hand it could be Ann Baker.'

'No!' Dee groaned.

'No,' Lisa agreed, laughing. 'One, as a minister she wouldn't have the time – or she shouldn't have the time – and two, she was rubbish.'

Dee stood up and went to the oven to check on their pizza.

'This forces our hand a bit,' Lisa observed. 'We need to cut you some slack if you're going to do this.'

Dee closed the door of the oven, turned down the temperature slightly and rejoined her on the sofa. 'Yes and I'd better find a cook. Ronan is going to be on my case until I do.'

'Ronan's an interesting character, isn't he?' Lisa mused. 'He comes across all easy going and relaxed, but there's a tough enough businessman underneath.'

'You'd better believe it,' Dee agreed. 'He has a softly, softly approach but he's a force to be reckoned with. I like him.'

'And his son,' Lisa nudged her.

Dee grinned. 'Yeah, him too.'

'Pity about the mother-in-law.'

'Oh, Julia's not so bad. She left a nice message on the phone today although she didn't like your boots.'

'Bitch.'

Dee laughed. 'She'll be so impressed if I'm on telly all the time.'

'You're going to have to go shopping,' Lisa announced.

'Why?'

Lisa rolled her eyes. 'Well, you can't wear the same skirt every week.'

Dee's face fell. 'I hadn't thought of that. What a pain, I don't have the time or the money for shopping.'

Lisa's eyes lit up. 'Maybe they'll give you an expense account or they'll dress you from their wardrobe department.'

'Oh, right. One week I'll be dressed as Snow White and the next I'll be Goldilocks.'

'You nut,' Lisa laughed. 'They must have ordinary, everyday clothes for their newsreaders and weathermen.'

'Weather people,' Dee corrected. 'Do you really think so?'

'Absolutely. That beautiful redhead that reads the nine o'clock news is in a different outfit every night; the clothes must be supplied as part of the job.'

'I hope you're right.'

'But,' Lisa looked her in the eye, 'that's not what we're here to discuss.'

Dee raised an eyebrow at the businesslike tone her friend had adopted and grinned.

'No, it isn't, Ms Dunphy, so let's talk business.'

Chapter 15

Dee was woken at five-thirty by Sam. 'What is it, sweetheart?' she asked when she opened her eyes to see him standing by her bed.

'There's a funny noise in my room, Mummy.'

Dee pulled back the covers. 'Want to come in here?'

He nodded eagerly and scrambled up on to the bed.

Dee tugged him in beside her and pulled the duvet up around their ears. 'Now, close your eyes and go to sleep.'

'Is it nearly morning time?' he asked.

'Nearly, but there's still time for a little sleep.' It had been a late night and Dee prayed that her son would go back to sleep for another hour.

'Mummy, what was that?' he whispered, his breath warm on her face.

She sighed. 'It's just the water gurgling in the pipes, now go to sleep.'

'Mummy?'

She opened her eyes and looked into his, less than two inches away. 'Yes?'

'My toes are cold.'

She took his tiny feet between her hands and rubbed them gently. 'Now, go to sleep!'

He smiled, closed his eyes tightly and snuggled even closer. Dee closed her eyes too and inhaled his unique smell, felt his small body squirm against her and wondered how she'd ever got to be this lucky.

They only got thirty minutes more sleep in the end and Dee's eyes were tired and sore but she still felt excited and upbeat at the prospect of her meeting with Carolyn Maher. She had arranged the food for the children's snack and lunch, just in case she didn't get back on time, and she would deliver Ronan's order on her way to the studio.

'On the way to the studio.' She giggled to herself at how cool that sounded and covering the chicken and broccoli pie with tin foil, she went upstairs to dress. Though she wasn't going to be on TV this time, there was a chance that she might be meeting some important people, so she'd done the sensible thing and asked Lisa what she should wear. They'd had several glasses of wine at that stage and Lisa waded through her wardrobe, tossing clothes left and right and complaining loudly about Dee's lack of taste, obsession with practicality and, most importantly, lack of quantity.

'Is this it?' she had asked incredulously.

'Yes,' Dee said defensively, 'it's all I need.'

Lisa looked at her and shook her head sadly. 'Don't you have any mistakes tucked away?'

Dee frowned.

'You know, those impulse buys,' Lisa prompted, 'the sparkly tops, impossible heels, slinky dresses that you never actually have the courage to wear.'

Dee shook her head. 'I had the dress I wore for our last night out but I caught it in the taxi door when I was getting out and it ripped.'

Lisa sighed. 'Seven TV are going to have their work cut out with you.'

Dee slumped on to her bed and watched miserably as her friend held up pair after pair of jeans and tracksuit bottoms. 'Maybe I should cancel.'

'You will not! We'll find something, don't you worry.'

And they had, but as Dee dressed in the simple white shirt, jeans and hacking jacket, she had her doubts.

'Accessories is the solution,' Lisa had pronounced and arrived in that morning with chains for Dee to drape around her neck, a large silver bangle to go on her wrist, and huge silver hoops for her ears.

She had also insisted that Dee use more make-up than usual. 'You saw how fabulous you looked after they made you up in the studio,' she'd insisted when Dee expressed her reservations, 'and make up and jewellery is the only way to carry off an outfit like this.'

And so Dee had carefully applied smoky-grey eyeshadow, eyeliner and tons of black mascara and some pale pink lip gloss. When she went down to the crèche to show Lisa her efforts, it was her son's reaction that said it all.

'Mummy, you look like a princess,' he'd said, wide-eyed, coming forward to throw his arms around her waist.

'Thank you, sweetheart,' she'd murmured, bending to kiss the top of his head.

'Smashing,' Martha had said, grinning excitedly. Lisa had told her where Dee was off to and she couldn't believe that she might end up working with a celebrity.

'What shoes are you wearing?' Lisa demanded.

'My trainers?' Dee said uncertainly.

'No!' Lisa shook her head furiously. 'That would ruin the whole effect. Wear your cowboy boots.'

'But they're ancient.'

'I'll give them a quick polish and they'll be fine.'

'It's okay, I'll do it,' Dee protested as Lisa bustled to the door.

'While you're wearing a white shirt? I think not! Where are they?' Lisa added as she made a beeline for the door.

'Er, in the cupboard under the stairs – I think.'

'Right, stick on a video for the kids and I'll be back in a minute.'

Sam's eyes widened. 'We can watch telly?'

Lisa nodded. 'But only if you're all as quiet as mice, okay?'

Sam and the other children nodded and, whispering

and giggling, they curled up on the rug in front of the TV while Dee put on *Postman Pat*. When the children were engrossed in their programme, she crossed the room to the baby section and bent to tickle a baby lying under a play gym.

'Don't get too close,' Martha warned. 'Lisa will murder you if you get dirty. I can't believe you're going to be on telly every week,' she added excitedly as she propped one of the older babies in a bouncy chair and gave him his bottle. 'Good boy, Joshua.'

'It may not even happen; I'm only going in to talk about it,' Dee cautioned.

'It will happen,' Martha said confidently, 'you were a natural on that programme, much better than any of the others.'

'Thanks.' Dee felt her cheeks redden.

Martha laughed. 'You'd better get used to being recognized. People will be coming up to you in the street and asking you for your autograph.'

Dee laughed. 'I don't think so. One, appearing once a week to talk about food doesn't exactly make me a celebrity and two, no one would recognize me without my make-up.'

'But everyone will know where you live and work,' Martha pointed out, 'so they'll be watching out for you.'

Dee's expression clouded. She hadn't given much thought to how this development would leave herself and Sam exposed and vulnerable. Still, she reasoned, really big stars lived relatively normal lives in Ireland, their celebrity accepted and often ignored – including her supposed relative, Bono.

'Here you go.' Lisa arrived back brandishing Dee's boots.

'They look like new,' Dee marvelled, bending to put them on.

Lisa glanced over at the kids. 'They should be okay for another five minutes; I'll walk you to the car.'

'Good luck.' Martha smiled.

'Thanks.' Dee went quickly to kiss Sam. 'Be good,' she murmured and then hurried after Lisa.

'I just hope this heap gets you there in one piece,' Lisa eyed up Dee's car with distaste. 'Maybe we should call a taxi.'

'I'll be fine.' Dee kissed her friend's cheek. 'Thanks for everything, Lisa.'

'No problem, partner.' Lisa gave her a quick hug. 'Give them hell.'

Dee's nerves disappeared almost the moment she walked through the door of Seven TV. The place was buzzing and she spotted at least three famous faces as she sat in reception waiting for Carolyn.

'I'm so sorry for keeping you waiting,' Carolyn said, sweeping into the room and stretching out a hand.

'No problem,' Dee said, taking it. 'I've been people watching.'

Carolyn laughed as she led the way through the swing doors into a long corridor.

'After a couple of days you won't even notice them. So tell me, what did your little boy think when he saw his mummy on TV? It's Sam, isn't it?'

Dee nodded. 'He was very impressed but then it's easy to impress a four-year-old.'

'Don't be so modest, you were great. All of the production team here thought you were a natural. People think it's easy to sit in front of a camera and talk but it takes a real talent to behave as if the camera isn't there and you have it.'

'Thanks,' Dee said, too overawed to say anything else.

Carolyn turned down another corridor. 'I'm taking you to meet Marty Vaughan, he's the director of programmes, and also Marge Preston is going to try and join us.'

'Right, great,' Dee said hoarsely and swallowed hard.

Carolyn stopped abruptly, rapped on a door and led Dee into a tiny office that seemed to have files and paper on every surface. 'Marty, meet Dee Hewson. Dee, this is Marty Vaughan.'

Dee held out her hand and found it enveloped in that of the older man who had stood to greet her and now towered above them both.

'Hewson—'

'No relation,' Carolyn said quickly as she glanced around the room. 'Shall we grab a meeting room?'

Marty laughed loudly and winked at Dee. 'That's her

way of saying my office is a disgrace. Let's go to the canteen instead and we can have a coffee.'

'Good idea.' Carolyn led the way and Marty stood back to let Dee follow her.

As they made their way down more narrow corridors, Carolyn stopped a couple of times to introduce Dee to other staff members and Dee felt her cheeks grow hot as Carolyn explained excitedly that they hoped Dee would be joining the *Right Now* team.

'Is everything okay?' Carolyn asked when they were finally seated in the canteen, steaming mugs and biscuits in front of them. 'You look very pale.'

'I'm fine, just a bit overwhelmed,' Dee admitted.

'Carolyn has that effect on everyone,' Marty said dryly. 'Carolyn, you haven't even explained the job to Dee and you're assuming she'll accept.'

Carolyn smiled apologetically and stood up. 'I'll just phone Marge and let her know where we are.' She went over to the phone on the wall and was back moments later. 'Sorry, Dee, if I got a bit carried away. It's just that I think a nutrition spot would be a wonderful addition to the programme and you would be the perfect person to be a part of that.'

'I love the idea too,' Dee assured her. 'Who else would be involved?'

'Well, we haven't teased through all the details yet,' Marty replied, 'but we thought that we might have you, a dietician and a different guest each week – and Marge would be in the chair, of course.'

'We could plan a few weeks in advance,' Carolyn continued. 'You could come in around eleven on Wednesdays, talk through and rehearse for the programme and then stay on for a couple of hours afterwards to discuss the material for the following week.'

'So you'd only need me here on Wednesdays?'

Marty nodded. 'Yes, anything else we should be able to handle on the phone or via email. Do you have an email address?'

Dee nodded. 'Yes, of course.'

'Great!' Carolyn beamed.

'So, before we go any further, Dee, do you think you would be able to commit to spending Wednesdays with us?'

Dee thought about it for a second and then nodded. 'Yes, I do. It would suit me a lot better than coming in a couple of times a week for a shorter period.'

'Excellent.' Marty looked up and grinned as Marge breezed through the door, fetched herself a coffee, and came to join them.

'Hello, everybody. Dee, hello! Great show yesterday.'

'Thanks,' Dee said, 'you made it very easy.'

Marge smiled. 'Oh, what a lovely thing to say!'

'We were just discussing the nutrition spot with Dee,' Marty explained.

'You will do it, won't you?' Marge urged. 'I need someone sensible and down to earth to tell it how it is. Some of these experts get too detailed, too technical and people switch off. We need someone real, someone who cares, someone ordinary—'

Carolyn rolled her eyes at Dee. 'Well put, Marge, how can she resist!'

'Oh, you know what I mean.' Marge shrugged at Dee. 'Don't you?'

Dee grinned. 'I know.'

'So as a viewer, Dee,' Marty leaned forward on the table and studied her, 'as a concerned mother, what topics would you like to see covered in this segment?'

'Quicker and easier ways of cooking,' she said after a moment. 'There are so many cooking programmes on television but they all concentrate on fresh produce, elaborate sauces and lots of work. Why don't they point out that microwaving vegetables is as quick and easy and a lot healthier than microwaving a ready-meal? Why aren't people told about the value of frozen or tinned fruit and vegetables? I'm sure there are lots of people who'd like to cook more but are just put off because it seems so complicated.'

'You're right,' Carolyn interjected, 'and it's an all-or-nothing attitude, isn't it? Only organic fruit and veg and they all rubbish the microwave.'

'We should check out the facts about the risks with microwaves, though,' Marty cautioned.

'I'll get someone on to that.' Carolyn made a note.

'Now, a nutritionist ... do you have anyone in mind?' Marty asked.

Carolyn nodded. 'There is a woman I think would be

perfect for the job; leave it with me, I'll call her today.'

'Anything else, Dee?' Marty asked.

'I'd like to see a piece on breakfast cereals but I don't know if you want to get into that kind of thing.'

Marge grinned. 'We like controversy, don't we, Carolyn?'

Carolyn laughed. 'Let's put it on the list and see what we come up with.'

'What about kids' drinks?' Marge suggested.

'Oh, yes, and school lunches,' Dee said, leaning forward. 'The amount of crap being marketed as healthy lunchbox fillers is scandalous.'

Marty nodded his approval. 'I don't think we're going to have any problems filling this spot. Carolyn, do you think we'd be ready to launch in two weeks?'

Carolyn nodded. 'Yes, if we have two full days to work on it, I'm sure we could. Dee?'

Dee nodded. 'Sure.'

'That sounds fine to me.' Marge looked at her watch and stood up. 'I need to leave you people. Dee, I look forward to working with you.'

Dee stood and shook her hand. 'Likewise.'

'Right,' Marty stood too, 'I think that's that.'

Dee glanced awkwardly from Marty to Carolyn. 'There were a couple of other points.'

Carolyn slapped a hand to her mouth. 'Oh, God, we haven't talked about money, have we?'

Dee shook her head. 'No and er . . .'

'Was there something else?' Marty asked.

Dee bit the bullet. 'Clothes.'

'Clothes,' he looked blank.

'It's just that Marge always looks so smart and I'm afraid I don't really have much in the way of good clothes. In my line of work jeans and tracksuits are more the thing.' This all came out in a rush and when she stopped, Marty was looking slightly bewildered.

'Carolyn?' He looked at the producer.

'I'll take care of it,' Carolyn said, leading the way to the door. 'Let's go to my office, I have your contract there.'

They paused at the junction of two corridors and Marty held out his hand. 'Dee, glad to have you on board. I'll see you next week.'

'Thanks, goodbye.' Dee shook his hand and then turned to follow Carolyn.

'I hope you don't feel we've steam rollered you into this, Dee.'

'Things are moving very fast,' Dee admitted, 'and I am a little bit nervous about the financial end of things.' She really wanted to do this job and she loved the idea of working with both Carolyn and Marge, but if it wasn't financially viable she'd have to consider turning it down. The thought depressed her hugely.

Carolyn nodded her understanding and then turned into an office even tinier than Marty's but immeasurably tidier. 'Please, sit down,' she said, going behind her desk and indicating the chair opposite. 'Now, I have a letter of offer here somewhere and, if you're happy with it, a contract for you to sign, well two, in fact – a copy for us, and a copy for you to keep. Ah, here we are.' She pulled out three A4 sheets and handed them to Dee. 'You have a look at that while I phone April Deevers. She's the nutritionist I'd like to be on the show, I think you'll love her.'

Dee was only half listening as she ran an eye down the letter of offer, unable to believe her eyes.

Carolyn made her call and when she was finished she set down the phone with a satisfied smile. 'Excellent, she'd love to do the spot. So, Dee, what do you think?'

Dee looked up, her face blank. 'Pardon?'

'Is the offer okay?' Carolyn asked.

'Yes – yes, it's more than generous.'

'And, with regard to clothes, you can use our wardrobe department if you like.'

'Is that what everyone does?' Dee asked.

Carolyn shrugged. 'It varies. Some of the guys come in from the golf course and then just borrow a jacket, shirt and tie. We were thinking of having you sitting at a desk for the nutrition segment in which case you could wear your jeans or jogging pants and just glam up above the waist.'

Dee laughed delightedly. 'That would be great!'

Carolyn made a note on a pad. 'Okay, consider it done.' She looked up and smiled. 'So, are you happy to sign the contract?'

'Absolutely!' Dee nodded eagerly. 'I can't wait to start.'

'Great. Well, put your thinking cap on over the next

couple of days and I'll call you on Monday. Then we can spend Wednesday brainstorming with April and decide what issues we're going to address over the first couple of weeks.'

Carolyn guided Dee back to reception and wished her a hurried goodbye. 'Sorry to rush you, but I'm late for my next meeting. Thanks for coming in, Dee, I'm really looking forward to working with you.'

Dee smiled widely. 'Me too.' She left the building and walked back to her car, where she sat staring at the letter of offer for a number of minutes. Twelve shows at eight hundred euros a show, bloody hell! Finally, realizing that it was well past lunchtime and she'd have to get her skates on, she switched on her mobile phone, slipped on her headset, and drove out of the car-park. Within seconds, it rang. She sighed and glanced down at the display, but it was a number she didn't recognize. 'Hello?'

'Dee?'

'Yes.'

'It's Neil. Can you talk?'

'Yes, but Neil—'

'Look, I'm sorry, I know I said I wouldn't ring—'

She sighed. 'It's okay, I was going to give you a call later anyway.'

'You were?'

'Yeah. I thought maybe we should get together and talk.'

'That's great, Dee. Do you want to come over here?'

'No,' she said quickly. 'Let's meet in town.'

'Okay, then.'

'I could get away tomorrow morning for a couple of hours.'

'Great. What about eleven at the Gresham?'

'Fine.'

'Thanks. Bye, Dee.'

'Wait – Neil, why did you call?'

There was a short silence. 'I was just hoping you might be ready to talk.'

'Okay, then, I'll see you tomorrow.'

'Bye.'

Instead of the trepidation that Dee had expected to feel, she was quite optimistic at the thought of the meeting but then nothing could really get her down today. She had a new job that was going to greatly improve her bank balance and the plans that she and Lisa had discussed made the future look a lot more secure. For the first time in a long time she felt that her head was above water again and it was a very good feeling indeed.

When she got back to the house, it was nap time and those children who weren't sleeping were resting quietly with Martha close by. Lisa hurried out as soon as she heard the car. 'Well?' she asked, as soon as Dee stepped out.

'I've got another job,' Dee said simply.

'Oh, wow!' Lisa said, grabbing her and swinging her around. 'What are you going to be doing? How long for? How much are they paying you?'

Dee laughed. 'Steady on, will you? I'll tell you everything but first I need to eat, I'm starving.'

Lisa looked disappointed. 'I thought they'd taken you off to lunch in some posh Dublin Four restaurant.'

'No, but they gave me tea and some very nice biscuits.' She led the way into the kitchen and rummaged in the fridge for the makings of a sandwich while Lisa put on the kettle. 'Oh, Lisa, it was such a buzz!'

'So, come on, tell me everything.'

The two girls sat down – Lisa with one eye on the clock – and between mouthfuls of food, Dee told her about her morning. When she'd finished, she produced the letter and spread it in front of Lisa.

'Bloody hell.' Lisa looked up at her and then back at the letter.

'Not bad, eh?' Dee grinned.

'Great.' Lisa nodded but didn't look at her.

'What?'

'Nothing.'

Dee wasn't fooled. 'Lisa?'

'Well, it's just that with an offer like this you don't really need to expand any more, do you?'

'Are you kidding?' Dee's eyes widened. 'The *Right Now* contract is only for three months and though the salary is generous, I don't think I can really afford to retire!'

Lisa grinned. 'Oh, okay, then. It's great that it will only take up one day a week, too.'

Dee nodded. 'Although, I will have some homework to do.'

'Which you will enjoy every minute of.'

'True,' Dee laughed.

There was a distant cry and Lisa stood up. 'Sorry, gotta go.'

'Lisa, I need to go into Dublin in the morning,' Dee said casually. 'I'm going to visit a couple of recruitment agencies. Can you manage without me?'

'Sure, no problem. I'll be asking you to return the compliment soon enough. I'm putting an advert in the paper tomorrow.'

Dee smiled at the excitement that shone in Lisa's eyes. 'That's brilliant. Have you told Martha our plans?'

Lisa shook her head. 'There's no time or peace to talk properly during working hours so I've asked her to meet me for a drink this evening.'

'She is going to be thrilled.'

'I certainly hope so. See you later.'

When she was alone, Dee cleared up after her lunch and began to prepare the food for the next day. She felt bad that she'd lied to Lisa about the reason for her trip into the city but she knew her friend would only worry and then pester her on her return about what had transpired.

But for now Dee needed to handle this alone. There

was so much to consider and she didn't want to be influenced by other people's prejudices. Lisa couldn't get beyond what Neil had done in the past but Dee knew, for Sam's sake, she had to be bigger than that. She *would* drop into a couple of recruitment agencies tomorrow and make full use of her time in the city. If she didn't, Ronan would be on her case again. Anyway, it looked like now she had no choice in the matter; she was going to have to share her kitchen with another cook. She just had to make sure that she found the right one.

Dee threw herself into her cooking for the remainder of the afternoon and then she and Sam went for a bracing walk, stopping off at the chip shop on the way home.

'Mum,' Sam said as they wandered back to the house munching their chips, 'tell me again about Daddy.'

Dee sighed. Sam often asked her about his father but somehow today it was even more poignant, given that she'd been talking to Neil only a few hours earlier. 'You know that story off by heart, Sam.'

'Please, tell me again,' he wheedled.

She put an arm around his shoulders and hugged him against her. 'Oh, okay, then. Your daddy's name was Neil and he was handsome and funny and he had curly brown hair, green eyes—'

'Just like me!'

She laughed. 'Yes, just like you.'

'But he doesn't know about me,' Sam said, bowing his head.

Dee gulped. 'No, we split up before I knew I was going to have a wonderful little boy.'

'But if he knew, he'd be here, wouldn't he?' Sam prompted.

Dee closed her eyes and pulled him closer. 'Yes, and he would be the happiest man in the world.'

'Can't we find him, Mummy?'

This was also a common question and Dee realized that there would be more and more as he got older. 'No, sweetheart, I'm afraid we can't.' She took a deep breath. 'But maybe someday, he'll find us.'

Sam stopped and craned his head so that he could look up at her, his eyes shining. 'Do you think so, Mummy?'

She shrugged and smiled. 'You never know and, in the meantime, remember you've always got me and Aunty Pauline and Uncle Jack. And how many children do you know that have a playschool in their house?'

Sam giggled. 'None.'

'And how many have Martha and Lisa to mind them when Mummy isn't around?'

'None.' He was smiling broadly now.

'And,' she added, 'how many of them have as many grown-up friends as you? There's Conor and Ronan and Julia.'

'And Vi and Doctor Bill and Sheila and Lauren,' he added.

'And Matthew and Ger,' Dee reminded him.

Sam's smile faltered. 'Ger isn't really my friend.'

'Sure he is.'

'No,' Sam shook his head firmly, 'he doesn't like me; he doesn't like kids.'

'I'm sure you're wrong,' Dee lied, amazed at her son's insight.

'And Aunty Peggy!' Sam's face lit up again. 'We forgot Aunty Peggy!'

'Now how did we forget her?' Dee said faintly, forcing herself to keep smiling. Dear God, she *had* completely forgotten Peggy. Forgotten the woman and how she fitted into this whole picture and what would happen if Sam's daddy did 'return'.

'But I still don't have a granny or granddad,' Sam said sadly.

'Maybe not, but I think we've established that you've got quite a lot of friends, haven't we?' Dee nudged him playfully.

'Yeah,' he grinned, digging into his chips once more, 'and we haven't counted any of the other kids yet.'

Dee groaned dramatically. 'Oh no, I'm never going to get to bed tonight!'

Sam giggled. 'Don't be silly, Mummy, there aren't *that* many.'

'Okay, let's see if you can name them all before we get home.'

*

After a bath and a story, Sam curled up with his numerous teddy bears and was asleep in minutes. Dee went into her bedroom, changed into pyjamas and went back downstairs. Getting a beer from the fridge, she took her pad and pen from the drawer and sat down on the sofa to think about possible topics for the *Right Now* programme. But though she was excited about the programme and eager to come up with some good ideas for Carolyn, all Dee could think of was Peggy.

It was strange that the woman hadn't been in touch, she realized now. She knew as well as Dee did that they were now in a very difficult situation. Sam was young but he wasn't stupid and it was going to be hard to explain to him what it all meant. Dee was still staring at her blank pad when the phone rang. She leaned forward to grab it and stuck it against her ear, spilling beer in her lap in the process. 'Shit! Hello!'

'Charming.'

'Sorry, Conor, just spilled beer all over myself.'

'Is that my fault?'

'Yep.'

'I could bring you a refill,' he suggested.

'Nah,' Dee yawned, 'I don't really want it. I'm heading to bed.'

'I could help there too,' he said, chuckling.

Dee was about to tell him to come on over but she knew she'd end up telling him about Neil and Peggy and then he'd start to advise her and—

'Dee? Are you still there?'

'Yeah, sorry, I'm just asleep on my feet.'

'I'd better go and let you get to bed.'

'Yeah, do you mind? I'd invite you over, only I'd probably be asleep before you got here.'

He chuckled. 'I'll try not to take that personally. Why don't I drop by in the morning to sample your muffins?'

She grinned. 'Okay, then – oh, no, sorry, I won't be here.'

'Oh, where will you be?'

She hesitated for only a second. 'I'm going in to Dublin to visit a couple of recruitment agencies to see if I can find a decent cook,' she told him, closing her eyes and cringing as she lied.

'That's great, Dee, you could do with the help.'

'So your dad told me.'

Conor was silent for a moment. 'He's just trying to help.'

'I know that, Conor,' Dee assured him, 'and he's right. Look, why don't I call you when I get back? I can fill you in on all the news then.'

'Great, talk to you tomorrow. 'night, Dee.'

'Goodnight, Conor, sleep well.'

Dee groaned as she put down the phone. She knew that Conor knew that she'd been a bit weird with him but he'd let it go. She knew he thought it all came back to Neil and, she supposed, he was right. She'd have to explain to him exactly what was going on and soon. But not yet.

Chapter 16

Sam slept like a baby which meant that when Dee rose at five-thirty she felt reasonably refreshed. Despite her worries she had slept well which was fortunate, given that she had until eight-thirty to pack in a day's cooking. Then she would wake Sam, make breakfast and get him dressed. She hoped he was not in a philosophical mood because she really didn't think she could handle any more questions about Daddy or, God forbid, Aunty Peggy.

She was feeling quite nervous about meeting Neil so she was determined not to think about it for now and instead threw herself into her work. To distract herself she decided to see if she could come up with topics for the *Right Now* show. She found she could always think clearly when she was working in the kitchen and had left her pad and pen nearby in case she was inspired. Her current preoccupation was to come up with rules for reading labels that would make them a bit easier to interpret. For instance, how many people knew, she wondered, that ingredients were listed in order of quantity? That would make them think twice if they saw sugar second or third on the list or in the case of most jams, first!

She finished kneading the wholemeal bread, cleaned her hands and picked up the pen. She felt a sudden buzz at the thought of helping people make better choices when they were filling their shopping trolleys. She thought about all the confusing facts about fats, and scribbled down another note before going to the fridge and taking out the fish she had to gut and fillet. There really were enough topics to keep a slot like this going indefinitely, she realized, and smiled happily. She had no wish to be famous but she was definitely enjoying the idea of dipping her toe in such a completely different pond.

For so long her life had been divided between the kitchen and the crèche and the highlight of her day had been dropping in to the café. The thought of visiting a TV studio every week as part of the team filled her with excitement and adrenalin and made her realize what a dull life she'd been leading. Still, she hadn't a lot of choice and she'd made the best of her lot. She had Sam and she enjoyed her work and that was more than most people could say, but there was no doubt that she was ready for more. Initially it had been all about money, and that was still important, but now it was also about fulfilment and Dee couldn't wait to get started.

There weren't going to be enough hours in the day at the rate her life was going, she thought, as she put the prepared fish back into the fridge and sat down at the table to peel potatoes. She really would have to get an assistant sooner rather than later. Before she'd gone to bed last night she had checked out the Golden Pages and was delighted to discover a recruitment agency that specialized in catering not far from the hotel where she was meeting Neil.

Meanwhile, Lisa had placed an advert in the paper for two childcare workers with both experience and qualifications. Dee had queried whether the latter was really necessary but Lisa was adamant, saying it would show commitment to childcare as a career. 'Too many girls use it as a stop-gap until something more interesting comes along and I don't want them. I want to put together a team of people who love children, are dedicated to the job, and can rely on each other.'

Dee thought this was probably a tall order, but she could understand how Lisa felt. Having worked alone for so long she was nervous of sharing her kitchen with someone else. Her other concern, she'd confided in Lisa, was the thought of bringing strangers into her home.

'Don't you worry, we'll check and double check their references,' Lisa told her vehemently. 'We're not bringing any weirdoes, robbers or perverts into this house. And before I hire anyone for the crèche, you've got to meet them and be sure you're happy with them too.'

Dee had appreciated her friend's sensitivity and promised to do likewise. Whoever was going to work in the kitchen would have to have the best of references and be good with children, too, or it would never work.

Dee dumped the bowl of potato peelings, filled the pot of potatoes with cold water, and put them on to boil. It was almost seven, the bread was ready to come out of the oven, the muffins were ready to go in, and it would take a little over an hour to prepare the fish pie. She wouldn't cook it as Ronan had decided, where possible, to finish the dishes off in the café and thereby entice the customers in with the mouth-watering aromas.

By ten o'clock, Dee was pulling up outside the café and Ronan looked surprised when he opened the door. 'You're early,' he said as he came out to the car to help her.

'I'm on my way into Dublin,' she explained.

'You look very nice. Are you going somewhere special?'

Dee ducked her head as she felt her cheeks flame. 'I'm going in to visit a recruitment agency.'

'Wonderful!' He beamed delightedly. 'I'm sure you're doing the right thing.'

Dee thought of introducing Sam to his daddy. 'Yes, I think I am.'

They carried the food into the restaurant and Dee turned to leave. 'Right, I'd better get going. All the instructions are taped to the lids.'

'That's fine; you go on and the very best of luck.'

She smiled, feeling guilty at the genuine affection and sincerity in his face.

'Thanks, Ronan.'

She hurried out to her car, praying that it would survive yet another journey into the city and for the first time that morning allowed herself to think about what she was doing. 'Why do I feel guilty?' she murmured to herself as she joined the slow stream of traffic heading into the capital. 'What choice do I have?' But she knew the issue wasn't the choices she was making but the deceit. She would tell Conor, of course she would; it just wasn't the kind of thing you discussed over the phone.

It had been a mad, chaotic week. She had hardly had time to turn around, let alone talk. She had a lot to tell him, she realized, quite apart from seeing Neil. Maybe they could go for one of their marathon walks over the weekend and while Sam raced ahead on his bike, she could bring Conor up to date. It would be nice to spend some quality time together and it would get Sam off her back. He had complained yet again this morning that it had been days since he'd seen Conor.

The traffic moved relatively quickly and soon Dee had parked the car and was walking briskly towards the hotel. It was five to eleven and Neil had never been the punctual sort so she probably had time to have some tea and catch her breath before he put in an appearance.

She was surprised, then, as she walked into the large, comfortable lounge, to see that Neil was already ensconced on a sofa near the window, a pot of tea in front of him and the newspaper spread out by his side. She stood watching him for a moment and, as if sensing her scrutiny, he looked up and waved, his face breaking into a wide, happy grin.

She walked across the room, conscious of his eyes on her. 'Hi.'

'Thanks for coming, Dee.' He quickly folded his paper and moved up on the sofa but Dee took the chair opposite and immediately a waitress appeared at her elbow.

'Tea or coffee?' Neil asked her.

'Tea please.' She smiled at the young girl.

'You look great,' he said, when they were alone again.

She shrugged. She was in her customary jeans, but she'd left her hair loose so it swung around her shoulders and she'd carefully applied some eye make-up and lip gloss, reasoning that she had to look presentable if she was going on to the recruitment consultancy. At least that's what she'd told herself.

'How's Sam?'

She nodded and smiled. 'He's great.'

'I've been thinking about him a lot and I can't stop looking at the photo they printed in the *Daily Journal*. He's gorgeous, just like you.'

'It's not a great photo, and he's actually more like you.'

His eyes lit up. 'Is he really?'

'Yes, and just as untidy.'

He laughed. 'I'm afraid that hasn't changed.'

'I have some photos with me if you'd like to see them,' she offered. She couldn't really believe that she was sitting here chatting in such a civil manner, but if he was going to be a part of their lives, she would have to make an effort to put the past behind her.

'Great!'

She sat back as the waitress served her tea and then passed him the envelope that she always carried with her.

Neil carefully took out the photos and studied them. The first was one of Sam playing in the snow, his cheeks red and his eyes bright with excitement as he stared into the camera. 'How old was he in this one?'

Dee leaned closer to see which photo he was looking at. 'Three. He'd had the flu and been in bed for days and he was terrified that the snow would be gone before he got a chance to play in it.'

Neil moved on to the next.

'That was in Lisa's garden last year; she had a barbecue to celebrate Ger's birthday.'

'Ger?'

Dee made a face. 'The boyfriend.'

'You don't like him.'

'He's not good enough for her,' Dee said simply.

Neil nodded and moved on to the next photo. 'Oh,

wow!' He stared in wonder at the tiny baby wrapped in a pale green blanket.

'That was taken the day we came home from the hospital,' Dee said softly.

'How did you decide on the name?' he asked, not taking his eyes from the photo.

Dee laughed. 'He seemed so tiny and frail and I wanted him to grow up big and strong so that no one could ever hurt him.'

He smiled. 'Samson?'

She nodded. 'But it's just Sam on the birth cert. Pauline was furious with me because I didn't give him a saint's name.'

'I think it's a great name.'

'Thanks.'

'Oh, look at this!' He held up a photo of Dee holding Sam up in the air, the child's head thrown back with glee. 'When was this taken?'

'Conor took it last year at Sam's fourth birthday party.' She got some satisfaction when Neil's mouth tightened.

'Do they get on well?' he asked.

'Yeah, Conor's great with him.'

'Good.' He looked at the last photo, one of Sam curled up in bed asleep, his thumb in his mouth.

'He was only about ten months old then,' Dee volunteered. 'He'd been crying all evening and had thrown his tea at me. I was tired and very fed up and I thought at one point I was going to hit him. Then eventually when he went to sleep I couldn't leave him. I just sat staring at him for ages thinking I couldn't live without him no matter how much he screamed. I went searching for the camera because he just looked so sweet and vulnerable. I've kept that photo close by ever since just to remind me that even when he's driving me nuts, I really do love him.'

'You don't need the photo,' he told her. 'It's obvious from the way you talk about him, that you adore him.'

'It's easier now that he's older but trust me, when he was teething or having temper tantrums or not sleeping at night I needed reminding. It's not easy looking after a baby, especially alone.'

'I wish I'd been there to help.' He stared miserably at the photo. 'I've missed out on so much.'

'Yes.' She watched him steadily, wondering if she could believe in his regret.

'You should have looked for me,' he said suddenly. 'You could have called Mum and told her about Sam, you could have given me a chance to be a proper father.'

Dee sat back in her seat, stunned by the sudden attack. 'A proper father?' she said incredulously. 'A gambler who would have spent the Children's Allowance on the three-thirty at Haydock? He didn't need a father like you.'

Neil flinched at her words then nodded slightly. 'You're right, I'm sorry, it's just so hard.' He looked down at the picture of Sam sleeping and stroked it tenderly.

Dee's anger was gone as quickly as it had come. 'I didn't need another dependant, Neil, I needed – *we* needed – someone we could rely on.'

'And have you found that in Conor?'

Dee hesitated, realizing that she wasn't sure of the answer. 'Conor is an important part of our lives,' she said carefully, 'but he's not Sam's father. Sam doesn't need a father, he's got me. I've looked after him since the day he was born and I don't think I've done too bad a job. He's happy, Neil, and I'm going to make sure he stays that way.'

His shoulders slumped. 'So you're not going to let me see him.'

'I didn't say that, but I need to know that you won't hurt him. I need to know that I can trust you and I'm not sure I can after all you've done.'

He nodded solemnly. 'I can understand that, but you have to remember that anything I did to you when I was gambling, well, it wasn't really me.'

'Oh, please!'

'It's true, Dee, it's a disease. I am so sorry I hurt you and that I stole from you, but it wasn't really me doing all that; it was the gambling.'

Dee sighed. 'In my head I accept and understand that but it doesn't change the fact that you hurt me and how do I know it won't happen again?'

'Because I'm better now.' He leaned forward in his

seat. 'Look at me, I'm successful, I drive a nice car, I own my own company. How would I have any of that if I was still gambling?'

'You may have stopped, but how do I know you won't start again – maybe not next week, but next year, or in five years?'

He shook his head, helplessly. 'You don't. I wish I could give you a guarantee, I really do, but I can't.'

Dee looked at him, at the defeat in his posture, the sadness in his eyes and the emptiness in his voice and realized that his happiness, as well as her son's, was in her hands. 'Is there anyone I could talk to?' she said finally.

'What do you mean?'

'When I leave here I'm going to a recruitment consultancy because I need a cook. I won't take a stranger into my home, though, unless all of the references are okay. I won't let anyone within a yard of Sam unless I've checked them out as much as is humanly possible. To all intents and purposes, you are also a stranger and I'd like to check out your references, too.'

Neil looked momentarily flummoxed. 'I suppose that makes sense.'

Dee stood up. 'Okay. When you come up with someone I can talk to, let me know.'

Chapter 17

'Where's my mummy?' Sam asked, his voice whiney.

Lisa counted to ten. 'I've told you, Sam, she had to go out. Have some lunch and she'll be back before you know it.'

'Don't want it. I feel sick.'

Lisa was immediately by his side, her hand on his forehead. He was warm but not alarmingly so. She studied him carefully and noted that while he was pale, his eyes were alert. They were also having fish pie for lunch, not one of Sam's favourites. She crouched down beside him and smiled up into his face. 'Would you like to curl up on the sofa and look at your Barney book while we have our food? Then maybe you could eat something later with Mummy.'

Sam nodded eagerly and scrambled down from his place at the table. Lisa continued to help the other children with lunch but kept a careful eye on him and was relieved to see that he was sitting up straight and happily flicking through the book. The children were just finishing the meal when Natalie knocked her milk all over Rebecca and while Martha fussed over the distraught child, Lisa cleaned up the mess. When they had finished Lisa led the toddlers out to the bathroom to tidy up and get ready for nap time. As she was shepherding them back inside, Dee walked through the door and smiled as the children ran to her.

'Hello there!' She bent to hug each child in turn.

'How did it go?' Lisa asked.

'Really well.' Dee shrugged off her jacket, dumped her bag on the hall table, and followed them back into the crèche. 'They have at least three people on their books who might suit, so we're going to try and set up interviews for early next week. Where's Sam?' she asked, scanning the room.

Lisa's eyes flew to the sofa but Sam was gone. 'Martha? Where's Sam?'

Martha looked up from where she was settling the children on their sleeping mats.

'He was there a second ago.'

Dee walked across the room. 'Sam? Are you hiding?' She moved towards the cabinet with the TV, expecting Sam to jump out on her – it was one of the children's favourite hiding places – but as she drew level with the sofa she pulled up short at the sight of the crumpled heap on the floor in front of it. 'Sam!' She dropped to her knees and rolled him over gently. His eyes were closed and there was no response. 'Lisa, call an ambulance.' She pressed her ear to his chest, listened and prayed. 'Oh, thank God,' she murmured when she heard the quiet but steady beat. Gently, she prized open his mouth but could see no obstruction and he seemed to be breathing okay. 'Sam? Come on, sweetheart, wake up. Mummy's here, Sam, Mummy's here.'

Lisa came back into the room. 'The ambulance is on it's way. Martha, let's take all the children in for their nap.'

'What's wrong with Sam?' Tom demanded, standing his ground.

'He's not feeling too well,' Martha said gently. 'Don't worry, the doctor is coming to take care of him but right now we need to leave him to sleep.'

She sat Tom on a cushion with a book and then settled the other children on mattresses while Lisa returned to Dee's side.

'How is he?'

'His breathing is normal and so is his temperature,' Dee said worriedly. 'I don't know what's wrong, but he won't wake up. How was he all morning?'

'He said he felt sick and wouldn't eat lunch but I checked his temperature and he was fine. I told him he didn't have to eat and sat him on the sofa looking at a book. He was quite happy and alert up until about five minutes ago.' She straightened as she heard the ambulance siren and hurried out to the door.

'Mummy?' Sam's eyelids flickered and he looked up at her briefly.

'Sam! It's okay, sweetheart, you're going to be fine.' Dee tried to smile at him but her eyes were full of tears.

'Hello, there.'

Dee looked up and through her tears saw a paramedic bending over her. 'He opened his eyes for a moment.'

'That's good. What's his name?'

'Sam.' Dee moved back to allow the man to examine her son. 'I checked his mouth but I couldn't see anything. We've no idea what happened. He complained of feeling sick but he was playing one minute and the next I found him on the floor unconscious.'

'Sam? Sam, can you hear me?' The paramedic checked Sam's pulse and lifted his shirt to inspect his body.

Sam opened his eyes again.

'Hello, Sam, how are you feeling?'

'A bit sick.'

'Poor you. Did you have a fall, Sam?'

He shook his head.

'You didn't hit your head, did you?'

'No.'

'Any headache?'

'No.'

The paramedic shone a light in Sam's eyes and then checked his neck for stiffness.

'Now, I'm just going to put this on your arm. Do you know what it is?'

'It's for checking my blood pressure.'

'That's right; you're a very clever boy.'

'He's quite familiar with all things medical,' Dee

explained. 'Sam suffers from asthma and eczema.'

'Does he now? Has he ever had an episode like this before?'

'No.'

'Okay. Well, your blood pressure is fine, Sam, but I think we'll bring you into hospital just to let the doctors take a look at you. Is that okay?'

Sam's lip wobbled. 'Can my mummy come?'

'Of course she can.' He turned to Dee. 'Do you want to put a bag together with some of Sam's things?'

'Oh, right.' She scrambled to her feet but Sam wouldn't let her hand go.

'Mummy's just going to get your teddy,' Lisa said, taking Dee's place. 'Can I sit beside you until she gets back?'

Sam looked from his mother to Lisa and nodded, releasing Dee's hand.

'I'll be straight back,' she promised and sped upstairs to pack pyjamas, teddy, toys and books into a small bag. Her heart was racing and she was terrified, but she knew she had to keep it together for Sam's sake. When she came back downstairs they had put Sam into a wheelchair and were taking him out to the ambulance.

Dee grabbed her bag and jacket and turned to Lisa. 'I don't know how long we'll be.'

'Don't worry, we'll manage. Shall I phone Conor and tell him what's happened?'

'Please, and you'd better get him to warn Ronan that it might affect tomorrow's menu.'

Lisa grabbed Sam's coat and hat from a peg in the hall and handed them to Dee.

'He'll need these later when he's coming home.'

Dee tried to smile but found she was close to tears. 'Oh, God, Lisa, I've never been so scared.'

Lisa threw her arms around her. 'I know, Dee, I know and I'm sorry. If there was something I should have seen, should have done—'

'Don't be silly, it's not your fault.'

'He's all loaded up,' the paramedic said from the doorway.

'Do you think he's going to be okay?'

'I'm sure he'll be fine. You know what kids are like; at death's door one minute and running around like wild things the next.'

Lisa walked with them to the ambulance. 'Call us when you can,' she said as Dee climbed in beside her son.

'I will.'

'Bye, Sam, see you later.' Lisa just had time to see Sam raise his hand before the paramedic shut the door and the ambulance drove away. Taking a few deep breaths in an attempt to control her own tears, Lisa went back inside. The children were all sleeping except for Tom who was sitting staring into space, his eyes wide and frightened. Lisa sat down next to him and gave him a hug. 'Don't worry, Tom, everything's okay now.'

'Where's Sam gone?' he asked in a shaky voice.

'To the hospital, but he's going to be just fine.'

'Will he be back soon? Will he be back in time for tea?'

'No, darling, I don't think so.'

'Is he going to die?' Tom said bluntly.

Lisa shook her head. 'No, of course not. The doctor will give him some medicine and he'll be fine.'

'Will they give him ice cream at the hospital?'

'Er, I'm not sure, maybe.'

He smiled up at her. 'Do you think I could have some too?'

She laughed. 'We'll see.'

The closer they got to the hospital, the better Sam seemed to get and by the time they were wheeling him into the emergency room, he was the life and soul of the party. Dee was relieved to see him so alert and happy but she still wanted to know why he had passed out in the first place. If it happened once it could happen again.

'Mrs Hewson?'

'Miss,' Dee said automatically, and she stood up to greet the doctor.

'I'm Doctor Berrane.' He smiled as he shook her hand and Dee thought she wouldn't mind being a patient if she had him to look after her. 'And it's Sam, is it?'

Dee nodded to where her son was crouched on the floor playing with a truck.

'That's him. He doesn't look very sick, does he?'

The doctor laughed. 'Thank goodness, but we'll check him out just to be sure.'

Sam climbed up on the bed in the small cubicle and the doctor carried out the same routine tests that two other doctors had already carried out. Then he asked Dee all about Sam's medical history and he wrote notes, nodding from time to time. 'Okay, then, thank you.'

'So what happens next?' Dee asked as he started to walk away.

He paused. 'We'll wait for his urine sample to come back from the lab and if that's all right then you can probably take him home.'

'But you don't know why he collapsed.'

He shook his head. 'No.'

'Then how do we know he's all right? How do we stop it happening again?'

'Let's wait for the tests to come back and we'll talk about it then.' And with a polite nod, he walked out of the ward.

'It's frustrating, isn't it?' said the man sitting beside the next bed. 'My daughter's been having fits on and off for months and they still can't get to the bottom of it.'

Dee looked at the girl in the bed who was busy playing with a doll. 'She looks fine.'

'Yes.' He chuckled. 'She always seems to improve once we walk through the door!' He stood up. 'I'm going to get a drink, can I get you something?'

She shook her head. 'No, but thanks.'

'I'll be back in a minute, darling,' he told his daughter and quietly left the ward.

Dee turned back to study her son. He was leafing through a book that she'd packed for him and looked completely fine. Maybe they all just felt safe when they got in here, she mused, looking around. She could understand that as the emergency ward, despite being crammed with beds, was bright and cheerful. A nurse walked in and Dee immediately hopped up and went over to her. 'Nurse, could you keep an eye on my son for a little while? I need to make a phone call and I think he's a bit nervous about me leaving him.'

'No problem at all. Sam, would you like to come into the nurse's station with me to get some crayons and paper?'

He nodded and stood up, slipping his hand into hers.

'I'm just going outside to call Lisa, Sam, okay?'

He nodded again and left with the nurse without a backward glance. 'And I think I'm indispensable,' she murmured, exchanging a wry smile with another mother.

Dee hurried back through the rabbit warren of corridors to the front door and joined the ranks of other worried parents outside, some on mobiles and some just staring into space. She shivered, realizing things could be a lot worse. She phoned the crèche and Lisa picked up the phone on the first ring.

'Dee! How is he?'

'He's fine, Lisa, in great form.'

'Oh, thank God.'

'I haven't got long; I can't use my phone in the hospital so I just ran out for a minute to check in with you. I don't have anything to tell you, really. They did some tests and we're just waiting now for results but they don't seem to know what's wrong with him.'

'Well, he's in the right place,' Lisa consoled her. 'I'm sure he'll be fine.'

'Did you talk to Conor?'

'No, he wasn't answering his phone so I rang Ronan. He sends his love and says not to worry; Zoe is going to make bolognese for tomorrow and he'll buy a couple of quiches from the supermarket.'

Dee winced. 'God, I hope he doesn't lose customers.'

'They'll survive for one day.'

'What about the children's tea? I was going to make them scrambled eggs on toast.'

'I saw the eggs, so I was going to boil them and make sandwiches, is that okay?'

'Dear God, Lisa, we'll make a chef of you yet!'

'Don't push it,' Lisa warned.

'I'm so sorry for leaving you in the lurch like that.'

'Don't be silly, as if it's your fault. Anyway, Paula's here. Her mother saw the ambulance and sent her over as soon as she got in from school.'

'That was very kind.' Dee felt a surge of gratitude for good neighbours.

'Is there anyone else you want me to call? Pauline?'

'God, no, she'd only get in the way and drive the staff crazy.'

'Okay, then, you go and look after Sam and don't worry about us; everything is fine.'

'Thanks, Lisa.'

Dee was about to go inside when a thought occurred to her. Maybe she should phone Neil? There was no real reason to; he hadn't been around all the other times Sam had been sick but that, she realized, was what was niggling her. He was here now. She could dial his number and in seconds he would know. It didn't make any difference to her, she still would not let him come in and see Sam but if he was being honest about his feelings, it would make a difference to him. If he cared about Sam he would want to know if he was sick, even if there was nothing he could do about it. Deciding to give him the benefit of the doubt, Dee searched for his number and dialled.

'Oh my God, Dee, is he all right?'

'Yes, he seems to be.'

'But he lost consciousness?'

'Yes, but I don't think it was for long.'

'You're not sure? Was he alone?'

Dee sighed irritably. He hadn't been around for five years and now he was passing judgement on her? 'No, he was in the crèche. One minute he was reading on the sofa and the next he was gone. We thought he was hiding but then,' Dee's voice wobbled, 'I found him on the floor in front of the sofa.'

'I'll come straight in.'

'No! No, Neil, there's no point; there's nothing you can do. I'll phone you when I have more news.'

'Dee?'

'Yes?'

'Thanks for letting me know.'

'That's okay. Bye, Neil.'

Chapter 18

When Dee got back to the ward, Sam was sitting up on the bed watching a Barney DVD on the small television in the corner. His eyes were heavy and Dee climbed up on the bed and slipped an arm around him. 'Are you okay?'

'Uh-huh.'

The nurse came over when she saw Dee was back. 'Are you tired, Sam?' He nodded, not taking his eyes off the screen. 'The doctor will be down to see you soon.'

'Are the results back?' Dee asked.

She nodded. 'Yes, Doctor Berrane needs to look at them. He's on his rounds now but I have paged him.'

'Thanks.'

The nurse moved on to talk to the little girl in the next bed and Dee wriggled around in an effort to get comfortable. 'Everything is going to be fine, Sam,' she said, cuddling him into her. 'You have a little rest.'

'Mrs Hewson? Mrs Hewson?'

Dee's eyes flew open and she looked up at the doctor

smiling down at her. 'Oh, I'm sorry!' She slipped her dead arm from under Sam and sat up.

'Sorry for disturbing you, you looked very comfortable.'

She looked down at her sleeping son. 'Is he okay?'

The doctor put a hand on Sam's wrist and listened before nodding. 'He's fine.'

'Is there any news?' she asked anxiously.

'Yes and no. The tests are all clear which is, of course, good news, but it means we don't know why Sam lost consciousness.'

'So what do we do now?'

'We can keep him in and run more tests if you like or you can take him home and bring him back if you're worried. If it's any consolation there seems to be a bug going round and the symptoms have been fainting and nausea.'

'He did say he felt ill at lunchtime and he didn't eat much at breakfast.'

'Let him sleep for the moment,' the doctor suggested. 'We'll take another look at him when he wakes, but I think the best thing to do is to take him home. If he doesn't want to eat, don't press him but make sure he gets plenty of fluids. If you're worried, bring him back in. You can come straight up to the ward and the nurse will page me.'

Dee smiled. 'Thank you, you've been very kind.'

'Good news?' The nurse came over and sat on the edge of the bed after the doctor had left.

Dee shrugged. 'I suppose so.'

'I know it's hard when you don't have all the answers, but you wouldn't believe how often it happens with children. They seem to get so seriously ill and so suddenly and then' – she snapped her fingers – 'just like that, they're better again!' She smiled. 'My mother says it's why God invented hair colorant.'

Dee chuckled and stood up. 'I've certainly got some grey hairs today! I'd better go and make some more phone calls. If he wakes, will you tell him I'll be back in a few minutes?'

The nurse stood up too. 'Sure, but I'd say he'll be out for a while; he's had quite a day.'

Dee turned back to Sam and laid a hand gently on his forehead. Thankfully he was as cool as he looked and so peaceful. She crept away from the bed and then hurried back outside to call Lisa and Neil and maybe she'd try to get through to Conor; it was odd he hadn't been in touch but then her phone had been off while she was in the hospital.

She stood on the steps and switched on her phone, nearly jumping out of her skin when somebody touched her arm.

'Sorry, Dee, I didn't mean to frighten you.'

She whirled around and did a double take when she saw Neil standing beside her. 'Neil, what are you doing here?'

He shrugged and looked sheepish. 'I didn't know what else to do.'

'You can't see him—'

'No, no, of course not, I just wanted to be close by in case you needed anything. I mean, I could get you stuff in the shops or something, food, clothes . . .' He shrugged again.

Dee nodded slowly and smiled, realizing how helpless he must be feeling. 'Thanks, that's very kind of you but we don't need anything.'

'So, is there any news?'

She sat down on the step and he sat beside her, his eyes scanning her face worriedly.

'He's fine. He's asleep at the moment but they'll probably let me take him home when he wakes.'

'So what's wrong with him?'

She sighed. 'They don't know. They think it's probably a virus of some sort. Apparently there's a lot of it about at the moment.'

He frowned. 'So have they given him anything?'

'No, the doctor said that I should take him home, give him plenty of fluids and keep an eye on him.'

'And are you okay with that?'

'There's not much I can do about it, is there? Of course I'm nervous, Neil, but Sam has come through so much in his short life I have to believe he'll come through this as well.'

He reached out to squeeze her hand. 'I'm sure he will.'

'Dee?'

She looked up to see Conor standing over them.

'Conor!' Oh, shit, this was all she needed. She felt colour flood her cheeks.

'I'm so sorry, Dee, I came as soon as I heard. How is he?'

'He's fine, Conor,' she assured him. 'Apparently he just has some virus that's going around.'

'Dad says he passed out.'

'Yes, it was awful, he gave us quite a fright.'

Conor nodded and looked pointedly at Neil and she realized that he probably thought she'd meant herself and Neil when she'd said 'us'. 'Oh, sorry. Conor, this is Neil.'

The two men sized each other up as they shook hands.

'Can I see him?' Conor asked, turning back to her.

'Well, he's asleep—'

'But I can sit with him.'

Dee noticed the determined set of his chin. 'Yeah, that would be great. I just need to call Lisa and I'll be right with you. He's in the emergency ward, just follow the signs; it's a bit of a walk.'

'I'll go on up then.' He nodded curtly at Neil. 'Nice to meet you.'

'And you,' Neil said, but Conor was already walking away. 'I don't think he was too pleased to see me here,' he murmured.

Dee refused to meet his eye; she had the feeling that he'd enjoyed that little drama.

'He just wasn't expecting you; neither was I.'

He stood up. 'Thanks for calling me, Dee, it was good of you.'

'I had to,' she said simply.

'Can I push my luck and ask you to call me again tomorrow?'

'I'll text you.' She stood up too. 'Now I must phone Lisa.'

'Well, unless you need me to do anything—'

She shook her head. 'No, that's okay.'

'Then I'll go. Bye, Dee, and thanks again.'

'Bye Neil,' she said and turned away to call her friend and bring her up to date.

Dee paused in the doorway of the ward and smiled with relief when she saw Sam sitting in the middle of the floor with Conor playing with a forklift truck. Both of them were intent on manoeuvring the vehicle to pick up some blocks and oblivious to her scrutiny, and she started when the nurse appeared at her side.

'He's thrilled to see his daddy, isn't he?'

'Oh, he's not—'

'Mummy, look what Conor brought me!' Sam called excitedly.

'Lucky you,' Dee murmured, going over to her son and crouching down beside him.

'It's a forklift truck just like the one Conor has on

his farm,' Sam told her, 'and I can work it. Conor says when I'm older I can learn how to drive his one.'

'Yes, well, we'll see about that. Did you say thank you?'

'Yeah.' But Sam still reached up to hug Conor once more. 'Thanks, Conor.'

'You're welcome, champ.' Conor looked up at Dee. 'The doctor was here; he says we can go home.'

'Oh, doesn't he want to talk to me?'

'Not unless you want to talk to him. He checked his blood pressure and listened to his heart and chest and said he was happy enough to discharge him.' Conor frowned. 'I'd have come and got you but he said he was talking to you earlier.'

'No, that's fine. I'll just go and have a word with the nurse and then we can get going. Sam, why don't you go to the toilet and then get your shoes and coat on?'

'But I want to play with my new toy,' he protested.

'You can play with it in the car,' Conor promised, lifting the little boy easily on to his shoulders. 'Now let's go to the loo; you can steer.'

The nurse looked up as Dee stuck her head into the nurse's station. 'Ready to go?'

'I think so.'

The girl handed her a piece of paper. 'That's the number of the ward. If you have any worries at all just call.'

'You've been really kind, thanks a million.'

'You're welcome. Sam's a smashing little boy.'

Dee smiled. 'Thanks.'

Sam chattered the whole way home, telling Conor all about his trip in the ambulance and the doctor letting him use his 'stetscope'. Dee sat back in the passenger seat content to listen, her son's voice sweeter than ever. To be taking him home was more than she could have hoped for and though she was still concerned that they did not know the reason for his collapse, she had confidence in the doctor and in Sam's own demeanour.

When she looked back to check on him she noted the sparkle in his eyes, the healthy colour of his skin, and the rapid-fire questions that he was raining on Conor. He was not behaving remotely like a sick child.

When they pulled up outside the house, Lisa hurried out to greet them.

'What on earth are you still doing here? It's almost seven.' Dee asked as her friend hugged her tightly.

'I couldn't leave without seeing him,' Lisa whispered, watching as Conor lifted Sam down from the jeep. 'He looks a lot better.'

'He is.'

'Lisa! Look what Conor bought for me.' He held the forklift up for her inspection.

'Cool! Let's take it inside and you can show me how it works,' Lisa said. As Sam skipped inside she turned back to Conor and Dee. 'Why don't you two go and have a cuppa? I'll keep him with me in the crèche for a little while and let you catch your breath.'

'I don't know, Lisa—'

Lisa put her hand to her mouth. 'Oh, God, you don't trust me with him, do you?'

'Don't be daft, of course I do!' Dee retorted. 'It's just I'm terrified to take my eyes off him. I don't know what I would do if anything ever happened.'

Conor slipped an arm around her shoulders as the tears started to fall. 'Sam doesn't need to see you like this,' he murmured. 'Let Lisa look after him and take a short break.'

Dee nodded silently and allowed him to guide her down the hall towards the kitchen while Lisa hurried after Sam.

'So,' he said once she was sitting down, 'what will it be?'

'Tea, please.'

'Want me to put something in it?' he asked as he filled the kettle.

'No, I'm tired as it is and I want to keep my wits about me. What if he passed out again?'

'I'm sure he'll be fine. I'm so sorry you couldn't contact me, Dee. I went into the market and my phone ran out of juice. Dad didn't manage to get through to me until I was back in the car and so I drove straight to the hospital – well, via the toy shop.' He carried two mugs of tea over and sat down beside her.

'Thanks for the present, he loves it.'

He gave a short laugh. 'Then that's about the only useful thing I did today.'

'There was nothing you could have done.'

'I could have been with you. Like Neil.'

She put a hand on his when she heard the hurt in his voice. 'Neil wasn't with me. I phoned him from the hospital to tell him what happened – I felt I had to – but I never asked him to come; he just turned up minutes before you did.'

Conor nodded. 'Are you going to let him meet Sam?'

'I don't know yet,' she said honestly.

'You must have told him something.'

Dee massaged her forehead with a weary hand. 'I told him this morning that I'd like to talk to someone who can vouch for his recovery.'

Conor's eyes narrowed. 'You were talking to him this morning?'

Dee flushed. 'Yes, I met him in town.'

'So you didn't go to see a recruitment consultant,' he said slowly.

'I did! I did that too.'

'But the real reason you went in to Dublin was to meet Neil.'

'Conor, I can't make any decisions without talking to the man,' she snapped irritably, 'and I could hardly invite him here.'

'Agreed, I just wonder why you felt you couldn't tell me about it.'

'I was going to—'

'When, Dee, after he'd moved back in?' He hadn't raised his voice a fraction but Dee could hear the anger in his voice.

'Conor, please, you are completely overreacting. It's been a crazy week and so much has happened and I was planning on telling you all about it; there just hasn't been an opportunity.'

'Okay, then you can fill me in tonight over dinner.'

'Dinner?'

'We're going out, remember? Paula is booked for eight o'clock.'

Dee had completely forgotten. 'Oh, Conor, I can't leave Sam tonight, not now.'

'Then we'll stay in and talk.'

Dee sighed. 'Can't we do this tomorrow, Conor, I'm really beat.'

He stood up abruptly, splashing his tea. 'Fine, then, I'll head off so.'

'Conor!'

'I'll just go and say goodbye to Sam,' he said and strode out of the kitchen.

'Shit,' Dee murmured. She really should follow him and make him listen but she felt so exhausted; too exhausted for the heavy conversation that would ensue. Anyway, she was a bit annoyed with him. He was being completely unreasonable. How could he expect her to go out and leave Sam tonight? Right now she wasn't sure she'd ever let him out of her sight again. Hearing the front door close, she went through to the crèche and smiled when she saw Sam curled up on Lisa's lap listening as she read him a story.

'Sam, it's time for your bath,' she said when Lisa had finished.

'Ah, Mum.'

'And if you're good,' Lisa interjected when his lip settled into a stubborn line, 'and your Mum doesn't mind, I'll read you another story when you're tucked up in bed.'

'Yes!'

'But only if you're really quick.'

He hopped up immediately. 'Okay, but Mum, can I have something to eat first?'

Dee nodded, delighted. 'Sure! Let's go out to the kitchen and see what we've got.'

He raced ahead and she turned back to Lisa. 'Thanks a million but don't you want to get off?'

'I'm in no rush and as Conor had to go I thought I could talk you into an extremely unhealthy takeaway.' She eyed her speculatively. 'I figured you might need the company.'

'I don't know what I'd do without you,' Dee said, hugging her.

'Mum? Mum? Are there any chocolate cookies?' Sam yelled from the kitchen.

Lisa laughed. 'I think he's on the mend.'

Chapter 19

Though Sam was a lot better the next day, Dee kept a careful eye on him and insisted they have a quiet day at home. It was for her benefit as much as his. Though Sam had slept through the night and woken in wonderful form, Dee had crept in every so often to check on him. She was exhausted when she woke and was happy to spend the day quietly, just the two of them.

Julia called on Sunday morning, insisting Dee and Sam join them at the café for Sunday lunch. 'I'm sure you could do with the break and I happen to know the food there is quite good,' she joked.

Dee agreed. She hadn't talked to Conor since Friday night. Although he had sent a text to ask after Sam, he didn't call and neither did she. She knew she should but there was too much to be said and it couldn't be done on the phone, especially with little ears close by. Maybe she'd get an opportunity today to set the record straight.

When they arrived at Better Books, Ronan and Julia and Conor were already seated and sharing a bottle of wine.

Immediately they saw Sam, they fussed over him, Julia producing a new football for the little boy. Conor, pleasant but distant with Dee, concentrated all his attentions on Sam and soon he, Sam and Ronan were arguing good-naturedly about who was really the best football team, Liverpool or Manchester United.

'You must have got such a fright,' Julia murmured to Dee as she poured her a glass of wine.

'I did,' Dee agreed. 'I'm still a bit nervous, to be honest. Who's to say it won't happen again?'

Julia nodded sympathetically. 'Still, he looks wonderful today and he seems to be in top form.'

'Yes.'

'You look tired,' Julia observed, 'you're doing too much.'

Dee smiled. 'You can talk!'

'I don't have a young child to look after,' Julia pointed out. 'Seriously, Dee, maybe you should re-evaluate things. I mean, if you'd been there when Sam took ill—'

Dee bit her lip. 'He was in our home with my best and trusted friend who happens to have a string of qualifications in childcare not to mention being fully trained in First Aid.'

'But Conor said you found him unconscious.'

She sighed. 'He was in the same room and it all happened in a matter of minutes.'

Julia shrugged. 'All I'm saying is no one looks after your children the way you do.'

Dee stood up abruptly. 'Excuse me, I need to use the loo.' She pushed open the door and crashed into Zoe coming the other way. 'Oh, sorry.'

'You're in a hurry.' Zoe looked at her and then frowned at Dee's flushed face and glowering expression. 'What's up?'

'Julia,' Dee growled.

'Oh.' Zoe nodded in understanding. 'What's she said this time?'

'Basically that if I'd stayed home and looked after my son, he wouldn't have been taken ill.'

'Silly old bat, ignore her,' Zoe advised. 'I always do.'

After splashing water into her face and taking a moment to calm down, Dee went back inside and was relieved to see Julia had gone over to another table to chat to a neighbour. Conor and Sam were at the jukebox and Ronan was sitting alone, sipping his wine. As she sat back down next to him, he topped up her glass. 'It seems we've been deserted.'

'I'm glad of a chance to talk to you,' she told him. 'I had quite a successful meeting with the recruitment people on Friday and I'm hoping to interview at least one person next week.'

'Oh, that's great, love. I hope you don't feel I've forced your hand.'

She shook her head. 'No, not at all and with the latest developments, I'd have had to get help anyway.'

'Oh?' He looked at her curiously.

'I haven't had a chance to fill Conor in yet so I'd appreciate it if you kept it to yourself until we've had a chance to talk—'

'Yes, of course.'

'—but I've been asked to do a regular spot on the *Right Now* programme.'

'Dee, that's wonderful! Congratulations!'

Dee grinned. 'Thanks. It will mean I'll be spending Wednesdays at the studio so I am going to need the help. But I don't want you to worry,' she added hurriedly, 'I promise that standards won't drop.'

'I know that,' he admonished, 'and look at the crowds your fame will draw in, I'll have to build an extension to the place!'

She laughed. 'I doubt that.'

'I'm delighted for you, darling.' He kissed her cheek. 'I think you will be wonderful and, if it doesn't sound too patronizing, I'm proud of you.'

'What's all this?' Julia said bustling over, her face curious.

'Dee is going to be a TV star!' Ronan told her, smiling broadly, and instantly forgetting his promise to keep the news to himself. 'She's got a regular spot on that programme she was on.'

'No!' Julia's face was a picture.

Dee groaned inwardly. 'Yes, it's true,' she confirmed, shooting a nervous glance in Conor's direction. 'They've decided to do a weekly spot on nutrition and they've asked me to be on the panel.'

'How exciting!'

'What's exciting, Mother?' Conor asked as he and Sam returned to the table.

'Dee's just told us about her new job,' Julia said as Ronan shot Dee an apologetic look. 'Why didn't you tell us?' she added with a reproachful look.

He looked blankly at his mother. 'I've no idea what you're talking about.'

'Mum's going to be on telly every week,' Sam told him, bouncing up and down excitedly on his chair. 'She's going to teach people how to eat proply.'

'Properly,' Dee said automatically. 'Sorry, Conor, I never got a chance to tell you. With all the fuss over Sam on Friday it completely went out of my head.'

He nodded and gave a forced smile at no one in particular. 'Congratulations.'

'Thanks,' she said dully.

Julia prattled on through the meal, asking questions and offering her views on what topics should be discussed. Dee nodded and smiled but it was hard to ignore Conor's coolness. She wished Julia would shut up. All she wanted to do was to get Conor alone so she could explain everything. When Zoe had served them coffee, Dee sent Sam off to wash his hands.

'I know,' Ronan said, 'why don't Julia and I take Sam to the cinema?'

Julia stared at him. 'I'm not sure there's anything suitable on. Anyway, Dee probably has plans.'

'You don't, do you?' Ronan asked.

'Well, no, but I'm sure you have better things to do with your Sunday afternoon.'

'We'd like to, wouldn't we, Julia?' He squeezed his wife's knee probably a little harder than necessary.

'Yes, yes of course.'

'And you and Conor can go for a drink or a walk or something,' he went on.

Dee shot a look at Conor. He didn't look at all keen on the idea.

'I was going to do some paperwork this afternoon,' he murmured.

'Nonsense,' his mother retorted, 'it's Sunday. The poor girl needs a break after the terrible time she's had.'

Dee smiled. This was true Julia. One minute she was an irritating old busybody and the next she was a sweetheart.

Conor caught her eye and smiled. 'Do you want me to take you out after the terrible time you've had?'

'A walk might be nice.' She smiled too, glad to see some warmth back in his expression.

'Good, then that's settled.' Ronan stood up as Sam came running back. 'Now, young man, what would you say to a trip to the cinema?'

'Yeah!' Sam cheered. 'Can I have popcorn?'

Julia looked anxiously at Dee.

'Popcorn is fine,' Dee told her, 'but just water if he's thirsty.' She pulled Sam to her and hugged him. 'Behave yourself.'

'I will.'

Julia stood up and stretched out a hand to the little boy. 'Then let's go.'

'Thanks.' Dee smiled at her and then at Ronan.

'The least I can do,' Ronan murmured.

'You two go and enjoy yourselves and we'll see you at home later.' Julia squeezed Dee's hand. 'I promise we'll take very good care of him.'

Dee watched them leave and snuck a look at Conor. 'Sorry,' she said when his eyes met hers.

He shrugged. 'None of it seems very important after what happened to Sam.'

She smiled. 'Thank you.'

He stood up and held out his hand to her. 'What's it to be, a walk or the pub?'

'Both?' she suggested, taking it. 'A walk first, I think.'

They didn't talk as they walked the short distance to the beach but Conor kept a tight grip on her hand. She squeezed it gratefully and tucked her head down into the neck of her jacket to avoid the cool breeze.

'So you're going to be rich,' he said finally with a sideways grin.

She laughed. 'No, but the bank balance will be a lot healthier. Mind you, that isn't saying much.'

Conor did a double take at her sober expression. 'Are you finding things that hard?'

'I was,' she admitted and was relieved that she finally could. 'It's been a tough few months.'

He stopped and looked at her. 'Dee, you should have told me, I could have helped you.'

Dee grinned. 'Oh right, Moneybags!'

'Okay,' he admitted, 'it wouldn't have been easy, but we could have worked something out.'

'Thanks, but it's all in the past now.' She tugged him on. 'Seven TV are paying me nine thousand, six hundred euros for twelve shows.'

'Good God!'

'I know!' She grinned. 'And Lisa and I have agreed a rent increase.'

'Oh, when was this, on Wednesday when you stood me up?'

'I didn't stand you up,' she corrected, digging him in the ribs, 'I had already agreed to make her dinner. Anyway, we had a really long talk about the crèche. Lisa has some great ideas. She wants to expand and take on more staff and provide a more rounded service.'

'Good on her.'

'I'll continue to do the food for her but I won't be helping out with the kids as much.'

'You'll miss that,' he observed.

'I know, but I'm really looking forward to the TV spot. I'll just spend Wednesdays in the studio so I get the buzz but it doesn't take over my life.' Her face lit up as she spoke and she stopped when she saw the look of amusement in his eyes.

'What?'

He hugged her close to him. 'Nothing. It's just that I've never seen you so fired up about anything before.'

She nodded slowly. 'Yeah, I am, and it feels good. I'll just have to be careful that Sam doesn't lose out.'

He sighed. 'Sam is fine, don't worry about him so much.'

'Can you blame me after what happened on Friday?' she protested. 'Anyway, your mother doesn't agree.'

'What do you mean?'

'She as much as said that he'd never have got ill if I had been looking after him instead of gadding about.' She waved a hand around wildly.

'That's ridiculous, and you should know better than to listen to her; I never do.'

Dee's lips twitched. 'Still, she's right; he's young and he does need me.'

'And he's got you,' he said impatiently. 'You're talking about spending one day a week in the city, not moving to another country.'

'I suppose you're right,' she admitted.

'I am.' They walked on in silence for a moment. 'So have you heard any more from Neil?'

She shook her head.

'But if he comes up with this "reference" you're going to let him see Sam.'

'Yes – yes, I am.' She looked at him. 'It's the right thing to do.' Conor nodded but he didn't look at her and in profile she could see his face was grim. 'You don't approve.'

'It's not for me to approve or disapprove.' He held up his hands. 'It's your decision; Sam's your son.'

Something about this answer disappointed Dee. 'Yes he is.'

'I just don't want Sam to get hurt.' He turned to look at her. 'I don't want you to get hurt either.'

She smiled and, ducking her head under his arm, nestled close to him. 'It's all going to be fine.'

When they got back to Ronan's house a couple of hours later, it was to find Sam sitting up at the kitchen table playing Snap with Julia.

Dee sat down next to her son and planted a kiss on his tousled curls while Conor went to raid the biscuit tin. 'Hey, you, have you had a good time?'

'Great.'

'What did you go and see?'

'*Happy Feet.*'

Dee pretended to look annoyed. 'Aah, I wanted to go and see that!'

'Don't worry, Mummy,' he assured her quickly, 'we can go again.'

'Can we now?'

'Yes.' He nodded confidently. 'And Conor can come too.'

'Thanks, champ.' Conor sat down the other side of him and tossed him a piece of shortbread.

'Mum?' Sam looked immediately to his mother for permission and she nodded.

She watched as the two of them discussed the movie, completely comfortable in each other's company and wondered if Neil would ever take Sam to the cinema, if he would ever have a relationship with his son.

'Penny for them,' Ronan said softly.

Dee looked up to find the older man standing over her. She felt the colour flood her cheeks. 'They're worthless,' she assured him with a light laugh.

Chapter 20

Vi, laden down with paints and brushes, banged on the back door with her elbow.

'Dee? Hurry up, for God's sake, I'm going to drop something.'

Dee ran to open the door and stood back as Vi pushed past her and unloaded the tools of her trade on to the kitchen table.

'Be a love and get the easel and canvas out of the car, would you, Dee?' she said moving towards the kettle. 'Lord, I'm parched.'

'Oh, Vi, do we have to do this today?' Dee groaned, 'I'm so busy.'

'You're always busy. Don't worry, you won't even know I'm here. Besides,' the older woman reminded her, 'you promised.'

'Okay, okay.' Dee obediently went to fetch the rest of the artist's stuff while Vi made strong coffee, a smug smile on her face. 'How do you lug this stuff around with you all the time?' Dee said, coming back panting.

'I don't, I get people like you to do it! Tell me, how's young Sam? I heard he was sick.'

'He passed out on Friday, scared the hell out of me,' Dee told her. 'We had to call an ambulance but, of course, he was fine once we reached the hospital and they couldn't find anything wrong.'

'And he's okay now?'

'Full of beans.' Dee glanced at the clock. 'I'm afraid I can't sit and chat, I've lots to do.'

'So I've heard.' Vi settled herself at the kitchen table. 'Would I be right in thinking your money worries are no more?'

Dee leaned against the worktop and smiled. 'What have you heard?'

'That you're about to become a TV star.'

Dee laughed. 'That's a slight exaggeration. I can't believe the word is out already, I only told Conor and Ronan on Sunday.'

'And Julia,' Vi reminded her, 'and you were in the café at the time.'

'Ah, yes, I take your point.'

'The difference in you today compared to last week is amazing. You were really worried, weren't you?'

'Yes,' Dee admitted. 'To be honest, I thought I was going to have to sell the house.'

'Would that be so bad?'

'Of course! It would have meant throwing Lisa out and Sam losing the only home he's ever known.'

Vi shrugged. 'It would be a blow but Lisa would find

new premises and as for Sam, he would adjust to living on the moon once you were with him.'

'I suppose.'

'What is it about this house?' Vi asked, curiously. 'Why has it got such a hold on you?'

Dee turned away. 'It doesn't, don't be silly.'

'It must be worth a few bob, what with its location and that huge garden. You could sell it and buy another place much better suited to your needs and probably still have cash left over.'

'But I don't have to any more,' Dee pointed out. 'Not only do I have this TV job but I've increased Lisa's rent.'

'Is it because it's the family home and your only link with the past?' Vi continued as if she hadn't spoken.

Dee concentrated her attention on her 'to do' list. 'It's just a house,' she laughed.

'Funny, that's what I was going to say. Any connections with the past are in here,' she pointed at her head, 'and in here', she moved her hand to her heart. 'You can't lose them, Dee, you carry them with you wherever you go.'

Dee turned when she heard the wobble in Vi's voice and was surprised to see the sadness on the woman's face. 'That sounds like the voice of experience,' she said softly.

Vi laughed and, pulling out a hanky, blew her nose noisily. 'I've experienced most things. That happens when you're as old as I am.'

'You're not old. You're younger than Ronan and Julia, aren't you?'

Vi immediately got to her feet and started to sort through her paints. 'No idea. Now, my dear, I hope you have plenty of cooking to do because I need at least two hours of your time.'

'That's fine,' Dee said, allowing her to change the subject, 'just don't expect me to smile all the time.'

'God forbid.'

It was going to be a busy week, Lisa realized, but an exciting one. She couldn't believe that after only advertising for a childminder on Friday, the emails had been flooding in and the phone hadn't stopped ringing. Now she had two candidates coming, one at twelve-thirty and one at one-thirty; she just hoped that they met with her long list of requirements. She could have arranged to meet them after work but it was important, she felt, to see the candidates with the children so Dee had agreed to step in to cover for her. It would also give her friend an opportunity to observe the candidates and Lisa was glad of that. She'd never carried out an interview before never mind hired someone and she would welcome Dee's input.

She had been on a high since her conversation with Dee although Ger's reaction had put a damper on things.

'You want your head examined. Offering to pay more rent and forking out for more wages; you'll be broke.'

'Extra staff means more children and more children mean more money. Also I won't have to put in such long hours.'

'You're kidding yourself,' he'd said with a snort, 'when you're the boss you always work long hours and more staff means more headaches, everyone knows that.'

Lisa had been disappointed at his reaction and a little unnerved; maybe he was right and she was taking on too much. But then Conor had dropped in yesterday and he was full of praise for her ideas and very encouraging about the future of Happy Days. It had given her a great boost. If anyone knew how hard it was to run your own business, it was Conor. Lisa was always impressed at the way he met the many problems associated with farming head-on and just got on with it.

'How do you keep going when it gets really hard?' she'd asked him.

He'd thought about it for a moment and then shrugged. 'I suppose it's because I love what I do.'

And that had been the best thing he could have said because although Lisa had many doubts about her own abilities, she knew she loved her job, adored working with children, and couldn't think of anything she would rather do.

She had been thrilled that when she told Martha of her plans, she, too, had been excited, especially about the plan to have a completely separate baby room.

'I'm so glad about that, Lisa,' she'd confided. 'I've always thought the babies needed more space and with the other children walking in dirt from the garden, it's hard to keep the little ones clean.'

'Do you want to stay with the babies?' Lisa had asked.

'Oh, yes.' Martha had nodded enthusiastically. 'The older children are great and I love them, but I just adore watching babies develop over the first year.'

Lisa had smiled, thankful that she had at least one employee who loved her job. 'I feel the most important thing is to find the right people,' she'd said finally. 'We have to have a good team so that we back each other up and give each other time-out when we need it. I think anyone I hire will initially be on a trial basis because no matter how good their qualifications are, if we don't get on or they're not fitting in, it won't work.'

Martha had been in full agreement and was even more delighted to learn she was getting a salary increase and would have more time off.

Lisa hadn't bothered to tell Ger any more of her ideas. She didn't need his negativity ruining everything. She couldn't be sure but she had a feeling that he was jealous, although why that should be, given his high-powered job in the council, she had no idea. For the first time she could remember, she'd turned him down when he suggested they go out on Saturday night.

She'd spent the day reading the numerous applications that had come in by email and had been really fired up by the experience. When Ger had called with his last-minute, casual invitation she'd realized that she'd prefer to stay in, have a hot bath and work a bit more on her plans. She hadn't said that, of course; she wouldn't deliberately hurt his feelings. Instead, she told him she was feeling a bit under the weather as her period had started and that had produced the desired effect. Ger wasn't the kind of guy who fetched hot water bottles and rubbed your back.

Lisa had quite enjoyed her night alone, she realized now as she cleaned down the table in preparation for snack time. It was amazing the effect this whole business was having on her. She had been in super-efficient mode all morning and she couldn't stop smiling. Several parents had even commented on it.

'Has he popped the question?' one father guessed, winking at her and nearly ruining her mood.

'Why do people always think that if you're happy it must be down to a man?' she'd complained to Martha but it hadn't bothered her for long; nothing had. She did a quick check on the children who were busy working on Mother's Day cards and then went over to Martha. 'I'm just going out to get the snack.' Martha looked up from where she was building foam blocks with the babies.

'Okay, but will you hurry? I need to change Olivia's nappy.'

Lisa wrinkled her nose. 'Yes, you do, don't you?'

Vi was painting away and Dee was cooking ratatouille when Lisa breezed in. 'Hiya ,Vi, how's the masterpiece coming?'

'You tell me,' Vi said, sitting back to allow Lisa a closer look.

'Oh, nice.' Lisa looked at the painting and then at Dee. 'Although I'm not sure her nose is quite that big.'

Dee's head whipped around. 'What?'

'Very funny,' Vi said, swatting Lisa away. 'You're next.'

Lisa snorted. 'You must be really desperate if you want to paint me.'

'Why do you say that?'

Lisa turned away from Vi's watchful eyes and went to the fridge to fetch the yoghurt and fruit. 'Well, let's say I'm not exactly Halle Berry.'

'No, you're the wrong colour,' Dee agreed.

'Funny.'

Vi frowned. 'Who's Halle Berry?'

Lisa rolled her eyes. 'Crikey, Vi, don't you ever go to the cinema?'

'I think *Breakfast at Tiffany's* was the last film I saw,' Vi said thoughtfully, 'or was it *Lawrence of Arabia*?'

'You're kidding,' Dee laughed. 'That must be nearly forty years ago.'

'That would be about right. It was when I was dating.'

Lisa giggled.

Vi shook her head in exasperation. 'I was young once too, you know. We used to go the cinema – the pictures, we called it – because it was the only place to go if you wanted a bit of comfort and privacy,' she winked, 'if you know what I mean.'

'I bet you were a right looker when you were young,' Lisa said enviously.

'I wasn't bad.' Vi's eyes twinkled.

'I can't believe you never married,' Dee said, ladling the vegetables into a container. 'Didn't you ever find Mr Right?'

Vi gazed wistfully into the distance. 'I think I probably did but of course I didn't realize it at the time.'

'What happened?' Lisa asked, turning and leaning against the counter, the snack forgotten.

'I was foolish and let him go, that's what happened and the moral of the story is, when you've got a good man hold on to him.'

Dee and Lisa were silent as they digested this and then they heard Martha calling.

'Damn. Olivia!' Lisa muttered, throwing the food on to a tray and hurrying to the door.

Vi looked puzzled. 'I thought the other girl's name was Martha.'

Dee laughed. 'It is.'

*

'Martha, I'm so sorry!' Lisa opened the door with her elbow and shot her assistant an apologetic look. 'Shall I take them through for their snack or do you want to change Olivia first?'

'*You* can change Olivia for your sins,' Martha retorted.

'Fair enough. Shall we move the gang into the dining room first?'

'Yes, please.' Martha handed Olivia to Lisa and went to fetch the other two babies.

'Come on everyone, line up,' Lisa said to the other children. 'Ready, steady, up two, three, four, up, two, three, four.'

Lisa marched the children into the other room, supervised them as they scrambled up on to their chairs, and waited while Martha strapped the two babies into their high-chairs. 'Okay, Olivia, let's go and get you a nice clean bum!'

The baby gurgled and smiled gummily up at Lisa as she changed her. 'Aren't you a real sweetie?'

The baby girl blew bubbles and waved her hands around.

'Wouldn't I just love to take you home with me?' Lisa sighed wistfully. 'I'd be the luckiest woman in the world if I had a little girl like you, wouldn't I?' She taped on the new nappy, put the baby's pink tights back on, and scooped her up in her arms. 'Now, gorgeous, let's go and get some food.' She kissed the top of Olivia's head and allowed herself one final sniff of that delicious baby smell.

She couldn't work with babies all of the time, she'd realized that a long time ago. It filled her with a yearning that was like a physical pain. For some reason she found the older children easier. They were little people with established personalities and though she loved them all, they were other people's children. But when she held a baby, the tenderness and emotion she felt was not that of a childminder but of a woman who longed for a child of her own.

She paused in the hallway to give Olivia one more quick cuddle. 'That's my fix for today,' she murmured and took the baby back in to Martha.

Chapter 21

After the crèche closed for the day, Dee and Lisa went into the kitchen to discuss the two candidates.

'I'm bored, Mum,' Sam complained, kicking his foot against the leg of the table. 'What can I do?'

'You can paint,' Dee announced.

'Yeah! Cool!'

When Dee had dressed him in one of her old T-shirts, set him up with an array of different colours, three large sheets of paper, water and a brush, she joined Lisa on the sofa and took a grateful sip of the tea Lisa had made. 'Oh, I needed that.'

She kicked off her shoes and tucked her feet under her. 'So, tell me, what do you think?'

'One almost definite,' Lisa said, her eyes twinkling with excitement. 'The first girl, Yvonne.'

Dee nodded. 'I didn't get that much time with her but she seemed to know what she was talking about.'

'She was great with the children, Dee. Firm and confidant but loving, too.'

'And does she have the references you wanted?'

Lisa looked at the CV in her hand. 'Yes, I'll give them a call tomorrow but she has impressive qualifications and her last job was in a crèche in the city, one of the big ones.'

'Does that mean she's unemployed now, though?' Dee looked concerned.

'Yes, but only because she left to nurse her dying father. He passed away last month.'

Dee still wasn't happy. 'Why didn't she get her old job back?'

'She sold her father's house and decided to move away; too many memories. I believe her, but, like I say, there are plenty of referees I can talk to.'

'And the second girl? Sally, wasn't it?'

Lisa shook her head. 'She looked good on paper and said all the right things but she just seemed a little cold and distant with the children.'

'I don't know if I'd say cold, but she definitely seemed quite reserved,' Dee agreed.

She stood up and went over to check on her son's progress. He was carefully painting purple planes of all shapes and sizes. Though Dee had set out a variety of colours, purple was the only one he was using and, these days, planes were all he wanted to paint. 'That's lovely, sweetheart. Why don't you paint some blue planes now?'

He shook his head, not looking up. 'They have to be purple.'

'He's a gas little man,' Lisa murmured when Dee

rejoined her. 'He always has very firm ideas about what he wants.'

'I know where he gets that from,' Dee whispered back.

'Neil.' Lisa nodded.

Dee smiled. 'He always knew exactly what he wanted from life, he was always very forceful and stubborn and yet now . . .'

'You've seen him again, haven't you?' Lisa's eyes searched her face.

Dee looked over to make sure Sam was still absorbed in his artwork and then nodded. 'I met him on Friday morning for a chat.'

Lisa shot her a reproachful look. 'You told me you were going into Dublin to find a new chef.'

'And I did, but I met him too. I'm sorry I didn't tell you, Lisa, but I was afraid you'd try to stop me.'

'Who do you think you're talking to – Pauline?'

'Sorry,' Dee said again.

'So did you learn anything?'

'Not much,' Dee admitted. 'But later on he was great.'

'Later on?' Lisa said blankly.

Dee sighed. 'I called him from the hospital. I had to,' she added when she saw the look on her friend's face, 'I just had to. He came over.'

Lisa's eyes widened. 'What?'

'Oh, he didn't come in; he was waiting outside for me when I came out to phone you.' Dee smiled wryly. 'Unfortunately, so was Conor.'

'God, I'd say that was an interesting conversation.'

'It was.'

'Go on,' Lisa urged.

Dee noticed that Sam had stopped painting and she shook her head. 'I think it's somebody's bedtime. Do you want to wait and I'll make us some tea?'

Lisa shook her head. 'Sorry, I can't, I promised Ger I'd meet him. He's a bit narky with me because I haven't seen him all weekend.'

'How come?'

'I was just busy,' Lisa said vaguely as she gathered up her papers and bag. 'Right, I'll check out Yvonne's references tomorrow and you know I have another interview on Thursday and one on Friday.'

'No problem, it's just Wednesdays that I can't do.' Dee walked her to the door.

'Are you looking forward to your first day in the studio?' Lisa asked.

'I'm nervous but yes, I'm excited too.'

'You'll be great. And I don't want you worrying about Sam, I'll have him glued to my side.'

Dee smiled gratefully. 'He seems absolutely fine again but it doesn't stop me worrying.'

'Of course it doesn't, he's your son.'

After Dee had waved her off she went back into the kitchen and smiled at Sam.

'Now, sir, how about some tea?'

'Is there any of your pizza left?' he asked.

'Yes, I kept you some, is that what you would like?'
He nodded. 'Yes, please.'

'Okay, then. Why don't you go and wash your hands
and I'll clean up here?' She bent to help Sam remove
his painting shirt and he trotted off to the bathroom,
whistling tunelessly.

Dee smiled as she cleaned down the table. It was
such a relief to see him behaving normally and looking
so much healthier than he had on Friday. In one way it
was a relief but in another it just frightened her that
something so random, so sudden and so violent could
attack her little boy. It made her feel vulnerable and
powerless and more determined than ever to keep her
son safe from everyone and everything.

Neil still hadn't been in touch about arranging for her
to talk to someone who had witnessed his epiphany
and that made her a little nervous. She saw the clothes,
the car, she heard his words, but she still couldn't risk
believing in him. She needed to hear his story from
someone else.

She tidied away the painting materials, turned the
oven on and put the remainder of yesterday's pizza in
to re-heat. She put on the kettle to make some tea and
poured milk into a plastic mug for Sam. She was just
pouring the water into the teapot when Sam skipped
back into the room and clambered up on a chair at the
kitchen table.

'Is Conor coming over?' he asked.

Dee set his mug down in front of him and went to

fetch two plates. 'The vet is coming to see a sick cow but he said he should be here by seven.'

'Which cow?' Sam asked anxiously.

'He didn't say.'

'I bet it's Darth Vader, he's always getting sick.'

Dee suppressed a smile. Sam had insisted that all the cows should have names and Conor had finally agreed as long as they weren't girly names like Buttercup and Marigold.

'As if!' Sam had looked at him in shocked disgust.

'Will I have time to play with Conor?' Sam was saying now.

'I tell you what, why don't you get ready for bed as soon as we finish tea and then you can be all ready to play when he gets here?'

'Great, thanks, Mum.'

Dee served up their food and sat down beside him to eat. 'You like Conor, don't you?'

Sam nodded and smiled through his mouthful of pizza. 'So do you, Mum, don't you?'

She laughed. 'Yes I do.'

'He's your boyfriend,' he said, with a shy grin.

'I suppose he is,' she agreed, amused at his embarrassment. 'Is that okay?'

His head bobbed up and down enthusiastically. 'I like him. He'd be a great daddy, wouldn't he?'

Dee gulped. 'Yes, I suppose he would.'

Sam chewed thoughtfully for a moment. 'Do you think he'd like to be my daddy?'

'Oh, sweetheart, it doesn't work like that.'

Sam watched her steadily. 'Why not?'

Dee looked away. 'It's just not that simple.'

He stuck his chin out stubbornly, looking, ironically, like his father. 'Why not? If Conor wants to be my daddy and I want him to be my daddy, why can't it be?'

'You're too young to understand,' she said, annoyed with herself for using this pathetic cop-out. 'Eat your food,' she added.

Sam glowered at her and quickly finishing her own meal, Dee went to the sink and started to scrub the oven tray. She hated it when Sam asked awkward questions and she hated that reproachful look he gave her when she couldn't or wouldn't answer his questions. As she dried the tray and slid it back into the oven, there was a rap on the back door and, with a nervous glance at her son, she went to answer it.

'Conor! You're early.'

He shook the rain off like a dog and came inside, bending to tug off his mucky boots. 'Yeah, the vet got out earlier than he thought he would.'

'Hey, Conor!' Sam was down from the table and hurling himself at Conor. 'How's the cow? Is it Darth Vader again?'

Conor steadied himself and grinned down at the little boy. 'It is, but he's going to be fine.'

'Coffee? Tea?' Dee offered.

'I'd prefer a beer,' Conor admitted, stretching. 'God, it's been a tough day.'

Dee fetched a bottle of lager from the fridge and handed it to him. 'Sam, why don't you get ready for bed and then you can come back down and play for a while?'

'I want Conor to come up with me.'

'No, sweetheart, Conor's having his beer.'

'No, that's okay.' Conor took a drink and then set the bottle down on the counter. 'Come on, champ, let's go.'

Dee went to follow but Sam stopped her. 'No, Mum, you stay here.'

Dee managed a weak grin. 'Oh, right, I know when I'm not wanted.'

Conor gave her an apologetic smile and followed Sam upstairs. Dee abandoned her tea and went back to the fridge to fetch another beer.

God only knew what the conversation was going to be like upstairs and if Sam carried on with the whole daddy business, she'd just want to curl up and die. Conor might even think she'd put him up to it! She took a gulp of her beer and crept into the hall to see if she could hear anything. Not surprisingly, given the thickness of the walls in the old house, she could only hear the occasional shriek of laughter from Sam. Still, that in itself was a good thing, she decided, as she went back into the kitchen and cleared away the remnants of their tea. If they were having a deep, intense conversation, then her son would hardly be giggling and laughing.

*

The kitchen was clean and tidy and she had almost finished her beer when they eventually arrived back down. She glanced nervously from one to the other but could read nothing from their expressions.

'Let's play snakes and ladders,' Sam said, pulling a box from the shelf under the television and sitting down on the rug.

'Conor might not want to play,' Dee started.

'No, I'd like to.' Conor, having rescued his beer, sat down on the rug beside the child, leaned his back against the sofa, and stretched out his long legs.

Dee looked down at their two heads bent over the game and felt a twinge of envy. 'Can I play?'

Sam grinned up at her. 'Of course you can, Mum, you can be yellow.'

She sat down beside them and Conor turned his head to smile at her. 'How are you?' he murmured.

She leaned across to kiss him. 'Fine.'

'Conor, you go first,' Sam ordered, 'you're blue.'

'Okay, then.' Conor shook the dice in his hand and threw them.

Sam poured over them, trying to add them up. 'Five!' he said, victorious.

'That's right, Sam, very good.' Dee smiled at him. 'Is it my turn?'

'No, me first, then you. I'm green.' He shook the dice and threw.

'That's eight, sweetheart,' Dee told him, and he moved his counter along. 'Right, my turn and watch out because I'm feeling lucky tonight.' She threw the dice. 'Double six! What did I tell you?'

'No!' Sam screamed, bouncing around on the rug, 'I'm going to win.'

'We'll see about that,' she replied.

'My God, you two are very competitive,' Conor said mildly, 'but I have to tell you, neither of you have a hope.'

They played three games, Dee and Conor playing skilfully to ensure Sam won two of them. 'Right, mister, that's enough,' Dee said, glancing at the clock, 'it's bedtime.'

'Conor, will you read me a story?' Sam asked, smiling sweetly up at him.

'Sure, but wouldn't you prefer your Mum to do it? She's much better than me.'

'He's fed up with me,' Dee said, grabbing Sam and tickling him. 'One story only, okay?'

He nodded, still giggling, and threw his arms around her.

Dee hugged him close. 'I'll be up to tuck you in before you go asleep.'

Conor pulled him up on to his shoulders and headed for the door. 'Duck!' he warned, as he always did, and bending his head and giggling, Sam said, 'Quack.'

Dee felt unexpected tears in her eyes as she listened to their noisy progress across the hall and up the stairs.

They seemed like any normal father and son and either Conor enjoyed their time together or he was a damned good actor. She tried to imagine Neil horseplaying with Sam, the three of them playing games together or Neil taking him for bath time, but she couldn't. Probably because she had never seen Neil with children and didn't even know if he had ever hoped to be a father. It was something that had never come up in conversation during the whole of their relationship; their main priority had been to have fun.

Dee guessed that if they had discussed it she would have been the one to say she definitely didn't want children. After the childhood she'd had, the misery she'd gone through when her mother died, and the distant relationship she'd had since with her father in this bleak, heartless house, she couldn't imagine being a parent herself. She shivered as she remembered how close she'd come to having Sam aborted. It really didn't bear thinking about.

'He's asking for you.'

Dee jumped.

'Sorry.' Conor put his arms around her and pulled her close. 'You were miles away. What were you thinking about?'

'Just daydreaming. Back in a minute.' Kissing him lightly on the lips, she slipped out of his embrace and went upstairs to her son. He was cuddled up under the covers but two eyes shone out at her.

'I had a nice time today, Mum.'

She sat down beside him. 'Good.'

'I wish Conor lived here, then I could play with him all of the time.'

'Who'd look after the cows if he was here all of the time?'

Sam frowned. 'I forgot about them.' Then his face brightened. 'I know, we can go and live there.'

'And what about Lisa and Happy Days?'

He shrugged. 'I could come each morning just like the other kids.'

She laughed and bent over to kiss him. 'Sleep, sweetheart, it's late.'

'It would be cool to live on a farm,' he mumbled, nestling down under the covers, his eyes already closing. 'I could help Conor, he'd like that.'

'Goodnight, Sam, love you.'

'Love you too.'

She closed the door and went back downstairs, shaking her head at her son's words. She hoped he'd have forgotten this business by morning; the last thing she wanted was him taking his great idea directly to Conor.

'What's wrong?' Conor asked when she came back into the kitchen frowning.

'Nothing.'

He stood up and put his arms around her. 'You're not still worrying about Sam, I hope; he's absolutely fine again.'

Dee moved away, irritated. 'I'll always worry about him, he's my son.'

'I understand that but—'

'You don't understand, you couldn't.'

His smile disappeared instantly. 'No, I suppose not.'

'I'm sorry for snapping, Conor,' she said tiredly, flopping down on to the sofa, 'but it's something that's very hard to understand unless you've experienced it. I was just thinking when you were upstairs that I never thought I'd have children. I didn't particularly want any but now I can't imagine life without Sam. In fact, if anything ever happened to him I wouldn't want to go on.'

He sat down beside her and squeezed her hand. 'You shouldn't even be thinking like that.'

'I'm not, not really, I'm just trying to explain to you how strong the bond is between us.'

His face softened and he traced the curve of her cheek with his finger. 'You don't have to explain that, it's evident in every word, every look and every touch.'

Dee twisted around on the sofa so that she could look up at him. 'Did you have a good childhood, Conor?'

'Yeah, fine.' He shrugged. 'Fairly normal, I'd imagine.'

'Who were you closest to,' she pressed, 'your mother or father?'

'Dad, I suppose, but that's probably because we both loved sport so much. He worked long hours during the week – you know he was a civil servant in the city before he took early retirement and bought Better Books – but at the weekend he came to every match I played and when we weren't outside doing something, we were in front of the box watching some sport or other.'

'Do you think your mum felt excluded?'

'Of course not.'

Dee smiled.

'What?'

She shrugged. 'Nothing.'

'You don't believe me, do you?'

'Sorry, but men don't really notice these things, do they?'

'Don't they?' he mimicked.

Dee bashed him with a cushion. 'No, you don't.'

'My mother has always been perfectly happy looking after as many people as will let her and the last thing she wanted was to stand on the sideline on a cold winter morning watching me playing rugby very badly.'

'Maybe she spent her time looking after other people because you and Ronan were so self-sufficient.'

'Oh, please!' Conor groaned. 'There's less crap up on the farm.'

She made a face. 'It was just an observation.'

'Yes, and if I make observations about your family I'm very quickly told to mind my own business.'

Dee reached out to take his hand. 'Let's stop this now before it descends into a silly argument. I don't want that.'

'Neither do I,' he assured her.

She leaned over and kissed him. 'Would you like another beer?'

He pulled back and looked at his watch. 'I should head back home and keep an eye on that cow.'

Dee kissed him again. 'I'm sure it will be fine for another while.'

Conor groaned as she climbed up on to his knee and started to open his belt.

'Of course,' she said, tracing kisses down his throat and on to his chest, 'if you've got to go, you've got to go.'

He closed his eyes and let his head fall back. 'I suppose I could stay a little bit longer.'

'So would you like me to get you that beer?' she asked, her hands on his belt.

'Not right now,' he murmured, his arms snaking around her, 'maybe later.'

Chapter 22

Dee's first official day at Seven TV passed by in a whirl and she enjoyed every minute of it. Carolyn told her that she and April would be the permanent panel members on the nutrition spot and that each week there would be a guest appearance from a variety of people from chefs to doctors to celebrities who felt strongly about the subject.

'Or who just want to promote their book,' Marge said dryly.

April laughed.

'Polly Underwood will be back one week,' Carolyn said, ignoring her colleague's cynicism.

'She's great,' Dee enthused. 'She hits the nail on the head every time.'

Marge nodded. 'Yes, she's a good panellist. So many people get technical but Polly keeps it simple.'

'So, topics for the first four shows,' Carolyn picked up a pad and pen and looked at Dee. 'What do you think?'

Dee gulped. 'Well, I'm not sure—'

Marge laughed. 'For goodness' sake, Carolyn, don't hurl the poor girl straight into the deep end, she hasn't done this before!'

'I did come up with some ideas,' Dee said quickly, afraid they would think she'd given the programme no thought since their last meeting.

'It's only twenty minutes,' Carolyn told her, 'so either we touch on a lot of things briefly or we take one topic and deal with it more extensively. April, what do you think?'

April Deevers, a small, sparrow of a woman with a wide smile and intelligent hazel eyes, consulted her notes. 'I don't think twenty minutes is enough time to do an in-depth piece on any one aspect. Also, I agree that we should keep it simple otherwise people will just tune out.'

'Dee was saying that the last day,' Carolyn told her.

Dee smiled nervously at April. What could she possibly tell a woman who had years of training on the subject? 'I just think that people are more receptive if you tell them of simple ways to improve their diets rather than expecting them to change their whole way of life overnight.'

April nodded. 'I couldn't agree more. Beating people up never works; I've learned that from experience.'

Carolyn turned back to Dee. 'So, Dee, as a mother, what things would you like to see covered?'

Dee glanced down at the page in her hand. 'Well, the first item on my list is the one that got me into all of this in the first place and that's food labelling. I thought we could come up with a shortlist of tips on what to watch out for.'

'That's a good idea,' April agreed.

'Like what?' Marge frowned. 'I thought the problem with labelling was the fact that labels can be double Dutch and they're all different.'

'You're right, but there are a few pointers we could give the viewers,' April explained.

Dee nodded. 'For example, ingredients are always shown in descending order of weight.'

'I didn't know that,' said Marge.

'And also, people need to be aware that if a produce is sold as low-fat, it's quite possible that it still may be high in salt or sugar, possibly even both.'

Carolyn shook her head. 'Unbelievable. Is this topic enough to take up a full segment, April?'

'Oh, I think so.'

'Good, then can you and Dee decide on the points to include? Given the time and allowing for Marge's introduction and wrap-up, it probably should be limited to five.'

Dee and April exchanged looks and nodded.

'Right. What else have we got?' Carolyn prompted.

After two hours they had come up with loose plans for four shows and some ideas about shows five and six too. After this meeting, Dee and April were going to iron out the exact details for the first two shows.

'Are we going to take calls from viewers?' Marge asked as she and Carolyn prepared to leave.

Carolyn nibbled her thumbnail as she considered this. 'I don't think so, it would just eat into our time. Maybe we could have a general phone-in once a month.'

'I think that's an excellent idea,' April agreed. 'Then we could answer questions on any aspect of nutrition.'

'Right.' Marge stood up and smiled down at them. 'I think this is going to be great! Dee, April, thanks for coming in.'

'Yes,' Carolyn agreed as she gathered her papers together, 'I think it's going to be a very popular spot.' She checked her watch as she stood up. 'I'll check back in with you in a couple of hours and then we can have a last run-through of the details next week. April, could you be here an hour before the show, or is that asking too much?'

'No, that's fine.'

'Great.' Carolyn smiled. 'See you later.'

When they were alone, April smiled at Dee. 'Well, we have a lot to do but well done you, Dee, for highlighting this area. I think it's wonderful that it's going to be a regular spot on the programme.'

'It's just something I feel strongly about,' Dee said.

'Carolyn says your little boy has allergies.'

'Yes. He has asthma and eczema. He's allergic to some foods and to dogs and cats and things like washing powder. He's not too bad, but he definitely improved dramatically once I changed his diet.

Sometimes, though, it can be really frustrating. He does well for months and then suddenly he's ill again and I've no idea why.'

April nodded in understanding. 'It is hard but you do know he will probably grow out of it.'

'Yes, that's what I've been told,' Dee laughed, 'but unfortunately it doesn't make me worry any less.'

'I know.' April patted her hand.

'Anyway, we're not here to talk about Sam. We'd better get stuck in.'

April's eyes twinkled. 'It's fun, isn't it?'

Dee laughed. 'It's brilliant!'

By the time Carolyn returned they had not only come up with the material for the first two shows but, carried away by their mutual enthusiasm, they had gone on to work on shows three and four. The producer had been delighted and after a brief visit to the wardrobe department, Dee was on her way home by two o'clock. If it was like this every week it would be the easiest money she'd ever made and the most fun she'd ever had.

As it was only mid-afternoon, traffic was light and she would be home a lot earlier than she'd expected. Given that all of her work was done for tomorrow, Dee decided to make the most of her free time and bring Sam back into town to get shoes and maybe treat him to a movie. They could take the train and it would be a double treat; Sam just loved trains. She phoned ahead to ask Lisa to check the movie times.

'*Happy Feet* starts at four-thirty but he's already seen that, hasn't he?'

'What's that got to do with anything?' Dee laughed.

'True.'

'So how are things with you?' Dee asked as she cruised up the M1.

'Great. Two of the children are going home early so it will mean a nice quiet evening for us.'

'Wonderful, you deserve it. Look, I should be home in about ten minutes, will you get Sam ready, please?'

'No problem, see you soon.'

Dee hummed along to the radio as she drove, happy at the thought of the free time ahead. When she had an assistant, she'd be able to do stuff like this more often, she realized. She had an interview set up for the following day with a girl who had previously worked as a cook in a nursing home. The recruitment consultant had said she was the perfect candidate for the job but Dee wasn't convinced.

'You only need someone to follow orders, though,' Lisa had pointed out reasonably, 'not a creative genius who'd want to take over.'

'I suppose you're right,' Dee had acknowledged, but she still wasn't sure. She felt that if she was going to have to share her kitchen with another cook it had to be someone who was committed and switched on by food. She knew she was probably being too fussy but, as she'd said to Lisa, this person wouldn't just be sharing her kitchen but sharing her home, too. Oh, well, she reasoned as she turned off the motorway, she'd find out very soon if the ideal candidate was, in fact, ideal.

As soon as she pulled up outside the house, she saw Sam waving excitedly at her from the window only to disappear and reappear seconds later in the doorway with Lisa beside him.

'Mum, where are we going?'

'I thought we could go into town for new shoes,' Dee said mildly but felt immediately guilty when his face fell. 'And then maybe you could take me to see *Happy Feet.*'

'Yes!' Sam punched the air and did a little dance.

Lisa raised an eyebrow. 'I think he likes the idea.'

'Okay, sweetheart, into the car, we'll have to hurry if we want to make the train.'

'We're going on the train?'

'Dear God, the child will burst with excitement,' Lisa laughed, as she helped him into the car. 'Put your seatbelt on, Sam, and have a great time.'

'Thanks!'

Dee drove the short distance to the train station, Sam singing loudly all the way. Fate was on her side as a car pulled out of a spot near the entrance and she hurriedly took it and switched off the engine. 'Come on, little man, we have a train to catch.'

*

'This is the best,' Sam said as they stood waiting on the platform. 'The only thing that would make it better would be if Conor could come too.' He whirled around excitedly. 'Mum, why don't you phone him and ask him?'

'I'm afraid it's too late for that, sweetheart. Conor would never make it on time.'

'I s'pose.'

'Anyway, this was a last-minute idea because I got home early. I thought you'd like a trip out, just the two of us.' She cringed at the peevish note in her voice. Who exactly was the child here?

'Of course I do, Mum,' he said hugging her, 'but I like spending time with Conor too and so do you. It's nice when the three of us go out.'

Dee didn't have to reply as the train rounded the bend and Sam was immediately distracted.

'Yippee, it's here. Let's get in the first carriage.'

Dee took a firm grip of his hand until they were safely ensconced in the first carriage, Sam bobbing up and down happily in his seat. She really had no need to take him to the cinema at all, she realized. He'd be happy enough with this little jaunt to and from the city on the train! Still, it was nice to have time together and wonderful to see him looking so healthy and happy.

Sam had been absolutely fine since his funny turn the previous Friday and Dee was starting to relax a little but a scare like that had made her realize how easy it would be to lose him. Lisa too had been troubled about how quickly he had gone downhill unobserved and she was taking steps to make sure it didn't happen again. When Dee had gone into the room on Monday evening it was to find the furniture in the crèche had been rearranged so that Lisa and Martha could see every area from their usual vantage points. Of course, there was no way to watch every child every minute of every day but they were still determined to be even more vigilant in future.

The train pulled into Tara Street station and Dee stood up. 'Come on, Sam, this is our stop.'

'Are we getting my shoes first, Mummy?' he asked, as they stepped down on to the platform.

Dee checked her watch. 'No, the film is starting soon so we'll go to the cinema first.'

'Cool!'

Sam skipped along happily at her side, his hand in hers as they left the station and made for O'Connell Bridge. They were halfway across the Liffey, the wind whipping Dee's hair around her face, when Sam broke free with a cry.

'It's Aunty Peggy! Aunty Peggy!'

Sam raced ahead and as Dee pulled her hair out of her eyes and hurried after him she groaned when she saw that he was indeed right. Bending to hug Sam was Peggy Callen, a horrified expression on her face as her eyes met Dee's and, standing slightly behind her, looking shocked and confused, was her son Neil.

Dee hurried over, her eyes flicking between mother and son, pleading with them not to say anything. 'Peggy, great to see you!' She kissed the older woman's cheek but her fingers dug into Peggy's arm.

'And you.' Peggy replied, her voice shaky.

'We're going to the cinema,' Sam announced, dancing around them.

'Well, aren't you the lucky one.' Peg smiled down at him.

But Sam had now noticed Neil and was looking at him curiously. 'I'm Sam, who are you?'

Neil opened his mouth to answer but Peggy jumped in before he could say a word. 'This is my friend Ne—' She stopped. 'Noel. This is Noel.'

'Nice to meet you.' Neil nodded at Dee and smiled at Sam. 'Hello, Sam.'

'Hi,' Sam said shyly.

'Hi,' Dee echoed. 'I'm sorry to run, Peggy, but if we don't hurry we'll miss the start of the film.'

But Sam wasn't ready to go quite yet. 'We haven't seen you in ages, Aunty Peggy. Does Prince miss me? That's Peggy's dog,' he added for Neil's benefit.

'Yes; yes, I know.' Neil looked from Sam to his mother.

Peggy reddened but kept her eyes on Sam. 'He's fine, love.'

'Can I come and see him soon?' he persisted.

'Of course you can, darling.'

'Come on, Sam.' Dee was actually dragging him away now. 'I'll call you, Peggy, and we'll set something up.' She avoided Neil's eyes completely.

'Great, love. Bye, now. Bye, Sam, have a lovely time.'

He waved furiously, walking backwards so he could still see her. 'Bye, Aunty Peggy,' he roared.

Dee quickened her pace and Sam was forced to turn around. 'Mum, you're going too fast.'

'Sorry, I just don't want us to be late.' Dee wondered if Sam could hear the wobble in her voice.

'Why haven't we been over to Aunty Peggy's, Mum?' Sam asked as Dee held open the door for him and they went into the lobby of the movie theatre.

'Mummy's been very busy,' Dee said, reaching into her bag for her purse.

'Can we have popcorn?'

'Sure,' she replied, knowing that right now she'd agree to anything.

When the movie had started and Sam was engrossed in the story, Dee slumped back in her seat and closed her eyes, grateful for the darkness that enveloped them. She felt physically exhausted although she knew her weariness was due to shock. She wondered how Peggy was doing and how she would explain all of this to Neil. Would he be happy that Peggy and Sam had a relationship or just furious that she had kept it from him?

Dee remembered vividly the first time she had come

face to face with Peggy Callen after Neil had left her. She had gone to the airport to pick up Pauline and Jack after their annual visit to a cousin in Atlanta and was wandering around the arrivals area in the vain hope of finding a seat. She had paused when she became aware of a woman staring at her and had been horrified when she realized it was Neil's mum and her eyes were firmly fixed on Dee's eight-month-old bump. Dee had turned away and moved to the other side of the arrivals hall but Peggy had followed her and with a firm grip on her arm, guided her towards the coffee shop and sat her down.

'I don't have time, I'm collecting my aunt,' Dee remembered protesting, but Peggy wasn't interested.

'I won't keep you long,' she'd said, her voice quiet but determined. 'Is it Neil's?' Dee's eyes met hers and she knew she couldn't lie. She'd simply nodded.

Peggy gasped and put a hand to her mouth. 'Oh, dear God.'

'You don't have to worry,' Dee had retorted, 'this is my baby and I'll raise it. I don't want anything from your son and I don't want him anywhere near us.'

'Oh, Dee, don't talk like that!' Peggy had been reproachful.

'Sorry, but can you blame me after what happened? Have you heard from him?' she'd asked then although she knew she shouldn't care.

Peggy's shoulders had slumped as she shook her head. 'He phoned last Easter and I gave him an earful about you as soon as I heard his voice. He hung up and I haven't heard from him since.'

'You're better off,' Dee had said bitterly but then she'd felt bad when she saw the wounded look in Peggy's eyes. They had always got on really well in the past and Peggy had been very kind when Dee's father had died. Whatever Neil had done it wasn't his mother's fault. Dee had stood up. 'I've got to go,' she'd said but put a hand on the woman's shoulder. 'I'll call you when the baby comes.'

Peggy had grabbed her hand and squeezed it, tears shining in her eyes. 'If you need anything, anything at all, you only have to ask.'

As promised, Dee had phoned Peggy the day she got home from the hospital and told her that she could see the baby on the condition that she never told Neil. Peggy had reluctantly agreed. 'I do understand, Dee, but I hope that if he comes back some day, you will change your mind.'

After that Dee and Peggy met up a couple of times a year but once Sam hit three, he demanded more contact with his Aunty Peggy, loving every moment with her. Dee was happy to oblige. It was wonderful to watch the close relationship develop between them and it was only slightly overshadowed by the fact that Sam didn't know that this was, in fact, his grandmother.

As Sam got older and started to wonder why he didn't have a father or grandparents, Dee had been sorely tempted to tell him the truth about Peggy but, realizing it would only confuse the child, she'd held her tongue.

As far as everyone else was concerned, Peggy was a cousin of her mother's who was slightly agoraphobic; hence the reason no one ever got to meet her and all the meetings took place in Peggy's house. Dee did wonder why Peggy hadn't gotten in touch when Neil returned. Maybe she was afraid Dee would cut off contact completely.

Looking down at her son now, his eyes riveted to the big screen, his hand mechanically feeding popcorn into his rosebud mouth, Dee knew there would be questions later. She hated the fact that it would mean she'd have to lie to him, but if she told him who Neil really was he'd know that she had been lying to him his whole life and that Aunty Peggy was in fact his grandmother.

Chapter 23

Sam went to bed without complaint that night and was asleep within minutes, a fact for which Dee was supremely grateful. Conor had called to say another cow seemed to have been hit by the same bug and he couldn't leave the farm and Dee was glad. She'd never told him who Peggy really was and she wasn't ready to do it tonight. She needed time to collect her thoughts and prepare herself for what lay ahead, whatever that might be. She decided to pour herself a large glass of the wine that Conor had brought over the previous night. En-route to the fridge, she switched on the answering machine. She was afraid that Neil or Peggy might call and she wasn't ready to talk to them either.

As she'd expected, on the journey home from town Sam had returned to the subject of Peggy. Dee had kept her answers both simple and vague and, as soon as there was an opportunity, she had turned the conversation back to the movie. Sam had been easily diverted but she knew that it was a temporary reprieve. He was a deep thinker who would mull things over at length and come back with questions days, weeks, sometimes even months, later.

She remembered the time a lady had collapsed at the supermarket, Sam was only three and was sitting in the trolley, and Dee had stayed with the woman until the manager arrived and had taken her off to his office.

'What's wrong with the lady?' Sam had asked.

'She's not feeling very well,' Dee had told him but he continued to quiz her as they walked home and that night as she was putting him to bed. Nearly a year later, he had brought it up over dinner one day. 'Do you think that lady's okay, Mum?'

'What lady?' Dee had asked, confused.

'The one in the supermarket.'

Dee had been amazed that he had not only remembered the incident but had also been so concerned about the woman. It had touched her but also alerted her to the fact that Sam was a lot more observant and sensitive than she had realized.

Dee's musings were interrupted by the doorbell and, with a heavy sigh, she set down her glass, stood up, and went out into the hall. She opened the door, stood back, and smiled slightly. 'Come in, Peggy.'

The older woman's eyes slid towards the staircase. 'Is he asleep?'

Dee nodded and led Neil's mother back out to the kitchen. 'Wine?' she offered, pausing by the fridge.

Peggy shook her head as she perched on the edge of a chair, twisting her hands in her lap, her eyes anxious. 'What did he say?'

Dee sat down on the sofa and reached for her glass. 'Not much. He was wondering how you were suddenly well enough to be out and why we hadn't been to see you in so long but, thankfully, he never asked about Neil.' She looked at Peggy, noting the dark circles under her eyes, the slump of her shoulders and the nervous way she was biting on her bottom lip. 'Was he annoyed?'

Peggy gave a laugh that was half a cry. 'You could say that. I tried to explain but I don't know how much he actually took in. Finally he just stormed off.' Peggy shot her a nervous look. 'I was afraid he'd come here.'

It was Dee's turn to look worried. 'He'd never do that, would he? I mean, that would get him nowhere. I wouldn't let him in. In fact, I'd never let him near Sam—'

'Are you going to let him near Sam at all?' Peggy asked quietly, her eyes searching Dee's face.

Dee looked away. 'I'm not sure.'

Peggy waited.

'I want to,' Dee explained, 'but I'm afraid.'

Peggy nodded. 'I can understand that.'

Dee looked at her. 'Has he changed, Peggy?'

Peggy thought for a moment. 'Yes, I think he has. He's been home for over two months now, and I've seen no sign of him gambling. Having said that, I'm not sure I'd know what to look for.'

Dee sat forward. 'Why didn't you tell me he was back?'

'I don't know. I wasn't sure what to do. He hadn't mentioned you and so I suppose I thought maybe it was better to say nothing. Then he saw you in the newspaper.'

Dee couldn't help feeling hurt. Neil hadn't been interested in seeing her again; it was all about Sam.

'I think if you let him get to know Sam, he might stay,' Peggy said, tentatively. 'He's been checking out commercial properties that would make a suitable depot.'

'Does anyone call looking for him?' Dee probed. 'Does he get any post?'

Peggy frowned. 'I'm not sure. I'm usually out when the postman comes. Why?'

Dee frowned. 'I asked him for a reference; someone who could vouch for his story but he hasn't come up with one yet.'

'I'm sure he will.'

'Are you?' Dee wasn't convinced.

'But look at him, Dee,' Peggy urged. 'Look at the way he dresses and look at the car.'

'He could just be on a winning streak,' Dee said dismissively.

'But he even sounds different from the way he used to when he phoned me,' Peggy insisted.

Dee nodded slowly. She had noticed that too. The

nervous edgy tone from his gambling days was missing and Neil sounded more like the outgoing young man she had first met.

'I know it's hard, Dee, but you don't have to rush into this. Sam has survived this long without knowing his father; he can survive a while longer. But please don't dismiss the possibility that maybe Neil could be a part of Sam's life, for my sake?'

Dee reached over to squeeze her hand. 'Even if I do agree, Peggy, have you realized how hard it would be to explain everything to Sam? How do you think he'll feel about us when he finds out he's had a grandmother all these years?'

Peggy sighed. 'We'll have to explain that we were just trying to protect him.'

The doorbell chimed again and they looked at each other in alarm. 'Do you think it's him?' Dee whispered.

'It could be.'

'I can't let him in, Peggy, if Sam should wake—'

'Of course you can't! Don't worry, I'll persuade him to come home with me.'

Dee let Peggy go first but she followed her, afraid that Neil would push past his mother and demand to see his son.

Peggy opened the door and peered out. 'Hello?'

'Er, hi.'

Dee groaned as she recognized Conor's voice. She immediately came to stand by Peggy's side. 'Conor, hi, what are you doing here?'

'You sounded a bit down on the phone so I just dropped in to see if everything was okay.' His eyes moved from Dee back to Peggy.

'I'll go,' Peggy said immediately.

'Oh, please, don't go on my account,' Conor protested.

Peggy smiled tightly. 'I was leaving anyway. Goodbye, Dee, keep in touch.'

Dee bent to give the woman a quick hug. 'I will, Peggy, drive carefully.'

'Why did you come to the front door?' she asked Conor, leading the way back out to the kitchen.

'I saw the car and didn't want to interrupt anything.'

She laughed as she bent to pick up her empty glass. 'Like what?'

'I'm not sure,' he said, leaning against the worktop and watching her.

'Want a glass?' she went to the fridge and took out the bottle.

'No, I'm fine.'

She splashed wine into her own glass. 'How's the cow?'

'Okay.'

She shot him a nervous look. 'Come and sit down.'

'I can't stay long,' he said, dropping into the chair opposite. 'I'm sorry, I wouldn't have come at all if I'd known you had company.'

'I wasn't expecting Peggy.'

'Peggy?' He frowned. 'That's your mother's cousin, isn't it? I thought she was housebound.'

'She's been getting some therapy,' Dee said lamely, taking a long drink.

'And she even drives herself, and in the dark too,' Conor marvelled.

'What are you saying?' she said sharply.

'I just think it's great; she's overcome a lot. Sam must be delighted. She'll be able to come and visit whenever she likes now.'

'Yes, I suppose she will.' Dee sighed. That hadn't occurred to her but of course Conor was right. Sam would now expect Peggy to play a fuller and more active part in his life and if she didn't it would mean telling more lies. Could her life get any more complicated?

'Dee, what's wrong?'

She looked up to find him watching her closely. 'Nothing.'

'Fine, don't tell me. I'll go.' He went to stand up.

She put a hand on his arm. 'Conor, don't go. Look, it's been a tough day, that's all.'

'Is this about Neil?'

'No!'

'You've seen him again, haven't you?' Conor persisted.

'No, I haven't.' She drained her glass and carried it over to the sink.

'Then you were talking to him.'

She turned around, her face incredulous. 'Conor, are you calling me a liar?'

'Would I be so wrong?' he countered. 'You're not exactly forthcoming, are you?'

'This is ridiculous!' she exclaimed. 'I don't have to tell you every single thing that happens in my life, do I?'

Conor looked at her and shook his head. 'No – no of course you don't.' He stood up and crossed to the back door.

'Where are you going?'

'I'm not going to stay where I'm not wanted.'

'Conor, don't be stupid!'

He stood in the doorway looking at her, waiting.

'Come back in.' She looked at him. 'Please?'

He closed the door again and leaned his large frame against it. 'It might be better if I went. It's not really working, is it?'

'Isn't it?' Dee said, confused.

'You've changed, Dee. I practically have to make an appointment to see you these days and I hear more about what's going on in your life from my dad than I do from you.'

'That's not true.'

'I'm on the edge of your life,' he continued as if she hadn't spoken, 'a peripheral. You don't see me as anything more than that.'

'That's rich coming from you,' Dee retorted.

Conor looked at her, exasperated. 'What's that supposed to mean?'

'You're a loner, Conor, a bachelor. You like to see me a couple of times a week, but you also like your own space. I'm fine as long as I fit into the part of your life you've allocated me but no more than that.'

'Of all the crap you've ever spouted—'

'It's okay, I went along with it,' she assured him.

Conor sighed. 'It's all about him, isn't it?'

She nodded, swallowing back the tears. 'Always.'

He nodded and smiled slightly. 'I suppose that's it then.'

She watched in shock as he turned, opened the door and stepped out into the darkness. 'Conor?'

He paused, his face in shadow. 'I want to see Sam. I don't want to just drop out of his life.'

She swallowed hard. 'That would be great.' She took a step towards him but he just turned away.

'Goodnight, Dee.'

Dee stared after him until his car was out of sight before stumbling back inside. Going upstairs, she slipped into Sam's room, settled him more comfortably on his pillow and kissed his forehead. Crossing the hall to her own room, she crawled into bed, dragged the covers up over her head and cried.

Chapter 24

Lisa sat at the kitchen table reading applications for the position of Dee's assistant. 'Some of these look really good, although I still don't understand what was wrong with the girl you met last week; she seemed fine to me.'

'You think?' Dee continued kneading bread.

Lisa sat back in her chair and frowned at her friend. 'What is wrong with you, Dee?'

'Nothing.'

Lisa turned her head to make sure the door to the hall was closed. 'Is it Neil? Has he been in touch?'

'There's nothing wrong, okay?'

'I haven't seen Conor around much, have you fallen out?'

'He took Sam up to the farm yesterday,' Dee reminded her.

'That was Sam, not you.'

Dee stopped kneading. 'We've broken up.'

'Oh, Dee, I'm so sorry!'

Dee went back to her bread-making.

'Is it because Neil's back?' Lisa pressed.

'It has nothing to do with him, Lisa.'

'So it was your idea.'

Dee shrugged. 'It was mutual.'

'Ah.'

Dee looked up. 'What does that mean?'

'Nothing.'

'He did not dump me.'

Lisa shrugged innocently.

'And I didn't dump him.'

'Maybe not consciously,' Lisa agreed.

Dee sighed. 'Spare me the amateur psychology, Lisa, I'm not in the mood.'

'I won't say another word on the matter. Now, let me phone a couple of these candidates and set up interviews.'

'I'm not sure—'

'You promised Ronan.'

Dee sighed. 'Okay, okay, but I can only interview on Monday or Friday afternoons.'

'Yes, ma'am.' Lisa saluted and flicked through the pages in front of her. 'I think Kitty Burns looks interesting and Des O'Shea.'

'I don't want to work with a man,' Dee said vehemently, 'for a whole load of reasons.'

Lisa chuckled. 'You're probably right. What about Vera Matthews?'

'That's the retired chef from Donegal?'

'Yes, she moved down here to be near her daughter

and is finding she has too much time on her hands.'

'Yes, she could fit the bill.'

'I'll call those two so.' Lisa stood up.

'No, leave it, you've enough to do; I'll call them both later.'

'It's no trouble—'

Dee smiled. 'It's okay, Lisa, I'm not nursing a broken heart and I'm not about to fall apart.'

'I know that but you could still do with a little TLC.'

'When I've finished up here I'm going to get my hair done,' Dee announced.

'Oh, God, no!'

'What?'

'You always do something drastic when you're emotional.'

'I do not and I am not emotional; I'm perfectly fine.'

Lisa shot her a knowing look. 'If you say so.'

'So, Dee, what would you like me to do?'

Dee studied her reflection and then met Louise Mulvaney's pretty eyes. 'I think I'd like to try something different?'

'Great!'

Dee listened vaguely as Louise talked. 'That sounds fine,' she said when she realized that the hairdresser was waiting for a response.

Louise smiled kindly. 'I'll get you a mug of tea and some magazines. You just switch off and relax for a while; we'll look after you.'

Dee nodded gratefully, and as one of the girls applied highlights to her hair, she buried her face in between the covers of *Cosmopolitan* and closed her eyes. The last thing she wanted to do was discuss holidays or celebrities or even her son; especially her son.

As if Sam knew that she and Conor had broken up, he seemed to talk about no one else. Dee had made it clear to Conor when he asked to spend the afternoon with Sam the previous day that she didn't want him to say anything.

'He doesn't need any heavy, detailed explanations,' she'd explained, 'it would only upset him. It's better if he just gradually gets used to us seeing less of each other.'

Conor had looked at her, his face grim. 'Until we don't see each other at all.'

'Like you said, it's a small town,' she reminded him, 'and I don't know about you but we're not planning on going anywhere.'

'What if he asks questions?' Conor had persisted.

'Answer them honestly, if possible, and keep it brief, but if there's anything you're not comfortable with, tell him to ask me.'

Dee had been a nervous wreck by the time Sam had arrived home, but he had been happy, dirty and tired. His only preoccupation was Boxer, Conor's Labrador.

'Do you think I'll ever be able to have a dog, Mum?'

'I don't know, sweetheart. You weren't near Boxer, were you?'

'No.' Sam had shaken his head sadly. 'Conor always locks him in the barn when I'm there.'

'Doctor Bill says it would be okay for you to have a budgie or maybe even a guinea pig.'

Sam had shot her a scornful look and turned over to go asleep but he hadn't mentioned anything about Conor who'd confirmed in their brief conversation on her doorstep that the little boy had been in good form and hadn't asked any awkward questions.

But eventually he would, of course, and between Neil, Peggy and Conor she wondered if she would be able to give him the answers he wanted and needed. She gave an involuntary sigh and the hair stylist stopped and caught her eye in the mirror. 'I'm sorry, did I hurt you?'

Dee smiled tremulously. 'No, someone just walked over my grave.'

Later that afternoon, Martha was walking across the hall with the nappy bucket in her arms when Dee walked in. She dropped the bucket and stared. 'Oh. My. God.'

'Is it that bad?' Dee asked nervously.

'No! No, it's lovely.' Martha rescued the bucket and smiled reassuringly. 'It's just . . . different.'

Dee put a self-conscious hand to her cropped, streaked hair. 'I fancied a change,' she said lamely.

Martha grinned. 'Great idea, although I'm not sure what Vi's going to say.'

'Vi!' Dee looked at her watch. 'Oh, shit!'

Martha laughed, holding the bucket aloft. 'I know what you mean.'

Dee took a deep breath and pushed open the kitchen door. 'Vi, I'm so sorry.'

'Yes, yes, of course you are,' the other woman grumbled without looking up.

'I, er, hope this isn't a problem.'

'I'm in no rush—' Vi looked up and the smile froze on her face. 'Oh, good grief, what have you done?'

'I felt like a change.'

Vi flopped down into a chair. 'Well, don't just stand there, put the bloody kettle on.'

'So what's this all about?' Vi asked as Dee turned on the tap.

'What do you mean?'

Vi sighed. 'Most women would be happy to wash that man right out of their hair but not you; you had to cut him out.'

Dee looked at her and said nothing, her eyes large and luminous against the feathered hair that framed her face.

'It's nice in a punkish sort of way,' Vi conceded.

Dee laughed. 'The stylist wanted to add a few pink stripes but I didn't feel that brave. Have I screwed up your work?'

Vi shrugged. 'No, I'm working on detail now although it's been rather hard given you weren't here.'

'Sorry.' Dee turned to make a strong coffee for Vi and a mug of tea for herself. Vi produced her hip flask and shot Dee a questioning look.

'God, no, not for me,' Dee laughed, carrying the drinks to the table and going to fetch the milk.

Vi added a liberal shot of brandy to her own mug and carefully screwed the top back on. 'So, Conor's gone then.'

'Lisa told you.'

'No.'

Dee sighed. 'I wish you wouldn't trick me like that.'

'Trick you?' Vi's eyes were wide and innocent. 'I was just stating a fact. Want to talk about it?'

'Not really.'

Vi nodded and sipped her coffee in silence.

Dee rested her chin in her hand and stared into her mug. 'It's all such a mess, Vi.'

'I thought everything was going so well. You have this wonderful new job, more money, and you and Conor seemed happy.'

'It's complicated.'

Vi smiled. 'It always is.'

Dee's eyes met hers. 'Really, really complicated.'

'You know what? You need to come over to my place for the next sitting.'

Dee blinked. 'What?'

'We can't talk here; someone is always crashing

through that door. How about tomorrow evening? Get that girl next door to look after Sam. Shall we say seven?'

Lisa burst through the door. 'Oh my God, look at your hair!'

Dee smiled at Vi. 'Seven should be fine.'

'It's lovely, really it is.'

'Lisa, stop!' Dee said, continuing to empty the dishwasher.

'It was just a shock. I've never seen it that short before.'

Dee straightened and fingered the hair that now only reached her chin. 'It's never been this short before.'

'So, did it work?'

'What do you mean?' Dee asked, knowing exactly what her friend meant.

'New haircut, new life. Do you think Neil will like it?'

'It's nothing to do with Neil.' Dee went back to emptying the dishwasher.

'Are you sure about that?'

'Please stop, Lisa,' Dee begged. 'I'm really not up to this interrogation.'

'Sorry, I'm just worried about you.' Lisa bent to help her. 'I don't want you rushing into anything.'

'I'm not stupid.'

'I know that but Neil can be persuasive and he's Sam's dad and he's apparently doing well for himself and it would all be so easy, so perfect, so simple, to slip back into a relationship.'

'I've no intention of slipping into anything,' Dee said through gritted teeth.

Lisa straightened and started to arrange the cutlery in the drawer. 'Dee, I've known you a long time and I know what you're like.'

Dee smirked. 'Oh, yeah?'

'Yeah, and I know you would do anything for Sam.'

Dee said nothing.

'Just don't try and give him the happy-ever-after without considering yourself in all this. He's only going to be truly happy if you are too.'

'Who's to say I wouldn't be?' Dee parried.

'Dee?'

'Don't worry, I'm just kidding.'

Lisa grinned and reached out to pat Dee's head. 'Good. I just wanted to make sure that it's only your hair that's gone!'

'I lost my marbles long ago,' Dee joked.

But Lisa didn't laugh. 'You're a great mum but don't forget that Dee Hewson's happiness is important too.'

'As long as I've got Sam I'm happy,' Dee said automatically.

Lisa rolled her eyes. 'Oh, please! Sam won't be a little boy for ever. Before you know it, he'll be on the phone pouring his heart out to some girl and you'll be finding dirty magazines under his bed.'

'My boy would never keep dirty magazines under his bed,' Dee said with a grin, 'he'd find a much better hiding place.'

But still, Lisa wasn't to be diverted. 'I don't want you to end up alone, Dee.'

'I won't, I'll have you. We'll both become silly old women together.'

Lisa finally laughed. 'But no cats, I can't stand the bloody things.'

Chapter 25

'I think I like it, Mum,' Sam said seriously.

'Great, now brush your teeth.'

Sam continued to study her hair. 'It's a bit like Tom's.'

'Not quite the look I was going for,' Dee murmured, putting paste on his brush and handing it to him.

'But Tom's great and his hair's cool.'

'Then I'll take that as a compliment.'

'Does Conor like it?'

Dee turned away to get a face cloth. 'He hasn't seen it yet, now will you please stop talking and brush your teeth?' Dee left him to it and went into his room to close the curtains, switch on the lamp and turn down the covers. In a way it was a relief that Sam was focussed on her hair rather than the more volatile issues that currently touched their lives.

Sam skipped into the room and bounced on to the bed. 'Mum, can Aunty Peggy come to see us?'

'Did you do your face and hands?' Dee parried.

He nodded. 'Can she?'

Dee folded his clothes and put them on the chair at the bottom of the bed. 'If she feels up to it, of course she can.'

'Cool! I could show her all of my Lego and she could meet Tom and' – he grinned from ear to ear – 'she could come up to the farm.'

Dee turned to him and smiled. 'We'll see. Now, what story would you like?'

Sam snuggled under the covers. 'I don't think I want one, Mum, let's just have a chat.'

'Good idea.' Dee groaned inwardly. 'What did you and Tom do today?'

He shrugged. 'Nothing much. Mum?'

Dee sat down beside him and resigned herself to an inquisition. 'Yes?'

He peered at her from under the covers. 'Could I buy a *Star Wars* transformer?'

Dee smiled with relief. 'Like Tom's?'

Sam nodded eagerly. 'I'll use my own money.'

'I'm not sure you'd have enough,' she prevaricated. She had made it a rule that big presents were for birthdays and Christmas but as it was Sam's own money that he'd received as gifts, what could she say?

'Conor said I would.'

'Oh, you've discussed this with Conor?'

He shrugged. 'It just came up when I was at the farm.'

'I'll bet. I hope you weren't asking him to buy it for you,' she said severely.

'I wasn't, Mum, honest! We were just talking, he likes *Star Wars* too.'

'Really?'

'Yeah,' Sam was sitting up now, 'and he says he saw a Star Wars transformer for nineteen euros in that shop around the corner from Better Books.' He scrunched up his face in concentration. 'I do have nineteen euros, don't I, Mum?'

'Well, let's check,' she said, standing and going to his money box. Emptying it on to the bed, she helped him count. There were two twenty-euro notes, one five-euro note and several coins. 'Forty-five euros and eighty-five cents,' she said finally.

'Yes!' he punched the air. 'I could buy two Star Wars transformers!'

'No; no, you couldn't, and even if you could, I wouldn't let you.'

'I'm just joking, Mum,' Sam said with an exaggerated sigh.

Dee laughed and put the money box back on the dressing table.

'So can we go and buy it tomorrow?'

'I'm not sure, Sam, I have a lot to do.'

His face fell.

'If we can't do it tomorrow, we'll definitely do it the next day,' she promised as she bent to kiss him.

Sam's arms snaked up around her neck. 'Thanks.'

'Night-night, sleep tight, and don't let the bugs bite,' she whispered, 'but if they do—'

He grinned. 'Bite them back! 'night, Mum.'

Dee went into her own room and changed into pyjamas, pausing when she caught sight of her reflection in the mirror. 'God, what have I done?' she muttered. She could see why Sam saw a resemblance to Tom; in her pyjamas she looked like a twelve-year-old waif. What on earth would Carolyn and Marge make of her new look?

She hadn't considered her TV image when she'd let Louise loose on her hair but still, she turned her head from side to side, it was a lot funkier than her usual boring cut. Oh, well, she reasoned, going downstairs, it was too late to worry about it now. She fetched a glass of sparkling water from the fridge, settled herself comfortably on the sofa and took up her pad and pen; it was about time she put some thought into Wednesday's show.

She was grateful that she and April had done so much work the last day because she certainly wasn't feeling very creative this week. She doodled around the edge of the page and tried to work up some enthusiasm for fresh foods or some indignation about labels, but nothing came to her. She went to the cake tin and took out a chocolate muffin. As she nibbled on her cake and stared blankly at her pad, her thoughts turned from the show to Conor. He was on her mind a lot. She missed him. How she'd love to be able to pick up the phone and ask him over. How she'd love to sit him down and explain all of the confused emotions she was feeling about Neil's return, but she didn't think he'd ever understand. He had already judged and sentenced the man, as indeed had Lisa, although that was more understandable.

Lisa had seen the wreck that was her life when she came home from Greece and she had been a witness to the difficult years that followed. But someone had to think about Sam in all of this and it seemed she was the only one who understood that. She sniffed, blinked back the tears and reached for her water. If only Neil would come up with a reference that would give her something to go on, some reassurance before she put her son into the firing line. She thought about talking to Peggy again but it was impossible for the woman to be objective and it would be unfair to expect it of her. Peggy was doing her level best not to take sides, and Dee realized how hard that must be and appreciated it. If only she could believe that Neil was half as good a person as his mother.

She kept reminding herself that he was suffering from a disease and that it wasn't his fault that he'd behaved the way he had but that just made her more nervous for the future. If she did let him meet Sam, if they did get to know each other, if Sam came to love him, what would happen if he turned out to be no good? What if he wanted shared custody or he took Sam on a holiday to Spain and didn't come back? She shivered uncontrollably as the tears slid down her face.

She thought of the alternative. Sam at eighteen, going

in search of his father and discovering that Neil was a pillar of society who had wanted to be a part of Sam's life but his mother had said no. How would he ever forgive her?

Whatever she chose to do, it seemed she couldn't win. However she looked at the problem, there was no solution. She went over to the kitchen counter and used a piece of kitchen roll to clean up her face. Maybe Vi would be able to help. Often it was easier to see the solution to a problem if you were detached from it and Vi had always struck Dee as a wise and intelligent woman. Also, she realized, there were charities and helplines who could probably advise her. She was only powerless if she let herself be. She needed to arm herself with as much information as possible and then she would know what to do for the best. Sitting back down in the chair, she started to make notes in her pad.

The next morning, Dee had to drop off the food at the café on her way to the TV studio. She was hoping that Ronan wouldn't be there; the last thing she needed was the air of disappointment that she knew would surround him when he found out that she and Conor had broken up. Still, Conor was a private man, hopefully he hadn't said anything yet. And at least she had some good news for his father. The two candidates that she and Lisa had agreed on were coming to see her on Friday afternoon; that should put a smile on his face.

She was feeling a little brighter, and was looking

forward to her visit to Vi's that evening. She knew she could rely on the woman for sound advice, a sympathetic ear and, most importantly, to be the soul of discretion.

Though they had never been that close, there was something about Vi that Dee trusted. Her mother would have been a similar age now if she'd survived cancer and perhaps that in itself was the attraction.

Dee often wondered what kind of relationship she would have had with her mum had she lived. She remembered her as being soft and kind, a woman who rarely raised her voice, but she didn't really recall anything about her spirit, her character or her essence. She had just been her mum and Dee, like every other child, had just accepted her presence. Her most outstanding memories were of the harsh reality of her loss.

She vividly remembered coming home from school to find Aunt Pauline alone in the house and though she asked where her mother was, Pauline had curtly told her to be a good girl and do her homework. She was sitting over her tea of a boiled egg and toast when her father had walked in, looking as if he was in a trance.

'She's gone,' he'd said, over and over, sitting at the table and staring at his hands.

'Where's my mum?' Dee had asked, hearing him but not wanting to believe the evidence of her ears and eyes. 'Where's my mum?'

When Pauline had explained that her mother had died, Dee had run to her father for comfort but his arms were loose around her and his eyes were vacant. She knew, there and then, that she was alone.

Now as she sat in her car outside the café the memory made her shudder.

'Dee! My God! Your hair!'

Dee whirled around to see Zoe standing on the pavement staring in at her. 'Hi, Zoe.' She grinned, climbing out of the car. 'What do you think?'

'It's so cool! You look like Natalie Imbruglia.'

'Oh, please!' Dee rolled her eyes and started pulling containers of food out of the back seat and loading Zoe's arms.

'You do, honest.' The girl grinned. 'Is this your new celebrity look?'

'No, this is my "fed up with the old me" look.'

'I know what you mean, I could do with one of them.'

Dee laughed as she followed the girl inside. Zoe looked more like she belonged on a catwalk than behind the counter of a café in a small town with her perfect face, hair and figure. It was unlikely she'd ever had a bad hair day!

Ronan was filling the coffee machine when they walked in and Zoe called out to him. 'Hey, boss, what do you think of our celebrity chef?'

He turned and raised an eyebrow at Dee's new hairstyle. 'Well, well, well, look at you.'

'He doesn't like it,' Dee said to Zoe.

'I do, it's just – very different.'

'He doesn't like it,' Dee repeated and Zoe laughed.

'Never mind what I think, what do I know about fashion or trends?'

Zoe looked pointedly at his flamboyant tie and check shirt. 'What indeed?' she drawled.

'Hey, cheeky, don't forget who pays your salary.'

'No, boss, sorry, boss.'

'So, what does my son think?' Ronan asked, leaning against the counter and crossing his arms.

Dee continued to unpack the containers. 'He hasn't seen it.'

'He'll love it,' Zoe assured her. 'Anyway, it wouldn't matter if you'd got it all shaved off, he'd still think you were the bee's knees.'

'True.' Ronan chuckled.

Dee sighed. There was no one else in the café and there wouldn't be a better opportunity than this; Conor would probably thank her for doing it. 'Conor and I have split up,' she said before she lost her nerve.

Ronan looked shocked for a moment and then, regaining his composure, patted her arm awkwardly. 'We all fall out from time to time. If I had a fiver for every time Julia and I argued, I'd be a very rich man.'

'We didn't argue,' Dee said quietly, 'we just decided to call it a day.'

Zoe looked from her shell-shocked boss to their calm, but sad-faced chef. 'I'll go and get the rest of the stuff out of the car. Sorry, Dee,' she added as she passed.

Dee smiled and nodded. 'Thanks.'

'Well,' Ronan said, 'I must say I'm surprised.'

She nodded silently.

'And there's no chance—'

She shook her head.

'I'm sorry about that. I thought you two, well,' he cleared his throat, 'you don't want to know what I thought. Just remember, Dee, that you may have split up with Conor but that doesn't mean you have to split up with me or Julia, and that goes for young Sam too.'

Dee's eyes filled up as she looked at him. 'Thanks, Ronan, I appreciate that.'

'Don't mention it,' he said, clearing his throat again.

'I'd better go,' she said, edging towards the door, 'I'm due at the studio in an hour.'

'Oh, right.' He smiled. 'Well, good luck, then, we'll all be watching.'

'Thanks, Ronan,' she said again and escaped before the tears threatened to spill over.

'You okay?' Zoe was leaning against the car, the last of the containers at her feet ,when Dee emerged.

Dee nodded and fumbled in her pocket for a tissue. 'Fine.'

'Good luck today, then.'

'Thanks.'

'And, by the way, I was wrong,' she added as Dee lowered herself into the driving seat.

'Sorry?'

Zoe smiled kindly. 'You don't look like Natalie Imbruglia, you're much more attractive.'

'Cheers, Zoe,' Dee said with a watery smile, and she drove away.

Chapter 26

Made-up, rather heavily she thought, with a fuchsia pink top and long dangly earrings, Dee made her way down to the set.

'Dee! Look at you!' Marge hurried over to hug her.

'Don't ruin her make-up,' Carolyn warned. 'Isn't her hair gorgeous, Marge?'

'Absolutely perfect.'

'Thanks,' Dee said shyly. 'Is April here yet?'

'In the loo, and today's guest has just arrived.'

'Oh, who is it?' Dee asked.

'Shay Dunne, you know, the personal trainer?'

Dee nodded. Shay was the man responsible for getting everybody who was anybody in Dublin fit and healthy. 'Is he interested in taking part in our piece on labelling?'

Carolyn nodded. 'Very. He thinks it's a great idea. Right, then, Dee. You can grab a seat back there or go and wait in the green room if you prefer.'

'I'd like to stay, if that's okay.'

'Fine, just don't talk when the on-air sign is on. You'll be on after the second break, so about thirty minutes, okay?'

Dee nodded excitedly. 'Fine.' She was quite looking forward to watching the show from the sidelines. The last time she'd been here she had been too flustered to notice anything much and then she'd been whisked in and out so quickly everything was a bit of a blur. The first thing that struck her now as she sat on the battered couch at the back of the room was how small the set was and how empty it was. Apart from Carolyn and Marge there were only two other people and Dee couldn't even see a camera. Within minutes, however, there was a sudden bustle, people came and went, April and Shay arrived in, and soon the tall dark girl in black – later introduced to Dee as the floor manager – called for silence. Marge took her place and the theme music for *Right Now* started.

'Exciting, isn't it?' April whispered, squeezing in beside her on the couch.

Dee nodded and smiled, afraid to open her mouth.

'It's okay, we're safe while the music is on. Are you nervous?'

'Terrified.'

'Don't be. You know your stuff and that's the trick. You won't believe how fast the time will go. If you forget anything or you get stuck, just give me a look and I'll dig you out.'

'Thank you.' Dee smiled gratefully.

'You'll be great,' April assured her, 'and I love the hair.'

Shay Dunne came over to stand next to them. 'Hi, April, how are you?'

'Not as fit as I should be!'

'You're in great shape, I'll never get any business from you.' His eyes moved to Dee. 'Aren't you going to introduce me to this lovely lady?'

'Sorry, Shay, this is Dee Hewson.'

His eyes widened. 'Oh! Any relation—'

'No, afraid not.'

'She's going to be famous in her own right soon enough,' April said loyally. 'Wait till you hear her, Shay, she's wonderful.'

'Oh, what's your expertise?'

'Shush!' The floor manager put a finger to her lips as the music came to an end and the 'on air' sign flicked on.

Dee got completely caught up in the show and couldn't believe it when Carolyn came to fetch her and April. Shay was already on set having been interviewed in the slot before them and he smiled encouragingly as Dee came to take the seat next to him. A girl came to touch up Marge's hair and the floor manager called 'One minute!'

'Dee, April, I'll introduce you, give your background and then it's pretty much over to you. Shay, please feel free to join in.'

He nodded. 'I'd love to; it's something I feel quite strongly about.'

'Then you and Dee have a lot in common,' Marge told him with a wink at Dee.

Dee felt herself redden but there was no time for embarrassment as the countdown began.

'Welcome to *Right Now*,' Marge said, smiling into the camera.

For the first time Dee saw it, the autocue underneath. It was nothing like the cameras she'd seen on TV, much smaller and quite discreet. Dee sat, her back straight and her eyes on the host, and listened carefully. She had no idea when the camera was on her and she didn't want to be caught out looking unprofessional.

Carolyn had told her that it was best to behave as if the camera didn't exist and to talk to the other panellists as if they were having a chat around her kitchen table. Dee wasn't quite sure she could do that but she understood what Carolyn meant. Marge addressed April first and it gave Dee a chance to catch her breath and take her cue from the articulate and lively older woman. April very quickly drew Dee into the conversation and soon she was taking them through the slide with the five points she and April had compiled, giving examples from her own experience. This was when Shay joined in with examples of his own and before she knew it, Marge was thanking them and announcing the next ad break.

*

'That was excellent!' Carolyn told them when they were off-air.

'Excellent,' Marge agreed. 'I'll come and find you after the show and we'll review the content for next week,' she told April and Dee. She blew them a kiss and then went off to meet her next guest.

'Why don't you two go down to the canteen?' Carolyn suggested. 'You deserve a nice cuppa after that. Shay, thank you so much for coming in and staying on for the nutrition spot; you were great.'

Shay shook her hand. 'No problem, I enjoyed it.' He turned to smile at Dee and April. 'I don't suppose I could tag along for that cuppa, could I?'

'That would be great,' April told him, 'you can give us your thoughts on what we have planned for next week's show.'

Shay spent half an hour with them, listening to their ideas and throwing in a couple of his own. Dee was disappointed when he finally got up to leave. 'It was lovely to meet you,' she said.

'The pleasure was all mine,' he said, smiling into her eyes.

'He's such a flirt,' April laughed when they were alone.

'Yes,' Dee agreed.

'He is very attractive though, isn't he? All those muscles and toned skin and that hair.' She saw Dee grinning at her. 'Hey, I may be getting older but I'm not blind.'

Dee laughed. 'He is attractive,' she admitted, 'but nice with it.'

'And intelligent too, not a combination you get very often.'

'Oh, I don't know about that,' Dee said wistfully thinking of Conor. She had always enjoyed being held in his strong, brawny arms and when it came to kindness, humour and intelligence, Conor was hard to beat. She sighed as she realized how much she missed him. They hadn't been able to go out on too many conventional dates but she was used to him dropping in and out, to him being a part of her day, and there was now a very large gap in it. Sam was beginning to notice.

'Penny for them,' April said.

'Oh, sorry, I was miles away.'

'I could give you his phone number if you like.'

'Sorry?'

'Shay?'

She laughed. 'Thanks, but I'm not interested.'

'Already taken, eh?'

'You could say that,' Dee agreed. 'Now, have you had any more thoughts on next week's show?'

Again, when she emerged from Seven TV and switched her phone back on, the messages started to roll in. She smiled delightedly as she read the congratulations from her friends, and was particularly touched by Conor's.

U WER GREAT, AS ALWAYS

He usually signed off with a kiss but, she supposed, that wasn't appropriate any more. With another heart-felt sigh, she slipped her headset on and drove out of the studio car-park. She had only just pulled out into the traffic when the phone rang. 'Hello, Dee Hewson?'

'Dee, it's Neil.'

'You're not supposed to be calling me, remember?'

He ignored her rebuke. 'I want to talk to you. I know you're in town, will you meet me, same place?'

'How do you know I'm in town?' Dee asked suspiciously.

'I phoned the house and asked for you and no, I didn't say it was me.'

'You still shouldn't have done it; you promised.'

'Dee, give me a break here, I've been very patient and kept my promise to stay away but after the other day—'

'Okay.' Dee could hear the frustration in his voice. 'I'll be there in about ten or fifteen minutes.'

When she walked into the lobby area, her eyes went to the table where he had been sitting the last time they'd met in the hotel and, sure enough, he was there. He spotted her instantly and was immediately on his feet.

'Thanks for coming,' he said when she had taken the seat opposite. He nodded at the pint in front of him. 'I felt like something stronger, how about you?'

'Just some sparkling water for me, please.'

'You never were much of a drinker,' he remarked after placing the order.

'No,' she agreed, thinking of the amount of wine and beer she'd managed to consume in the last few weeks. 'How are you?'

He shrugged. 'I'm not sure. The other day was a bit of a shock.'

'I can understand that but don't blame your mum, Neil. I told her I'd never let her see Sam unless she promised not to tell you.'

'I realize that but it's still hard for me to accept that she's known him all this time and said nothing.'

'You should be grateful,' Dee told him. 'At least he's had a grandmother, if not a father.'

'Do you hate me that much, Dee?'

'No, I love him that much, Neil.' She stopped as the waiter arrived back with her water and took a sip. 'As far as I was concerned Sam had to be protected from you; that can't come as a surprise.'

He looked down. 'No, I suppose not.'

'You didn't help matters by not keeping in touch with your mother.'

'I did!'

'A few brief phone calls hardly count.'

He sat back on the sofa and looked at her. 'But what was the point, Dee? What could I tell her?'

She shrugged. 'I don't know, but you must have realized that as your mother she would always want to know that you were okay.'

His smile was cold. 'But I wasn't.'

But Dee wasn't about to start feeling sorry for him. 'And what about when you turned things around and made a success of your life? What was to stop you calling her then? You could have flown her out for visits, she would have loved that.'

Again he looked away. 'I wasn't ready.'

'You were – are – her adored son. There is nothing she wouldn't have done for you. She would have been over the moon to know that you were well and happy and you deprived her of that. How long is it now since you kicked the gambling?'

'A couple of years.' He didn't look up at her and his face wore a sullen scowl.

'You surprise me,' she said softly. 'Usually a recovering addict can tell you the exact number of months, days and hours since their last drink or drug or bet.'

'I didn't want to bore you.'

She continued to watch him carefully through narrowed eyes. 'You never did come back to me with a referee. Can't you find one, Neil?'

'Not one that speaks English, as it happens, no.'

'You're not helping yourself here, Neil. I'm beginning to wonder if you really want to be a part of Sam's life after all.'

Neil sat forward now, his face close to hers, his eyes blazing. 'How can you make a statement like that when you won't even talk to me? How can you base everything on two chats? How can you decide what kind of person I am now based on so little?'

'I can't,' she hissed back, 'but you're not giving me anything else to go on, are you?'

He sighed. 'The only way forward is if you get to know me again and make your own decision.'

She shook her head, her eyes full of confusion. 'I don't know—'

'What have you got to lose?'

She glared at him. 'I would have thought that was obvious, even to you.'

'Okay, listen, I have an idea. You've already introduced me to Sam as Mum's friend, why can't we continue like that? I could get to know him, he could get to know me and if at a later stage you decide you can trust me, well, then we can tell him the truth.'

She frowned. 'I don't know, that would mean more lies. As it is it's going to be an awful shock for him to find out that Peggy is his granny, never mind that you are his dad.'

'It might be a very pleasant one,' he pointed out. 'Hasn't he ever said that he'd like a daddy or grand-parents?'

Dee looked down at her hands. 'I need to think about this.'

'Okay.'

'I have to be honest, Neil, I'm not comfortable that you haven't got someone to vouch for you. That makes me suspicious.' He opened his mouth to protest but she cut him off. 'You can't really expect me to trust you after all you've done.'

'No,' he hung his head, 'no, I suppose I can't.'

She studied him for a moment and then nodded. 'Let me think about it, okay? I'll call you.' She stood up.

'When?' He stood up too.

'Soon.'

'But—'

'Don't push it, Neil,' she warned.

He smiled. 'Okay, sorry, and thanks.'

'I'm not making any promises,' she warned.

'I understand. Thanks for listening.'

Walking back to the car, Dee felt under huge pressure to make a decision and was glad that she'd be able to unload some of her worry this evening on to Vi's sympathetic shoulders. It would help to get a completely objective slant on the problem, and it certainly wouldn't hurt. She wondered what the woman would make of the whole thing. Dee had never told her anything about Sam's father and she wasn't sure if Vi knew the story but was just too discreet to mention it. She was not the prying sort and she wasn't exactly forthcoming about her own life either, Dee realized as she drove home. Vi had been back in Banford for around four years now and though Dee knew that the artist was originally from the area, she knew very little else about the woman. In fact, the comment she had made about her trips to the cinema when she was dating was the only personal information Dee could ever remember her offering. How strange that she was such a central figure to the town and yet she seemed to be a total enigma. Had she ever been married, Dee wondered? She must have been stunning when she was young. She was still very attractive with those amazing cheek bones, Roman nose and piercing green eyes and she positively oozed personality. It was hard to understand how she was alone. Maybe after a couple of glasses of wine, Dee would find out why.

Chapter 27

'Come in.' Vi smiled warmly and drew Dee into the warm, cosy cottage. She led the way into a small sitting room decorated in red and cream with a huge fire crackling in the grate.

'This is lovely,' Dee said, flopping gratefully into an overstuffed chair.

Vi produced a bottle of red wine and a bottle of brandy. She held up the latter. 'Don't suppose I can tempt you?'

Dee shook her head, laughing. 'I'd never get anything done tomorrow.'

Vi sat in the armchair opposite her and, pouring wine into a large glass, pushed it across the coffee table to Dee. 'Cheers,' she said raising her brandy balloon.

'Slainte. I've never been in here before.' Dee looked around her appreciatively. The walls were adorned with paintings of all shapes and sizes and a huge variety of styles but none of them were Vi's own work. The four armchairs were an unusual charcoal-grey and inordinately comfortable with numerous cushions in different shades of red, all made of sumptuous materials with beading and tassels. An enormous red wool rug covered the plain wooden floor in front of the fireplace and two lamps with maroon shades threw a pleasantly subtle light across the room.

'It's lovely.' Dee smiled.

'This is my evening space,' Vi told her, 'my place to unwind.'

'I thought I was here to sit for you.'

Vi's eyes twinkled in the firelight. 'You didn't really.'

Dee laughed. 'No, I didn't.'

'I'm nearly finished with you, anyway. I've got enough sketches now to allow me to incorporate you into any painting I want.'

Dee shuddered. 'What a scary thought.'

Vi laughed. 'The good news is that I won't need to hog half of your kitchen any more.'

'Oh,' Dee said, surprised at the disappointment she felt. 'I've got kind of used to having you around.'

Vi chuckled. 'I'll come back soon to paint Sam,' she promised.

'That would be wonderful.' Dee's eyes lit up. 'Although trying to get him to sit still for more than a minute at a time will be a challenge.'

'There are tricks to painting children.'

'So when can I see what you've made me look like?' Dee asked, trying not to sound too eager.

Vi's smile was ambiguous. 'Soon enough but, I warn you, you probably won't recognize yourself.'

'Why's that?' Dee asked nervously.

Vi shrugged. 'Not everyone does. They expect to see the person they see in the mirror or in a photograph and that's not the way I work.' Vi watched her thoughtfully. 'I paint from the inside out.'

Dee shrugged. 'I don't mind. I quite like the idea, especially if other people don't recognize me either.'

Vi nodded, pleased. 'Good. Now, why don't you tell me what's been troubling you?'

'You don't hang about, do you?' Dee said, taking a sip from her glass.

'I don't see the point these days. Don't tell me anything you don't want to but I'm happy to listen if you need an ear.' She raised her glass to her lips and waited.

'I do need to talk but I'd like some impartial and objective advice too, Vi. I have quite a dilemma and I'm afraid I can't see the wood for the trees at the moment. I'm absolutely terrified of doing the wrong thing simply because I'm confused.'

Vi shot her a look of disbelief. 'You are a very impressive and intelligent young woman and in your heart you probably already know the right thing to do.'

Dee smiled. 'Now you see that's why I came to you! It's kind of you to say that but I'm not so sure.' She sighed. 'Where do I begin?'

'Take your time,' Vi advised, settling herself more comfortably. 'There's no rush.'

Dee took another sip and hugged a large, corduroy

cushion to her chest. 'Sam's dad has turned up. He wants to get to know him and I'm not sure if I should let him.'

Vi nodded thoughtfully. 'I see.'

'Do you know anything about him?' Dee asked. 'Please, if you do, just say so. It will save me the hassle of going through the whole sorry saga.'

Vi frowned. 'I did hear something a long time ago. You lived abroad with him, split up and then you came home alone, is that right?'

'Not quite alone.' Dee smiled. 'It was a bit more gruesome than that, I'm afraid. Neil had taken to gambling and when I couldn't take it any more and told him I was leaving, he decided to leave first, taking my money and some jewellery with him.'

'That's disgraceful!'

Dee nodded. 'It was a shock to say the least. Luckily, I was able to pay for my flight home with my credit card and I still had my house to come back to. I thought I could probably still go to college if I worked nights and weekends. I wasn't afraid of hard work as I'd had more than three years of doing nothing.'

'And then you found out about Sam,' Vi surmised.

'Yes. What a shock that was, although it turned out to be a blessing. I'll be honest, though, they were tough times but I was lucky. I had Lisa who was so kind to me and even my Aunt Pauline was supportive when she finally got over the shock.'

Vi frowned. 'And I suppose you had Peggy too, your mother's cousin?'

Dee sighed and shook her head. 'No, not at first. You see, Peggy isn't my mother's cousin.'

'Oh, I must have got it wrong.' Vi laughed. 'I do that a lot these days.'

'No, you got it right. That's what I told everyone.'

Again, Vi waited silently for Dee to explain, leaning over to top up her glass.

'Peggy is Sam's grandmother.'

Vi's eyes widened but she said nothing.

'To cut a long story short, she found out about the baby and wanted to be a part of his life. I agreed as long as she promised never to tell Neil – that's Sam's father.'

'I can understand that you were angry with him, he behaved abominably.'

'It was more than that, Vi. He had become addicted to gambling. That's why we split up and that's why he robbed from me. He couldn't think beyond his next bet; it was always going to be the one that would make him rich and, of course, then he would promise it would be his last. I decided that if he ever did show up again, I would never let him be a part of Sam's life. I knew I couldn't rely on him. Not only would he be in and out of the picture but he'd probably end up stealing from the child's piggy-bank.'

Vi sighed. 'I'm sure you're right; addiction is a terrible thing.'

Dee nodded. 'And even if Sam didn't have a father at least he had Peggy. It didn't seem to be important that he didn't know exactly who she was. He loved her and she loved him and that's all that mattered.'

'But now he may find out the truth.'

'Exactly. If I agree to Neil meeting him he will find out that I've lied to him and then what's he going to think? And not only have I lied to him but Peggy has, too. How is that going to make him feel?' She closed her eyes briefly as she felt the tears welling.

'Has he changed?' Vi asked softly, reaching over to top up Dee's glass again.

'Oh, don't! I'll never be able to get up in the morning.'

'I'll make you some tea before you leave,' Vi promised. 'So, Neil, has he changed?'

Dee rested her cheek against the cushion and stared into the fire. 'That's the six-million-dollar question, isn't it? He says he has. He's got a successful business in Spain – or so he tells me – he drives a big car and he's being very reasonable, understanding and patient.'

'But you don't trust him.'

'How can I?' Dee wailed. 'What if I do introduce him to Sam and in six months or a year he disappears and we never see him again? Or what if Neil really is successful and rich and decides to seek custody? Or worse, maybe he'll just snatch Sam and I'll never see him again!'

By now tears were streaming down Dee's cheeks

and Vi put down her drink so she could reach across and take her hands. 'Oh, darling, please don't upset yourself. That is not going to happen.'

Dee shook her head. 'You don't know that. Oh, God, Vi, I've gone through every scenario possible in my head and I don't see any way that this can work out without either Sam or me getting hurt.' She took a tissue from her bag, mopped up her tears and blew her nose.

'Tell me about Neil,' Vi said gently when Dee had calmed herself. 'Tell me about the boy you fell in love with.'

Dee smiled slightly. 'I couldn't believe he was even interested in me. I was a bit of a mouse, whereas he was funny and popular and older.'

'Where did you meet?'

'Lisa dragged me along to this charity dinner dance in town with the soul aim of finding a man. She fancied Neil's friend and so the four of us ended up spending the evening together. As it turned out, their relationship came to nothing but Neil and I clicked straight away. Aunty Pauline didn't approve of my having anything to do with boys before I finished my exams so we used to meet up at his place or in town or sometimes he'd come over to Banford and we'd hang out in Lisa's house.'

'And you were happy.'

Dee nodded. 'Yes. He made me feel very special and right from the start I felt I could tell him almost anything. He didn't like Pauline at all, thought she was a right old dragon and he gave out about Dad neglecting me. Neil said he was spending all of his time grieving for his dead wife instead of making the most of his time with his daughter who was still very much alive. I used to tell him to shut up and leave him alone but at the same time I liked the fact that he felt that way.'

'It sounds like he cared about you.'

Dee nodded. 'I really think he did. He worked for his uncle in a clothes shop and hated every minute of it and he just wanted to take time out and go and see the world. He talked of nothing else and I was terrified of losing him.' Dee paused to blow her nose again. 'And then Daddy died. It was shortly after I left school. He went to work as usual and I got a call to say he'd been taken ill and was in hospital. By the time Pauline and I got there he was already dead.'

'Heart attack?'

Dee nodded.

'You poor thing, that must have been such a shock. You were what, seventeen?'

'Eighteen. I was shocked, I suppose, but not desperately upset, not the way I was when my mother died. That sounds terrible, doesn't it?'

Vi shook her head. 'Not at all. You probably weren't as close to him as you were to your mother.'

'I wasn't, and we seemed to grow even further apart after she died.' She paused to take a drink and when she spoke again her voice was steadier. 'The day we buried him, Neil asked me to go away with him. I didn't hesitate.'

'Your aunt must have been furious.'

'Apoplectic. We had a huge argument and she called me a lot of really horrible names.'

'But you made up?'

Dee shook her head. 'No. We left for the States the following December and she still hadn't talked to me. Then when I returned home, pregnant, she was even more disgusted. It was only when Sam was born that we finally buried the hatchet.'

'So you went to America,' Vi said, taking her back to her story.

'Yes. Dad had left me some money, it was supposed to be to put me through university but because I had turned eighteen, the solicitor said it was up to me what I did with the money. I had always intended to return to my studies the following year. I thought we'd be away for six months tops and then I'd come home and start my new life. It was actually three years and four months, in the end, before I stepped on Irish soil again.'

Vi's eyes widened. 'My goodness! And were you travelling all of that time?'

'Pretty much. We slowed down a bit towards the end, spent about six weeks in Morocco and nearly two months in Greece. That's where we finally broke up. We had actually been getting on quite well just before it happened. I had been ill and Neil was always at his best when I was low; very kind and attentive. Anyway, this night I sent him off to get something to eat and when I woke hours later, he still wasn't back. I went looking for him and finally tracked him down to this town square where he was betting on a cock fight.' She shuddered, remembering. 'I'll spare you the details but I'd never seen anything so disgusting, nor have I since. Anyway, it was clear that it didn't disgust him; he was enjoying every second. I knew then that I'd have to leave him.'

'But I thought he left you,' Vi said.

'He came back to our room and found me packing and persuaded me to wait until morning. He was remorseful, kind, tender, and he held me in his arms as I went to sleep. When I woke he was gone.'

'With the money.'

'And a couple of other things too.'

'You poor thing, you must have been devastated.'

'Shocked more than anything,' Dee said as she remembered the trance-like state she was still in when she'd landed in Dublin airport. 'I had realized he had a problem although I tried to ignore it for a long time but I still thought that he was basically a good person. The fact that he had sunk so low that he would actually rob from me I found astounding.'

'When did you first realize his gambling might be a problem?' Vi asked.

Dee winced. 'Within the first year,' she admitted. 'We went to Las Vegas and we had great fun in the casinos but I soon realized that he was too turned on by the whole experience.'

'And did you say anything then?'

'Oh, yes, absolutely; we talked, then we quarrelled, and then I insisted we left. I was hoping it was just the atmosphere of the place and that he would be fine once we moved on but it wasn't that simple. He just went underground and lied to me.'

'He may have started gambling when he was still in Ireland,' Vi mused. 'It would have been easier to hide from you when you weren't living together.'

Dee shook her head. 'I don't think so. He seemed to change personality after Vegas and he was often very high or very low. I should have left as soon as I noticed but,' she smiled sadly, 'I so wanted it to work.'

'That's completely understandable; you loved him.'

Dee nodded, tears in her eyes. 'Yes, I did. The thought of losing Neil was a devastating one; worse in a way than losing Daddy. And the thought of coming home to live in that house alone . . .' Dee shivered.

'Those first few weeks in Dublin must have been hard,' Vi said softly.

'Awful,' Dee admitted. 'Lisa was wonderful but I just couldn't seem to get my act together. She got me information on different courses, on part-time jobs and on what benefits I might be entitled to, but I wasn't interested. And then I discovered I was pregnant. Once I'd decided to keep it – him,' she smiled, 'I decided to forget about university.'

'There are plenty of single mothers who go on to third-level education,' Vi pointed out.

'Yes, I know, and I thought I would return to it some day, but it just didn't work out like that. Once Lisa opened Happy Days and I got into cooking I realized I didn't have to. I still might do an advanced cookery course after Sam starts school.'

Vi smiled. 'You could probably teach it!'

Dee shook her head. 'No, believe me, I've still got a lot to learn.'

'But you'd found your niche.'

Dee nodded. 'Yes, I had.'

'Did you ever hear from Neil once you got home?'

'No, nothing, and even though I was furious and hurt over what he had done, I still worried about him. I thought about contacting Peggy but I didn't want her to know about the baby. Then we bumped into each other at the airport one day.' Dee laughed. '"Bumped" being the word. I was eight months pregnant! She begged me to keep in touch, to let her know when the baby was born, and I agreed. She had always been kind to me and it wasn't her fault that Neil had behaved the way he did.'

'Did he keep in touch with her?'

'He phoned occasionally over the years but once she started asking him questions about where he was and what he was doing, he would hang up.'

'And then, out of the blue, he walks through the door, what, five years later?'

Dee frowned. 'Yes, he came back a couple of months ago, apparently. I don't think he had any intention of getting in touch with me until he saw the picture of Sam and I in the newspaper.'

'And his mother hadn't told you he was home?'

She shook her head. 'I think she was afraid too.'

Vi pondered all of this for a second. 'So why did he come home?'

Dee shrugged. 'That's what I don't understand and it's one of the things that makes me suspicious; why now? I can't help feeling there's a hidden agenda.'

'And what does Peggy think?'

'She's happy to have him back, obviously, but I think she has a lot of questions herself—'

Vi nodded. 'And she's probably afraid to ask them in case she loses him again.'

'Probably,' Dee agreed. 'They had a row when he found out she knew about Sam; he couldn't believe she'd kept it from him, especially since he's been home.'

'It must be a difficult situation for her; she's torn between her son and her grandson.'

'Yes, and she adores Sam. I am so glad now that I let her be a part of his life, she's very important to him.'

'Which brings us neatly back to your predicament. Do you think that maybe Neil could become important to Sam too?'

'I've no doubt that he would, Vi, that's what worries me. Sam is a loving and giving little boy but what if

Neil just takes and leaves?' Dee nibbled her thumb anxiously.

Vi shrugged. 'I'm no expert, Dee, but don't they say you should always give children as much information as they can handle?'

'What are you saying?'

'Just that you don't have to tell Sam everything in one go, but feed it to him a little bit at a time. Neil turning up like this is a shock, and I can understand your anxieties, but Sam would have started asking questions sooner or later and you would have had to tell him something.'

'I already have,' Dee assured her. 'I told him that his daddy and I broke up before he was born and that it had nothing to do with him. I've never bad-mouthed Neil and I always told Sam that I was sure his daddy would never have left if he'd known I was going to have a baby. I told him I didn't know where Neil was which was true, of course, but by not explaining who Peggy was I lied to him and deprived him from talking to her about his father. She could have told him what Neil was like as a child and shown him photographs.' Tears started to fall again and Dee didn't even bother trying to check them. 'I deprived him of that.'

'Yes, you did,' Vi acknowledged, 'but you were just trying to protect him. Anyway, it's not too late. Neil is alive; he's here, as is Peggy. You can change all of that, it's within your power to fix.'

'But how can I trust Neil? What if I make this big

announcement to Sam that his dad's back and they get to know each other, they start to build a relationship and then Neil bugger's off again? Or worse, he starts to gamble again and Sam gets to witness his downfall first-hand?'

Vi sighed. 'You can't protect him from everything, Dee. Other children grow up with parents' failings, some get through it okay and some don't. At least he'll always have you. By all means, keep a tight leash on Neil until you feel you can trust him again but maybe it's time for Sam to know the truth. And I think at some stage he should know exactly what his father did and Neil should be the one to tell him that.'

Dee looked vaguely shocked. 'I think that's a bit much, Vi, he's only four!'

Vi smiled. 'Yes, you're probably right, but like I said, he will ask questions and I think that you should feed him the truth in bite-size pieces.'

Dee absorbed these words in silence.

'You must remember, Dee, that this is very big in your head. Neil coming back into your life has been a huge shock, but as far as Sam is concerned, nothing has changed. He's still little more than a baby and you have plenty of time to get this right. Having said that, please don't let me or anyone else pressure you into doing something you're not ready to do.'

'Neil has suggested that I introduce him to Sam as Peggy's friend and then, if that works out, we can tell him the truth at a later stage.'

'It's an option,' Vi agreed, 'but it is also adding to the lies.'

'Yes, that's what I thought. Oh, Vi, I just don't know.' Dee dropped her face into her hands. 'It's all too much responsibility and I'm not sure I can handle it.'

'You can,' Vi said fiercely, 'you know you'd walk over hot coals for that child.'

Dee let her hands fall into her lap and she nodded slowly, suddenly drained. 'I would, Vi, I really would.'

'Then that's all you have to remember.'

Chapter 28

In Vi's bathroom, Dee splashed water on to her face and stared at herself in the mirror. She looked like she'd run a marathon or climbed a mountain; her eyes were red, her skin blotchy and with her new hairstyle she looked more like a waif and stray than ever. Burying her face in one of Vi's soft towels, Dee took a moment before going back outside.

'I'm out here,' Vi called and Dee made her way out to the small, cluttered, crazy kitchen that she always thought oozed Vi's personality.

'I thought you might be ready for some tea,' Vi was saying as she cut two pieces from a large chocolate cake, 'and a sugar hit. It's shop-bought, I'm afraid – my talents don't run to baking – but it's delicious, none the less.'

Dee sat down at the table and smiled. 'You are amazing, you know that? I would never think of feeding someone chocolate cake when they're going through a crisis but you know what? It's just exactly right.' Greedily, she bit into the cake and closed her eyes as she savoured it. 'Gorgeous. You know, you're totally wasted. You should be the mother of a huge brood of children.' She eyed Vi curiously as the woman nibbled delicately on her own piece of cake. 'Wouldn't you have liked that?'

Vi didn't meet her eyes. 'You can't have everything you want, life isn't that simple.'

'Tell me about it,' Dee laughed.

'And you didn't have a child alone, not in my day. If you got pregnant you went away until you had the child and then gave it up for adoption.'

Dee shook her head. 'I was shocked when I found out I was expecting Sam and I admit I thought about my options, but I can't imagine what it must have been like not to *have* any options.'

'It was hard,' Vi agreed.

Dee paused, her cake halfway to her lips. 'Vi?'

Their eyes met and Vi smiled slightly. 'What can I say?'

'You had a child?'

Vi nodded. 'He'd be thirty-six now, my baby.'

'My God, what happened?'

Vi shrugged. 'I got into trouble. The father was, let's say, already involved and there was only one thing for me to do. I was working as a florist at the time, here in Banford, and it would have been a terrible scandal if it had got out.'

'The father was a local too?'

'Yes, and it was a much smaller community back

then; you couldn't do anything without everyone talking about it. My parents were devout Catholics and very involved in the parish and I knew they'd be devastated to find out that their only daughter had got herself into trouble.'

Dee stared. 'You never told them?'

Vi shook her head. 'I never told anyone. I said that I was fed up with life in a small town. I was twenty-two and all of my girlfriends were either married or engaged and I was starting to get these pitying looks.' She swallowed hard, her eyes suspiciously bright. 'I told Mam and Dad that I'd had enough of being the town spinster and I was off to the bright lights of London to find myself a man and/or a career.'

'They must have been upset.'

She shrugged. 'Maybe, I don't know. I never really fitted in and they were never quite sure what to do with me. It was probably a relief when I left.'

'And did you go to London?'

Vi shook her head. 'Lord, no, for all my weird ways, city life never held any attractions for me. First I went to Bournemouth and I got a job working in another florists'. I told them I was a widow and they were very sympathetic. I had a good pregnancy and I was able to work right up until I went into labour. I had already made arrangements for the child to be adopted and they came to the hospital for him three hours after he was born.'

'Three hours,' Dee gasped, 'Oh, Vi, you poor thing.

I can't imagine having to hand over Sam just like that.'

Vi stared into the fire, obviously reliving the moment. 'That was the hardest part,' she said, her voice barely audible. 'I had never considered keeping the child, I knew it would be better off in a proper family, but I never realized that I would have some time with it, with him.' She sighed. 'He was so beautiful he took my breath away. I couldn't stop looking at him and I inspected him from head to toe trying to memorize every precious inch. The nurses wanted to take him away but I wouldn't let them. I had only this small amount of time with him and I wasn't going to give up any of it.'

'Do you have a photo?'

Vi shook her head as she reached into her sleeve for a lacy handkerchief. 'I never even thought of it, but I wouldn't have been able to afford a camera even if I had. But it's okay because I have a picture right in here.' She smiled at Dee as she tapped her finger on the side of her head.

After allowing Vi a moment Dee asked the question. 'Do you know what happened to him?'

Vi nodded. 'He went to a lovely family in the locality; they already had two young sons so I'm sure he must have been very happy.'

'But he's never tried to contact you?'

Vi shook her head. 'No.'

'How would you feel if he did?' Dee persisted.

'I have no idea, but it's hardly likely at this stage.'

'Did you leave Bournemouth after you—'

'Gave him away?' Vi said, her voice sharp.

'Vi! I'm not judging you!' Dee looked shocked and hurt.

Vi patted her hand. 'No, darling, I know you're not. I suppose I'm still a little sensitive on the subject, even after all these years. I moved to the Isle of Man and got a job—'

'In a florists'?'

Vi nodded, smiling. 'Indeed. I worked for this lovely lady for fifteen years, Daphne Valentine, and when she died she left the shop to me. I had started to paint in my spare time and I decided to take her name; it seemed a much more appropriate artist's name than McDonald!'

Dee laughed.

'I struck up a friendship with a local artist, John Drake,' Vi continued. 'He taught me a lot and we had some good times together.'

Dee raised an eyebrow. 'Oh, yes?'

Vi smiled. 'It was a very casual, relaxed sort of friendship and yes, we became lovers, but it was out of loneliness more than anything else. He died five years ago and that was when I decided to sell up and come home. And' – she smiled at Dee – 'here I am.'

'My God, Vi, you've been through so much.'

'No more than anyone else. At least I had somewhere to come back to and a few bob to buy my lovely little house.'

'And you have lots of friends,' Dee added as the sadness lingered in the older woman's eyes. 'Me, Conor, Lisa and Ronan and Julia.' She grinned. 'Well, maybe not Julia!'

Vi smiled too, but her heart wasn't in it.

'I think I should get going.' Dee stood up. 'Oh, I feel a bit dizzy!'

'You did drink a bottle of wine,' Vi reminded her.

Dee groaned. 'I didn't, did I? I'm going to be in a right state in the morning. Still, I don't care, it's been great. Thank you, Vi. Not only for listening to me, but for trusting me with your story.'

Vi stood too and embraced her. 'Likewise.'

'Will you be okay?' Dee's eyes searched her face.

'Of course!' Vi assured her. 'Will you?'

Dee nodded and smiled. 'Yes, I think I will. I think I know what I have to do.'

As she walked home, Dee's head was reeling with all that Vi had told her and for once she was completely distracted from her own problems. The poor, poor woman! How awful it must have been for her to go through all of that alone. Dee couldn't begin to imagine it. If she hadn't had Lisa she'd have been consumed by loneliness and even Aunt Pauline had been supportive in her own peculiar way. Vi was obviously a strong woman, even stronger than Dee had always imagined. She was surprised and touched that she had confided in her. It had brought their friendship to a new level and

Dee knew that it would not be the last time that she turned to Vi.

'You're out late.'

Dee jumped as Conor appeared from nowhere at her shoulder. 'Conor, you scared the hell out of me!'

'Sorry. I did whistle all the way up the road. You must either be very drunk or very preoccupied.'

She smiled sleepily. 'A little of both.'

'Where were you?' he asked lightly. 'I didn't see you in the pub.'

'No, I was in Vi's,' Dee said, liking the fact that he was interested.

'Oh, are you still posing for her?'

'We're finished now.'

'I'm looking forward to seeing the results.'

'I don't know if I am,' Dee admitted, thinking about how Vi said she painted from the inside out; a frightening thought given the turmoil that had been going on inside Dee's head over the last few weeks.

'How are you?' he asked softly as they continued the short distance to her house.

'Okay. You?'

'Fine. Nice haircut.'

She laughed. 'Liar. How are the cattle?'

'Healthy again, thank God. It was looking very dodgy for a few days but it looks like they've all come through it unscathed. Is Sam okay?'

She turned to smile at him. 'You only saw him the other day.'

'Yeah, I know.'

'He misses you too,' she assured him. 'When I was going out this evening he wanted to know why you couldn't mind him instead of Paula.'

'You know you can ask me anytime.'

They stopped at her gate and she looked up at him. 'I'm not sure that would work.'

He rested his hands lightly on her arms. 'Dee, I miss him and I miss you too.'

She looked up at him. 'Conor, I don't know whether I'm coming or going at the moment and I don't want to mess you around.'

'Do you miss me?' he persisted, pulling her closer.

'Yes,' she whispered, 'but—'

He put his finger to her lips. 'Let's just take it from there, shall we?'

Her eyes held his and she kissed his finger and then, parting her lips, ran her tongue along it.

Conor groaned. 'Don't do stuff like that unless you mean it.'

She didn't answer but closing her eyes, pulled his head down to hers and kissed him hungrily.

Conor pressed her back against the garden wall and his hands moved up and down her body.

Dee knew that this shouldn't be happening but she couldn't bring herself to stop it. It had been a while since Conor had kissed her like this and she couldn't even remember the last time they'd made love. She shuddered as his mouth moved to her neck and throat and one hand slipped into the waistband of her jeans, his fingers playing with the flimsy lace of her pants.

'Dee?' He pulled away to look at her, his breathing ragged.

'Wait here, I'll get rid of Paula.'

Chapter 29

Dee woke in the early hours to Conor kissing her shoulder and slipping out of the bed. 'Where are you going?' she asked, lifting her head off the pillow to look at the clock and regretting it. There seemed to be a hammer banging relentlessly at her temples and her eyes hurt.

'I didn't think you'd want Sam to see me here,' he whispered.

'Yeah, you're right, it might confuse him,' she conceded. She watched sleepily as he pulled on his jeans and sweatshirt. 'He won't be up for ages yet.'

Conor sat down beside her and gave her a long, lingering kiss. 'I need to get back. I've no car and it will take me nearly an hour to walk.'

She searched his face. 'Are you sorry you came back with me last night?'

'No, of course not, Dee. How can you think that after what we've just done?'

She shrugged and yawned. 'That was just sex.'

He stiffened. 'Was it now?'

She grinned. 'Yes and very good it was too.'

He rose to his feet and grabbed his jacket. 'Glad I could be of service. Goodbye, Dee.'

'Seeya,' she murmured, ducking back under the covers and closing her eyes.

'Get up, Mummy, get up!'

Dee woke to find her son bouncing up and down on the bed beside her. Reaching up she pulled him down and tickled him.

'Stop, Mummy, stop,' he said, shrieking happily.

She relented, dropped a kiss on his cheek and then swung her legs out of bed. Immediately her head started to throb and she winced. Peering at the clock through leaden eyelids, she cursed softly. 'It's seven-thirty, the damned alarm didn't go off.'

'Yes it did, you just didn't hear it.'

She turned to grab him and tickle him again. 'Then why didn't you wake me?'

He put a hand to her cheek and smiled into her eyes. 'I thought you might need to sleep. You work very hard, Mummy.'

Dee hugged him briefly. 'Get your slippers on and we'll go and have some breakfast.' When he was gone, she stood up and pulled on her own robe, conscious of a slight tenderness around her thighs, a reminder of the passionate night she'd shared with Conor. Her smug smile faded, however, when she remembered his abrupt departure in the early hours. She couldn't quite

remember what had been said but she had the distinct
feeling he'd been annoyed with her.

Going downstairs, she set Sam up with a bowl of
cornflakes and a glass of apple juice and went in
search of her phone. It was in her bag on the floor
just inside the back door where she'd dropped it last
night and she flushed as she remembered how desperate she had been to get rid of Paula and drag Conor
inside.

'Morning, how are you?' she typed into the phone
and sent it to him. That was an innocent enough
message. She'd find out if she was in his bad books
or not when she saw his reply. Her phone beeped as
the message was sent and then beeped again as the
message was received but although she kept it beside
her as she made tea and started to plan her day, there
was no reply from Conor. Still, he had a habit of leaving
his phone in the house when he was outside on the
farm and this was his busiest time. She could phone
the house and leave a message on his answering
machine but there was probably no need. He'd call or
text when he had time.

'Mummy, my arm is itchy,' Sam complained, pushing his bowl aside and rubbing his skin roughly.

'Don't darling,' Dee said, going to him and frowning
at the red blotches all down the side of his arm. Now
what the hell had caused that? 'Did you have anything
to eat with Paula last night?'

He shook his head.

'Please tell me the truth, Sam, you won't be in trouble.'

'I didn't have anything, Mummy, I promise,' he protested, tears welling up in his eyes.

'I'm sorry, sweetheart, of course I believe you.' She hugged him quickly. 'Let's get you into a cool bath and then I'll put some cream on your arm. You'll be right as rain in no time.' She smiled confidently at him, scooped him into her arms as if he was a baby, and took him upstairs.

Once Sam was playing happily with a plastic submarine in the bath, Dee gathered his clothes and bed linen in her arms and ran downstairs to stick them in the washing machine. Then she quickly hoovered the floor and sofa before going upstairs and hoovering every surface of his bedroom. She was about to put the hoover away when she remembered Sam had been in her room as well and, just in case, she hoovered in there and stripped the sheets from her bed too. She would have been changing them anyway, she realized as she smelled the faint aroma of Conor's aftershave. Last night seemed an eternity ago now.

'Mummy, I'm getting cold,' Sam called to her.

'Coming,' she yelled back and after she'd brought all the laundry downstairs and put the hoover away, she went up to dry him carefully in a soft towel and applied the cream to his arm. It didn't look that much better but at least Sam wasn't complaining too much.

She had just plonked him in front of a video and made herself another cup of tea when Lisa breezed in.

'Is my name in the pot?' she asked. 'Hiya, Sam.'

Sam waved vaguely, his attention on the TV.

'Is everything okay?' Lisa asked, realizing that Sam was in pyjamas and his hair was damp.

Dee fetched another mug. 'He has a rash on his arm.'

'Oh, anything serious?'

'It looks quite angry but it doesn't seem to be spreading. I think I might keep him here with me today.' She brought the tea over to the table and flopped into the chair opposite Lisa's.

'Wouldn't it be better if he came into the crèche?' Lisa said, adding milk to her mug. 'It would be a distraction for him and anyway, you look exhausted.'

'Yeah, well, I've just hoovered everywhere and stripped the beds too. The fact that the rash is localized suggests exposure to something, probably animal hair but I've no idea how it could have happened. Do any of the kids have a new pet at home?'

'Not that I know of and all the parents know about Sam's allergy, so they're pretty vigilant.'

Dee shook her head in resignation. 'Then I just don't know. Maybe I'll call Paula and see if she has any ideas. Unless—'

'What?'

Dee was remembering Sam rolling around her bed earlier and wondered whether Conor had left a souvenir of Boxer there.

'What is it?' Lisa repeated.

'Conor was here last night,' Dee mumbled.

Lisa grinned delightedly. 'You've only just broken up!'

Dee sighed. 'I know.'

'So it's all back on again.'

'Wipe that silly grin off your face,' Dee said, but she was smiling too. 'I'd had a few drinks with Vi and I was on my way home when I bumped into him and ' – she shrugged – 'well, one thing led to another, you know how it is.'

Lisa sighed. 'Not really, Ger's not the impulsive type.'

Dee chuckled. 'Anyway, I'm not sure whether we're on or off. I vaguely remember that he was a bit pissed off with me before he left but I'm not sure why.'

'Ask him.'

Dee rolled her eyes. 'Oh, yeah, that would go down really well. "Conor, what did I do to upset you, only I was too drunk to remember."'

'Well, you don't say it quite like that, stupid.'

Dee shot a look at the clock and sprang to her feet. 'Oh, well, I've no time to think about it now, I have to prepare lunch for the café.'

'What are we having?' Lisa asked, quickly draining her mug and heading for the door into the hall.

'Chicken casserole,' Dee told her, 'and just beans on toast for tea, I'm afraid.'

'They love beans,' Lisa assured her. 'Are you going to let Sam come inside?'

'I'll keep him here for the moment,' Dee decided, 'maybe later.'

'Okay then, see you later, Sam.'

'Bye.' Sam waved at her and then wandered over to his mother. 'Am I not going into the crèche today, Mummy?'

'Let's see how it goes,' Dee said, inspecting his arm. 'How does it feel?'

He shrugged. 'Okay. Can Tom come in and play with me?'

'Oh, I don't know, Sam—'

'Please?' he begged.

'We'll see.'

He sighed impatiently. 'So can I watch TV until then?'

'I thought we could listen to a story while I cook.' Sam had several CDs of stories that Dee sometimes let him listen to when he couldn't sleep.

'Cool!' he said and sped upstairs to choose one.

Dee was relieved that he was so easily diverted. Often rashes reduced him to tears but thankfully this one seemed mild. It was possible that some of Boxer's hair was responsible. Though Conor was always very careful that he didn't carry any dog hair into her house, he hadn't expected to see her last night, never mind end up in her bed. As she started to prepare the vegetables for the casserole that would feed both the crèche and Ronan's customers, she remembered the feel of Conor's hands and lips on her body and realized exactly how much she'd missed that closeness.

'Mummy, I've got one!' Sam was back and was scrambling up on to a kitchen chair.

'Give it here then.' Dee smiled at him and, wiping her hands on her apron, she went over to put the disk into the CD player and fetched Sam some yoghurt on the way back.

As Sam ate and his eyes glazed as he got caught up in the story, Dee thought that, despite all the complications in her life, she really was a very lucky woman.

Chapter 30

Lisa was sitting at her kitchen table a few days later, applications and notepad in front of her and a pen clenched between her teeth, when she came to a decision. She had interviewed two more candidates but neither had come close to Yvonne. Now, if Dee agreed, she would ask the girl to join them for a month's trial to see how they all got on. Happily she had Martha's backing; her young assistant had been equally impressed by Yvonne's handling of the children. Lisa had hoped she would be able to hire two candidates straight away but she wasn't going to settle for just anyone. She would keep looking until she found another girl as talented as Yvonne; it was just a matter of time, she decided optimistically.

Dee didn't seem to be having as much luck when it came to hiring a cook, but then Lisa thought her requirements were almost impossible to fill. The truth was that Dee just didn't want to share her kitchen and was putting obstacles in the way to delay the inevitable. But Ronan had made his feelings on the subject clear and then there was the added stress of Dee working at Seven TV; she couldn't carry on alone for much longer.

Despite the hard work, she thought, Lisa could see how much her friend was enjoying the new challenge but, ironically, as a result of the publicity, she was receiving more calls than ever about catering work. She had to turn down most of it but Lisa was convinced there had to be a way of cashing in on the situation.

'Let's go for a pint,' Ger said, putting down his newspaper and smiling at her.

'Aren't you meeting the lads?' Lisa looked up from her notebook, surprised.

'No, not tonight.'

'Okay, then, why not?' She smiled at him. 'Just let me go and get ready.'

'Now don't be all day up there,' Ger groaned, 'it's just the local we're going to.'

'Five minutes,' she called over her shoulder and headed for the stairs. Up in her bathroom she quickly applied some eye-shadow, mascara and lipstick, combed her hair and went into her bedroom to ransack her wardrobe. After dismissing a number of outfits as 'too much' or 'too tight' – there were an increasing number of the latter and she blamed Dee's food – she chose a silky-blue top and her most flattering jeans. They were extra long and with her highest boots she looked almost slim. She called them her Lauren jeans because when she wore them she didn't feel quite as enormous when she was standing beside her tiny friend.

When she went back downstairs, Ger eyed her up and down. 'You look nice,' he mumbled.

Lisa nearly fell over. His usual greeting would have been 'What took you so long?'

'Shall we go?' he was saying now, holding the door open for her.

Lisa blinked. Ger had obviously been abducted by aliens but she quite liked his replacement. Either that or he was in trouble or had some bad news to impart; much more likely, she thought resignedly. Still, at least it would be done over a Bacardi and diet Coke.

When they arrived in the pub, Sheila and her husband Matthew were at a table in the corner.

'Do you want to join them?' Ger asked as Lisa waved to them and then looked around for another table.

'You want to sit with my friends?' She eyed him suspiciously.

He shrugged. 'I don't mind, he's a nice enough bloke.'

'Yes, still, they look a bit cosy, maybe they'd prefer to be alone.' She knew in her heart that Sheila didn't particularly like Ger and there was always an awkward atmosphere when they were together. 'Let's sit at the bar.'

'Sure, if you like.' Ger held out a stool for her and then turned to the barman to order.

Lisa watched in stunned silence. Ger had told her the

burned sausages and mash had been lovely, then he'd held the door for her, pulled out her chair, and now he was ordering a drink without the usual prevarication, allowing her time to rummage in her bag for her purse. 'Is everything okay, Ger?' she asked when they had been served.

'Fine, why?'

'You just don't seem yourself tonight,' she said tactfully.

He sighed. 'I suppose I'm not.'

'What's wrong?' she prompted. 'Is there a problem at work?' Ger hardly ever talked about what went on at the office other than to tell her that he was surrounded by idiots and definitely underpaid.

'In a way.' He shot her a nervous look. 'I think I'm in a bit of a rut, Lisa.'

'Oh?'

'I'm thirty next June and I feel as if my life is going nowhere.'

'Oh, I wouldn't say that. You have a successful job, a house,' she playfully punched him in the arm, 'me.'

He didn't return her smile. 'Lisa, we need to talk.'

Again, she stared at him. Whoever heard of a man uttering those four words, especially a man like Ger? 'Well, that's what we're doing, right?'

'I think I need a break,' he blurted out.

'Well, I'd need to wait until Yvonne has settled in but that shouldn't be a problem. Somewhere in the sun, or do you fancy your chances on the piste?'

He looked at her solemnly. 'Not that kind of break.'

Some of Lisa's drink went down the wrong way and she got a coughing fit.

'Are you okay?' he asked, banging her enthusiastically on the back.

'Fine, fine,' she gasped, warding him off. 'Are you telling me you want to break up with me, Ger, is that it?'

'It's not that I want to, Lisa, but I think I should. I don't think we're going anywhere and it's wrong of me to hold on to you when you could find happiness with another man.'

'Have you been reading those self-help books again?'

'Lisa, I'm trying to be serious here.'

'Sorry.'

He frowned. 'Do you understand what I'm saying, Lisa?'

'I'm not totally thick, Ger, of course I realize what you're saying. I'm just a bit confused as to why. We're getting along fine, aren't we?'

He scratched his ear and coughed nervously. 'Like I said, with thirty approaching I'm re-evaluating my life.'

'Oh, please,' she laughed, 'you're not on *Oprah*, just give it to me straight. Is there someone else?'

He hesitated for a second and then nodded.

Lisa stared. When she'd asked the question she hadn't dreamed that the answer would be yes. 'Who is she?' she demanded, through gritted teeth. 'It's not skinny Sally from accounts, is it?'

'No!' He looked shocked. 'She's only twenty, I'm not a cradle-snatcher!'

'Then who?' Lisa persisted. 'I have a right to know.'

'It's Esther,' he said, a sloppy smile creeping on to his face.

Lisa stared at him. 'Esther, with the bottle-lens glasses? You're kidding me, she must be fifty!'

'She's only thirty-nine and she's a very nice person. Looks aren't everything, you know,' he added piously.

'You've spent nearly all of our time together having a go at me about my weight or my hair or my clothes; I was never good enough for you.' Lisa blinked back tears.

He winced slightly. 'Yes, I realize I haven't been exactly kind to you and I'm sorry about that. Esther has made me see that you have to look inside someone, not be distracted by the packaging. She says that people are too cruel to each other by far and that there would be a lot less strife in the world if we all tried to be kinder to each other.'

'Esther's got quite a lot to say, hasn't she?' Lisa said bitterly, wondering if they could really be having this conversation. She felt as if she was in the middle of a bad soap opera.

He smiled. 'No, she's actually very quiet and shy; she's quite a restful person to be around.'

'Unlike me, you mean?' Ger seemed completely oblivious to the hurt he was causing.

'No, no, Lisa, please don't think I'm making

comparisons. You're a lovely lady and I hope you find your soul-mate, I really do. You deserve only the best.'

Lisa stood up and glared down at him. 'Finally you've said something I agree with.'

'Where are you going? You haven't even finished your drink yet.'

Lisa picked up her glass and drained the contents. 'There. Goodnight, Ger. Have a nice life.'

'Oh, but Lisa, what about my stuff at your place—'

'It will be in a bag on the doorstep first thing in the morning.'

'There's really no need to be like this,' he sniffed. 'I'm sure we can both still behave like adults.'

'That's where you're wrong.'

'Well, if that's the way you want it.' He shrugged sadly. 'Take care of yourself, Lisa, be happy.'

'I intend to be, Ger, I intend to be.' And turning on her heel, she marched back through the pub and out into the night air. She just hoped that no one had seen the tears rolling down her cheeks.

Chapter 31

Ten minutes later Dee opened the door to find her best friend on the doorstep.

'If Conor's here I'll go,' she said straight away.

'He isn't,' Dee said pulling her inside. 'What on earth are you doing here at this hour of the night?'

'I was in the pub,' Lisa told her.

'Want a coffee?' Dee asked, leading her towards the kitchen.

'Only if you don't have alcohol.'

Dee grinned. 'Will wine do?'

'If there's nothing stronger,' Lisa acquiesced gruffly.

'There isn't, and I'm afraid I have no idea what this wine is like; it's a bottle left over from Christmas.'

'If it's alcoholic it will do.'

'Would it be fair to say this has something to do with Ger?' Dee asked as she opened the wine and poured it into two glasses.

'It would.' Lisa snatched a glass from her and emptied half of it.

Dee filled it up again and watched as her friend took

another gulp. 'Let's sit down and you can tell me all about it.'

Lisa flopped down on the sofa, her glass shaking precariously. 'That won't take long; he dumped me.' And she burst into tears.

Dee immediately sat down and put her arms around Lisa. 'I don't believe it!'

'It's true,' Lisa sobbed.

'He's a fool.'

'Yes,' Lisa agreed and took a drink, her tears dripping into her glass.

'I just can't believe it,' Dee said again.

'It came as a bit of a shock to me too,' Lisa said before glugging down more wine.

'Did he tell you why?'

Lisa looked up, her eyes brimming with tears again. 'He's found his soul-mate.'

Dee was incredulous. 'He's been cheating on you?'

Lisa shook her head. 'No, at least, I don't think so. He's fallen for this woman at work and honestly, Dee, I look better than her on my worst day.'

'Well of course you do,' Dee said, patting her hand.

'No, Dee, I really mean it. She looks about fifty. He says she's only thirty-nine but that's bullshit – her hair is all straggly with grey bits, she wears these milk-bottle lens glasses and get this,' Lisa's voice was shaking with emotion, 'she's at the very least a size eighteen.'

'No!'

'Yes!' Lisa nodded furiously.

'But Ger always hated it when you put on even a few pounds.'

'Exactly!' Lisa banged the coffee table with the palm of her hand and this time slopped wine on her jeans and the sofa. 'Oh, now look what I've done!'

'It doesn't matter, Lisa,' Dee said pushing a tissue into her hand and going to fetch some kitchen roll. When she returned Lisa was dabbing at the stains with her tissue. 'The tissue was for you,' Dee said, gently taking the sodden tissue off her and pressing a piece of kitchen roll into her hand instead. Taking another piece, she quickly soaked up the wine and then refilled Lisa's glass. 'Good job it was white, eh? It would be a shame to ruin those jeans.'

Lisa sniffed. 'He even told me I looked good. I should have known straight away there was something up. He was nice all evening. Sheila and Matthew were in the pub and he even suggested we sit with them.'

'He didn't!'

'I know, like I said, I should have known he was up to something.'

Dee frowned. 'He mustn't have been planning to tell you tonight if he wanted to sit with them.'

'Oh, he did, the spineless git was just putting it off. And then he starts all this "you're a lovely person, Lisa, I hope you find someone too" crap.'

'I can't believe this.' Dee shook her head in wonder. 'Has he found God or something?'

'No, he's found Esther,' Lisa said bitterly and burst into tears again.

Dee held her as she cried and then ran to get more tissues and the wine bottle.

'You know, maybe it's not such a bad thing,' she said tentatively after Lisa had calmed down again. 'I'm not saying you didn't care about Ger but maybe you were more in love with love than you were with him.'

Lisa rolled her eyes. 'You're as bad as him now with all this amateur analysis.'

Dee grinned. 'You do it to me often enough.'

'Ah, but I know what I'm talking about,' Lisa shot back.

'Maybe you and Esther have something in common after all. No, forget I said that,' she said hurriedly when she saw Lisa's face. 'What are you going to do now?'

Lisa shrugged. 'What can I do?'

'Go on the hunt for a replacement?' Dee suggested.

'Absolutely not! No, I'm taking a break from men for a while.' She sat up straighter. 'I'm going to put all my efforts into Happy Days and make it the best crèche in Banford.'

'It already is.'

'Then in North County Dublin,' Lisa said firmly. 'I mean it, Dee. I've got a real buzz out of making all these new changes and I've still got lots of ideas.'

Dee smiled. 'I know you have, I think you're great.'

Lisa nodded her thanks. 'Yvonne will work out fine, I'm sure of that but I really need at least one more girl.'

'Person,' Dee corrected.

'Girl.' Lisa was adamant. 'The only men allowed on the premises are the fathers.'

Dee laughed.

'But we have to sort you out too,' Lisa continued, a determined look in her eye.

'Why do I need sorting out?'

'Because you're burying your head in the sand.'

'What's that supposed to mean?'

Lisa looked her straight in the eye. 'Dee, you don't want to take on a cook, do you?'

'I wouldn't say that but it's very hard to find the right—'

'Dee?'

'Okay, okay, I'm not keen on the idea but I don't have a lot of choice, do I?'

'We all have choices,' Lisa said with a sigh, her eyes filling up again.

'Oh, Lisa!'

'I'm fine, I'm fine. We're talking about you now. We just have to figure out what your choices are.'

'When you come up with an answer let me know,' Dee murmured.

Lisa scowled. 'I wish you'd take me seriously, Dee, I'm trying to help you here, despite the pain I'm in.'

'Sorry.'

'Look, you still have this old house to maintain and your television contract is only for twelve shows, isn't it?'

Dee nodded. 'Yes, but I have a better income now thanks to Seven TV and you.'

'That will soon be gobbled up with gas, electricity and food bills not to mention your health insurance.'

'Oh, cheer me up, why don't you,' Dee groaned.

'I'm just being realistic, you must think about the future. You might want to send Sam to private school one day and, according to my brother, that costs a bloody fortune.'

'Okay, okay, I'll hire a cook,' Dee cried, holding up her hands in submission.

'You're not listening.' Lisa shook her head impatiently. 'You have to think about what it is you enjoy doing and incorporate that into your plans.'

'I enjoy cooking,' Dee told her, 'alone.'

Lisa gave her a look and took a moment to consume some more wine. 'How did the show go today?' she asked eventually.

'Fine.'

'What were you talking about?'

Immediately, Dee came to life. 'Homemade products versus processed products. We had the buyer from ValueMart supermarkets on and he was saying that customers are a lot more discerning these days and there's huge demand for specialized products.'

Lisa's eyes narrowed, her misery forgotten. 'Like what?'

Dee shrugged. 'Jams, pâté, breads, that sort of thing.'

Lisa burst out laughing.

'What?' Dee smiled. She was delighted to see her friend laughing again even if she had no idea why.

Lisa sighed. 'I love you dearly, Dee, but sometimes you can be incredibly thick.'

'Thanks very much!'

'Well, I'm sorry, but you can.'

'Lisa, I have no idea what you are on about.'

'Right, you like cooking alone, yes?'

Dee nodded.

'So you could produce your own range of foods. You already have recipes for chutneys and jams, breads and cakes, it's just a matter of packaging and marketing them.'

Dee stared at her. 'I'm assuming that it's the shock of being dumped that has unhinged you, hopefully temporarily.'

'No, listen, Dee,' Lisa said, her eyes alight with excitement. 'This could really work. You have the talent and now you have the contacts and the celebrity status. People would queue up to buy your produce and because of your connection with the *Right Now* nutrition spot, the supermarkets will be begging to stock it.'

Dee shook her head. 'Even if you were right it would take a huge investment to set it up; I would need to come up with a brand name, a logo, someone would have to design and make the packaging and then there's the small matter of production. I would need a commercial kitchen to produce food on that kind of scale and half a dozen chefs to help me and then there's the distribution – it's impossible.'

'Nothing is impossible. We'd need help on all of the design stuff and administration, admittedly, but I have an answer to the production problem.'

'Go on.'

'You could hire some people like that woman you interviewed, the one who moved down from Donegal to be near her daughter.'

'Vera.'

'And that other girl, Kitty, she has young children, doesn't she?'

'Yes, but where exactly would I put them, Lisa?' Dee said impatiently.

'That's just it, you wouldn't have to put them anywhere. They could work from home.' Lisa smiled triumphantly. 'You give them your recipes, supply them with the ingredients, tell them what quantities you want and voilà!'

'But what about the cost of their electricity and equipment and all that sort of thing?'

Lisa waved a hand expansively. 'You could incorporate all those costs into their salaries.'

Dee looked at her. She seemed to have an answer for everything. 'I don't know, Lisa, it's an enormous undertaking.'

'It would be a lot of work setting it up,' Lisa acknowledged, 'but once you were up and running it would be straightforward enough.'

'It's an interesting idea,' Dee agreed slowly, 'but I'd need a loan to get it off the ground and who's going to give me one?' She thought back to the last meeting with her bank manager and realized he'd laugh in her face if she came looking for money.

'Banks will be beating a path to your door to give you money, Dee, you're hot property now.'

Dee shook her head, smiling. 'Lisa, I've appeared on television three times for a matter of minutes, I'm hardly a celebrity.'

Lisa leaned forward and looked at her, her expression serious. 'You have made waves, Dee, with your stance on this whole labelling issue and Joe Public trusts you and listens to you. Why do you think these journalists keep phoning you for your opinions?'

It was true that hardly a day went by now without some member of the press calling for her views on some issue or other. Dee felt a flicker of excitement stir deep within her. 'I suppose it wouldn't cost me anything to look into it a bit more.'

Lisa grinned triumphantly. 'It wouldn't cost at all! And now that I'm a single woman again I can devote all my lonely evenings to helping you.'

Dee watched as the tears welled up again in Lisa's eyes.

'Oh, Dee,' she wailed, 'what am I going to do?'

Dee rocked her gently as she cried. 'You're going to make Happy Days the best crèche in North Dublin, remember?'

Lisa sniffed and nodded into Dee's shoulder.

'And when you're not busy with that,' Dee continued, 'you're going to help me set up my new business.'

Chapter 32

Peggy had finished cleaning the bathroom and was about to go back downstairs to make a sandwich for lunch when she had second thoughts. Neil was out and she hadn't been inside his bedroom in over a week; the floor must need hoovering and she should probably change his sheets. She didn't like to invade his privacy but if he couldn't be bothered to do his laundry, she reasoned, someone had to do it. She stripped the bed, tossed the dirty laundry down into the hall and then threw open his bedroom window to let some air in before going in search of clean sheets.

As she made up the bed, her eyes darted occasionally from the papers on his bedside table to the open suitcase in the corner. Would it be so terrible if she had a little rummage? All she wanted was some evidence that he was telling her the truth. Some little nugget that she could take to Dee to prove to her that Neil was trustworthy. Of course, if he would only talk to her she wouldn't dream of stooping to such behaviour but no matter how much she begged and pleaded, he told her nothing. In fact, he'd told Dee more than he'd told her.

Peggy's eyes filled up and she quickly wiped them on her sleeve. Neil had never confided in her before, why would he start now? Even when he was Sam's age he'd been a secretive little monkey and it would have concerned her more if he hadn't been so good-humoured and outgoing. She wondered now, though, if that character trait had had any bearing on his addiction and if there was something she could have done to change it. Maybe if his father hadn't died of a brain haemorrhage when he was only fourteen he wouldn't have strayed from the straight and narrow. Certainly, Mick would have stopped him going off around the world. But it was the very fact that she had lost her husband when they were still relatively young that had made Peggy realize she had to let her son go. Life was too short and she wanted him to experience it to the full. She loved getting the postcards every month – although she knew it was Dee who sent them – from exotic places and she was happy that he was doing it with such a lovely girl. She'd been proud of the way Neil had taken Dee under his wing. The young girl had been so shy and reserved when he had first brought her home but had positively blossomed as the relationship deepened. Peggy had had her doubts about Dee giving up her college place to go travelling and she had understood why Pauline was concerned that Dee was squandering her inheritance, but she had never doubted that Neil loved the girl or that he would take good care of her.

Peggy slumped down on to the freshly made bed, letting the tears run unheeded down her cheeks. She had felt physical pain when she found out what had happened out in Greece and though he was her son and she loved him, she found it hard to come to terms with what Neil had done. It didn't help that he had always refused to discuss it with her.

'I've made my peace with Dee, Mum, and recompensed her and that's all that should concern you,' he'd told her, several times, but it wasn't enough for Peggy. She wanted him to tell her what had made him do such a terrible thing; what it was that had turned him from being a confident and happy young man into a deceitful, pathetic excuse for a man. She wanted him to talk to her about the gambling and to rely on her for support if he needed it. Again, he dismissed her entreaties, saying that it was all in the past and she shouldn't worry about it. But she did.

The first Peggy knew about the whole incident in Greece was when Pauline Fogarty, Dee's aunt, had made a brief but extremely angry phone call the night after Dee got home. It wasn't until after Sam was born that Dee gave her the full history of Neil's downward spiral into addiction. It had been hard to hear but after the long silence, Peggy had welcomed the information, feeling now she could at least help if ever Neil wanted her to.

He had called briefly soon after the break-up and had

merely told her that things hadn't worked out and that he was continuing his travels alone. When she'd questioned him about what Pauline had told her, he'd hung up.

When Peggy first found out about her son's behaviour she went through a variety of emotions. The first, predictably, had been denial, but as the days passed and Dee refused to talk to her, she began to realize it must be true. Then had come anger; how could her son have done such a thing? She had brought him up better than that! She hadn't had much to give him when it came to material things but she prided herself that she had given him her moral code and she was horrified and furious that he could turn out so badly. Then had come guilt; what had she done or, indeed, not done, that had resulted in him turning out this way? And why, if he was really dealing with an addiction and all that that entailed, had he not felt he could turn to her?

It was then that she'd phoned first the Samaritans and then Gamblers Anonymous. The people she had talked to in both organizations had been kind, informative and had given her the same advice; wait. Her son had a disease and it was impossible to help him until he was ready to be helped.

'I don't even know where he is!' she'd wailed.

'He'll probably come home when he reaches rock bottom,' she was told. 'You just need to be there for him when he does.'

After that, Peggy had borrowed books on the subject from the library, determined that when Neil eventually came back to her she would be fully equipped to help him but instead of the broken shell of a man that she'd been expecting, a prosperous and confident one had walked through her door, one who very politely informed her that he didn't need her help, it was 'sorted'.

That was what unnerved her most and stopped her from begging Dee to give him a chance. She would never say it aloud, but she wasn't quite sure she trusted Neil.

Wiping her eyes, Peggy stood up to go – it wouldn't do for him to find her in here – when her eyes came to rest on the papers by the bed. They were probably just bills, he certainly wasn't going to leave anything important lying around; he was almost obsessively secretive. She bent and strained to read the small print; her glasses were downstairs but she was afraid to go and fetch them in case Neil returned. Neither did she want to pick up the documents in case she put them back in the wrong order and he noticed. Since when, she thought tiredly, had she become so afraid of her own son?

The top document was, as she'd suspected, a bill. It was for seven hundred and eighty euros from a garage near the airport. She frowned. It seemed like too new a car to need a service and if anything had gone wrong with it, surely it would have been taken care of under warranty? She would think about that later when she had more time. She moved it slightly to one side so she could see the page underneath. The words made no sense to her, presumably it was Spanish. There was only one page left and it was slightly crumpled and, her pulse quickened, it was handwritten. The writing was small and untidy – definitely not Neil's – and Peggy struggled to make out the words, not even sure if they were actually in English.

She froze as she heard Neil's key in the door and jumping to her feet, she quickly smoothed down the bedspread and fixed the pages back the way she'd found them. She was standing in the doorway, trying to look composed when he reached the top of the stairs.

'What were you doing in my room?' he asked, frowning.

'And hello to you too,' she laughed.

'Mother?'

When had he stopped calling her Mam, she wondered? 'I was changing your sheets.'

He shot her a suspicious look and then brushed past her to go into the room.

'You're welcome,' she muttered, heading for the stairs.

'Sorry, Mam, thanks.'

She turned back to see him standing in the doorway looking slightly shamefaced.

She smiled. 'You're welcome. Neil—'

'Sorry, Mother, can't talk now, I have to make a call.'

'Sure, no problem.' She went downstairs and started to make some ham sandwiches for their lunch.

Every time she tried to get close, tried to talk to him, he just backed off, she thought, feeling frustrated. Sometimes, he had paperwork to do or he had a meeting to go to, or like now, he had an important call to make. Peggy sincerely hoped he was as busy as he made out and it was business and not gambling that was preoccupying him. She wondered if she would get another opportunity to look at that letter; if only she had read it first maybe she would have had time to make sense of it before he had interrupted her. And then there was the mystery of the bill from the car dealership; what on earth could it be for?

She wished she had someone she could ask; she cut the sandwiches with a little more force than was strictly necessary. She felt so alone and isolated; the only person she could really turn to was Dee and she couldn't do that; it would be the ultimate betrayal. There was her family and Mick's, all of whom were close but, despite that, she'd never told them about Neil's gambling problem. She told herself it was because she wanted to protect him but she knew that it was really because she felt embarrassed and ashamed. She understood it was an illness but she doubted that other people would believe that and so she bore her burden alone.

When Neil had come back she had called Gamblers

Anonymous again and asked the lovely man who answered if she could believe what her son was telling her.

'It's possible,' he had said cautiously, 'but I would advise you to be careful. Don't give him access to any of your bank accounts and if he asks you to invest in his business, don't.'

'It seems wrong to be suspicious of my own son,' she'd replied.

'You have to be.'

'Is it normal for addicts to be so secretive?'

'They are all very secretive when they're gambling for obvious reasons but when they start on the recovery process it's usually a huge relief to be able to talk about it. Perhaps he's just too embarrassed to tell you how bad things got. Is there anyone else he might talk to?'

Dee was the only one Peggy could think of and she told the counsellor the story and how Neil wanted to get to know his son.

'It would be good to get him to open up to her and, at some stage, even talk to his son about his addiction. But at the same time, and this goes for you too, you have to protect yourselves. It's up to him to prove to you that he's trustworthy again.'

Peggy set the sandwiches on the table, made some tea and then went to the door.

'Neil, lunch,' she called.

She was sitting at the table on her second sandwich by the time he joined her. 'The tea might be too strong for you.'

'It's fine,' he said, filling a mug. He grabbed three sandwiches and turned to leave.

'Couldn't we at least have lunch together?' Peggy asked. 'I hardly ever see you these days.'

He hesitated and then came to sit down. 'Sorry, but there's a lot involved in setting up a business.'

'So you've definitely decided to stay in Ireland,' she said, trying to keep her voice light and conversational.

'It's early days.'

'And if you did, would you sell the business in Spain?'

He frowned. 'I'd prefer not to, but Ireland is an expensive place so I may have no choice.'

Peggy stiffened. 'Could you not just get a loan?'

'Banks aren't very keen on lending money to someone who doesn't have a financial history in the country.'

'But surely your bank in Spain could vouch for you,' Peggy pressed.

'It's not that simple, Mother.' He shoved the last piece of sandwich into his mouth and stood up. 'Got to get back to work, thanks for lunch.'

'You're welcome.' Peggy watched him walk away and wished she didn't feel so suspicious. She needed more information, she decided, and as soon as he went out again she would be back in that bedroom.

She needed to know whether she could trust him. More importantly, she needed to know if he really deserved to know his son.

Chapter 33

The mystery of Sam's rash was cleared up the following week when Paula arrived for babysitting and went pale when Dee told her what had happened.

'Oh, God, Dee, I'm sorry, I think it was my fault.'

'But you don't have any pets, Paula.'

'No, but I was visiting my friend and she had just bought this new puppy. He curled up on my jacket and went asleep and though I brushed it when I get home, there could have been some hairs still on it. I am so sorry.'

Dee smiled and patted the young girl's shoulder. 'Don't worry about it, Paula, it's impossible to protect him from everything. I'm glad that the mystery has been cleared up, though, I hadn't a clue what it was that had triggered the rash and that's much more frustrating.' Dee pulled on her jacket and looked around for her handbag. 'I'm only going to the pub for a quick drink, Paula, so I shouldn't be long.'

'No problem.' Paula grinned. 'Is Conor taking you?'

'No, he isn't,' Dee said briefly. 'I'm going out with the girls.'

'Have a nice time, then.'

After Dee had run upstairs to say goodnight to her son, she let herself out of the front door and began the short walk to the pub. She wished Paula hadn't mentioned Conor as it had reminded her of exactly how miserable she was. It seemed, like Lisa, she had been dumped. When Conor hadn't returned her text after their night together, Dee had finally got up the courage to call him that night but he had been distant and after a few minutes of stilted conversation, Dee had made her excuses and hung up. He hadn't asked to see her again or made any comment about the previous night and she was completely confused and very frustrated. Now, almost a week later, he still hadn't been in touch and Dee realized he must have regretted their night together after all.

When she walked into the pub, Lisa and Lauren were already there, a bottle of white wine and three glasses in front of them.

'What's up?' Lauren asked, pouring her a glass. 'You look miserable.'

'It's Conor,' Lisa told her.

Dee shot her a warning look. 'We're not going to talk about boyfriends, now, are we, Lisa?'

Lisa smiled apologetically. 'No, we're here to talk about Dee Hewson Inc.'

'Yes, tell me more,' Lauren said, leaning forward.

'It's probably not an option,' Dee started. She had given a lot of thought to Lisa's idea and the more she thought, the more anxious she got.

'Oh, don't be so bloody defeatist,' Lisa told her and then, turning to Lauren, filled her in on her idea. 'I thought with your marketing experience, you might be able to help,' she said when she'd finished.

'Well?' Dee looked at Lauren expectantly.

'I think it's a great idea,' Lauren said enthusiastically.

'But it would cost a fortune to get it off the ground, wouldn't it?'

Lauren shrugged. 'It's been a while since I worked on a project like this so I'm not sure how much the costs have increased but I can easily find out. Your USP, of course, would be the fact that you're marketing fresh, home-cooked food.'

'USP?' Dee looked at her.

'Unique Selling Point,' Lisa said with a grin, 'even I know that.'

'The fact that you are now a minor celebrity certainly helps and will open doors with both the banks and the supermarkets. I like Lisa's idea about this being a cottage industry type of operation. It will keep the costs down and convince people that this really is about homemade food. I also think you should go for very simple, natural packaging.'

'We'd need advice on all of that,' Dee told her, 'I don't know the first thing about what type of packaging is necessary to prolong shelf-life. And that's another problem. How do we decide on things like "best before dates"?'

'There will be guidelines from the government departments for that sort of thing,' Lauren assured her confidently. 'There's a lot of help out there for new businesses, you just have to know where to look.'

'And I don't.' Dee looked glum.

Lauren winked. 'But I do.'

'But you have the twins to mind, how can you possibly help?'

'It will be a welcome break,' Lauren assured her, 'my brain is beginning to seize up and the twins have two grannies and three aunties queuing up to mind them.'

'And you really think it's a good idea?' Dee asked, beginning to feel excited.

Lauren's eyes sparkled. 'I think it's a bloody great idea!'

'So where do we start?' Lisa asked.

'Hang on a minute,' Dee put up a hand, 'we need to agree on something before we go any further. If you two are going to help get this business up and running, you have to be a part of it. You should be my partners.'

'No, that wouldn't be fair,' Lisa said. 'You're the one who'll be doing all the real work.'

'But I'm not going to let you help me for nothing,' Dee said.

'You can hire me as a consultant,' Lauren told her. 'I could do with the extra money and it would be a nice way to wean me back into life as a business woman.'

'That would be fine, except I don't know exactly what I need you to do,' Dee admitted.

Lauren laughed. 'Why don't I put together a proposal and an estimate and we'll take it from there?'

Lisa's eyes widened. 'Ooh, you'll be sorry you mentioned money, Dee!'

Dee shook her head. 'No, I'd prefer to do this on a proper business footing from the start. I haven't a clue how to go about any of this and I'd hate to have to depend on a stranger to help me.'

'Well I'll be the lackey and you just tell me what to do,' Lisa told her. 'And you can pay me with food. Now that Ger's gone I have no intention of wasting any of my time cooking ever again.'

Dee laughed. 'That's a deal!'

'What are you going to call it?' Lauren asked.

'It has to incorporate her name,' Lisa said.

Dee made a face but Lauren nodded her agreement. 'It would be madness not to, Dee.'

'I suppose.'

'Dee Hewson's Food,' Lisa suggested. 'Or just Dee's Delights?'

'That sounds more like a naughty lingerie shop,' Lauren drawled.

'Or a massage parlour,' Dee agreed.

'How about Dee's Delicacies?' Lauren said.

'Not bad,' Lisa admitted.

'I quite like that,' Dee said.

'Good, Dee's Delicacies it is for the moment.' Lisa held up the empty bottle. 'Can we have a drink to celebrate?'

'I'll get them, it's the least I can do,' Dee said, standing up. 'Thanks, girls, I wouldn't ever dream of doing something like this without you.'

Going to the bar, she ordered a bottle of champagne.

'What's the occasion?' the barman asked curiously.

'Life, Eamon, just life,' Dee said unwilling to reveal her plans just yet. If she told the barman it would be all around the town in no time.

After some rummaging, he located a dusty ice bucket, filled it with ice and brought it, the champagne and three clean glasses to the table.

'Champagne!' Lisa clapped her hands in delight.

'What do you say, ladies, will I give it a shake?' Eamon gave them a lewd wink.

'Only if you're going to pay for it,' Lauren retorted with a withering look.

After he'd poured the champagne and left them, Dee raised her glass to her friends.

'Thank you for your faith in me,' she said feeling slightly tearful.

'To Dee's Delicacies,' Lisa said.

'May it make the top one hundred companies list

within five years!' Lauren joked, but there was a determined glint in her eye.

The pub door opened letting in a blast of cold wind and the three girls looked up.

'Oh, no,' Dee muttered.

'So, is it on or off?' Lisa whispered out of the corner of her mouth.

'Wish I knew,' Dee muttered back.

'Conor! Come and join us!' Lauren called with a wide smile.

Conor hesitated a moment before coming to stand by their table. 'Hi.' He nodded to each of the women, his eyes coming to rest somewhere to the left of Dee's chair.

'Champagne, very nice. What's the occasion?'

'We just felt like it,' Dee said quickly, her eyes flashing a warning as Lauren opened her mouth to contradict. 'Are you meeting someone?' she asked politely.

He nodded. 'Dad, he should be here any minute.'

'You're welcome to join us,' she offered half-heartedly. He looked so obviously uncomfortable in her company that it made her want to crawl into a corner and die.

'Thanks,' he said, equally polite, 'but we're going into the back lounge to watch a match. I'd better go and get a couple of pints in; it will be starting in a minute.'

Dee smiled brightly. 'Oh, right, well, enjoy.'

'Yeah, you too.' He nodded at Lisa and Lauren. 'See you later.'

'What the hell was all that about?' Lauren asked

when he was out of hearing distance. 'Have you two broken up?'

'Broken up, made up and broken up again,' Lisa told her. 'I think. I can't keep up at this stage.'

'What happened?' Lauren asked Dee.

'She doesn't know,' Lisa continued before her friend could get a word in, 'and she's too bloody pig-headed and proud to ask.'

'Lisa, will you please leave it?'

'Well, I'm sorry, but I think it's really stupid.'

'You don't know the full story.'

Lisa snorted. 'Neither do you! She was too drunk to remember what they rowed about,' she told Lauren.

'Lisa!' Dee hissed.

Lauren smiled slowly. 'The first time or the second?'

Dee sighed. 'The second. I've tried to find out but he's just giving me the cold shoulder.'

'You should tell him the truth, shouldn't she, Lauren?'

Lauren shrugged. 'It would be a lot simpler, if you want to get back with him, that is.'

'Of course I do, but he's not interested, he's made that very clear,' Dee said glumly.

'I wouldn't agree with that. I mean you did say he was very passionate the last night—'

'Lisa, will you please shut up? ' Dee muttered.

Lauren shrugged her slender shoulders. 'Look, if you don't feel you can confide in your new business partner, that's fine.'

'Oh, Lauren, please don't be like that. Honestly, there's nothing to tell, Lisa is just winding me up, aren't you?' She shot her best friend a stony glance.

'Yes, sorry.' Lisa nodded. 'It's just that she and Conor are so good together I think it's a shame if they break up.'

'Is it because he hasn't asked you to marry him, is that it?' Lauren asked.

'No! I have absolutely no interest in marrying him or anyone else!' Dee said louder than she intended.

'Evening.'

Dee looked up to see that Ronan had just walked through the door and was standing looking down at her, an uncertain smile on his face.

'Oh, hi, Ronan.' She smiled weakly. 'Conor's in the back bar.'

'Great, thank you, see you later maybe.'

'Shit.' Dee glared at her two friends. 'Now that I have been totally humiliated, do you mind if we talk about something else?'

Lauren rolled her eyes and turned to Lisa. 'What about you and Ger, any hope of you two getting back together?'

'God forbid.'

Dee shot her a look of disbelief. Lisa had been crying on and off all week.

Lauren raised her eyebrows. 'Seriously?'

'Absolutely,' Lisa said, ignoring Dee. 'Ger has done me a favour.'

'Well, for what it's worth, I agree,' Lauren told her.

'Me too,' Dee said and smiled to show Lisa that they were friends again. 'You must know that you were way too good for the guy.'

'Do you know, I'm beginning to think you're right,' Lisa admitted. 'And the sad thing is that I probably would have married him if he'd asked.' She shuddered. 'What a mistake that would have been. But I'm turning over a completely new leaf. No more men for me, I'm going to concentrate on my business. I'm also going to get fit.' She grinned at them. 'I've joined the gym.'

'You hate the gym,' Lauren reminded her.

'I know, but now I have all this free time in the evenings I decided I had to do something proactive with it. If I sit home alone thinking, I'll just get depressed, feel sorry for myself and eat.'

'I think it's a great idea.' Dee patted her arm.

'But it's still as boring as I remember,' Lisa admitted.

'You should go to a class,' Lauren told her, 'that's what I did after the twins were born. It's more fun, you don't really feel like you're exercising at all.'

Lisa eyed Lauren's svelte figure. 'Is that all you did to lose weight?'

Lauren laughed. 'No, I pushed a double pram back and forth to the park and the shops and ran up and down the stairs a million times a day.'

Lisa sighed. 'That would do it.'

'I tell you what, Lisa, you go to the gym and I'll cook

you low-fat meals that are so gorgeous you won't even know they're low-fat,' Dee promised.

'Really?' Lisa brightened.

'Really,' Dee said, standing up. 'Now I must go to the loo.'

Lauren winked at Lisa. 'The loo that just happens to be in the back lounge?'

'That's hardly my fault,' Dee pointed out archly, annoyed that she was so transparent.

When she opened the door into the other lounge, she tried to have a quick look around without being too obvious. There were quite a few people in the darkened room and she thought she could make out Ronan's head but she couldn't see Conor. Feeling disappointed, she made her way along the back wall towards the toilets. As she pushed open the door she collided with someone coming the other way.

'Oh, I'm sorry – oh!'

'Hi, Dee.' Conor stepped back so she could get through the narrow doorway.

'Hi, Conor. How are you?' Dee smiled nervously, conscious of how close he was and how tall he seemed when she was wearing trainers.

'Fine. How's Sam?'

'Yeah, he's okay, the rash healed up quite quickly thank goodness.'

'Rash?' He frowned. 'What rash?'

'Oh, right, I forgot you didn't know. The morning

after we' – she felt her cheeks grow hot – 'met, he got a rash on his arm but it's fine now.' She peered up at him from under her eyelashes. 'Have I done something to annoy you, Conor?'

'Sorry?'

She sighed. 'Look, I know I said something to upset you that night, but I'm afraid I don't know what it was. I'd had quite a lot to drink at Vi's.'

He looked at her, frowning. 'So you don't know what you said to me?'

She shook her head. ''Fraid not. Do you want to tell me?'

He smiled slightly. 'It doesn't really matter.'

'It mattered enough for you not to call me,' she retorted. 'And when I phoned you, you were really off with me.'

'I'm sorry, I feel a bit stupid now.'

'Why?' she moved closer and put her hands on his chest.

'Because I forgot that you'd been drinking.' He frowned again. 'I hope you don't feel that I took advantage of you.'

She smiled. 'I do and I loved every minute of it.'

The door opened and they sprang apart, grinning at each other like school kids as they waited for the woman to pass. She shot them a suspicious look before going into the ladies'.

Conor pulled her close and she could feel his breath

on her cheek. 'Are you going to be here for much longer?' he murmured.

'Not long. You?' She licked her lips.

'The match should be over in about an hour. Were you planning an early night?'

He held her waist with his hands and slid his thumbs under her shirt to stroke her skin lightly.

Dee closed her eyes briefly. 'I think that would be a good idea,' she murmured.

He straightened, so that he could look at her, his eyes dark. 'Want some company?'

'Oh, yes.' She reached up and pulled his mouth down to hers and wouldn't let him go even when the woman pushed past them again, tutting loudly.

'Oh, God,' Conor groaned when they finally pulled apart. 'I hope it doesn't go to extra time!'

Dee laughed. 'You'd better go before Lisa or Lauren come looking for me.'

'Would it matter?' he asked.

'No, but it's kind of exciting having a secret assignation.' She kissed him one more time and then pushed him towards the door. 'I'll leave the back door open. Come straight up.' And blowing him a kiss, she disappeared into the ladies'.

Chapter 34

'So why did you cut your hair?' Conor asked as they lay in bed, drinking beer and talking quietly. They had a lot of catching up to do.

'I felt like a change.'

'Or did you do it because you were annoyed with me?'

'Maybe,' she admitted, moving closer and kissing his chest. He'd always loved her hair and hated it when she got it cut. 'Stupid, huh?'

He sighed. 'We both were. Still, sometimes it takes a break to make you realize what's important.'

She sat back against the pillow so she could look into his face. 'What do you mean?'

'I mean we have something really special and we nearly threw it all away.'

'Twice,' Dee pointed out.

He winced. 'Yes, twice. Do you think we can try to be more careful in future?'

She smiled. 'We can try.'

He was silent for a moment and then he took her hand. 'Can I ask you something?'

He kept his eyes down so she couldn't read his expression. 'Of course.' She squeezed his hand in encouragement.

'Do you want Neil back?'

'No, Conor, of course I don't!'

He looked up, his eyes searching hers. 'Are you sure about that?'

Dee sighed. 'Yes, I am.'

'But you loved him once.'

'Yes, I did, but that was more than five years ago. We could never move on from what happened back then and I wouldn't want to. I don't believe he would either. He wouldn't have even come to see me if it wasn't for Sam.'

'Idiot,' Conor muttered. 'So are you going to let him meet Sam?'

'I suppose I should.'

'But do you want to?' Conor asked gently.

Dee thought about it for a second. 'I just want to make Sam happy. It would be wonderful if he could have a special relationship with his father but how do I know I can trust Neil not to hurt him? I've done a lot of research into gambling and I know it's a disease and I must make allowances for that but I have to put Sam first.'

Conor nodded firmly. 'Of course you do.'

'The problem is', she continued, 'even though he might be okay now, there's no guarantee that he will stay that way.'

'No.'

'It's so hard, Conor, I don't know what to do for the best. Peggy says—'

'Peggy?' Conor frowned. 'What's she got to do with it?'

Dee sighed. 'Oh, God, I'd forgotten you didn't know about any of that.' She sat up and swung her legs out of bed. 'I'll get you some more beer, it's a long story.'

'No,' he glanced at his watch, 'I've an early start. Put on some coffee and I'll get dressed.'

'I think that's everything,' Dee said, standing up to put on the kettle again.

Conor was still looking at her. 'I can't believe you've kept this to yourself all these years.'

'I had to, Conor. I couldn't risk someone letting it slip to Sam.'

He looked at her. 'Don't you know that I would never repeat anything you said to me in confidence?'

'Yes; yes, of course I do, but you must remember that this all happened before we met. By the time you and I got together, I had been keeping it a secret for so long that I suppose I began to believe it myself. It wasn't until Neil returned that Peggy's position in Sam's life came into question.'

He shook his head. 'You're starting up a new business, your cousin is really Sam's granny, is there anything else I should know?'

She grinned. 'No, how about you?'

'Me?' he chuckled. 'I'm an open book, what you see is what you get.'

'I don't know if I'd agree with that,' she said lightly, setting a fresh mug of coffee in front of him.

He held out his hands, his eyes innocent. 'What?'

'You are such a closed book,' she told him, sitting down opposite him and pulling her knees up to her chin. 'I know hardly anything about your student years or your time in Clare. If it wasn't for your mother boasting about your achievements, I wouldn't know anything at all!'

He shrugged. 'You know me, Dee, I'm just not the chatty sort.'

She kept her head down and said nothing.

'What?' he prompted. 'Come on, Dee, out with it. I refuse to break up with you again.'

She smiled. 'I suppose I've always wondered why you came back. You were pretty settled in Clare, weren't you?'

He shook his head. 'No, not really. I was an employee on a farm and it was always my goal to buy my own place.'

'But why not a place down there where your friends were?' she persisted. Now that she'd finally got him talking, she was determined to find out all she could.

'Mum and Dad had moved back here by then and it seemed like the obvious thing to do. I am their only child,' he pointed out, 'and they're not getting any younger.'

Dee watched him silently. That made sense, she had to admit. 'So there was no woman you were running away from or that had broken your heart?'

'Would that bother you?' he said, looking pleased with himself.

She made a face. 'No! I was just curious. You just never talk about your time down in Clare.'

He looked surprised. 'I do.'

'You told me about the cattle and the pigs and the fact that Aidan's mother made the best apple tart you'd ever eaten—'

'She still does,' he assured her.

She ignored him. 'But you never told me what you got up to when you weren't working.'

'Slept, went to the pub,' he shrugged, 'pretty much what I do now.'

'Oh, Conor,' she said with a weary sigh.

'What is it you want me to say?' he asked reasonably.

'I suppose I'd just like it if you shared a bit more.'

He muffled a snort.

'What?'

'Nothing.' He bit his lip.

She scowled. 'Go home.'

He stood up, laughing softly, and pulled her to her feet.

She cuddled into his embrace, reaching up to cup his face in her hands. 'You look tired.'

'And whose fault is that?'

She grinned. 'I didn't hear you complaining.'

'Nor will you.' He looked into her eyes, his expression suddenly serious. 'Thank you for telling me everything.'

She shrugged. 'I would have sooner but—'

'I was too busy being a moody bastard.'

She smiled. 'I was to blame too. It's just been such a crazy time I don't really know whether I'm coming or going. Do you think I'm mad even considering this business venture?'

'I think you'd be mad not to. It's a brilliant idea. Lisa is a very clever girl.' He shook his head in wonder. 'I still can't believe that Ger dumped *her*. Still, I always said he was a pillock.'

'She was devastated but talking to her tonight, she seems to be coming to terms with it.'

Conor hugged her one last time. 'I've got to go and you should get some sleep.'

'I will.' She walked with him to the door, pulling her dressing gown tighter around her as he opened it and cold air rushed in.

'I'll call you tomorrow,' he promised.

As Dee went back to bed, a dreamy grin on her face, she realized that she still hadn't found out any details about his love life at all. 'Bugger,' she murmured, climbing into bed and falling into a deep and dreamless sleep.

Chapter 35

The next few weeks sped by as Dee, Lisa and Lauren worked on their new project. Lauren was making contacts, talking to designers and, together with Dee, drafting a business plan. Dee still thought it was a waste of time approaching her own bank manager but Lauren suspected he might have a change of heart when he saw what Dee had achieved over the last couple of months.

'But we'll approach a couple of other banks too,' she told Dee. While they worked on that, Lisa talked to the chefs who had impressed Dee most to see if they were interested in working from home. She also went back to the agency Dee had originally talked to and told them of the change in their requirements. The consultant was very optimistic that it would be easy to find people who wanted to work from home.

Each night when Sam was in bed and Conor sat reading or watching television, Dee would work at the kitchen table coming up with suitable recipes. She had got great help and advice from Polly Underwood and April, the chef she had met on her first *Right Now* show. Also, the various government agencies involved in new businesses and food legislation had bent over backwards to help.

'I had no idea there was so much involved in starting up a new business,' she had confessed to Lauren, 'but I'm very impressed at how much help there is out there.'

'You're a future employer and tax-payer, it's in their interests to help you,' Lauren had pointed out.

'Cynic.'

'Realist,' Lauren had retorted.

Conor had been wonderful, spending lots of time with Sam and giving Dee plenty of opportunity to work on her new venture. He'd even suggested, tentatively, that maybe Sam could spend a night at the farm. The idea frankly terrified Dee. Apart from the fact that Boxer wandered in and out of the house at will, there were traces of the animal everywhere.

'You don't trust me, do you?' Conor had accused her.

'I do, Conor, you know I do, it's just I don't think you realize how hard it is to protect him. Look at that episode with Paula.'

'I do realize,' he'd insisted, 'and I will do whatever's necessary to keep him safe, but if it means that you would just sit here worrying yourself sick then there's no point.'

Dee knew how much Sam would love it and that it would be a huge display of her trust in Conor, so she'd agreed. 'But you'll have to do a major clean-up first,' she'd said, only half joking, 'and we don't tell Sam until the day or he'll have driven me mad talking about it.'

Conor had seemed genuinely delighted and assured her she wouldn't recognize the place when he was finished with it. They'd agreed on the Friday of the following week and Dee knew what she had to do on her night off. It was time to see Neil and put him out of his misery.

His patience had grown thin over the last couple of weeks and he had called Dee a number of times. Things came to a head when she went to the supermarket one morning and found him waiting for her when she came out. 'How did you know I was here?' she'd said angrily, looking around to see if anyone was watching them.

'I followed you,' he admitted.

'What the hell are you playing at? Do you think I'm going to let you near my son if you start stalking me?'

'I'm not stalking you, Dee.' He held up his hands. 'Look, I'm sorry. I just need to know, one way or the other, what's going to happen. All this hanging around is doing my head in.'

She sighed, wearily. 'I do realize that it must be hard for you, Neil, but it's not exactly easy for me either. Look, I've decided to let you meet him.'

Neil's face lit up. 'Really?'

She smiled. 'Yes, but before you get too excited, it's not going to be today or tomorrow. I need to work out the best way to handle this. I'll need to prepare him, but also, you have to understand, there will be conditions.'

'Of course! Oh, Dee, I am so grateful. You won't regret this, I promise you.'

'I hope I don't.'

'So what happens next?' he asked, trying but failing to stop smiling.

'We need to sit down and talk about what we're going to tell him; you, me and your mother.'

'My mother?' He frowned.

'Yes, Neil. She's going to go from being his aunt to his granny overnight so she needs to be involved.'

'Right, okay. So, when?'

'I don't know yet, I'll call you.'

Neil looked at her impatiently. 'Please don't leave it too long, Dee,' he begged.

'I won't. Now I have to get back; I'll call you. And Neil?'

'Yes?'

'Don't follow me ever again or the whole deal is off.'

'I won't,' he promised. 'Thanks, Dee.'

As soon as she was in the car, Dee phoned Peggy to tell her of her decision. Her words didn't get the reaction she was expecting. 'Peggy? Are you okay?' she'd asked finally.

'Yes, sorry, I'm just in the middle of something and it's hard to talk.'

'Sorry, I won't keep you but will you meet me next Wednesday? I'd like to talk to you before we meet with Neil.'

There was a moment's pause and then came Peggy's voice again, slightly stronger. 'Yes, Dee, I'll meet you.'

After they'd agreed a time and place, Dee had rung off but she couldn't shake the feeling that Peggy hadn't really wanted to meet. Nor had she seemed that excited about the prospect of Neil finally getting to meet his son. Perhaps she was nervous about how Sam would take the news that Peggy was not a distant cousin but his granny. Yes, she decided, that was probably it.

Dee wasn't so worried any more, thanks to Vi Valentine's words of wisdom. She believed her relationship with her son was strong enough to withstand the situation and that she had the strength to deal with it and with Neil if necessary.

Dee stood in the kitchen, her hands in a bowl kneading bread, her thoughts miles away. The only time she really got to think these days was when she was alone in the car or baking bread. This morning, her thoughts had turned to Vi Valentine and her own revelations about her past. Dee thought it was an incredibly sad story and she was amazed that something so terrible had happened to such a seemingly happy person. It was a testament to her courage and strength that she had survived, never mind become a talented artist.

Though they had met up a couple of times since that night, they hadn't revisited the subject and, Dee realized, they probably never would. But there was no doubt that their bond had been strengthened by the exchange and Dee was glad of that. Vi had become a good friend and Dee was grateful that she'd come home to Banford. It couldn't have been easy, the town must have many painful memories for Vi. It must be something about the air here, Dee mused; we all come back eventually. Ronan, Conor, Vi, and Dee herself, of course.

She couldn't escape Banford and her family home quick enough all those years ago but now she was back and happy and she didn't think she'd ever leave again. She couldn't help thinking that her mother would be glad with how things had worked out.

'Dee?'

She started as she heard Martha call her. She quickly wiped her hands on her apron and went to the door. 'Yeah?'

'The staff loo seems to be blocked again.'

Dee sighed. 'Okay, I'll ask Conor to have a look at it.' This happened from time to time and Conor could usually sort it but she knew she would need a plumber sooner rather than later. She might have come to grips with this house emotionally but there was no doubt that it was a financial nightmare.

As she was ahead of schedule, Dee decided to call up to the farm on her way to the café. Perhaps if she bribed Conor with some muffins, he'd be more willing to get to work with his plunger.

She went in to Lisa to tell her she was off and to steal a quick hug from her son. As usual, he was engrossed in play; Tom, like glue, at his side.

'What are you making?' she asked as they were surrounded by Lego.

'A rocket,' Tom told her, not even looking up.

'Very impressive.' She crouched down and pulled an unwilling Sam into her arms.

'Mum!' he groaned.

'Sorry!' She grinned at Lisa and stood up. 'I'll be stopping off at the supermarket on my way back, do you need anything?'

'No, I don't think so.'

They walked out into the hall together and stopped outside the dining-room door. They could hear Yvonne singing nursery rhymes with the children inside and couldn't resist peaking in.

'How's she doing?' Dee whispered.

'Really well,' Lisa enthused, 'I don't know how we managed without her.'

'She seems very sweet-natured.'

'She is, but she's good fun too.'

Dee softly closed the door again. 'I'd better get going. I want to drop by the farm and ask Conor to fix the loo.'

Lisa rolled her eyes. 'Any excuse.'

'True,' Dee admitted, laughing.

Twenty minutes later she was stepping out of her car and breathing in the sharp morning air. It was still a little cool for April but there was a definite air of spring about the place. Conor's farm was only a ten-minute drive from the town but when she came out here she felt as if she were in the middle of nowhere and loved the feeling of peace that descended on her.

She wandered around the side of the house, but there was no sign of Conor or Boxer so she called him on his mobile.

'Hey, you.'

'Hi. Where are you?' Dee asked.

'At home.'

'Yes, but where? I'm in the yard.'

'Oh, have you brought me something nice for my elevenses?'

She grinned. 'I might have.'

'I'm in the bottom field, give me five minutes.'

Dee hung up and walked down the track. Within seconds she could hear the tractor's engine and shortly after, the vehicle rounded the bend slowly and she waved. A brown figure charged ahead like an Exocet missile and as she braced herself for Boxer's welcome she was glad she was wearing the old duffle coat that she kept in the boot especially for her visits to the farm. 'Hello, Boxer,' she said, patting him lightly and then firmly lifting him off her. 'Down, boy, good dog.'

Rummaging in her pocket, she found the biscuits she'd brought for him and threw them across the track. Boxer scampered after them and she hoisted herself up on the fence to wait for Conor.

She sighed happily as she looked around her at the rolling hills, a checkerboard of browns and greens dotted with sheep that looked more like little clouds from this distance and in the fields nearer, the magnificent Aberdeen Angus cattle that were Conor's pride and joy.

It would be good for Sam to spend some time up here with Conor. He was surrounded by too many women mollycoddling him all of the time. Still, now he was getting older that would all change. He would start school in September and that would give him a new feeling of independence. While she was nervous about school from a health perspective she had no such concerns about her son fitting in. The plus about growing up with a crèche in his home was that Sam was well used to being surrounded by people of all ages and he'd always seemed to love the interaction. Also, his best friend Tom would be starting school, too, so they would be able to support each other as they adjusted to the new routine.

'Hello there.' Conor pulled up beside her, switched off the engine and swung himself down. 'This is a nice surprise,' he murmured pulling her to him.

Dee put her arms around him and kissed him. 'I can't stay long,' she said, finally drawing back with regret.

'Are you sure?' he said, pulling her back for another kiss.

Dee laughed and pushed him away. 'You'll have to settle for a muffin.' She held up the bag she was carrying

'Fair enough,' he agreed, grabbing the bag off her and shoving a cake into his mouth.

She shook her head, pretending disgust. 'You'd better not eat like that when you're minding my son. I don't want him learning bad manners.'

'It's a compliment to your wonderful cooking,' Conor assured her, leading the way into the kitchen and putting on the kettle.

Dee stopped in the doorway and looked around her.

He looked back at her, expectantly. 'Well? What do you think?'

Dee realized that Conor was waiting for her reaction but she was lost for words. The faded three-piece suite that Conor had inherited from his parents was gone and had been replaced by a dark green leather armchair and a two-seater sofa. The marked, brown lino that curled at the edges had been removed and the floorboards polished and now a large, brightly patterned rug lay in front of the stone fireplace. The rest of the kitchen was the same but cleaner and, Dee realized, completely free of clutter. Conor had always used the kitchen table as a makeshift desk and the worktops as a filing cabinet but there wasn't as much as an envelope in sight. The final touches were a mug tree with six colourful mugs, flanked by a gleaming new stainless-steel kettle and toaster, and brightly striped curtains adorned the large window.

'Well?' Conor repeated impatiently.

'It's fantastic,' she said, hugging him quickly before crossing the room to touch the soft leather of the armchair. 'Beautiful.' She sat down and wriggled into the seat. 'It's all beautiful.'

'I thought the leather would be a healthier option and the rug is polyester; it can be shoved into the washing machine. Dad helped me with the floor and Mum bought the other bits and pieces.'

Dee felt her eyes fill up. 'Did you do all of this just because Sam's coming to spend one night?'

He smiled. 'Well, I was hoping that it might be a more regular occurrence and that maybe sometimes his mum would come too. Let's go upstairs; I want to show you his room.'

'His room?' she echoed, following him upstairs. There were three bedrooms upstairs; Conor slept in the largest, kept the second as a guest room and the third was piled high with junk. But now he was leading her past his room and past the guest room and to the door of that very room. He grinned at Dee before throwing open the door with a flourish. 'Ta da!'

Dee stepped in and stared around her at the freshly painted blue walls, the Star Wars border, the matching duvet and curtains and the polished floor boards. 'Conor, I don't know what to say,' she said as tears stung her eyes.

'Do you think he'll like it?'

'I think he'll love it. What little boy wouldn't?'

'I was going to get a football duvet but I wasn't sure which team—'

She put a finger to his lips. 'It's perfect, Conor. I am completely in shock. How on earth did you get the time to do all of this?'

He shrugged modestly. 'It didn't take that long. I ripped up the lino and threw the suite out in the yard the night you told me about Paula bringing the dog hair into the house.' He shook his head, his face grim. 'I'd never forgive myself if he got sick while he was here with me.'

Dee stared at him, completely lost for words. How had she not realized how much this man loved her son? How had she ever doubted him? She turned away and crossed over to the window.

'What is it, what's wrong?' He came to stand beside her and slid an arm around her shoulders.

'I just don't know why you bother with me,' she sniffed. 'I don't deserve you.'

He grinned. 'Does that mean I can have more than just muffins for elevenses?'

'No, sorry' – she looked at her watch – 'oh, crikey, look at the time!' Dee pushed past him, allowing herself just one last glance at the beautiful little room. 'I'm sorry, but I really have to go, I have your dad's delivery in the car.'

'Phone him and tell him you're running late,' he urged, pulling her back and kissing her.

She returned his kiss hungrily before pushing him away and running downstairs. 'Sorry, can't let my biggest customer down.'

'You're no fun,' he said, following her.

She laughed. 'I am, and I'll prove it to you if you want to come over tonight.'

'You're on.'

'It's all really beautiful, Conor,' she said again, waving a hand around her as they walked back through the kitchen.

'And I'm not finished yet,' he told her. 'I'm converting the back room into a proper office; I've already bought a desk and a filing cabinet and I've ordered a new PC and printer. And,' his eyes twinkled down at her, 'my new king-size bed is being delivered tomorrow.'

'Have you won the lottery or something?' she asked as they went outside to her car.

'You could say that,' he said lightly.

She whirled to face him. 'You're kidding!'

'I am, but I have had a bit of luck. I'll fill you in tonight.'

She groaned as she climbed into her car and wound down the window. 'Conor, you can't make me wait until then.'

'You'd better hurry, your customer will be waiting.'

'You are so cruel,' she grumbled, starting the car and putting it into reverse.

He laughed. 'I know.'

She smiled up at him. 'Thank you so much, Conor.'

'For what?'

'For the room, the sofa, the floor.' She shrugged, her eyes shining. 'It's all amazing, thank you.'

He ducked his head in to kiss her. 'You're welcome.'

She was still smiling when she arrived at the café. Seeing Ronan through the door, restocking his shelves, Dee set down her load on the counter, went into the bookshop and, throwing her arms around him, planted a noisy kiss on his cheek.

'Oh! What was that for?' he asked, putting his hand to his face. 'Not that I'm complaining!'

'I've just been up at the farm,' Dee told him.

'Ah!' He smiled. 'It looks well, doesn't it?'

'It looks marvellous and I believe you had a lot to do with it.'

'Not at all,' he said modestly, 'Conor did the lion's share and Julia did all the shopping – no hardship there.'

'You all did the most wonderful job, I'm really touched.'

'Has the little lad seen it yet?'

She shook her head. 'No, I just popped in to ask Conor— oh, damn.'

'What?'

'I went up to the farm to ask Conor if he would bring his tools over later and fix the loo but, in all the excitement, I completely forgot.'

'Are you stuck? Do you want me to come and take a look at it now?'

'Not at all, we can use the one upstairs, don't worry.'

'Well, have you time for a cup of tea?' Ronan asked, leading the way back into the café.

'Nope,' she grinned, 'but I'll have one anyway.'

'Zoe? Can we have one tea and one coffee, please?'

Zoe smiled. 'Hi, Dee, how's it going?'

Dee sat up on a high stool. 'Busy but good, how about you?'

'Great, thanks.'

'Zoe's started a cookery course,' Ronan told her, leaning against the counter.

'No, really?' Dee looked from Ronan back to Zoe.

'Do you think I'm mad?' Zoe smiled.

'No, not at all, I think it's a great idea. What do you want to do when you're finished?'

Zoe shot Ronan a sidelong glance. 'I'm not sure . . .'

Ronan chuckled. 'It's okay, Zoe, I was going to tell Dee about our plans today anyway.'

'Plans?' Dee eyed him curiously.

'Yes, well, as you're going on to bigger and better things, I thought it was time I made alternative catering arrangements.'

Dee looked horrified. 'Oh, Ronan, I hope you don't

think I was planning to leave you high and dry; I would never do that!'

He patted her arm. 'Of course I know that, Dee, calm down. But I think – and young Zoe here agrees with me – that this new business of yours is going to be a lot more successful than you think. We see first hand every day how highly the customers think of your food and the prospect of being able to prepare something like it in their own home will be very attractive.'

'But Ronan, I'll have other chefs working for me, I'll still be able to cook for the café.'

'Well, that would be great in the short-term but we're hoping that Zoe will be able to take some of the load off your shoulders.'

'I'm not trying to steal your job,' Zoe said hurriedly, 'it will probably be ages before I'm good enough to go it alone.'

Dee nodded silently.

'Oh, please, say something.' Zoe looked at her anxiously.

'I think it's a great idea,' Dee told them.

'You do?' Ronan looked relieved.

'Yes, it's perfect. We can continue on as before but as Zoe settles in to her new position, she can try a few of my dishes from scratch.'

'That might take a while,' Zoe warned Ronan.

'It won't take that long,' Dee assured him before looking back at Zoe and smiling. 'You're a natural. I don't know why we didn't think of this before.'

The bell went in the shop and Ronan stood up, taking his mug with him. 'Must go, Dee, but I'm glad we've had this chat.'

'Me too,' she assured him.

'If Conor can't help you with your plumbing, give me a shout.'

She laughed. 'Thanks, I will. So,' she turned back to Zoe, 'you're going to be a chef.'

'I'm really looking forward to it, Dee, but I'm a bit nervous at the same time.'

'Don't worry, we won't throw you in at the deep end. And remember, even if you have the occasional disaster at the start, my freezer is only minutes away.'

Zoe laughed. 'I'll remember that.'

'I'd better get going.' Dee drained her mug. 'See you tomorrow.' After waving goodbye to Ronan, she walked out of the restaurant with a smile on her face. All in all it was turning out to be rather a good day. On impulse, she went into the florist across the road, bought a small bunch of white roses, and walked the short distance to Ronan and Julia's house.

'Dee, what a surprise.' Julia smiled brightly and held open the door. 'Do come in.'

'I can't stay, I just wanted to bring you these to say thank you.' She handed over the bunch of flowers and pecked Julia's cheek.

'How sweet of you, but what have I done to deserve

these?' Julia led her through to the kitchen and took a small, cut-glass vase from the window sill.

'I've just come from the farm and I saw all of your wonderful handiwork.'

Julia's smile widened. 'Oh, good, I'm so glad you like it. And what does Sam think?'

'He hasn't seen it yet but I know he'll be thrilled, although Conor may live to regret it; Sam won't want to come home! I love your little finishing touches, like the mugs,' Dee continued. 'You have a real flair for interior design. You should go into business.'

'As if I'd have the time,' Julia trilled.

'True,' Dee said apologetically. 'Well, I must go. Thank you again.'

'You're very welcome,' Julia said, walking back down the hall with her, 'and thank you so much for the flowers. I do love roses.' She opened the door and waved at the rows of white roses outside the door.

Dee's face fell. 'Oh, right, good. Well, goodbye, then.'

'Goodbye, Dee, love to Sam.'

Chapter 36

Peggy watched Neil swing the BMW away from the curb and then hurried up the stairs. She went into her own bedroom first and took the Spanish dictionary from the back of the drawer in her bedside table before hurrying into Neil's bedroom. She had realized after her fourth foray into her son's bedroom that she wasn't going to get anywhere unless she found someone who could read Spanish or – she had a flash of inspiration – she bought a dictionary. Now, after waiting all morning for Neil to leave, she finally had an opportunity to use it.

Quickly, she found the documents that had sparked her interest and got to work. She no longer felt guilty about invading Neil's privacy. When she read that bill from the garage more carefully, she discovered that the car he had boasted so much about was, in fact, just leased. He had lied to her and she needed to find out why, for Sam's sake as much as for her own sanity. She didn't want to uncover any sordid or dishonest details about her son or his life in Spain but she couldn't shirk from the truth either. He had hurt Dee once already and she couldn't – wouldn't – let him do it again.

When Dee had phoned asking her to meet up next Wednesday her first instinct had been to refuse, balking at the idea of being the bearer of bad news. But there was no point in putting off the inevitable. Instead she decided to find out everything she could, good or bad, so she could give Dee the full picture.

She took the first page, unfolded it carefully and started to work her way through the main words, jotting down the translation on the inside of the back cover of the dictionary. As she progressed, her heart sank. The key words she had uncovered were 'warning', 'notice', and 'debt' and the amount – she hadn't realized before that it was a number because it was spelt out – was seventy-three thousand euros. She dropped the page into her lap and put a trembling hand to her mouth. 'Dear, God,' she murmured, closing her eyes. After a moment, she forced herself to go on; she had no idea when Neil would be back so she had to make the most of her time. She carefully refolded the document and put it back where she'd found it. She took a deep breath before picking up the next page, the handwritten note, and, hoping that it wouldn't prove too difficult to decipher, Peggy started to read.

'You're kidding.' Dee stared at Conor. The children had all gone home for the day, Sam was helping Lisa and

Martha tidy up and the couple were alone in the kitchen having a cup of tea. Dee had been on tenterhooks all day wondering what Conor's secret was and now that he'd told her, she couldn't believe her ears.

He smiled happily. 'Nope, it's true.'

'Someone has paid you a quarter of a million pounds for half an acre and it has no planning permission?'

'Yep.' He laughed. 'The property boom, don't you just love it?'

'I can't believe it. So apart from doing up your house, what are you going to do with the money?'

'Probably build up the herd and I was thinking of going into venison production.'

'You're kidding?'

He laughed. 'No, and will you stop saying that? Why are you so surprised, do you think you're the only one capable of innovation?'

'No, of course not, it's just you've never mentioned it before.'

'You never mentioned your new business plans either,' he reminded her.

She laughed. 'That's because I didn't have any. It was all Lisa's brainwave and if it wasn't for her badgering and Lauren's brilliance it would never have even got this far.' She shook her head. 'I really don't know what I'm getting myself into; I'm not entrepreneur material.'

'That's rubbish, what about Dee's Deli Delights?'

'That was a lucky accident. If it wasn't for Sam's allergies I'd never have got into cooking.'

'I wish you wouldn't belittle your achievement. You turned a passion into a career and as a result you are now on television and being quoted in newspapers.' He smiled at her. 'You are a huge success, Dee Hewson.'

She laughed. 'It's all a bit surreal.'

'Yes, well, that's the way I felt when the estate agent told me how much that tiny piece of wasteland was worth.'

'I'm thrilled for you.' She hugged him. 'You've worked so hard, you deserve it. Now, before I feed you, can I ask you something?'

'Sure.'

She smiled sweetly. 'Will you fix the loo please?'

An hour later they were sitting at the table tucking into Dee's homemade burgers and chunky chips and Sam was regaling them with stories of his antics with Tom in the garden.

'I'm going to start a worm farm,' he told Conor finally.

Conor nodded. 'Good idea. It's called a wormery.'

Dee looked from him to her son. 'No way.'

'Ah, Mum!'

'Maybe we could have one up at the farm,' Conor suggested. 'Not in the house, though, we'd have to keep it in the barn.'

'What about Boxer?' Dee said. The barn was where the dog slept and where Conor kept him when Sam was around and she had to suppress a shudder at the thought of her son going in there.

'I'm in the process of clearing out the barn and I've built Boxer his own kennel and run,' Conor told her.

Dee smiled and reached over to squeeze his hand gratefully. 'Sam, do you realize how lucky you are to have a friend like Conor?'

The child nodded. 'Do you, Mum?'

She laughed and her eyes locked with Conor's. 'I certainly do.'

'So I'll be able to look after the worms,' Sam said, grinning from ear to ear.

'I'm also planning to get some chickens,' Conor told him.

'Cool!' Sam jigged up and down excitedly. 'Can I help you look after them too?'

'Only if your mum thinks it would be okay.'

Dee shrugged. 'It should be fine.'

'Brilliant!'

Dee shook her head as Sam bounced precariously on his chair again. 'Be careful, Sam, you'll spill your milk.' She looked back at Conor. 'So does this mean you'll be supplying me with fresh eggs?'

'Fresh organic eggs,' he told her.

'Brilliant,' Dee echoed her son and Conor laughed.

'When can we get them, tomorrow?' Sam asked.

'No, champ, sorry, it will take a little longer to organize that. First we need to build them a nice comfortable house. Then we have to build a fence around it to make sure that they are safe. And then,' he leaned closer to Sam, 'we have to find the right kind of chickens that will give us the best eggs.'

'Is there a chicken shop that we can go to?'

Conor chuckled. 'No, but there's a poultry farm down in Tipperary where I think I can get what we need, maybe you and your mum could come with me when I'm choosing them.'

'Can we, Mum?'

Dee looked at his eager little face and smiled. 'Of course we can.'

'Oh, this is great, wait until I tell Tom!' Sam was almost beside himself with happiness. 'Can I phone him and tell him right now?'

'No,' Dee said firmly. 'You can finish your dinner, have a short playtime and then you're going upstairs for a bath.'

Sam's face fell.

'Don't,' she warned him. 'You are a very lucky little boy and I didn't even hear you say thank you to Conor.'

Sam smiled shyly at Conor. 'Thank you.'

The child finished his food and drained his cup. 'Can I go and play with my Power Rangers in my room, Mum?'

She looked at him from under raised eyebrows.

'Thanks and please?' he said, dutifully.

Conor laughed.

'Go on then,' Dee smiled and shook her head as he

sped off. 'You have made one little boy very, very happy.'

'Good, although I'm sorry I told him about the chickens. I should have run it past you first.'

She shook her head. 'Don't worry, it's fine, he seems to be impervious to feathers. We visited the farm at the zoo last year and before I could stop him, he was holding a little chick in his hands; thankfully with no ill effects.'

He smiled. 'I know, I remembered.'

'You are a very good man,' she said, leaning across to kiss him.

'I think I should make the most of this gratitude,' he murmured, pulling her over on to his lap.

Dee reluctantly pulled away after a few minutes. 'That was very nice but I have a bath to run.'

'For me?' he asked, his eyes twinkling.

'No, but if you play your cards right, you might be in luck later.'

'Sounds good.' He ran his fingers through her short hair, combing it back from her face. 'Happy?' he asked.

She nodded, smiling. 'Oh, yes.'

'So, is now a good time to tell you that your loo has had it?'

'Oh, no, you're kidding.'

'Nope, sorry.'

'But how can that be?' she groaned, standing up. 'It was only installed four years ago; it's the newest thing in the house!'

'I'm afraid the plumber must have been a bit dodgy.'

'I don't have much luck with plumbers,' Dee grumbled as she cleared away the dirty dishes. 'The bloke who replaced the boiler definitely overcharged me.'

'There's a new guy in town and I've heard very good reports about him. If you like I'll ask him to come and take a look.'

Dee sighed. 'Yes, I suppose so. It has to be sorted.'

'And if you can't afford to pay him, I will,' he told her firmly. 'For once I'm in a position where I can help out.'

She smiled, bending to kiss the top of his head. 'Thanks, but I should be okay.'

'But if you're not,' he persisted, 'tell me. No more secrets, okay?'

'No more secrets on either side,' she amended.

His eyes widened as he held up his hands, all innocence. 'I've never had any secrets.'

Dee threw a tea towel at him. 'No, but you don't tell me anything either, and that's just the same as having secrets.'

He shrugged. 'What can I say? I'm just not the chatty sort.'

'Don't I know it,' she muttered.

He laughed, reaching for her again. 'Okay, I'll make you a deal. You can ask me one question a week and I promise, whatever it is, I'll do my best to answer it.'

She studied him suspiciously. 'About anything?'

He nodded. 'That's what I said. Go on, you can ask me the first one right now.'

'No way.' Dee slipped out of his grasp, a wide grin on her face. 'I have to have a think first.'

Conor rolled his eyes dramatically. 'Oh God, what have I let myself in for?'

She went to the fridge to put away the milk and took out two beers. 'Want one?'

He nodded. 'Just the one, I want to get home early and start work on the back room. My computer equipment should arrive in the next couple of days.'

'You've gone completely mad with this money, haven't you?'

'Well, every penny has always gone into the farm in the past. It's nice to be able to spend something on the house for a change.'

'It was a bit basic,' Dee acknowledged. In the two years since Conor had moved to Banford, he had done nothing to the house but as he had spent most of his time on the farm, in his parents' house or with her, it hadn't been a problem.

He sighed. 'I must be getting old, I kind of like my comforts. I blame you, you've spoilt me.'

She laughed. 'I'll take that as a compliment but I wouldn't get too focussed on your house just yet because now that you've told Sam you're going to get chickens, he'll be on your case until you build that chicken house.'

'Don't worry, it shouldn't take long but you're right.' He drank the last of his beer and stood up. 'I'd better get back to work.'

Dee moved into his arms and hugged him tightly. 'Thank you, Conor, for everything, but especially for your kindness to Sam.'

He kissed her. 'He's a wonderful little boy.'

'Do you want to go up and say goodbye or will I call him down?'

'I'll go up.' Conor gave her another quick kiss and walked out of the kitchen.

Dee smiled as she listened to him take the stairs two at a time, knowing he'd be up there for at least twenty minutes with Sam possibly even wangling a story out of him. There was a time when she would have followed him up and told Sam that it was time to say goodnight and that Conor had other things to do. It had taken a while for her to realize that Conor spent time with Sam, not because of her but because he wanted to and their relationship was a completely separate thing. Sometimes – and she hated to admit it even to herself – she was jealous of their closeness but most of the time, like now, she just thanked her lucky stars.

Chapter 37

'Change of plan for today's show,' Carolyn announced as soon as Dee walked through the door. Marge and April were already sitting at the table and Dee slipped into a chair and took the A4 sheet Carolyn held out to her.

'The opposition party have just announced that if they get into power after the next election, they will introduce the same traffic-light food labelling system that was introduced in the UK last year,' she explained to Dee.

'Wow, that's interesting.' Dee said, scanning the press release.

'Are you for or against?' April asked, sitting back and taking a sip of coffee.

'Definitely for,' Dee replied, looking up. 'Aren't you?'

'I'm not too sure. It may cause even more confusion in the long run. I mean, fruit is high in sugar but with this labelling a perfectly natural, healthy smoothy could be labelled red, which is very misleading. Also, the foods are graded in relation to other foods on the market so you may get oven chips that are coded green but that just means that, as chips go, they're healthier than other brands.'

Marge sat back in her chair and glanced at her watch. 'Can you explain it to me very simply, April?' she begged. 'I have to leave in fifteen minutes and this press release is too long and complicated.'

April nodded. 'Okay, it basically works the exact same as ordinary traffic lights. Red is danger and is used to warn you if a food is high in fat, sugar or salt. Orange shows that the level of these constituents is acceptable, and green shows that the levels are low. So, for example, you might have a ready meal that has a green light for sugar, orange for fat and orange for salt.'

'What about red?' Marge asked.

'I don't think we'll see many foods with a red light,' April said. 'They won't sell if there's a healthier option.'

'Has the system worked in Britain?' Marge asked.

'It's got mixed reviews,' Carolyn told her. 'Some of the big manufacturers don't like it.'

'That's a plus for a start,' Dee said.

'Why?' Marge asked.

Dee shrugged. 'Like April says, they're going to have a harder job shifting products that have red lights on the front of the package so it will probably force them to produce healthier products and that can't be a bad thing.'

'Yes, true,' April agreed, 'but it's still misleading. Just

because a processed meat pie has three green lights, it doesn't mean it's a healthy option.'

Dee nodded. 'Yes, April, but the people who eat meat pies are going to eat meat pies no matter what; at least this way they may choose one that is slightly healthier. Also, all the nutritional information and the guideline daily amounts would still be shown somewhere on the packaging.'

'But the traffic lights will be on the front,' Carolyn added.

'So you're for, Dee,' Marge said, making a note, 'and you're against, April?'

'Not against,' April corrected, 'but cautious.'

'That's great,' Carolyn said. 'We will be joined by the party spokesman on food and agriculture – what's his name again?'

'No, idea,' Marge replied.

Carolyn laughed. 'I'll confirm that with you later. You get the politician to explain how the system works, Marge; Dee, you could be the consumer's representative. Have you any questions you could ask?'

'Oh, yes.' Dee started to scribble notes in the margin of the press release.

'And I'll be the Rottweiler,' April said with a grin.

'Excellent.' Marge stood up.

Carolyn smiled. 'Well done, ladies, thank you.'

The spot went like clockwork and afterwards they went to the canteen to celebrate.

'This is great, we don't have any work to do on next week's show now,' April reminded Dee.

'True,' Carolyn said, 'but you might have some other things to discuss.'

'Oh?' Dee looked at her curiously.

Carolyn smiled. 'I had a meeting with Marty this morning and he's very pleased with the way the nutrition spot is working out. So much so that he thinks we should continue it until the end of the series.'

'Oh!' Dee smiled delightedly. 'That's wonderful.'

'You and April have been wonderful,' Marge confirmed. 'We have had more emails and texts about diet than about anything else covered on Wednesdays.'

'How many weeks are we talking about?' April asked.

'A further twelve weeks on top of your original contract,' Carolyn said, looking from one to the other. 'Are you both up for that?'

'That's fine with me. Dee?' April said and looked at Dee.

'No problem at all,' Dee said, happily thinking that she should definitely be able to pay a plumber now.

Peggy arrived early at the busy café on Grafton Street and buying a black coffee, she carried it carefully to a table by the window. As she waited, she fiddled nervously with her spoon and when she raised the cup to her lips, her hand shook so badly, she slopped the hot liquid over her hand and into the saucer. She mopped half-heartedly at the mess with the paper napkin and stared out of the window at the passing crowds, wondering what Dee would say.

Neil had noticed there was something wrong with her and when he had observed that she was very quiet she had said she wasn't feeling well. It wasn't a lie. She had been feeling positively nauseous since she had figured out exactly what those papers meant. She had felt like setting fire to the dictionary, irrationally blaming it for revealing her son's lies, but in the end she had tucked it back in the drawer of her bedside table. No doubt she would need it again.

Her very first instinct had been to confront him but then if he left after Dee had decided to let him see Sam, it would be her fault and she couldn't live with that responsibility. No, she had decided, instead she would present Dee with the facts, or the few that she had, and it would be Dee's decision what to do with them. It was a cowardly act but Peggy couldn't think of any way around it. Whatever the outcome was for Neil she didn't want to give up her grandson. It didn't matter if he called her Aunty Peggy until her dying day, it would be infinitely preferable to losing him. She groped in her pocket for a tissue and was dabbing at her eyes when Dee walked in.

'Sorry I'm late.' Dee beamed down at Peggy, her face still made up for the camera, and Peggy thought how beautiful and sweet and honest she looked. 'I'll just get myself a cup of tea. Do you want anything?'

'No, I'm fine,' Peggy told her with a faint smile.

She watched as Dee went to the counter, watched her return, and waited as the girl settled herself opposite and shrugged out of her jacket.

'So, how are you?' Dee asked, looking at her properly for the first time, her smile immediately fading. 'Peggy, is everything all right?'

Peggy shook her head.

Dee grasped her hand. 'What is it, Peggy, are you ill? Is there something wrong with Neil?'

Peggy laughed but her eyes were dead. 'Yes to both questions, really. There is definitely something wrong with my son and I am sick, so sick of him.' She hid her face in her hands. 'Oh, Dee, I'm sorry.'

'Peggy, please, you're scaring me.'

Peggy took her hands away and looked at Dee with red-rimmed eyes. 'I'm sorry.'

'Please, just tell me.'

Peggy nodded silently and clasping her hands together again she began to tell Dee about how she had been stealing into Neil's room on a regular basis over the last few weeks and rifling through his luggage.

Dee looked vaguely shocked but when Peggy paused and looked at her for a reaction she just shrugged. 'I'd probably have done the same thing. He hasn't done much to inspire our trust.'

'That's what I thought. But it wasn't just that, Dee. I thought it was wrong that he wasn't talking to me about his gambling and it seemed to me that there could be only one reason for that.'

'That he hadn't actually stopped,' Dee guessed.

Peggy nodded. 'Or that he had relapsed. Either way I couldn't help him unless I knew the truth. I talked to a counsellor and he told me that gamblers were consummate and very skilled liars—'

Dee nodded. 'They told me that too.'

'So that's why I invaded his privacy, Dee.'

'You don't have to explain yourself to me, Peggy.'

Peggy nodded her thanks and took a deep breath before continuing. 'I found three things. The first was a bill from a garage. That car he's driving? It's just a rental.'

'I suppose there could be reasons for that,' Dee said.

Peggy's smile was grim. 'Yes, except Neil had bragged to me about what a good deal he had struck with the dealer.'

'Oh.' Dee's face fell.

'It gets worse, I'm afraid,' Peggy warned her softly.

'Go on.'

'There was a document about a loan – I'm not sure of the details, it was in Spanish – but I could figure out the words "final notice" and it was printed in red.'

Dee stared at her. 'How much?'

Peggy swallowed hard. 'Seventy-three thousand euros,' she whispered.

Dee put a hand over her mouth. 'Was there a date on it?'

'I couldn't find one, no.'

'So maybe it was an old bill and he's paid it.'

'Oh, come on, Dee, he'd hardly be carrying an old bill around with him and how would he have ever been able to pay off that kind of money?'

'He owns his own business now,' Dee reminded her, clutching at straws.

Peggy frowned, that hadn't occurred to her. 'But it was a final notice,' she said doubtfully.

Dee shrugged. 'Isn't that the way big business works? You don't pay bills until you absolutely have to.'

'I don't know, do you really think so?'

Dee nodded confidently. 'I'm sure there's a simple explanation but you know what? We're going to ask him. You are going to bring him over to my place on Friday and we are going to talk all this through with him. What's more, if he wants to see Sam he's going to have to start going to Gamblers Anonymous meetings on a regular basis. He has to be straight up and honest with me, Peggy, or I can't go ahead with it.'

Peggy nodded hesitantly. 'It could be exactly what he needs or—' She sighed.

'Or what?'

'It may frighten him away for good.'

Dee reached over and took her hand. 'I know that would be very hard for you, Peggy, you've only just got him back, but I don't see what choice I have.'

Peggy squeezed her hand tightly. 'You don't and neither do I. You see, I haven't really got him back, Dee. He doesn't talk to me at all about what's going on in his life either now in Ireland or when he was in Spain. He won't even talk about his time with you.' She smiled faintly. 'The only subject that's not taboo is Sam and even that was out of bounds for a while after he found out about "Aunty Peggy".'

'So, are we agreed? Friday, at my place, we confront him.'

Peggy frowned. 'Will Sam be in the house?'

Dee shook her head. 'Absolutely not. So, what do you say?'

Peggy thought about the crumpled, handwritten note in the bag under the table and then made a decision. She had been saving it for last or maybe she had never planned to show it to Dee at all. It probably wouldn't matter one way or the other. Still, if this was going to work, the truth, all of it, would have to come out. She smiled tremulously and nodded. 'Okay then, Dee, let's do it.'

Chapter 38

'Thank you so much for coming to see us, Emma, it was lovely to meet you.' Lisa shook the girl's hand and smiled warmly. 'I'll be in touch in a couple of days.'

After she had closed the door, Lisa went through to the kitchen, a definite spring in her step. Sitting down at the table, she picked up the folder containing Emma Dawson's details. She was perfect for the job, Lisa thought as she read through the pages once more. Perfect on paper but, more importantly, perfect in the flesh. Lisa and Martha had exchanged delighted smiles when they saw her drop to the floor and start to crawl around on all fours, making the toddlers giggle helplessly. After finding someone as wonderful as Yvonne, Lisa couldn't believe that she'd found another contender who would fit in so perfectly with their little team. Once she got Martha and Dee's okay, she would hire Emma and get to work on bringing Happy Days to the next level.

First, she would advertise a new Montessori school

and an after-school service. Yvonne, she'd decided, would be responsible for the school in the morning that would cater for three- and four-year-olds and in the afternoon she would take care of the older children coming home from primary school. Emma would look after the one- to three-year-old children in the mornings, Martha could stay with her beloved babies and Lisa would float between the groups covering for the other girls during break-time or if one of them was on holiday or on sick leave.

She had been working hard on a new floor plan for the crèche and she was dying to run it past Dee. It would be costly, of course, but Lisa thought they could afford it and had put together a spreadsheet to show how. Now all they had to do was find time to discuss it, not an easy thing to achieve at the moment.

They were both running around like maniacs. When Dee wasn't cooking, she was working on her TV programme, in meetings with Lauren, or on the phone to an agency or a government department.

Lisa wasn't much better. Apart from her already busy job and developing her plans for Happy Days, she was a willing slave for Lauren, making phone calls and writing letters to beat the band.

She felt exhausted and was in bed by ten most nights but she was enjoying life more than she had in years. She couldn't believe that less than a month ago she was content to sit in front of the telly most evenings, stuffing her face. That was the other plus about being this busy, she didn't get time to eat as much! That and the fact that Dee had kept to her promise and was making her wonderful, low-fat food, meant that already she'd lost a few pounds and was able to squeeze into some of her old jeans.

Tidying up her papers, Lisa stood up and went to the door. The children would be having lunch soon and she would help supervise while Martha took her break. As she walked out into the hall, the doorbell rang and she changed course to go and answer it. A tall man was standing in the porch with his back to the door. 'Hello, can I help you?' she asked.

He turned around and smiled slowly, his eyes travelling up and down her. 'I certainly hope so.'

Lisa gulped and unconsciously sucked in her stomach. God, he was gorgeous! That curly, blond hair, those amazing blue eyes and just look at that jaw-line! He could have walked straight off a movie set.

'Am I in the wrong place?' He was scratching his head and frowning now.

Lisa realized that while she'd been staring he had been talking. 'Sorry, what did you say?'

'I'm here to fix your loo,' he grinned, 'and anything else that needs fixing.'

She smiled. 'Come on in. I'll show you where the toilet is.'

'Any chance of a cuppa?' he asked with a wink.

'You haven't done any work yet and you're looking for tea?' She was trying to look stern but it was hard with those twinkling eyes smiling down at her and that incredibly sexy smile.

'I'll earn it, I promise,' he told her.

'Oh! Okay then.' Pointing him towards the loo, Lisa hurried to put on the kettle and then went off to find Martha. 'Can you manage without me for a little bit longer?' she asked. 'Only there's a plumber working on the staff loo and I want to keep an eye on him.'

'You're probably right,' Martha agreed. 'My mam says you should never take your eyes of these trades- men or they'll sit around doing nothing and still charge you a fortune.'

Lisa smiled happily. 'I've always thought your mother was a very wise woman.'

Dee stared at Lisa. 'You've got a date with our plumber?'

'Yes, great, isn't it?'

'I thought you'd sworn off men for the foreseeable future.'

'Ah, but I hadn't met Freddy,' Lisa said, a dreamy look in her eye.

'Freddy?'

'Fabulous Freddy! Oh, wait until you meet him, Dee, he's a hunk.'

'Oh, Lisa—'

'Don't start, Dee,' Lisa held up a hand, 'you'll under- stand after you've met him.'

'But looks aren't everything.'

'No, but they help,' Lisa quipped. 'But no, it's not just his looks. He's funny and clever and a great plumber.'

'I'm not sure you're qualified to judge that,' Dee said dryly.

'He fixed the leaky tap in the children's bathroom and that noisy cistern in the upstairs loo.'

'Really?' Dee looked impressed. 'How come he ended up there?'

Lisa reddened. 'I was just telling him about our previous bad luck with plumbers and he offered to help. Honestly, Dee, he's so nice and kind and really, truly gorgeous. And, what's even more amazing is, he seems to like me.' She beamed at Dee and did a little dance.

'I'm very happy for you, Lisa, but—'

Lisa covered her ears. 'No, don't "but", please don't "but".'

'It's just that if he's so gorgeous, he's bound to have a wife or girlfriend already, isn't he?'

Lisa kept her hands over her ears. 'I can't hear you,' she sang.

'Okay, okay.' Dee held up her hands in surrender. 'I won't say another word.' But she decided to talk to Conor later about this 'Fabulous Freddy' and find out exactly how honest and nice and reliable he was.

'I don't know him that well but he seems like a nice guy,' Conor assured her that evening. 'Ask Matthew, they play rugby together.'

Dee shook her head worriedly. 'But Lisa says he's gorgeous, so how come he's single?'

Conor shrugged. 'I don't know, but he's hardly going to get away with two-timing in a small place like Banford.'

She brightened. 'That's true. Where does he live?'

'In the flat over his premises down on Church Road.'

'Oh!' That was indeed good news. It would be impossible for him to have a woman stashed away in a tiny place like that. 'How long has he lived here?' she continued, however. She had to look after her best friend, after all.

'Six months or so.' He grinned. 'Would you like me to ask him for his CV?'

She made a face. 'No, he's coming back in the morning so I'll check him out then.'

'Don't scare him off,' he warned, 'or Lisa will kill you. She positively soared out of here this evening.'

'I know and that's why I'm afraid of her getting hurt again. She's only just getting over Ger.'

Conor put his arms around Dee and kissed her hair. 'I know how much you care about Lisa, Dee, but I really don't think there's anything to worry about. And even if there is, she has to make her own mistakes; we all do.'

Dee sighed. 'Okay, don't worry, I won't interfere but I am going to be here in the morning just to see for myself what he's like. There's nothing wrong with that, is there?'

*

'Hi, how are you doing?'

Okay, so he was definitely a hunk. Dee smiled and held out her hand. 'You must be Freddy, I'm Dee Hewson.'

He shook her hand. 'Nice to meet you.' He held up a small piece of piping. 'I just need to install this and I'll be out of your hair.'

'Really?' She followed him down the corridor to the staff loo. 'Conor thought you might have to replace the whole toilet.'

'I may have to, but I thought I'd give this a try first. Why spend all that money if you don't have to?'

'I'm all for saving money,' she assured him, 'but at the same time this is a business and we can't really afford to have it breaking down every week.'

He looked slightly shocked. 'Oh, it won't do that. If it goes again, I'll be out within the hour to replace it.'

'Oh, okay.'

'But I'm pretty confident that this will do the trick. Now, I'd better get on.'

'Would you like some tea or coffee?' Dee offered.

'Not for me, thanks. I don't touch the stuff.'

Dee shot him a suspicious look. 'But Lisa said you had tea yesterday.'

He grinned shyly. 'I walked right into that one, didn't I?'

'Yes you did.'

He sighed. 'I just wanted to keep her talking a bit longer. She's gorgeous, she is, and so nice, too. I threw the tea down the toilet when she wasn't looking, but don't tell her, will you?'

'I won't,' Dee promised. 'I hear you're going out tomorrow night.'

He nodded. 'I booked a table at the Pink Elephant in Swords but then I was afraid she might not like Thai food.'

'She loves Thai food,' Dee told him, 'and she adores the Pink Elephant.' Not that she can afford to go there often, she thought to herself. Ger certainly never brought her; the miserable sod only ran to the local burger joint and even then he'd be rushing Lisa out of work so they could order from the 'early bird' menu. But there was obviously money in the plumbing business and Freddy was out to impress.

'Good.' He smiled happily.

'I'll leave you to it,' Dee said. 'Call if you need anything.'

He hesitated. 'I don't suppose she's around, is she?'

Dee smiled. 'In the garden with the children; she should be coming this way in about five minutes.'

'Great!'

Dee left him to his work, chuckling quietly to herself as he started to whistle 'Love is in the Air'.

'He's here,' she told Lisa as they all traipsed through the kitchen on the way back to the crèche.

'What do you think?' Lisa demanded, searching her face.

'I think he's lovely,' Dee admitted.

'Yes!' Lisa hugged her quickly.

'Lisa, are you very happy?' one of the little girls asked, smiling up at her.

Lisa scooped her up in her arms. 'I certainly am, Rebecca!' she said dancing around the kitchen. The other children started to join in until Dee finally called a halt. 'Okay, children, let's go into the dining room, it's snack time. And you,' she said to Lisa, taking the little girl out of her arms, 'are taking a break. But before you do, could you check up on that plumber for me?'

Lisa beamed at her. 'Consider it done.'

Chapter 39

'We've got it!'

Dee held the phone away from her ear. 'Lauren, is that you?'

'Yes! Dee, did you hear me? We've got a loan. Dee's Delicacies is off the ground.'

'No way!' Dee breathed, dropping into the nearest chair.

'Way!' Lauren told her.

'I can't believe it.'

'It's true. They were very impressed with our business plan; mind you, why wouldn't they be? It was brilliant.'

'It was, thanks to you,' Dee agreed. 'So what do we do now?'

'Take the products to the market place and see what the buyers think.' They had agreed on initially marketing four preserves, three types of muffin and two breads. The second stage of the plan would include soups and full meals but they wouldn't be introducing them for at least twelve months. 'Have you got any chefs on board?'

'Two,' Dee confirmed. 'I've given them both three recipes to try out so I can see how accurately they follow my recipes.'

'Great. Can we have a meeting early next week? I'm afraid the hard work is only just starting.'

Dee grinned. 'Bring it on.'

'Good woman.'

'Thank you for everything, Lauren, I couldn't have done this without you.'

'That's okay, darling, it's been my pleasure. My husband and two little babies are grateful too; Mummy has been much nicer since she started to use her brain again.'

'Good, I'm glad. Why don't you drop over around twelve on Monday? We can talk and you can stay for some lunch. Bring the girls, they can play with the other babies while we work.'

'That sounds perfect, Dee, see you then.'

Dee went in search of Lisa and found her in the baby room, sitting, watching Olivia sleep.

'Is everything okay?' she whispered, crouching down beside her.

Lisa started and then smiled. 'Oh, yes, fine. Olivia and Patrick have been a bit fractious this morning so I sent Martha out for a breather.'

Dee looked around at the other cots. Patrick was awake and playing with his toes and Millie was out cold, one pink, chubby foot sticking out through the rails. She crouched down beside Lisa. 'I just got a call from Lauren, we got the loan.'

'Oh, Dee, that's fantastic!' Lisa hugged her.

Dee nodded. 'Yeah, it looks like this might actually happen.'

'There's no might about it. So what do we do next?'

'I'm not too sure, but Lauren is coming over for lunch on Monday to discuss it. I told her she could drop the girls in here, is that okay?'

'Sure.'

'And if you could join us it would be great.'

'Let me talk to Martha, but it should be fine. I was hoping you and I could have a meeting about the crèche too, Dee. How about tomorrow night?'

Dee shook her head. 'I'm sorry, Lisa, I have something on.'

'Oh, I thought with Sam up at the farm you'd be at a loose end.'

Dee sighed and glanced around to make sure there was no one else in earshot.

'Neil and his mother are coming over tomorrow night.'

Lisa's eyes widened. 'Oh?'

'I've decided to let him see Sam but I want to have a long talk with him first.'

'I can understand that but why have you invited his mother?'

Dee realized there was no way she could go into all that now. She would tell Lisa the full story another time. 'We're joining forces to make sure he stays on the straight and narrow.' The door of the main room opened and Dee saw that it was Martha returning. 'I'll fill you in another time.'

Lisa nodded. 'Sam is looking forward to his sleep-over, he's talked of nothing else.'

Dee rolled her eyes at Martha. 'I hadn't planned on telling him until tomorrow but it kind of slipped out. I'll never get him to sleep tonight.'

'Tell him if he doesn't get a good night's sleep tonight he won't be able to go,' Martha suggested.

'Do you know what they're going to do together?' Lisa asked.

'Not a clue,' Dee laughed, 'and I think I'm probably better off not knowing.'

'Have you given him a long list of do's and don'ts?,' Lisa teased. Anytime Sam went somewhere without Dee she usually packed him off with a list of instructions, contact numbers and anti-histamine cream.

'No, I haven't, but I will be providing some food and a few extra bits and pieces just might find their way into Sam's bag.' Dee was smiling a little too broadly and she could see that Lisa saw right through her.

'He'll be fine, don't worry.'

Dee nodded. 'I know, it's just this is his first night

away from home without me so it feels a bit weird.'

Martha stared at her. 'But he's nearly five, Dee. Are you saying you haven't had a break from him in five years?'

Dee nodded. 'But I didn't want one,' she added hurriedly. 'I love my holidays with Sam. I was actually thinking of taking him abroad next month. I'd like him to have a nice holiday before he starts school but I hate the idea of going during the summer months, it's too hot.'

'May would be much nicer,' Lisa agreed, 'and the resorts are quieter too. It's a great idea, Dee, but you should still try and get away for a couple of days, just you and Conor. I could move in here with Sam and then you wouldn't have to worry about different food or sheets or anything.'

'I couldn't ask you to do that,' Dee protested.

'You didn't; I offered,' Lisa pointed out.

'Every couple needs some time alone,' Martha told her.

'You could go to one of those country house spas,' Lisa said dreamily. 'Good food, long walks, turf fires and long, lazy mornings in bed, wonderful.'

Dee laughed. 'You'll have to get Freddy to take you. Are you all set for the big date?'

Lisa rolled her eyes. 'It's really very weird,' she confided. 'I haven't a clue what to wear, there's no time for me to go and get my hair done and my eyebrows and legs badly need attention, but I don't care. It's not that it doesn't matter,' she struggled to explain, 'it's just that I know it won't be important to him. He met me here looking like this,' she gestured down at her baggy jeans and top and her smile lit up her face, 'and he liked me.'

Dee hugged her, feeling tears prick her eyes. 'What's not to like?'

Beside them, baby Patrick woke up with a scream, making them all jump and then laugh.

'Come here, little man,' Martha reached in to pick him up and kissed the soft down on his head. He stopped crying immediately and looked around with interest. 'Are you trying to figure out why you're surrounded by soppy women?' she asked.

Dee stretched out a finger to tickle his toe. 'This soppy woman has got to go. I'm off to Better Books. Lisa, do you need anything from the shops?'

'Get her a razor,' Martha advised. 'I'm thrilled that you're so laid back about your date, Lisa, but honestly, you'll feel much better if you're smooth.'

'You're right.' Lisa laughed. 'Dee, would you?'

'Consider it done.'

Dee hurried out to load up the car and was soon on her way to the supermarket. When she'd picked up a few bits and pieces for Lisa – she'd taken it upon herself to add some expensive shampoo and conditioner to the list – she drove the short distance to Better Books and took the food inside. There was a much bigger crowd than usual, but then she was later than usual, and it took a moment for her to spot Vi in the corner.

'Tea?' Zoe asked her.

'I'd love one.' Dee smiled. 'And whatever Vi is having and a slice of chocolate cheesecake.'

Zoe made the drinks, cut the cake and seconds later, Dee carried the tray over to Vi's table. 'Can I join you?' she asked.

Vi eyed the cake. 'Only if that's for me.'

'It is,' Dee laughed, sliding the coffee and cake in front of her. 'How are you?'

'Fine, my darling, and you?' Vi spooned some cake delicately into her mouth.

'Pretty good. Neil and his mother are coming over to my house tomorrow night to sort a few things out.'

Vi raised an eyebrow. 'I see.'

'I talked to Peggy and we agreed that we would confront him together and I won't agree to him seeing Sam unless he goes to GA meetings on a regular basis.'

'That seems fair. How did he react?'

'He's thrilled that I'm allowing him to meet Sam but he doesn't know all the conditions yet.'

'Have you told Sam anything yet?'

Dee shook her head. 'No, I didn't want to do that until everything's agreed with Neil. I hope he's going to be sensible.'

'I'm sure it will work out fine. He's been completely reasonable up till now, hasn't he?'

'Yes,' Dee admitted, 'he has.'

'So where will Sam be while this meeting takes place, not in the house, surely? I could take him if you want.'

'No, that's okay. He's staying at Conor's for the night.'

'I see.'

Dee grinned. 'What does that mean?'

'Nothing,' Vi said innocently. 'He hasn't stayed with Conor before though, has he?'

Dee shook her head. 'I was always terrified he'd get sick if he stayed in the house, what with the dog and everything. Don't get me wrong, Conor's very careful, but still . . .'

'So what's changed?'

'Oh, Vi, you wouldn't believe it. He's been secretly decorating the house over the last few weeks. He's thrown out his old scruffy sofa, and torn up the lino in the kitchen, and he's created the most wonderful little bedroom for Sam. Tomorrow will be Sam's first time to see it.'

'Conor's a good man.' Vi's eyes followed Ronan as he picked his way through the tables and went behind the counter to talk to Zoe. 'He's a lot like his father.'

'Yes.' Dee nodded. 'So, tell me, have you any finished paintings to show me?'

'I've just sent one off to be framed, it should be ready on Monday. I'll bring it over as soon as I get it and then maybe I could do some sketches of Sam.'

'You don't have to, you know.'

'I'd like to,' Vi assured her. 'As long as I won't get

in the way; you must be very busy with all these new business plans.'

'I am,' Dee agreed, 'but I must admit, I'm enjoying every minute. The bank has agreed to give me a loan so it's full steam ahead.'

'Well, I wish you luck with it, my darling, you deserve it.'

Dee leaned across to kiss her cheek. 'Thanks, Vi. I'd better get going.'

'Okay, darling.' Vi smiled. 'Take care and good luck tomorrow.'

Dee waved at Zoe and Ronan and went back out to her car. She was about to drive off when she realized that she'd left her phone behind her. Quickly retracing her steps, Dee threaded her way back to Vi's table, pausing when she saw Ronan at the older woman's side, his hand on her shoulder. She watched them as they talked quietly, Vi's eyes smiling up into his. Ronan turned suddenly and saw her.

'Dee, you're back.' He smiled. 'Did you forget something?'

'My phone.' She reached across him and pulled it from behind her cup and saucer. 'I'll forget my head one of these days.'

'Join the club,' he told her and they all laughed.

'Well.' Dee stood awkwardly for a moment. 'Must go. Bye.'

Vi held her gaze. 'Goodbye, darling.'

Dee pushed her way back through the café, went out

to her car and got in. 'Bloody hell,' she muttered as she sat trying to understand what she had just witnessed. 'Bloody hell.'

Chapter 40

It was three o'clock on Friday afternoon before Dee and Sam finally set off for the farm. Sam had spent nearly an hour trying to decide what to bring with him until Dee finally threw a few toys into his bag and dragged him out to the car. 'You're only going for one evening, Sam, and you probably won't have time to play with everything. You're going to the farm to spend time with Conor, remember?'

'Yeah, okay, Mum,' he'd agreed, grinning happily as he hopped into the back seat. 'What do you think we'll be doing?'

She smiled as she closed his door and slid into the driver's seat. 'I've no idea.'

'I'll probably have to do some farm work,' he said importantly.

You'd better not, Dee thought to herself, wondering if she should say something to Conor. But he knew her and he knew Sam and he knew what was possible and what wasn't. She also realized that it was important for their relationship for her to show some faith in Conor.

'We're here!' Sam yelped, squirming impatiently in his seat as Dee turned the car through the front gates and into the yard beside the house. Immediately, Boxer started to bark and she looked around her to see where he was. She smiled when saw him charging up and down in a run that spanned the length of the yard and sported a large kennel at the end. 'Look, Sam, Boxer has a new home!'

As she got out of the car, Conor came around the side of the house to greet them.

'Well, hello, there, this is a nice surprise.' He opened the back door and helped Sam open his seat belt. 'I wasn't expecting a visit from you today.'

Sam's face fell. 'But Conor, I've come to stay.'

'Really?' Conor frowned. 'I thought we were doing that tomorrow.'

'But, but,' Sam stammered, his lip trembling.

'Just kidding, Sam.' Conor grinned and swung the child up on to his shoulders.

Sam pulled his hair. 'That was mean.'

'Ouch! You're right, I'm sorry. Will you forgive me if I bring you on a tour of my house? It's changed a bit since you were here last.'

'I suppose,' Sam said doubtfully.

'But it's a long tour, so we'd better stop off in the

kitchen and get you a biscuit to keep you going.'

Dee watched as a wide grin spread across Sam's face.

'Okay,' he told Conor.

Conor winked at Dee. 'Right, then, let's go.'

They went into the kitchen and Conor crouched down so that Sam could help himself from the plate of biscuits on the counter top.

'Mummy made these,' he giggled.

'She sure did; we only have the best in this house. Now, what do you think of my new chairs?' He swivelled around so Sam could see the new leather suite.

'Nice,' Sam said, showing more interest in his biscuit.

'Oh, right, not impressed, eh? What about this, then?' He moved further into the room and turned to face the wall opposite the sofa where a new flat-screen TV hung.

Sam's jaw dropped. 'Wow! It's huge!'

Conor grinned at Dee. 'Okay, that was one change that was for me,' he admitted.

She laughed.

'Can we put it on?' Sam asked.

'No, we have to do the rest of the tour,' Conor told him.

'Are there more TVs?' Sam asked hopefully.

''Fraid not, champ,' Conor laughed. 'Now, this is my office.'

He threw open the door of the back room and Dee gasped. 'Conor, it's fantastic.'

'You've got a new computer, Conor!' Sam said excitedly.

'Yes, and a colour printer and I'm connected to the Internet. We might go online later, Sam, and see if we can find any *Pokémon* games.'

'Cool!' Sam patted Conor's head affectionately.

As they talked, Dee looked around her. The room was a warm green which looked well against the oak desk and filing cabinet and Conor had bought himself a black swivel chair. Again, he'd stripped the floorboards and thrown down another rug.

'I love your rug,' Dee said, admiring the modern design in a variety of pale greens and browns.

'I got that for thirty-five euros in that new place that just opened on Market Square. You should drop in, they have some great bargains.'

Dee grinned.

'What?'

'It's just that you sound so domesticated.'

'That's me, wait till you see my frilly apron.'

Sam nearly fell off trying to bend down to see into Conor's face. 'You don't really have a frilly apron, do you, Conor?'

'No, champ, I promise. Now, are you ready to go upstairs?'

Sam kicked his heels against Conor's ribs. 'Yeah, giddy-up, horsey.'

Conor coughed. 'Right.'

'Go easy, Sam,' Dee warned, following them upstairs.

'That horse isn't as young as he used to be.'

Conor pulled a face. 'Charming. Right, Sam, that's my room in there.'

Sam barely looked but Dee's eyes widened when she saw the bed.

'Good, eh?' Conor grinned at her expression.

'Plenty of room for you to stretch,' she agreed.

'Where do I sleep?' Sam demanded.

'Down in this room, Sam. It's where I keep all my stuff but I've cleared a corner for you to sleep in so you should be okay.'

Dee could have cried at the look of doubt and fear that crossed her little boy's face.

'Conor, open the door and stop messing,' she mumbled crossly.

'Sorry,' he said and carefully lowered Sam down to the ground. 'Go on in, Sam, see what you think.'

With a cautious look at his mother who nodded her encouragement, Sam slowly turned the handle and pushed open the door. He stood there for a moment just looking and Dee and Conor exchanged worried looks.

'Who's room is this?' Sam asked, looking around.

'It's yours, Sam,' Conor said gently.

Sam looked up into his face, his eyes wide. 'It's just for me?'

'Yes, if you want it. I thought that if I set up somewhere nice for you to stay, your mum might let you visit more often.'

'Cool,' Sam said, going over and sitting on the side of the bed and running his hand over the cover. He smiled up at Dee. 'Isn't it great, Mum?'

'I think it's amazing,' she agreed.

'So can I come to stay any time I want?' he asked.

She laughed. 'That depends on Conor. He might not want you once he knows what you're like. Did I tell you he snores, Conor?'

'I don't!' Sam giggled. 'Mum does sometimes.'

'Don't I know it,' Conor murmured and received a sharp dig in the ribs from Dee.

'You're a very violent family,' he complained. 'So what do you think, Sam? Will it do?'

'It's ace!'

'Is there anything you want to say to Conor, Sam?' Dee prompted.

Sam threw himself into Conor's arms. 'Thank you!'

Conor smiled at Dee over Sam's head. 'You're welcome, champ. Now, let's go and check out the barn, I have a job for you to do.'

Conor and Dee walked slowly down the stairs, Sam speeding ahead. When they reached the back door, Dee turned to Conor and smiled. 'He's thrilled, Conor, thanks.'

'No problem.'

She glanced at her watch. 'I'd better go and prepare for my guests.'

Conor's expression darkened. 'Will you be okay?'

'Yes, I'll be fine. Now that I know what I'm doing I feel in control. I hope Neil goes along with the plan, but if he doesn't,' she shrugged, 'then that's that.'

Conor looked around to see what Sam was up to. The child was over talking to Boxer but he was careful not to get too near the fence. 'I hope it goes well. Please don't worry about Sam, I promise I'll take care of him. Boxer's under lock and key, the sheets are new and—'

She put a finger to his lips and smiled. 'I'm not worried. Oh and by the way, I've thought of a question.'

'Sorry?'

'One question a week, remember?'

He groaned. 'Okay, then, go on.'

'Have you ever been in love?' she asked. She struggled to keep her voice light but she watched closely for his reaction.

He seemed to think about it for a moment and then nodded slightly. 'Yes, I have.'

'Conor, come on!' Sam ran back to them and tugged on his arm. 'What's my first job?'

'I'll leave you to it,' Dee said with a forced smile and started for her car.

'Dee, wait,' Conor said quietly, following her and grabbing her arm.

'I can't, Conor, I have to get back. Anyway, this is a boys' evening.' She dropped to her knees and held out her arms to Sam. 'You do whatever Conor tells you, okay?'

'I will.' Sam hugged her tightly.

'Call me in the morning and I'll come and get him,' Dee said, getting Sam's bag from the car and handing it over to Conor.

'Oh, but I was hoping to take him to buy the chickens tomorrow. You could come too and we'd get some lunch on the way.'

She shrugged. 'I'm not sure, Conor, I've such a lot to do.'

'Call me later,' he murmured, 'when they're gone.'

'It will probably be late.'

'It doesn't matter. Please, Dee?'

She nodded and turned her face so that his kiss landed on her cheek. 'Thanks for this,' she said brightly, getting into the driver's seat and starting the car. 'Bye, Sam.'

'Bye, Mum!' He roared above the noise of the engine and ran after her to the gate, waving until she was out of sight.

Dee drove away feeling slightly embarrassed and very annoyed with herself. Of course he'd been in love, he was thirty-two, for God's sake! What a dumb question to ask and what difference did it make anyway? She resolved there and then that she would not be asking any more questions. If he wanted to tell her things about his life, present or past, that was up to him, but she would not pester or beg for information like crumbs from the table. She was too old for such silly, schoolgirl behaviour and, she decided, as she thought of the evening ahead, she'd more important matters to think about.

Chapter 41

Neil and Peggy sat at the kitchen table while Dee made tea. Neil seemed quite relaxed, she thought, but the same certainly couldn't be said for his mother.

'I feel like I'm in a time warp when I sit in this kitchen,' Neil said, looking around him. 'Nothing seems to have changed.'

'No, with the exception of the equipment, it hasn't really,' Dee agreed. 'Any money I had I put into adapting the house to cater for the crèche's needs. We partitioned the sitting room, installed toilets downstairs for both the children and staff and then we put a special surface down in the garden to make it a child-friendly zone.'

Dee carried a tray with tea and biscuits to the table and was just lifting the pot when the phone rang. She excused herself and went to answer it. 'Peggy, would you pour?' she called back before lifting the receiver. 'Hello?'

'Hello, Dee.'

Dee sighed. 'Hello, Aunt Pauline. Is everything all

right?' She was usually the one to phone her aunt and even then she knew better than to phone after six.

'Everything's fine although Jack's knee is playing up again.'

'Oh, I'm sorry to hear that. Please, tell him I was asking for him.'

'You never called on Monday,' Pauline carried on regardless, 'you always call me on Mondays.'

'I'm sorry, Aunt, but like I told you last week, it's very busy at the moment.'

'You should never be too busy for your family,' Pauline retorted.

Dee thought of Sam and the conversation she should be having in the kitchen that would affect his whole future. 'You're quite right. Now I'm afraid you're going to have to excuse me, Aunt Pauline, I have guests.'

'Guests? Who?'

'I'll call you tomorrow, Aunt Pauline.'

'Now hold on one minute—'

'Goodnight, thanks for the call.' Dee put down the phone and went back into the kitchen. 'Sorry about that. It was my aunt.'

'Pauline?' Neil gave a short laugh. 'Did you tell her I was here?'

'What do you think?' Peggy hadn't poured the tea and Dee lifted the pot, shooting the silent woman a questioning glance.

'I remember sitting here the night of your father's funeral,' Neil was saying. 'Pauline was furious with me because someone made a joke and I laughed out loud.'

'You weren't her favourite person.'

'Can we get down to the reason we're here, please?' Peggy broke in, her voice sharp.

Dee, taken aback at her grim expression, nodded. 'Of course. Are you okay, Peggy?'

'Fine.'

'Okay then, shall I start?'

Peggy's eyes moved from Dee to her son. 'No. I think I will. I have some questions I'd like to ask Neil.'

Her son rolled his eyes at her, grinning. 'You're not going to shine a light in my eyes, are you, Mother?'

Peggy didn't return his smile. 'Tell us about the car, Neil.'

'What about the car?'

Peggy shrugged. 'Where you bought it, how much it cost, that sort of thing.'

Neil looked from his mother to Dee. 'You know all of this, and I don't see what that has to do with Sam—'

'Humour me,' Peggy said, not taking her eyes off him.

'We just want to know a bit more about you and your life, Neil,' Dee said. 'It's not a problem, is it?'

He shook his head. 'No, of course not. I bought the car from McCarthy's garage out beside the airport. It was seventy-eight thousand euros.'

'Liar.'

Neil stared at his mother. 'Excuse me?'

'You're a liar. You didn't buy that car, you're leasing it.'

'So what?'

'Why lie, Neil?' Dee asked.

'It's not a lie, for God's sake! I wasn't sure how long I'd be staying in Ireland and the dealer said that if I sold it again so quickly I would lose out. He suggested a lease instead so that's what I did.'

'So why lie?' Dee repeated.

'I just wanted to impress you, okay?'

Dee looked from him back to Peggy. 'Anything else?'

Peggy nodded and reached into her bag for a photocopy of one of the documents she'd found in Neil's room. 'Can you explain this?'

The two women watched as Neil took the document from his mother. 'Where did you get this?'

'I found it in your room,' Peggy said calmly.

'You had no right,' he said angrily.

'I had every right,' she shot back. 'If you want to come back into our lives you have got to be honest with us. Once I knew the car was a lie I decided to see what else you were hiding.'

Neil tossed the page on to the table. 'It's in the past, it doesn't matter any more.'

'So you don't owe that money?' Dee asked hopefully.

'No, not really.'

'Either you do, or you don't, Neil, which is it?'

'Life isn't always so black and white, Mam,' he said tiredly.

'Isn't it?' she said. 'Well, I wouldn't know what your life's been like, Neil, because you've never told me. All

I know about you is that you stole from Dee and you've been lying to us about money. That would suggest to me that you haven't stopped gambling at all. For all I know maybe the only reason you're here is to con me and Dee out of more money.'

'No!' He slammed his hand down on the table making Dee jump.

'Why did you come back, Neil?' Peggy went on. 'You never did say, did you?'

'To see you,' he said quietly.

'Oh, please, you've hardly spent more than ten minutes in my company since you got back. You're out most of the time and you never tell me where you go or why.' She threw up her hands in frustration. 'And then you expect Dee to let you meet Sam.'

'Enough!' he shouted, sitting forward in his chair, his face red.

Peggy backed away and Dee instinctively put a hand out to cover hers. 'Please don't shout, Neil,' she said quietly.

He stood up and went to the sink. 'I'm sorry,' he said finally, turning around and leaning against it. 'It was stupid of me to think I could get away with this.'

Dee stiffened but she said nothing, just watched him. Sweat glistened on his forehead, his breathing had quickened, and he was drumming his fingers nervously on the draining board. 'What is it you were trying to get away with, Neil?'

Peggy sat back in her chair, her shoulders slumped

and a defeated expression on her face. 'Just tell us, love. Tell us everything. Please?'

He sighed. 'It's hard to know where to begin.'

Dee watched him for a moment. She should feel angry and if Conor was here, Neil would probably be out the door on his ear by now but she felt she had to know the full story. 'Begin at the end,' she suggested, surprised at how steady her voice was. 'Begin when we broke up.'

He nodded and came back over to sit down. 'I left Greece immediately after that. I went to Morocco and bummed around Marrakesh for a while but I soon got through the money. I decided to head back to Spain. I figured I'd pick up some bar work there easily enough.'

'Did you sell my ring and Dad's watch?' Dee asked curiously.

He nodded. 'I'm sorry. Anyway, I told you the next bit about how I came to stop gambling.'

'Did you tell us the truth?' Dee asked, holding his gaze.

'Yes, I did.'

'And the bit about working as a bus driver?'

'Yes, that was all true.' He stopped.

'But you didn't set up your own business,' Peggy surmised.

He shook his head. 'No. Continental Coaches was the name of the company I worked for. Like I told you already, I worked long hours and it kept me out of harm's way. Andrew, my boss, was very pleased with my work. I never took sick leave, never gave any trouble and I was always on standby if any of the other drivers let him down. As a result, nearly two years later when he decided to open another branch in Ibiza, he put me in charge of the Benidorm operation.'

Dee frowned. 'So when was this?'

He thought about it for a moment. 'It would have been November, 2004.'

'Go on,' Peggy prompted him.

'It was the best thing that ever happened to me. I had never been given that level of responsibility before and I loved it. I worked my butt off when Andrew went to Ibiza; I wanted to prove to him that he'd made the right decision and that he could trust me.' He gave a short, humourless laugh and took a sip of his tea.

Dee and Peggy exchanged glances but neither of them spoke.

'Then one day a customer gave me a tip for a horse, said it was a sure thing. I thought that it wouldn't do any harm if I put on just one bet.'

'And it lost,' Peggy said.

'No.' He laughed. 'If it had lost, I'd probably be still running the company today. No, it won and so I went to collect my winnings and thought, while I'm here, I may as well put on just one more bet,' he shrugged, 'and that was that. I went back day after day putting more and more money on and losing it all. I was earning quite a good wage by then but it didn't take me long to go through it all. Then I started to dip into the petty cash . . .' He shook his head. 'It went downhill from there.'

'But how on earth did you get away with it?' Dee asked.

'I didn't. Oh, I managed to cover my tracks for a few months but Andrew got suspicious and sent in the auditors. I was arrested soon after that.'

'Dear, God.' Peggy crossed herself.

'I went to prison for six months,' he continued, staring into his glass. 'I got out Christmas week.'

'What did you do then?' Dee asked.

'I got some odd jobs here and there but nothing that paid very well. Then I bumped into Andrew again and he gave me a job as a driver.'

Peggy shot him a look of pure disbelief. 'You robbed from him and then he gave you a job?'

Neil nodded. 'Amazing, isn't it? But it turns out his father was a gambler and he knew exactly what I was going through. He told me he'd take me on as a driver but that I'd never be any more than that. I would never get near any cash and I would be monitored constantly.'

'That must have been tough,' Dee said cautiously.

He looked at her and smiled. 'No, Dee, it was the happiest I'd been since our time together in the US. Andrew took away all of the temptation. Everyone knew what I was like and not to trust me and, I can honestly say, it was a huge relief.'

'So what went wrong?' Peggy asked.

'Nothing. I haven't gambled since I got out of prison.'

'But what about this?' Peggy held up the page that detailed the huge debt.

He looked her straight in the eye. 'It's not mine.'

'Oh, please!' Dee shot him an angry look. 'Do you think we're stupid? Don't try to hoodwink us just because it's in Spanish, we know what it says and we know it's yours.'

'No, you don't, Dee,' he insisted. 'It is a debt and I am paying it back, but it's not mine.'

'You're trying to tell us that you're paying off someone else's debt?'

He sighed. 'Yes.'

'How can we believe you?' Peggy protested, her eyes filling with tears. 'Who in their right mind would take on someone else's debt? You have to prove to us that this is true or else . . .' She shook her head.

He reached across the table and took her hand. 'I'm telling you the truth, Mam. I've done a lot of terrible things but those days are behind me now. I'm sorry I lied about the car, it was a stupid thing to do. I just wanted you to be proud of me. I thought if I came back looking wealthy and successful it would make you happy.'

'All you have to do to make me happy, love, is to live an honest, decent life.'

'Then, in that case, you *can* be proud of me, Mam.'

Dee looked at the expression on Peggy's face and saw that Neil's eyes were bright with tears and immediately began to feel suspicious. 'Your story still doesn't make any sense.'

His face darkened. 'It's not a story.'

'Then explain this debt?' Dee challenged him.

Peggy waited in silence for her son's reply.

'I have a friend who was also a gambler. She—'

'She?' Peggy's eyes widened.

He nodded. 'Women gamble too, Mam. Anyway, Benita had taken money from the shop where she worked. She never took a lot, but she did it on a regular basis. Like me, as she got more desperate, she grew careless and she was caught. Her employer was an old family friend and so he agreed not to call the police if she paid it back and continued in her job for free.'

'So, where do you come in?' Dee asked.

'As soon as I got out of prison I started to attend Gamblers Anonymous meetings. That's where I met Benita. We became very close quite quickly. We've been together now for two years.' He shot her a nervous look.

'Isn't it a bad idea to get involved with another addict?' Dee asked.

'Absolutely,' he agreed, 'but thankfully it hasn't worked out that way for us.'

'So you've taken on her debt?' Peggy asked incredulously.

'Yes.'

Dee shook her head. 'And how do you know she's not using you the way you used me?'

'She's not; she loves me.'

Dee flinched. 'You can't always believe what people tell you, Neil,' she said bitterly, 'especially a gambler.'

'Dee, I am so sorry for how I treated you and if there was any way I could take it back, I would. I'm sorry if I'm hurting you again by telling you that I'm in love with another woman, but you wanted the truth.'

'You still haven't explained why you came home,' Dee said sharply. 'And where is this girlfriend of yours?'

Neil looked away. 'She's in Spain. I'm here because I'm working. Andrew had to come here on business, he's the one thinking of starting up in Ireland. He was in an accident a couple of months ago and busted his wrist and ankle and he can't drive so he brought me along to drive him.'

Peggy blinked. 'You're a chauffeur?'

He nodded, clearly embarrassed. 'The car is only in my name because he finds it so painful to use a pen and it was easier to let me take care of the paperwork.'

'But why didn't you just tell me that?' Peggy cried. 'I would have been thrilled to know that you were working, that you were okay and that you'd found someone special,' she shot a quick apologetic smile at Dee, 'again.'

'I'm sorry, Mam, I just wanted to be a big shot. I did intend to tell you everything but you were so impressed and proud. Then I picked up that newspaper and saw Dee and Sam and' – he held up his hands and shook his head – 'I was in shock. I knew immediately that I wanted to see Sam but I didn't know how Dee would feel. I thought it would add insult to injury if she knew I was with someone else and—'

'And?' Peggy prompted.

He hesitated for a moment. 'I just decided to say nothing.'

'You told us that you were thinking of moving back to Dublin for good,' Dee reminded him.

'I'm sorry, but I thought if I told you I was going to live in Spain you really wouldn't let me get to know Sam.'

'I don't know what to make of all this,' Dee said, wearily. 'How can we trust you? There have been so many lies.'

'And there's still something you haven't told us, isn't there, Neil?' Peggy was watching him steadily.

'No, that's everything.'

She closed her eyes briefly. 'Don't, Neil, please? You've come this far, don't stop now.'

He shook his head. 'I'm sorry, Mam, I really don't know what you're talking about. If there's something else, then I've forgotten it.'

Frowning crossly, she put a hand into her bag and, producing the handwritten note, tossed it across to him. 'How can you forget that?'

Neil picked up the note and smiled slightly and then in front of Dee and his startled mother, began to cry.

*

Neil had excused himself and gone out into the garden and Dee turned to Peggy.

'What? What's going on? Why is he so upset?'

Peggy shook her head. 'I don't know.'

'What was that letter about?'

'It was from a girl, presumably Benita, I couldn't read the signature. She was telling him she missed him and that she didn't care about the money. She wanted him to be with her because it was nearly time and she didn't want to have their baby alone.'

'She's pregnant!' Dee exclaimed. 'But why would that upset him?'

Peggy sniffed and pulled a handkerchief from her sleeve. 'She must have lost it. I'd better go out and see if he's okay.'

While Peggy followed Neil outside and disappeared into the shadows, Dee went to the fridge and took out a bottle of wine. She felt as if she'd just gone three rounds with Mike Tyson and she wasn't sure if it had been worth it. Where did this leave them? Where did it leave Sam? She poured wine into a glass and drank thirstily, pacing back and forth, occasionally pausing to look out the window into the darkness. It might be April but they'd freeze if they stayed out there much longer. She was just about to refill her glass when the door opened behind her and she watched as first Peggy came in and then Neil, both of them subdued and red-eyed.

'Can I use your loo?' he asked Dee.

'Sure.' She took him out into the hall and pointed him towards the staff loo and then went back in to Peggy. 'Well?'

'Good news and bad. She was expecting twins but she lost one last month.'

'Oh, God, that's awful. When is she due?'

'Eight weeks.'

'I still don't understand why he wouldn't tell us.' Dee took down two more glasses, poured the wine and handed a glass to Peggy.

'He was still afraid it would affect your decision about Sam and also he thought it would be bad luck to talk about the baby. He seems to be fairly traumatized by the loss and he hates being away from Benita at such a time.'

'Then why doesn't he just go back?' Dee said.

Neil appeared in the doorway. 'Because if I hang on here with Andrew for another five weeks I will have enough money for an apartment for us. I can't let Benita and the baby come home to a room in a boarding house, what kind of start in life would that be?'

'If you want to be with her then you should go,' Peggy told him, 'I'll give you the rest of the money.'

'Oh, no, Peggy,' Dee started.

Neil flopped into his chair and shook his head in disgust. 'Dear God, she thinks I've made this all up just to get money out of you.'

'I didn't say that,' Dee protested.

'But you thought it.' Neil stood again and going to

the counter, took up Dee's pad and pen. 'Thanks for the offer, Mam, but no. In fact, if you want to help me, please don't ever offer me money again. You can buy something for the new house or for the baby, that would be very kind, but never offer me or Benita money.'

'What are you doing?' Peggy asked as he sat down at the table and started to write.

'This is Benita's number. I want you to call her and talk to her and get her side of the story. Her English is very good so you should be fine. And this is Andrew Charles's number, he's my boss. He'll be able to verify the whole story.'

'Oh, Neil, why didn't you just tell us the truth in the first place?' she asked, tears rolling unchecked down her face.

He smiled sadly, his own eyes full of tears. 'I was ashamed, Mam. To admit what I had done to Dee was hard enough but to tell you that I had gone to prison.' He shook his head. 'I just couldn't do it.'

'Is that everything now?' Dee asked, dashing a hand across her eyes.

He nodded. 'That's everything. I'm so sorry for all the lies and the hurt and I can't prove to you that I won't gamble again in the future. All I can tell you is that I've never had more reason to try not to.'

Chapter 42

Once Neil finally opened up it was as if he couldn't stop. There were tears all round as he told them of some of the lengths he'd gone to to finance his gambling, and his horror when he'd found himself in a Spanish jail. He explained, quite movingly, how he felt he couldn't face Peggy as he'd let her down so much.

'You always taught me the importance of honesty and having a good name and I thought you would be ashamed of me if you knew how much I'd lied and cheated,' he said.

'I'm your mother,' she cried. 'There is nothing you could do or say that would ever make me disown you.'

She explained to Neil how she had found out everything she could about the addiction and how she'd talked to the counsellors and asked for their advice.

'And I bet they told you to protect yourself,' he guessed.

She nodded. 'But the reason I didn't trust you and I went through your things was because they said that if you'd really stopped gambling, you would be able to talk about it.'

'But it was different because I was out of the country,' he explained. 'You hadn't seen me at my worst and I thought I'd got away with it. I thought I'd be able to swan back here looking rich and successful and you'd be proud of me.' He looked at her from tear-filled eyes. 'Pathetic, I know.'

Peggy took him in her arms as if he was still a child and Dee crept out of the room to give them some privacy. She went up to Sam's room and sat on his bed and wished he was there so she could hold him.

After twenty minutes or so, she gathered up some photo albums and returned to the kitchen. 'I thought you might like to see these,' she said, setting them down on the table in front of Neil. Within minutes they were all laughing and smiling as they flicked through Sam's life in pictures.

'Dear God, Pauline is laughing in this!' Neil gasped in amazement at the photo of Sam as a toddler, sitting on his great-aunt's knee. 'I don't think I ever saw the woman crack a smile.'

'Sam brings out the best in her,' Dee agreed, 'and I've never heard Jack talk as much as he does when he's with Sam.'

'That's because he never usually gets a word in edgewise,' Neil laughed.

With the atmosphere less charged they finally began to discuss how they could introduce Sam to his father.

'I can't believe you're going to let me do this,' Neil said. 'Thank you, Dee.'

'I'm doing it for him as much as for you, but please understand that it will be a while before I can let you spend time with him alone,' she replied.

'And you'll be going back to Spain in a few weeks so we have to be careful that he doesn't feel he's found you and lost you again, all in a very short time,' Peggy fretted.

'They can talk on the phone and write, or email,' Dee reminded her.

'I don't have a computer,' Neil said, 'but there's an Internet café very near the apartment.'

'I think that will work out fine.' Dee sighed. 'I'm not so sure, though, how he's going to feel when I tell him that Peggy is his granny.'

'I've given that some thought,' Neil said slowly, 'and I think we have to tell him that I haven't been well and that you were protecting him from me but that you wanted Peggy to be in his life, even if it wasn't possible to tell him exactly who she was.'

'That's a good idea,' Peggy agreed. 'It will make sense to him, he's used to us always trying to protect him and he's a very clever little boy. Maybe you could ask Lisa what she thinks. She knows him well and she's trained in childcare.'

Dee nodded. 'I'll do that.'

After she'd locked up, Dee curled up on the sofa and called Conor. He picked up on the second ring.

'Hi,' she said.

'Hi. Are you okay?'

'Yeah, fine. Is Sam?'

'He's great,' Conor said and she could hear the smile in his voice. 'We've had a busy evening feeding the cows, playing football, cooking—'

'Cooking?' Dee couldn't believe her ears.

'Well, barbecuing but don't worry, Sam was in charge of the marinade and the salad.'

Dee laughed. 'Sounds like fun.'

'Yes and we were just settling down to watch a programme about whales when Mum and Dad arrived so he spent the rest of the evening trashing us all at Snap.'

'He's fast,' Dee said proudly. 'Was he okay about going to bed in a strange room?'

'He conked out within minutes of his head hitting the pillow,' Conor assured her. 'So, tell me, how did it go?'

'Really well, although it's been a very traumatic evening. Peggy looked ten years older at the end of it and Neil wasn't much better.'

'And you?'

She thought about it for a moment. 'I feel more relaxed and at peace than I have in a long time.'

'I'm glad.'

She went on to give him a quick synopsis of the evening's conversation and finished up with the news that not only was Neil in a relationship but he was going to be a father again.

'I finally feel that he has been completely straight and honest with us,' she said when she'd finished, 'and he's working hard to make a new and better life for himself and Benita.'

There was a short silence on the other end of the phone. 'Are you okay with that, Dee?'

She smiled at the hint of doubt in his voice. 'I am one hundred per cent okay with that, Conor. I've told you Neil is Sam's father, nothing more. I loved him once but that was a very long time ago.'

'So when are you going to introduce them?'

'Probably some time next week. I want to talk to Lisa first, she might be able to advise me on the best way to broach the subject with Sam.'

'No one knows Sam like you do; follow your instincts.'

'Thanks, Conor.' Dee yawned. 'Oh, I'm sorry.'

'That's okay, I won't take it personally,' he said with a chuckle. 'You've had a rather tiring and stressful day. Go to bed. You need to be here at ten sharp tomorrow morning.'

She groaned. 'But Conor—'

'No buts, Dee,' he said firmly. 'Sam and I are going to buy some chickens and you're coming with us.'

'Okay, then,' she agreed, too tired to argue, 'see you at ten.'

Dee dragged herself out of bed and into the shower at eight o'clock the following morning. Though she was very tired she also felt exhilarated and high on life. Things really couldn't get much better. Then she remembered the ridiculous question she'd asked Conor. Well, maybe things could be a bit better, but she wasn't going to dwell on it. She certainly wasn't going to ask any more stupid questions. Conor had put so much money and effort into transforming his home just for her son; if that wasn't a declaration of love, what was? She dressed quickly in her denim skirt, white T-shirt and cowboy boots. Grabbing her jacket, bag and the apple tart she'd made for Conor yesterday before Peggy and Neil arrived – it may not be as good as Aidan's mother's but he still loved it – Dee went out to the car. She was just turning back to lock up the house when she saw Vi standing at the gate. 'Vi!'

'Hello, Dee.' Vi came towards her, a nervous smile on her lips. 'I was hoping for a quick word, but I can see you're going out.'

'I have a minute. Come inside.'

Vi followed her into the hall and stood looking at her, obviously uncomfortable.

'I'd offer you a cuppa only I'm expected up at the farm,' Dee said.

'That's okay, I can't stay.'

Dee waited but Vi was busy studying her feet and not showing any sign of talking.

'It was Ronan, wasn't it?' Dee said eventually. 'He was the father of your baby.'

Vi nodded, still not looking up.

'Does he know?'

Vi lifted her head and her eyes met Dee's. 'No.'

'Oh, Vi, how can you live like this? How can you see him every day and not say anything?'

Vi shrugged. 'What's the point in saying anything now? It's too late and it would only hurt him and maybe Julia too.'

'You still love him, don't you?' Dee said softly. 'Don't you find it hard being so close to him but not, if you know what I mean?'

Vi's beautiful eyes glittered with tears. 'It's nicer than not seeing him at all.'

'He's very fond of you too, I could see that yesterday.'

'Maybe, but he's married to Julia and he's a wonderful, honest, loyal man; I wouldn't have it any other way.'

Dee stepped forward and put her arms around her. 'You are a very special lady.'

Vi smiled. 'Thank you, my darling, you're very kind. Now, can I ask you to keep this little secret of mine, secret?'

'Vi, of course! I would never tell a soul, you know that.'

'Yes, I suppose I do; it's just that with you being with Conor—'

'You have my word,' Dee said solemnly.

'Thank you, my darling.' Vi gave her another quick hug and turned to go.

'And I'm always here if you ever want to talk about –
anything.'

'Likewise,' Vi said and was gone.

Dee pulled into the farmyard to find a very excited
Sam waiting for her. He chattered non-stop about his
evening with Conor and she sat and drank the tea
Conor had made her, listened to her son, and watched
the man move gracefully around the kitchen as he
cleared up after their breakfast.

It was a lovely, fun-filled morning and as well as
going to the poultry farm, they visited a donkey sanc-
tuary. On the way home, Conor took them to eat in a
cheery pub in the middle of nowhere that served the
most delicious home-cooked food.

'How did you find this place?' Dee marvelled as they
sat back and surveyed their empty plates.

'I used to stop off here on my way to and from Clare,'
Conor told her. 'Great, isn't it?'

'Wonderful.' Dee studied the menu with interest.
'I could adapt some of these dishes and use them in
the crèche and the café.'

'Work, work, work,' he teased, 'you high-powered
entrepreneurs are all the same.'

Sam fell asleep almost as soon as they were back in the
car and they were finally able to talk.

'Are you still feeling okay about what you agreed
last night?' he asked, careful to keep his voice low,

just in case. 'No second thoughts?'

Dee shook her head. 'No, I feel absolutely fine. In a way it's as though a weight has been lifted from my shoulders. I love the idea that we' – she nodded into the back at her son – 'won't have any more secrets between us. I'm still a little nervous of that first "chat", I have to admit.'

'It will be fine, you'll be fine.' He put a hand on her thigh and smiled at her. 'You look tired; why don't you take a leaf out of your son's book and have a nap?'

Dee yawned and shifted in her seat slightly. 'You wouldn't mind?'

'Of course not, you must be exhausted. Recline your seat a little. Dee? Dee?' But she was already gone.

'Okay, you two, we're home.' Conor had already unloaded the trailer and the chickens were now checking out their new home.

Sam rubbed his eyes sleepily and groaned. Conor came around, opened his door and his safety belt. 'Don't you want to check on your new babies?'

Immediately, Sam's eyes were wide open and he was scrambling down and running towards the hen house.

'Dee,' Conor said gently, 'we're home.'

Dee stretched and opened her eyes. 'Speak for yourself,' she complained, 'I still have a ten-minute drive.'

'Not yet you don't,' he said, helping her out of the jeep. 'I want to show you the barn.'

Dee smiled. 'Great.' She was a lot more interested in

a cup of tea than in seeing the barn, but the least she could do was show some enthusiasm and give Conor the same support that he'd shown her.

When they walked through the door, she didn't initially notice any difference other than that it was tidier than usual. Then she realized it looked smaller. 'This is going to be a general storage area and, of course,' he waved a hand towards the glass case on the floor in the corner, 'the wormery.'

'You don't have to go to all that trouble for Sam,' she protested.

'Are you kidding? A wormery is a great way of converting waste into compost.'

She smiled. 'If you say so.'

'Come on.' He took her hand and led her back outside and around to the side of the barn and stopped at another door.

'I never noticed this before,' she said.

'That's because it wasn't here before.' He opened it with a flourish and flicked on a light switch. 'What do you think?'

Dee walked into the brightly lit room and stared around her. The walls were lined with white units at both floor and eye level with long, narrow stainless-steel handles and a sophisticated black-granite work-top. But it was the large island in the centre of the room, also with a granite worktop, a double sink and a place for a hob, that really took Dee's breath away. 'Wow! What on earth are you going to do in here?'

He watched her steadily. 'Nothing.'

She laughed. 'I don't understand.'

'Well, it's like this. Lisa has lots of plans for Happy Days and she really could do with more space and I thought that if you and Sam moved out she'd have more room.'

Dee opened her mouth to speak but he held up his hand and hurried on.

'You're going to need more space for the new business, too; there's no way you can do it all from your own kitchen even if you do outsource some of the cooking. There's plenty of room here for you to both cook and store goods. I didn't install any appliances because, well, I don't know anything about them and I knew you'd have very firm ideas about what you wanted and needed.'

'I don't know what to say,' she said faintly, dragging her eyes from the kitchen back to his face.

He looked at her. 'You asked me a question yesterday—'

She pressed her hands to her hot cheeks. 'Oh, please, forget that!'

He ignored her. 'And the answer was yes. I have been in love. Just once.'

She nodded silently, not taking her eyes off him.

'And I still am.' He smiled. 'I love you, Dee. You and you alone. There's never been anyone else like you. Not in Clare and not in Dublin. You're the only one for me.'

'Oh, Conor.' Dee almost fell into his arms, her eyes bright with tears. 'What a lovely thing to say.'

He smiled. 'Well, it's about time, I suppose.'

'I was beginning to wonder,' she admitted. 'I knew you liked me but you never seemed to want it to grow into anything more. That's why I got it into my head that there must have been someone special in Clare.'

Conor shook his head. 'There was no one special. I'm sorry that it's taken me so long to say all of this, Dee, but you see, I didn't feel I had any right to ask you for any kind of commitment. I've spent every minute of my time since I started this farm scrimping and saving. I had nothing to offer you and you had Sam to think of. Be honest, you never would have brought him to live here in the state this place was in. You hated him even visiting!'

'That's not true.'

He raised an eyebrow and she smiled. 'Okay, maybe it's a little bit true.'

'I'm an old-fashioned kind of guy, Dee, and there was no way I was going to propose unless I could afford to offer you and Sam a decent life.'

'Propose?' she murmured.

'And then Neil turned up in his big car and his business in Spain and I thought that was that.'

'Oh, Conor.'

But he'd started, and he was determined to finish. 'So I went to my accountant and asked him if he had any ideas of how I could raise money.'

'Oh, Conor,' she said again.

'And he came up with the idea of selling that piece of land.' He smiled broadly. 'He earned every penny of his exorbitant fees that day. So, now, before your son comes in and ruins the moment,' he shot a glance at the door, 'Dee Hewson, will you marry me? And move in here, you and Sam? And run Dee's Delicacies from here? Oh, and I have the appliances brochure up at the house. It's for proper catering stuff and you can pick whatever you like, there's still plenty of money and—'

Dee reached up and put her hand over his mouth. 'Will you please shut up and let me answer?'

He nodded.

She smiled. 'I'd love to.'

'What?' he said, his voice muffled under her fingers.

'I'd love to come and live here, I'd love to run my business from this amazing room.' She looked around, smiling, and then her eyes returned to his. 'But most of all, I'd love to marry you, Conor Fitzgerald.'

'Really?' he asked, pulling her closer.

She nodded, moving her hand up to cup his cheek. 'Really. I thought you'd never ask. In fact, most of Banford had given up on you.'

'Like I said, it was just because—'

'Yes, yes, yes, you said.' She sighed. 'In fact, I've never known you to talk quite so much. How about a kiss to seal the deal before Junior gets back?'

He grinned. 'I think I can manage that.'

Chapter 43

'Can I have a treat, Mum?' Sam said as they drew abreast of the corner shop.

'You have a biscuit in your lunch box,' Dee reminded him.

'Oh, go on, Dee, it is his first day,' Conor wheedled. 'Just a small packet of those sugar-free fruit sweets.'

Dee grinned. 'All right, then, but be quick. We don't want to be late or you'll be in trouble with your teacher.'

Conor and Sam went into the shop and Dee rested against the wall and held her face up to the September sun. She couldn't believe that it was finally here; Sam's first day at school. He had grown over the summer and as Dee helped him dress this morning, she had marvelled at how much older he looked in the grey school uniform.

'It's a beautiful morning, isn't it?'

Dee opened her eyes and saw Vi Valentine standing in front of her.

'Vi!' She hugged her quickly. 'I haven't seen you in ages. What are you working on?'

'Oh, this and that, nothing important. What are you doing up in this neck of the woods?'

Dee smiled. 'We're taking Sam to school, it's his first day.'

'Oh, my, that is exciting! I'll have to do another portrait for you, this time with him in his school uniform.'

Dee smiled. 'Don't, you'll reduce me to tears and I'm trying very hard to be strong.'

Vi patted her shoulder. 'You're bound to be emotional, darling, but just remember that this is the beginning of another chapter in his young life.'

Dee nodded. 'Yes, I know. Don't worry, I'll be fine after today. It's just another first, do you know what I mean?'

'Vi, how are you?'

The two women turned as Conor and Sam emerged from the shop, Sam clutching a packet of sweets.

Vi smiled. 'Fine, Conor, thank you. Hello, Sam, I believe it's a big day for you today.'

'My first day at school,' Sam told her. 'I'm going to be in Miss Murray's class.'

'I'm sure you'll have a marvellous time.'

'You must come out and visit us at the farm,' Conor told her. 'You could do some bovine portraits.'

Vi laughed. 'That's an idea; I've never painted cows before, at least, not four-legged ones! How are the wedding plans coming along?'

Dee made a face. 'Slowly. There's just so much else on at the moment.'

Conor winked. 'She's testing the waters first, Vi, to see if she can live with me.'

'I'm not,' Dee protested. 'I just have a launch to organize first, then I can concentrate on our wedding.'

'And how do you like living on a farm, Sam?' Vi asked.

'It's ace.'

'That means he likes it,' Conor translated.

'We'd better get going,' Dee said, 'we don't want to be late on your first day, do we, Sam?'

'No way!'

She put an arm around her son. 'See you later, Vi.'

'She looks well,' Conor remarked as they carried on down the road, Sam skipping ahead.

Dee smiled. 'Yes.'

'I'm amazed she hasn't found a partner, she's still very attractive.'

Dee shrugged. 'She's probably too set in her ways to settle down with anyone at this stage.'

'I suppose.' Conor frowned. 'That reminds me, where is that portrait that she gave you, Dee?'

'It's around somewhere,' she said vaguely, 'I'm not sure where.'

'I'll find it and we'll hang it in the hall. It will remind me what you look like when you're at work.'

Sam looked up at him. 'That's silly, you only have to switch on the telly to see Mummy.'

Conor laughed. 'That's true, Sam, I never thought of that. You hate it, don't you?' he murmured to Dee.

'What?'

'The portrait.' He nudged her. 'Come on, you can't fool me.'

'Okay, okay, I don't like it,' she admitted.

'But why? I think you look gorgeous, all delicate and fragile and vulnerable.'

Dee made a face 'Exactly! I look like a victim.'

'Rubbish, you do not. You know what? You look like you do when you're watching Sam, all tender and loving.'

She turned her face up to his. 'Really?'

'Really. Vi is a very clever artist, she captured something that very few people notice. Now, can we hang it in the hall?'

She laughed. 'I'll think about it.'

'Mummy, look! It's Tom!' Sam bounced up and down and waved frantically at his friend across the road. 'Can we cross over?'

'Okay, but hold my hand, please.'

Sam came back and slipped one hand into hers and the other into Conor's. They crossed the road and as the boys chattered noisily, Dee and Conor said hello to Pam, Tom's mother.

'Look at you lot, all tanned and gorgeous,' the woman marvelled. 'Where were you?'

'We were in Spain visiting Neil, Sam's dad,' Dee told her.

'I've got a new baby brother,' Sam boasted. 'He's

Spanish and he's called Luis, that's Spanish for Louis.'

'That's wonderful, Sam, congratulations.'

'Is he going to come and live with you on the farm?' Tom asked.

'No, he lives with his mum, Benita, and Neil in Spain but they'll come to visit us and we'll go and visit him, won't we, Mum?'

'Absolutely.' Dee rolled her eyes at Pam.

'He seems to have adapted well to the situation,' Pam murmured as Conor and the boys moved ahead of them on the narrow path.

'I know, it's amazing. He was a bit nervous the first couple of times he met Neil but after that he just took it in his stride. Then I was afraid he might be jealous of the baby, but as you've just heard, he's as proud as punch.'

'It probably helps that they live so far away,' Pam said.

'Maybe; whatever the reason, I'm not complaining.' Dee smiled. They had come a long way since that first, nerve-racking meeting in the park. Sam, initially cautious and full of questions, had quite quickly come to grips with the situation and had welcomed Neil into his life as easily as he would a new child in the crèche.

They arrived outside the school and Dee crouched down so she could look into Sam's face. 'Okay, sweetheart, have a lovely day and remember, your nana is coming over to tea later to hear all about it.'

'Great!'

Dee smiled. 'Okay, then, are you ready?'

'Ready. Bye, Mum!' Sam said and sped off without a backward glance, Tom hot on his heels.

'This isn't quite the way I imagined it,' Pam said, tearfully. 'I mean, don't get me wrong, I'm glad they're both so happy and confident, but a hug would have been nice.'

'Sam, wait!' Conor shouted, brandishing his camera. 'I have to get a photo.'

Sam stopped and looked back. 'But—'

'Back here, please,' Conor said firmly. 'You too, Tom, we have to have a photo so that we have something to tease you about when you're eighteen.'

The boys came back, Sam groaning dramatically. 'Sorry, Tom, my dad is just *so* embarrassing.'

Dee and Conor exchanged a stunned look. *Dad*? Conor recovered first and organized them all into little groups, snapping away, a wide grin on his face.

'Okay, you can go now,' he finally told the children.

'Just one minute, *Dad*.' Pam grinned as she took the camera from him. 'Now it's your turn.'

'Oh, man!' Sam grumbled.

Conor and Dee crouched, one each side of him, and smiled at each other over his head.

'Okay, everybody, look this way and say cheese!' Pam ordered.

Sam put an arm around each of their necks and giggled. 'Gorgonzola!'